A DOUBLE DOSE OF HARD CASES AND SOFT HUSSIES —

ONE LOW PRICE!

SILVER CITY CARBINE

"Anything else you want to confess before you eat dirt and die, Plummer?"

"Not a damn thing. Just a small bet. Bet you ain't even got your hands on that Colleen yet. Right?"

Lee felt a twinge of anger, but pushed it down. That was Plummer's try to rile him, so he wouldn't be ready.

Lee stared at the other gunman. There was no eye movement, no hands quivering, no advantage.

Always draw first in a face-down, Buckskin Frank Leslie had taught Lee. It gives you a split second advantage as the other man sees your move and starts his own. Sometimes it's enough to keep you alive....

CALIFORNIA CROSSFIRE

"Let the lady go!" Morgan shouted.

"Mind your own business!" The man took one hand from the terror-stricken woman and threatened to draw. "Ease off, stranger, and stay alive."

Morgan took one more step toward the man, whose hand darted for leather and drew a .44 out of his holster.

With an arcing movement of his right arm, back and up, Morgan brought the blacksnake whip into action.

The whip tore a bloody trail across the other man's hand. The gun dropped to the street. He howled with pain, let go of the woman, and grabbed his injured hand.

With a flick of his wrist, Morgan recoiled the whip. "Now what the hell were you saying, tough guy?"

SILVER CITY CARBINE
CALIFORNIA CROSSFIRE

BUCKSKIN

KIT DALTON

LEISURE BOOKS   NEW YORK CITY

A LEISURE BOOK®

September 1992

Published by

Dorchester Publishing Co., Inc.
276 Fifth Avenue
New York, NY 10001

SILVER CITY CARBINE

BUCKSKIN

1

The grandfather clock in the Johnson Jewelry and Clockworks store on Main Street chimed the noon hour as Skinny Victor peered up and down Main Street from the mouth of the alley next to the Bird's Nest Saloon. Sweat beaded his pale forehead under a weathered black cap. He again looked both ways, gray eyes wary, alert to any danger. For a moment he panted to catch his breath. He wasn't used to running that far.

After another thirty seconds scanning Main Street he relaxed a little, took a few tentative steps onto the boardwalk in front of the timekeeper's store and then walked toward the edge of the planks and the drop off to the street.

He angled toward a saddled bay mare that had recently been tied there at a hitching rail. Again he checked both directions, then much more calmly than he felt, he untied the reins from the hitching rail and lifted his foot for the stirrup.

So suddenly he never knew how it happened, a man kicked sharply at Victor's upraised left foot, rammed it another two-feet into the air and dumped the slender man on his back in the dust of the street by the bay's front feet. He fell directly on fresh horse droppings and bellowed in protest.

"What'n hell?" Victor brayed as he looked up from the ground at the figure looming over him. The boot he saw coming caught him in the side before he could roll out of the way. Victor scrambled to his feet only to meet a solid right handed punch that jolted him back two-feet.

His eyes glazed and he shook his head to clear it. He looked and blinked and then into focus came the surly face of Sam Plummer. He knew Plummer. One of the enforcers for the Silver Strike Mine. Everyone knew Sam Plummer. He was a man about two inches shy of six feet, with white hair and a white moustache that had curls at the ends—a handlebar type. Sam was ugly as sin and twice as mean.

"Victor, you are an asshole, which ain't so bad for you, but you're a shit dumb asshole. Drop that hog leg in the dirt with one finger and your thumb. Now!"

The voice cracked like a bull whip over the backs of a dozen oxen. Victor took a deep breath that came out as a disgusted sigh, caught his worn .44 and let it drop into the dirt.

"Going for a ride somewhere, Mr. Victor?" Sam asked.

"Yeah, just up the street."

"Or maybe down to Hawthorne."

"No! No sir, Mr. Plummer. Not me. I'm a working man."

"True, you used to work at the Silver Strike Mine. We don't tolerate thieves at the Silver Strike. Empty out your pockets."

"I don't see no need . . . ."

Sam Plummer slammed the side of his .45 Colt across Victor's head, drawing two gashes that pumped blood at once, and slammed the slender man into the dirt again.

"Get up, Victor, and empty out your miserable pockets before I kick you square in the balls!"

"Oh, damn, that hurts!" Victor crowed, touching the long gouge marks on the side of his head. "Look there, I'm bleeding!"

Sam lifted the side of his six-gun again and Victor held up both hands.

"All right, all right." He reached in his pants pockets and pulled out a plug of tobacco, makings for smokes, a handful of change and a small rock that showed white quartz.

"Put that and everything else on the boardwalk," Sam ordered.

Victor shrugged, put the quartz and a small purse and the other items on the thick planks.

"Step back and lace your hands on top of your head."

Victor did.

Sam picked up the quartz and turned it over. He nodded. "Just a rock, huh? What you told the guard? Just a damn rock of quartz for your kid."

The back side of the quartz held a free gold nugget almost as large as a walnut.

"That's six ounces of gold, at least, asshole. You know what the Silver Strike does with thieves? Especially thieves who steal a nugget worth more than a hundred and thirty dollars, more than half a year's pay for a working man—"

"I was gonna bring it back—" Victor tried.

Plummer stared him down. "Pick up your shooter and put it in leather, Victor. I'll give you a chance."

"No sir. I ain't gonna draw on you, Mr.

Plummer."

"You draw on me, asshole, or you die without drawing. Take your pick."

A crowd had formed around the two men. The boardwalk was filled with thirty or forty people, mostly men, a few women. A dozen stood in the dusty street watching. Nobody stood behind either man, leaving an open space for a few wildly fired bullets should it come to that.

"Go ahead, Victor. Put your iron back in leather, right now."

Victor looked at the crowd. "Ain't somebody gonna help me? A man don't get killed for taking a little chunk of gold!"

He stared at the crowd. One or two men turned away, wouldn't meet his gaze. A woman brushed at tears on her cheek.

At last Skinny Victor took three steps to his six gun, reached down slowly and picked it up, then as quickly as he could he turned and fired at Sam Plummer.

Victor's shot got off first. Plummer had figured he had the man browbeaten enough. The round from Victor's .44 slid between Plummer's arm and his side, missing human flesh by an inch.

Before the sound of the first shot had faded, Plummer whipped his hand down, drew and fired so fast some in the crowd said they hardly saw his hand move at all. Then Victor's weapon spun out of his hand and he held his right wrist where one of the bones had been shattered by the big lead slug.

"That was stupid, Victor," Sam said quietly when the sound of the two shots had faded after echoing off Desperation Mountain behind the town.

"You gonna kill me anyway. I had me a chance."

"One chance, Victor, no more."

The wounded man stared at the crowd again.

"Don't you people see what's happening? You're letting Colonel Ralston be the law in Silverton. That what you want, some southern rebel army officer running our town? You gonna stand there and let this outlaw gun me down in broad daylight?"

Before he was through talking, Victor charged forward. Again he caught Plummer by surprise. The smaller man jolted into Plummer just after he holstered his weapon and drove him to the ground. Plummer slammed his fist into Victor's shot up wrist and the miner howled with pain and rolled away.

Plummer jumped to his feet, drew his Colt and shot Victor in the right knee joint.

For a moment it was quiet on Main Street. Then Victor's scream of agony filled the street. He sat up hugging his shattered knee. Tears streamed down his cheeks. He keened in unbearable pain.

The crowd started to drift away.

Victor saw them going. He screamed at them. "You're letting him do it again! How many men has Ralston killed in this town? A dozen, two dozen? I'm just one more. This bastard Sam Plummer is nothing more than a killer, a wanted man in Arizona and New Mexico. Wanted for murder."

A shot slammed into the stillness. Victor's left elbow disintegrated as the lead hit it and broke into a dozen pieces plowing forward into bone and muscle and some of the bullet coming out into the air again.

Sobbing replaced the sound of the shot as it faded.

"Letting this bastard get away with murder! Ain't right. Plummer, one day you'll meet a man you can't beat. I'll watch from hell as you go down in the dirt and beg for mercy. You're a whore, Plummer. Doing another man's killing. You like to kill. May you rot in hell for a thousand—"

Sam Plummer's Colt roared again, the round

boring a small hole in Skinny Victor's forehead and taking a two-inch chuck of skull, brains and blood with it as it jolted out the back of his head.

The thin body that had once belonged to Edward Skinny Victor flopped into the dust.

The last of the people on the sidewalk drifted away. One woman who had been biting her lip during half of the ordeal, left the post she had been holding onto that held up the overhang in front of the hardware store. She stepped off the boardwalk and ran forward.

She stood no more than five-feet three-inches tall, and wore a proper brown dress. She carried a reticule by a strap and as she ran forward, she swung the reticule like a rope and slammed it into Sam Plummer from the side. She hit him with the big purse four times before he recovered and grabbed the missile. He had drawn his six-gun with the first blow, now held it loosely.

"Whoa now there, lady," Plummer said laughing. "You're a little late to defend this thief."

"You're a monster! If I was a man I wouldn't live in this town another minute until I'd tried to kill you! You don't deserve to live another second!"

"Oh, God! It's that Irish temper. Sure and it's Miss Colleen O'Reily, the proud owner of the O'Reily #1 Silver Mine." His tone shifted from one of surprise and humor to a stern warning. "This is none of your affair, Miss O'Reily."

"Murder on the streets of Silverton is my affair, Mr. Plummer!" She scowled at him. "This is my town, too. Why don't you take your gun somewhere else to murder people?" She turned to the men on the boardwalk who had stopped to listen.

"You men there. How can you let a wanted killer like Sam Plummer run loose in our town? Are you all cowards? Are you all spineless, sniveling yellow bellies who won't stand up and defend your own town!''

The four men who had stopped turned away muttering.

She shook her head. ''God help us,'' she cried. ''It doesn't look like anyone else is going to.''

She stared at Plummer again, walked over and looked down at the body and blinked away tears. Then Colleen O'Reily marched back to the boardwalk and into the General Store.

Plummer watched her leave, shrugged, holstered his six-gun again and pointed to two men on the boardwalk.

''You and you. Come out here and get this dead trash off the street. Haul him down to the undertaker. Somebody might claim him.''

The two men hesitated, looked at each other.

''Come on, come on! I ain't got all day to stand around here. You coming or not?''

Plummer let his right hand swing down and brush the butt of his six-gun. Both men moved at once, picked up a hand each and dragged the mortal remains of Skinny Victor down Main Street to Nevada and north toward the undertaker's place.

Plummer watched them a moment, then nodded and walked down Main toward the stage office as he saw the Wells Fargo team of six racing into town.

The arrival of the stage from Carson City was usually the biggest event of the day. The stage brought in mail, parcels sometimes, a little fast freight, but most important, residents returning from small trips and new faces and new people for the community. It was their one link with the outside world.

For the past week, Sam had met the stage every day looking for somebody called Morgan. He was the last man on the security team at the mine, and

could be coming in any time. Plummer leaned
against the Johnson Jewelry Store window and
watched the passengers get off. Today everyone had
paid the extra two dollars to ride inside out of the
sun and any fall showers.

Two women stepped down from the high coach.
One a dowdy, frumpy, middle-aged woman, the
other a younger woman with a face that was
unpainted but told a story. She had an aloof smile
and Plummer knew at once she was a whore. He just
knew, and she didn't care if everyone knew.

Her thin smile said that none of her private places
were off limits and that all any man had to do to see
them and use them was pay her. Then the moist, soft
hidden pleasure places would be all his—for a half
hour. Plummer evaluated her through the dress and
nodded. He would see her face and figure soon, he
was sure, in one or the other of the twelve saloons
and bawdy houses in Silverton.

Next came out a small, fat man who had drummer
printed on his forehead and a sample case under his
arm. The last man out was maybe six-feet tall,
looked sturdy enough and wore fringed buckskins
and a tied down holster.

Plummer shook his head. The tall man didn't look
mean enough to be a gunfighter. Maybe a scout for
the army, or a gambler, or a foreman for the mine.
Damn sure he wasn't a gunsharp.

Plummer snorted and walked across to the Bird's
Nest Saloon opposite from Johnson's Jewelry Store.
He had earned a beer. He felt of the gold nugget in
his pocket. Col. Ralston wasn't absolutely sure there
had been a nugget. He only suspected.

For one brief moment Plummer thought of
keeping it. No, too many people had seen it, Ralston
would hear. He'd turn it in right after he had a beer.

Lee Morgan waited for the shotgun guard to

unlash the gear on the top rack of the Wells Fargo
Concord stage and toss down his carpet bag. Then he
shouldered it and looked over the town.

Silverton, Nevada, about 1500 people at almost
nine-thousand feet. No place to be in winter. The
town had one long Main Street and a cross street that
ran north up to the mines. One of them would be
where he would find his new boss.

First he wanted to have a beer and get some of the
trail dust settled. He'd never been on this flank of
the Sierra Nevada Mountains before. High country
was high country. That's where the gold and silver
seemed to be.

This strike was well south of Virginia City and its
mother lode, and fifty miles north of the gold mine
bonanza at Bodie, California.

Lee stood against the side of the Wells Fargo office
and reread the letter. It had caught up with him on a
two week stay in Denver. It was short and pointed:

> Mr. Lee Morgan. I need a man who can handle a gun
> and follow orders. Come to the Silver Strike Mine,
> Silverton, Nevada. Pay is $100 a month, food and
> ammunition.
>
>   Col. Cleve Ralston

Morgan walked across the street and looked up at
the hill behind town where he could see the
diggings, the tailings, the dry holes and eight or ten
operations that looked to be working. Two were
larger than the rest.

He watched a well dressed man approaching and
held up his hand. The man looked at his tied down
gun and stopped at once.

"Sir, which one up there is the Silver Strike
Mine?"

"Oh, yes, it's the larger one on the left. That's it.

Anything else?''

Lee smiled, thanked him and the man hurried on looking greatly relieved. That was strange, Lee thought. He looked up at the mine, shrugged and began walking down Main toward the other street that led up the hill. Might as well get on with it. He could have a beer later.

For a moment, Lee Morgan thought of Spade Bit as he headed up the hill. The flowing, marvelous horse ranch he once owned in Idaho a half day's ride out of Boise. His father had left him the ranch when he came up with a case of lead poisoning at the hand of gunsharp Harve Logan.

His daddy, William Buckskin Frank Leslie never did find out if he was faster than Logan. Both men had drawn and fired in a fraction of a second, so fast the eye could hardly see their hands move, both had shot straight and true, and both men died seconds later.

Buckskin Frank Leslie had worked both sides of the law, led a wild, gun-for-hire life and wasn't too particular who was right or wrong as long as he got paid. He'd been on a few wanted posters, then settled down somewhat to raise blooded horses on the Spade Bit far off the gunsel trail.

Lee Morgan was the bastard offspring of Frank Leslie and for a time that made Morgan hate his father. He had taken off as soon as he was big enough to make his way and soon earned his living with his gun as well. After all, he'd been taught to shoot by one of the fastest guns ever to slap leather.

He'd lost the Spade Bit, mostly to the Mexican hoof and mouth disease that attacked both ends of a horse and wound up wiping out his herd. Since then he'd done a little bit of everything, from swamping out saloons for grub and a bed, to working in a hardware store for pennies a day and a drafty warehouse to sleep in nights.

Out on the trail he'd been hungry more often than not.

Never again. He'd manage to rustle up some money from now on, even if it meant doing it at the business end of the Bisley Colts he carried on his right hip. His well worn holster was tied low to hang tight to his leg and not move at all when he made a fast draw. All the motion went into the weapon lifting out of the leather. That hundredth of a second could mean the difference between living and dying.

For a time he was on a wanted up in Idaho. He'd gunned down a man who deserved to be killed. Done it after he'd taken off a deputy sheriff's badge. Saved the county the expense of having a trial and the possibility that the killer might go free. A technicality, yeah, but lawmen didn't hanker much to the difference.

He'd been to Mexico a few times, all over the west and the southwest. Even did a turn in the tall timber up in the green lands of Washington south of Seattle.

Lee Morgan shrugged, let the bag of possibles drop off his shoulder and swing below on his left hand. His right was usually empty, ready, waiting to be used if necessary on the Bisley.

He passed two small mining outfits, then went up the last grade to the Silver Strike Mine. It was not all underground. A stamping mill hammered away to the left pounding the ore into small enough chunks so the processing vats could work on it. To the right he saw a small painted building that had the mine name over the door and a smaller sign that said: ''Office.''

He trudged that way, pushed open the door and went inside. At once the clanging of metal on metal of the stamp mills quieted. He was in a room that served as office and reception center. A half dozen chairs sat to one side.

A long counter across the room cut off the back of it and a young man with close clipped hair, wire rimmed eyeglasses and garters holding up his white shirt sleeves. He cleared his throat and looked at Lee. "Yes sir. May I help you?"

"I would hope so. I am to see Col. Ralston."

The young man smiled. "I'm sure you are. What is your name, please?"

"Lee Morgan."

"Just a moment," the scrubbed clean youth said and vanished through a heavy door at the back of the room. Quickly he came out and held the door open.

"Please come around the counter and right this way, sir," the fop said.

There was a new tone of respect in his voice. His glance went at once to Lee's tied down holster which held his Bisley Colts.

The young man pushed the door open, waved Lee inside, then closed it at once. Lee found himself in a large room that was more den than office. It was finished in dark wood paneling. Two elk heads had been mounted on one wall. A large window was heavily closed with drapes but high windows lighted the room.

Standing behind a massive mahogany desk stood a man who must be the colonel. He had a military bearing, stood at least six-three and was thick at the shoulder and chest. A big strong, forceful man. His dark hair was longer than the usual style and he wore a full dark beard tainted only slightly with stains of gray. Thin rimmed eyeglasses covered his watery blue eyes.

He held out his hand at once, a craggy face breaking into what passed for a smile.

"Ah, Morgan. Glad your mail found you. I've been told you're hard to get hold of."

"Sometimes, Colonel."

The man sat down, motioned for Lee to do the same and he sank into an upholstered chair across from the heavy desk. Now he saw that the Colonel must have real trouble seeing. There was a hint of a scar that showed through his beard on his left cheek. The men studied each other a moment.

"I'd expected a rougher, older man," Ralston said abruptly.

"Age has little to do with pulling a trigger, sir. I've seen a fourteen-year-old who could outshoot men three times his age. Remember that Jesse James was only sixteen when he rode with Quantrill and massacred the Jayhawkers at Lawrence, Kansas, and when Quantrill's men trapped and killed 75 union soldiers at Centralia, Illinois. The plain fact is, I'm somewhat older than I look."

Lee had heard a touch of a southern accent in the colonel's voice and guessed he must be from the south. At the mention of Quantrill, the former officer's smile blossomed.

"Yes, Charles Quantrill. One of the South's true victories in the recent unpopular affair." He cleared his throat. "Well, to the business at hand. You're known by your reputation, Mr. Morgan. No doubt about that.

"My questions are few. First, I demand unswerving loyalty to me and my operation. You will be working with three extremely good men. You'll be the junior member, so you'll take direction from any one of them.

"I demand that my orders be carried out without question, exactly like in the military. In case you're wondering, I did serve with the Confederacy and led a regiment of infantry. We served our cause well on many occasions.

"Briefly, I'm hiring your gun, your skill with it, not your morals or your ability to think. I don't want you to think. Do what you're told to do and we'll get along fine.

"Incidentally, I met your father once. Not too long ago. I understand he's dead now. He was the toughest god-damned gunman I ever knew. You're said to be like him. Not as fast as he was, but plenty fast. Don't disappoint me."

He stared at Lee for a moment, then stood, ending the interview. Before Lee could move he spoke again.

"My top man, Sam Plummer, will show you around, introduce you to my people, get you settled. You stay at the house next to mine down on Mountain Street. I've got a cook there for eight or ten of my top people."

The colonel nodded as he watched Lee who had stood.

"You know anything about mining, Morgan?"

"Not much, sir."

"Good. That's not your job. You're my army, my regiment, my enforcers. The tougher the better. Nobody fucks around with me or my people and gets away with it. If they do, they answer to that Bisley you seem to favor."

The colonel nodded again and Lee turned and walked out the door he had come in. A second man in the outer office signalled to Lee and led him out a side door. The man had a black patch tied over his left eye and appeared to be about thirty-five. He held out his hand.

"Lee Morgan, proud to make your acquaintance. I'm Thomas, orderly to the General. He was a General, but he likes Colonel better since that title has the best memories for him. I was with the Colonel during the war, and before and ever since. He saved my life."

They walked down the hill.

"I'm to show you your room and find Mr. Sam for you. Sam Plummer. You know him?"

"Heard his name a time or two."

Twenty minutes later, Lee was ensconced in a ground floor room of a big comfortable house on Mountain Street. He had the spot to himself, and it had a real mattress on the bed, a wash stand, a closet and a chifforobe. There was a dining room where three meals a day were served at seven, twelve and six. He had just washed up and changed shirts when someone knocked on the door.

Lee opened it and looked down at a shorter man with white hair and black eyes and a silly looking white handlebar moustache. The gent's six-gun was tied low and tight.

"Be damned, you were the one. I'm Sam Plummer. Saw you get off the stage but didn't guess you was Lee Morgan." He held out his hand. "We'll be working together, if you can take the guff off the old man."

"Sam Plummer. I've heard stories about you. You as fast as all them stories tell?"

"Hell no! You know how stories grow. I've heard some wild tales about Lee Morgan and six silver dollars thrown into the air."

They both laughed.

"Nobody's ever done six," Lee said. "Saw my daddy do four once, but he said it was luck. Two is good."

"You settled in? I'll introduce you to the other two men. Both with good reps. Glad I don't have to go up against either one of them. You neither, course."

They went down the hall and he met Johnny Hardin. The short Hardin was younger than he had expected, no more than twenty-five with a full black beard. He was too heavy for his five-foot two-inch frame, but the hog leg hung low away from his belly.

Hardin looked at Lee and nodded.

"Don't think we've met," Hardin said with a surprisingly soft voice. No one would take him for a gunman.

"Heard of you by reputation," Lee said smiling. Just because he thought Hardin was a backshooting snake was no reason to be unpleasant face to face. No telling how long he might be associated with the man. In a gunfight he would more than pull his weight.

"You're from Texas," Lee said.

"True, and a few other spots. As I recall, Idaho was your first home."

They watched each other a minute, then the smaller man nodded at Plummer. "Yeah, he's all right. Don't see any problem working with Lee here, if that was your question, Sam."

"No question, just stopped by to say howdy." Plummer grinned, waved and moved down the hall to the next door.

Bob Cassidy was already in the doorway watching. He was the opposite of Hardin, at least six-feet tall and as slim as a sapling. He moved into the hall, feet spread in a shootout stance, his hand hovering over the butt of a six-gun.

"We do it right here, Sam?" Cassidy asked, his voice high, excited.

"Quit your funnin', Bob. This here is our new gun hand, name of Lee Morgan."

Cassidy's scowl turned into a grin. "Hell yes! Buckskin Frank Leslie's drop. Heard you was around trying to outdo your daddy."

"Not a chance," Lee said. "Couldn't out gun him or out-rep him if I tried, so I ain't trying. Just doing what I can to make a living."

Cassidy's eyes sparkled. "Yeah, yeah. Same here. It's like being a cowboy or a miner or a sodbuster.

We just do it with our trigger finger." He laughed.
"Yeah, Idaho. Welcome to Nevada before it gets so
cold it'll freeze your prick off if'n you try to piss
outside."

He laughed again and Sam even grinned.

"Well, now you know all the players. See you for
supper at six, then we'll roam around the town a
little and find out what we can kick up for your
entertainment." He hesitated, then walked back
toward Lee's room with him.

"Figure I better mention it. The colonel is easy to
work for. Just follow orders and stay away from his
woman. Her name is Debbie Sue, she's a feisty
redhead who loves to spread her legs. If the colonel
finds somebody messes with his woman, that
hombre gets himself killed. Happened three times so
far since Spring. If Debbie Sue gets any ideas about
you, you put her off quick. She's just dangerous as
all hell."

Lee waved and went on to his room. It had a
number 4 on it and was in the corner. Probably
colder than the inside rooms. He'd be surprised if he
was still here during the winter. Course it didn't
make no never mind to a miner what kind of
weather it was topside, not with him beating his
brains against rocks half a mile underground.

Lee closed the door and sat on the bed. Best one
he'd been on in a time. For a moment he thought
about the beautiful Spade Bit in the Spring, three
hundred acres of the finest horse raising land he'd
ever come across. Gone. But maybe not gone
forever. Maybe someday he'd get back to Grove and
ride the Spade Bit again and even own it again.

Maybe.

He checked his Waterbury and saw that it was
only a little after two. Time for a good nap before
supper. He had just stretched out on the bed, boots

and all, when he heard the door open softly. He sat up quickly, the Bisley in his fist.

A woman in a bright red dress to match her hair stood there, a smile on her pretty face. She pulled the top of her dress apart where it had already been unbuttoned. Her big breasts swung into view and Lee caught his breath as he came to his feet.

"Hi, Lee. Welcome to Silverton. I'm Debbie Sue." She walked forward, her breasts swaying and jiggling. "Lee," she whispered. "If the colonel finds out you fucked me, he's gonna kill you. If you don't flip me over and fuck me good right now, I'm the one who is gonna want to kill you."

She put her arms around his neck, pulled his face down to hers and kissed him hard. Then she jammed her tongue at his lips until they opened and her hot branding iron stabbed inside his mouth, claiming it as her very own—at least for the next two hours.

2

Debbie Sue let go of Lee and hurried back to the door where she put a straight backed chair under the knob to serve as an effective lock. At the window she pulled the blind down from the side, then she did a little dance as she slipped out of the blouse making her generous breasts bounce and jiggle.

"I'm in heaven," Lee said softly.

He watched her dance. She wore no shoes. Her skirt was shorter than the floor dragging kind. Her body writhed and humped, her hips pounding forward suggestively as she ground toward him, her breasts keeping up with the beat only she could hear. At last she cupped her breasts and lifted them toward him until he kissed each one.

"Oh, my yes!" she whispered. "You are going to be so pleasured that I'll spoil you for any other woman who touches you. A treasure of delights. Anything you want to do with my body, anything . . . without blood."

She dropped to her knees and kissed his crotch, rubbing it and rubbing it until his erection began and then surged into full size. Eagerly she opened his fly pulling down his pants and his short underwear until his privates were raw naked.

"Glory!" she whispered, then took him in her mouth, sucking him in until her lips touched his hairy roots. She bobbed her head and he felt his pressure rising.

Gently Lee pushed her away from him as he worked at the fasteners at the side of her skirt. She unbuttoned them and pulled the fabric free. She wore nothing underneath. Her belly was flat, legs slender and strong, a blush of real redhead hair forested a triangle at her crotch.

Lee bent her over, pushed her hands to the floor and spread her legs. Kneeling, he went past the soft rose pucker between her tight cheeks to the pink slot that showed excited, eager juices already. He licked the soft lips, then drove his tongue into her as far as he could bringing a soft yelp of delight from her. She ground her round ass against his face urging him deeper, and let a quick, nearly silent climax surge through her slender body.

He came away, carried her to the bed and dropped her, producing a gentle giggle. Then he let her undress him.

"One fast time before you explode," she whispered in his ear.

Lee stood her against the wall, lifted her long, slender legs around his hips and pressed her back against the wall. Then he worked down and burrowed his shaft into her slot, bringing a gasp of pleasure and amazement from her.

"First fucking time ever this way!" she whispered.

Lee hardly heard her. His pressure had been

building for the last ten minutes and now the explosion went off before he wanted it to, ramming her back into the wall with every thrust, smacking her round bottom into the wallpaper as she chewed on his earlobe and took the thrustings with excited satisfaction.

Later they sprawled on the bed, he nibbling at her breasts. He sat her up and devoured the mounds again.

Lee grinned at her. "I'd guess you just love to fuck."

"Every day. I need a man every day or I get snotty and impossible. Cleve is almost fifty. Some days he can't even get it up. I hit him when he's like that. So I fuck around. Too often he finds out. I'm careful, damn careful. But if I get too nice to him, he gets suspicious. So I pretend I hate him all the time now."

"How'd you get hooked up with him?"

"I worked one of the best houses in Carson City before almost anybody here now was in town. He liked me, pulled me out and made me a lady. He thought. I still need to get poked twice a day, but I settle for once. Usually. Except for strokes of luck like this."

"You've done the other gunhands?"

"Sure. Ten, twelve, fifteen times, each. Nobody can put out my fire. Not even you."

Lee tried to prove to her that he could. He put her on top and let her ride him like a frisky Spring colt, but he was satisfied long before she was. She took out a bottle of whiskey she had brought with her and then both drank from the bottle.

"Morgan, you are good. Sometime I'll find out if you could last all night."

Lee got up and grabbed her legs and stood her on her head on the bed. He spread her legs and his tongue found her clit and he twanged it a dozen times until she rattled and shook in a furious climax that left her breathless and moaning in delight. He dropped her back on the bed and she squirmed until she cuddled against his naked form.

"So good!" She sat up and looked at him. "I may keep you as a pet. I'll ask the colonel."

Lee looked at her and waggled his finger at her.

Debbie Sue giggled. "I won't. But I promise that I'll see you just as often as I can."

"Not more than twice a day, afternoon and midnight. I have to get some rest."

She laughed softly at him and began dressing.

"I have to get back. I'll go out the window, safer that way."

A minute later she was gone and he lowered the window softly. Lee shook his head, half in wonder at the eagerness of the woman for sex. He'd heard about women like her. How long could she last that way? The fact that she had been a whore had no meaning for him. He'd known half a dozen ex-whores who got out of the business and were good wives and mothers.

Supper in the big dining room was served family style, with more then the seven men could possibly eat. A Chinese girl served the food. Plummer said her father cooked and was great at his job. The little Chinese girl was also available for all nighters for three dollars.

"Her father approve?" Lee asked.

"Hell, yes. Who do you suppose gets the three dollars!"

After supper Lee and Plummer went out on the town. They came into a saloon and found two men starting a gunfight. Plummer took one, knocking him to the floor, and Lee grabbed the other one and slammed the gun out of his hand.

"You assholes want to punch holes in each other, fine by me," Plummer said. "Just don't do it where you gonna hurt some Silver Strike workers. Get your asses the hell out of town if'n you want to start whaling away at each other with hot lead. Chances are neither of you can hit a shit stick at two feet. The barkeep will have your iron when he thinks you're fit enough to carry it."

Outside, Plummer looked sideways at Lee. "Sure you're cut out for this kind of work?"

"Never liked it none being a damned lawman, which is about what we're doing."

"Yeah? Well it gets more interesting. You hear what happened this afternoon?"

Morgan shook his head.

Plummer told him. "Damned thief had to be dealt with. Was gonna put him on the next stage tied hand and foot. But when the fucker shot at me, I just couldn't let him walk away. Another two-inches and I'd be out there on boot hill. Had to teach the asshole a lesson that the rest of the town would understand, too."

"I'm a gunhand, not a damned lawman," Lee said again. "We gonna have any real gun work?"

Plummer grinned. "Don't be so damn anxious. Lots of times when we shoot at folks, somebody shoots back. Could be harmful to our health that way."

"Happened before."

"Leastwise, Morgan, every damn miner in this town is gonna think twice now before he grabs any free gold and tries to steal it. I done that. I put the fear of hot lead into them."

They had come out of the Bird's Nest Saloon and stood in the spill of light from the two big windows and the bat wing doors. Main Street was ink-black most of the way, except for a few of the saloons that had front windows and belched out yellow puddles of light on the boardwalks.

Most of them didn't have front windows since they were prime casualties in a shootout inside the saloon. After a window had been replaced two or three times, most of the saloon owners simply boarded them up and lit another lamp.

Lee saw the kid coming toward them out of the darkness. He looked to be about twelve, thirteen maybe and small. He wore bib overalls and a dirty shirt, no cap and no shoes.

He stood just inside the spill of light for a moment, stared at both of them, then his right hand came up with a hog leg half as big as he was. He grabbed it with both hands and before Lee could bellow a warning, the kid fired. The lead nicked Plummer in the left arm and brought a scream of rage as he drew and fired so fast Lee lifted his brows.

The shot came suddenly with only a brief glance at the target, but the round hit precisely what Plummer aimed at: the kid's right wrist holding the old Colt .44. The polished lead slug drilled cleanly through the wrist, slammed the weapon out of the youth's hand and brought a wail of pain.

The boy held the bullet hole with his left hand and glared at Sam Plummer.

"You killed my pa today!" the boy spat at Plummer.

Plummer kicked the weapon away and pulled the boy more into the light.

"I did? Only shot one many today, Skinny Victor. You kin?"

"He was my pa. I'm Josh Victor and I'm gonna kill you! I owe you. What Ma and us kids gonna do now?"

"Damned if I know, kid. Should have wondered that of your pa when he stole from the Silver Strike."

Plummer caught the boy's left arm, held his wrist with one hand and his elbow with the other and brought the limb down sharply over his lifted knee. Both forearm bones cracked as they broke.

Young Josh screamed and then passed out.

Plummer snorted, dropped the boy onto the board walk and signalled Lee to continue walking down the planks.

"Damn fool kid could have got himself killed," Plummer said. "I let him off lucky. Like as not he'll remember today for a damn long time."

Lee didn't say a word. It wasn't his place. He was low man in the outfit. It wasn't his place to criticize.

They looked in two more bars. Most of the other stores were closed up tight. Almost every store had an overhang on the second story, built out eight feet over the boardwalk and held up by sturdy posts. It provided cover for the rain, and a natural tunnel when snow piled up in the streets as high as to the second floor level.

Plummer leaned against the Archer Meat Company store front and reloaded the spent round in his six-gun.

"One real problem in town right now, and her name is Colleen O'Reily. Her pa used to run the O'Reily #1 up the hill to the left. She runs it now, and by God, she does a pretty good job of it. Good enough so the colonel is troubled.

"Little Irish lass stands up for what she believes, I'll give her that. She pounded on me today after I nailed that thief in the street. She could be problems, real problems down the line. Me, I don't hanker to be the one to straighten her out. But the day might come when somebody has to." He shook his head. "I ain't never killed a woman, leastwise on purpose."

"Her father die in a mine accident?" Lee asked.

"Oh, hell no. He got lead fever. About six slugs in

him as near as I can remember. Got himself mixed up in a gunfight he had no business in. Least that's the way it looked to everybody.''

They patrolled the three block long main street until a little after eleven that night, then wound their way up to Mountain Steet and the house.

Lee found his room, made sure the window was locked with the twist fitting on top, then put a chair under the door knob. He was bone weary after the coach ride, and the sex ride with Debbie Sue, and patrolling the town. Tonight he needed some shut eye.

He got it.

The next morning after breakfast, Sam and Lee saddled horses and rode out along the limits of the four mining claims that the Silver Strike had stakes on. At the last one out on Desperation Mountain in the least likely looking area, they found one of the small miners who had started his dig close to the claim line and then sent his tunnel four-feet over into Silver Strike territory.

The little operation was called the Diablo. It had no stamp mill, might have a dozen men working the still short tunnel with no shafts sunk into the mountain at all. The mine owner, a tough looking stump-thick man pushed the hat back on his head and squinted up at the two riders.

"Plummer, ain't it? Yeah. Let me tell you this, Plummer. I got me tunnel in the right spot. I know hard rock mining. I'm on the line, perfectly legal, then I'm going to drop in a shaft to about a quarter of a mile.''

"Streib, you're talking yourself into an early grave!'' Plummer thundered. "Col. Ralson says your Diablo tunnel is on his property. You'll angle it away and back onto your own dirt at once or I'll come back with four men and rifles and shoot any man who trespasses on Silver Strike land. You understand my meaning, you little German bastard?''

Streib stood taller. "Plummer, you know, rifles shoot both directions. Look over there at the office.''

As Plummer and Lee looked that way a rifle snarled and the round cleared Plummer's head by not more than three feet.

His hand automatically darted to his hip.

"You touch that iron and you're dead where you sit. Lift your hand away, both of you. Keep them on the saddlehorn and you just might live long enough to ride off my claim. Either of you try to come back, you'll be killed on sight. Now get your gunslick asses off my Diablo claim!''

Plummer looked at Lee who nodded. "We can't beat that hand. Let's ride.''

"I'll be back, asshole!'' Plummer shouted at him, but kept both hands on the saddlehorn as they rode away, walking the mounts until they were over the crest of the rise and could relax.

"That one doesn't scare easily,'' Lee said.

Plummer was too worked up to say a word. He kicked the horse into a trot and then a gallop as he headed back to the Silver Strike. As they put their horses in the company stable, Plummer's face was still nearly purple with rage.

"Streib is a dead man,'' he blurted. "It's just a matter of a few days. I've got to go see the colonel. You can stay down at the house.''

Morgan went to the house, washed up and set his high crowned Stetson on his head exactly right, then walked downtown. He needed to learn more about the place, meet some of the people. He walked the length of the town trying to remember the names of the stores and where they were from the Patterson Undertakers at the east end of town to Benson

Bottling Works at the west end. The bottling works was really a small brewery.

He stopped in at the General Store to find a new folding pocket knife. He had lost his old one somehow on the stage. He bought one for a quarter, and was paying for it when he saw a pretty girl come into the store. She was on the short side with dark brown hair and he guessed about nineteen or twenty. He took his change and when he looked up the girl was standing in front of him.

"Mr. Morgan?" she asked.

"Yes, ma'am," Lee said touching his hat brim.

"I thought so." She shook her head and he saw that she was extremely pretty, with darting dark eyes, a snub of a nose and soft clear skin.

"I see that your gun is tied low, like the others. But you do seem different. You don't look like a mindless killer like the other three do. Oh, I know a paid killer can look almost any way, but you just don't seem to fit the norm."

Lee smiled. She was pretty. He understood what she said, but didn't take offense.

"Pardon me, my manners. I'm Colleen O'Reily. I run the O'Reily Mine #1, the one your boss is trying to shut down. How on earth. . . ." She stopped. Then she took a deep breath and stared at him with wonderment. "I just don't see how you can work for a killer like Cleve Ralston. He had a man killed, shot down in the street yesterday. Killed him because he stole a gold nugget from his mine! We have no law at all in Silverton, only the law that Colonel Ralston wants enforced by his three . . . no four, killer gunmen. How can you do it?"

Before Lee could answer, the woman lifted the hem of her long skirt and swept out of the store and to the boardwalk. Lee turned toward the clerk who he guessed also owned the store.

"Is Miss O'Reily always so outspoken?" he asked.

"Yes sir. Sure is. That Colleen says just about what she thinks, not a bit bashful about it. Gets her in trouble sometimes."

"What else can you tell me about her?"

"Oh, well. Let's see. She's single. She runs the mine, like she said. Her manager does most I imagine. His name is Warren Quade, a tall man, formal, sticky, a bookkeeper. He's been trying to marry the girl for the past year. You knew her Pa was killed in a shootout. Just what it was all about is a bit murky."

"Is her mine making a profit?"

"Yep. Good run outfit. Not as big as the Silver Strike. But run good. Some of them gypo miners should watch what she does, how they run her mine. They could learn a heap."

Lee thanked the man and wandered around the town. For a mining camp it was well laid out. Main Street was wide and straight as a plumb line. The cross street, called Nevada, went at a precise right angle heading up the hill toward the mines. The businesses were well spaced and had one alley through Main.

Houses were all pushed well back of the business section. Whoever set up the town figured on it staying for a while. Lee wandered into a drinking establishment, the Sierra Saloon, and saw that it was a real barrelhouse, with sawdust on the floor and no food or dancing girls. They had two items for sale, whiskey and beer, nothing fancy. He had a cold beer.

A town this high must have an ice house. There would be plenty of ice from the East Walker River. He hadn't seen an ice pond that was flooded in the fall so it would settle down before it froze, but there must be one. Then all a man had to do was saw the

ice into blocks and haul it to an ice house kind of a
barn and stack it in between layers of straw or hay
so it wouldn't melt together. Ice sure made beer a lot
tastier.

Lee had two beers, watched a card game for a
while and saw both men cheating, then wandered
back to the company house on Mountain Street.

When Plummer reported to Col. Ralston after his
ride out to the German's Diablo mine, both men
were angry.

"He actually fired at you, near you? He threatened
you?"

"Sure as hell did, sir."

"He dies. We'll work out the method and the time,
but he dies!"

Col. Ralston stalked around his office, took off his
glasses and wiped his watering eyes. He stared at
Plummer and changed the subject abruptly.

"Morgan. How is he working out?"

"Fair. No real test of him yet. But then he ain't had
no hard work, no killin' work to do."

Col. Ralston sat down at his desk, took off his
glasses and rubbed his eyes gently.

"Killing times. Yes, the years with the Confederacy were some of the best of my life. The drama,
the scope, the sweep of a great battle. I was in a lot
of the big ones, Plummer, war is man's greatest
game! The odds are so tremendous—life and death!

"One great mass of men, horses, machines and
weapons, pitted against another equal number of
men, horses, machines and weapons! God, I love it!
Five years of glory, then defeat and shame. You knew
my mansion, my barns, my fields, everything
burned or ruined by the Yankees. The bastards also
killed my wife and two children in an artillery
bombardment of my home. Christ but I hate you
Yankees!"

He shook his head in anger and loss.

Col. Ralston looked up and tears streamed down his cheeks. "Now because of my eyes, I have to hire men like you to do the killing for me. I shot a dozen Yankees one day myself! I'm not afraid to kill!

"Now I use people. I use you, the miners, the people of this town. The miners work all day for 90 cents. Fourteen hours by the time they get home again. Damn right I use them!

"Sam, you have to know that I'm going to take over, run out or kill every mine owner on Desperation Mountain. This whole damned silver field will be mine! I'll own it. I'll pay fifty cents for fourteen hours work and the men who won't work for that will damn well starve to death!"

He spun around and peered out through the heavy drapes. Sun streamed in and he turned his eyes away.

"Before any real law comes to town we'll own everything, have it all sewed up all legal and proper if we have to forge papers on every claim we don't own now. Then we'll start to make some real money!"

Ralston took out a pad of paper. He had each of the nine mines listed, with the owner's name, the number of men who worked in the mine and an evaluation of the owner's tenacity.

"Eight small mines, Plummer. Know damned well we can buy out three of them, for about half of what they're worth. You'll scare them into signing. Three of them that are making a small profit will be harder. They will start having *accidents* below and above ground. A twenty dollar gold piece here and there can buy a lot of problems underground. A fire or two, and the profit making mine is on the ropes and almost broke.

"The O'Reily mine will be the tough one. Might have to really damage it and shoot up a bunch of people, including Miss Mouth herself, to win on that one. That will be the last one we take over."

He handed Plummer a sheet of paper. "Here's the first target. We can't move too fast. So we do one mine a week. Wait three or four days, then get out there and do it. You have the extra gunhand. Take him along. Test him. I want the Desperation Mine burned out and destroyed within a week. I'll have another target for you as soon as this one is out of the way.

"That's all, Captain Plummer. Get to your men, make the assignments and pick up any equipment and arms that you will need."

"Yes sir!" Plummer said, playing the military game with the colonel whenever he seemed to need it. He took the sheet of paper and hurried out of the office and back down the hill to Mountain Street and his room. There he slowly, laboriously, read the sheet of paper with the instructions. At least he had it all straight. He'd talk to Morgan about it in two or three days after he'd studied the operation, and figured out just how best to ruin it with the least amount of damage.

It was three days later that Lee felt as if this whole job was nothing more than being an insulting and overbearing policeman. Col. Ralston certainly had no need for four gunmen of the caliber now on his payroll. Not unless he was going to start robbing banks, trains and stagecoaches.

Two of the last three nights Lee had walked the town from six to midnight. Only once had he touched his gun, and that was to win a bet with an unruly bar patron. The man was half drunk, had just won thirty dollars in a poker game and was crowing to the world what a fast draw he was.

Before he could demonstrate Lee had grabbed him

by the shirt and jerked him around face to face.

"You're fast?" Lee asked with a sneer.

"Damned fast," the man said. He looked at one of his friends and whispered. "Who is this guy?"

"One of Ralston's gunhands, Lee Morgan," his friend said.

"Oh, shit." The miner stared at Lee, quickly becoming sober.

"No lie, you really Lee Morgan from Idaho?"

Lee nodded.

The miner held up both hands. "You're faster than me. But just how fast are you? How about a little contest. Say I toss a beer bottle in the air and you bust it."

Lee snorted. "I've seen twelve year old boys do that with two tries. Get to something hard."

The miner scowled. "Say I hold the bottle shoulder high and drop it. You have to break it before it hits the ground. Draw and fire and hit the sucker!"

Johnny Hardin, who was making the rounds with Lee that night, chuckled and watched Morgan. Wasn't a man in a hundred who could draw that fast.

Lee shook his head. "Sorry, I don't put on demonstrations for free. Is there any betting money in the house?"

The miner grinned. "Now you're talking! What kind of odds you want?"

"I break the bottle, you owe me ten for every dollar I bet," Lee said.

"Not a chance. Two-to-one."

Morgan stared at the miner, shrugged and took four double eagles from his pocket. He handed the coins to the barkeep. "You hold the money, can you gents cover eighty dollars two-for-one?"

In five minutes the money was down. Everyone

moved away from the alley wall and the tall miner
held an empty pint beer bottle in his right hand.

"Barkeep will call, set, ready, drop!" Morgan said.
"Then you drop it and I draw. One shot. One try."

The saloon had filled up as word of the contest
spread and Lee had to growl at a couple of men to
keep them back so he had room to draw. He stood
back ten feet from the bottle, stared at the level
where the miner would hold it and made his
calculations. He had to take it about a foot from the
floor.

Lee stood in a gunfighter's pose, hand hovering
over his iron. He'd already slid the Bisley in and out
of the leather twice to be sure it wouldn't hang up.

Then he shook out both hands and relaxed. He
looked at the barkeep.

"I'm ready," he said.

The barkeep watched him a moment, then looked
at the miner.

"Set, ready, drop!" the barkeep barked.

The bottle dropped from the miner's fingers.

Lee Morgan jolted his hand upward jerking the
weapon from leather, his thumb cocking the
hammer and his hand-eye coordination aligning the
muzzle at the falling bottle. His finger stroked the
trigger all at the same time and the Bisley roared.

Through a thin pall of blue smoke, Lee saw the
bottle falling, then shatter a foot from the floor. It all
happened in less than a second. The men in the
saloon roared in approval.

Lee punched the spent round from the Bisley,
added a fresh one from his belt and holstered the
weapon.

The barkeep brought him his own 80 dollars and
the 160 wagered dollars in gold and paper. Lee gave
the barkeep a five dollar bill.

The men quieted and watched Lee.

"Like I said gentlemen, I don't use my weapon for sport. I'm a working man, only I work with my Bisley. I just hope I don't need to use it against any of you."

The silence was broken at last by a small voice from the back of the room.

"Christ in a bucket! Not against my draw!"

The jibe broke the tension and the men hooted and clapped and went back to their drinking and their faro and poker games.

Outside as they walked the street, Hardin got in his say. Lee had seen him holding in.

"You took a hell of a chance in there, Morgan."

"Not really. You see how tall that miner was, well over six feet. Now if I'd had a man five feet tall drop the bottle, I'd have a foot less to work with."

"Son-of-a-bitch, you've done that before," Hardin said grinning.

"Not the same way. Usually I work with a whiskey glass with bigger odds. Here I had a larger target and another foot of drop."

"And you made a profit of a hundred and sixty dollars. Almost two month's pay."

"More important I sent a message to the great unwashed. I'm a gunhand who can shoot fast and straight. Tends to keep some of the hotheads in line. My old dad used to tell me that half of being a fast gun was making the other guy believe you were good and could beat him."

"You did that for damn sure," Hardin said. "Even I believe it." He grinned. "I believe it, even if I am faster than you."

3

The next morning Lee walked down to Main Street. He knew the town now, every store and crook and alley. He moved straight to Johnson's Jewelry and Clockworks and admired the big grandfather clock just inside the screen door. The day was as warm as an Arizona afternoon, the sun out hot and bright and hardly any wind at all. Unusual.

He talked to Dale Johnson and showed him the Waterbury on a fine silver chain.

"Fifty cents for a good cleaning," the jeweler said. "Well worth it. Bet she's been losing time lately."

"About two minutes a day," Lee said. He'd never paid more than a quarter for cleaning the fine watch before. At last Lee nodded. "I need it tomorrow about this time."

Johnson grinned, wrote Lee's name on a piece of paper with a string attached and tied it to the stem. "Yes, sir, Mr. Morgan. Be ready before noon tomorrow."

Lee left knowing he'd been suckered for two bits, but every man had to have a few small victories.

As Lee stepped out of the jewelry store, Miss Colleen O'Reily stood waiting for him. She nodded, her expression serious, even grim. No smile from the pretty girl this morning.

"Mr. Morgan, I wonder if I might have fifteen minutes of your valuable time. I'll also buy you a cup of coffee and a cinnamon roll down at the Silverton Hotel. Don't get any wild ideas, this is a business meeting."

Lee grinned. He wanted to laugh. She was trying so hard to be precise and formal and tough. But if he laughed he knew she would turn and walk away. A business meeting? He was at the least curious.

"I'd be pleased to have a cup of coffee, Mine Owner O'Reily. The cinnamon roll sounds delightful."

She turned and started for the hotel which was on the same side of the street, just across the alley and past a small store that was filled with women's clothes and run by a seamstress.

"Mr. Morgan," she said as they walked the planks. "I know you are employed by Col. Ralston, but I think I have a situation that will interest you."

"Always ready to listen."

Lee had walked through the hotel lobby, but never been in the dining room. It was well set up for a mining town, with tablecloths and china. They sat to one side at a table for two and she ordered.

"As you know, Mr. Morgan, I own the O'Reily mine. I am also in the process of bringing the other miners together into an alliance, an association so we can protect ourselves from the Silver Strike."

"Mighty big job," Lee offered.

"Naturally, I thought of you. I'd met you, you're not a wild-eyed, crazy gunslinger. I want you to come to work for me. At first, as my chief of mine security, and as my general mine protector and my own bodyguard.''

''I have a good job, Miss O'Reily. I make a hundred dollars a month.''

She looked up, dark eyes frowning. ''So much? Gracious, I hadn't thought . . .'' She brushed at moisture in her eyes.

Lee smiled. She was some rough and tough businesswoman.

''It's more than just the business. I . . . I also want you to prove that Ralston, Cassidy, Hardin and Sam Plummer gunned down my father in cold blood. I want all four of them tried for the murder of my father. That means I want you to get the facts we can take to the county sheriff.''

Lee looked at her sternly over the rim of his coffee cup.

''Now that's what I'd call a tall order, Miss Colleen. It's a cold trail. A year ago, you said. Nobody can follow a trail that old. Just can't be done. People move, witnesses forget.''

''I'll never forget. Plummer picked a fight with Daddy and got him to go in the street for a shootout. Cassidy and Hardin were on a roof somewhere or in the alley. It was all arranged. People say they heard five shots.

''Daddy never pulled a tigger. Sam's gun had only one fired round in it and they called it a fair shootout. It was a planned backshooting, bush-whacking murder and nobody would do anything about it. The sheriff's deputy here in town is a coward who won't wear a gun, mostly collects taxes and does paperwork. I need you, Morgan!''

She damn well did. He knew exactly what she was up against. Lee also knew she didn't stand a chance in hell of getting the law on Ralston. But she was so damned cute! He wanted to put his arms around her and kiss away her tears and hold her tight and tell her everything would be all right. But it wouldn't. Ralston had her right by her tits and he was going to squeeze hard until she gave in and sold out or gave up.

"I'm sorry, Colleen. I'm working for your enemies. I can't help you. At least I won't tell them about this talk."

"The association needs you, too. We need you to be our chief ramrod."

"I'm sorry."

"Ralston is a murdering bastard! Can't you see that? He's a cheat, a killer, he treats his miners like animals and kills people he doesn't like or who get in his way. Morgan, you're on the wrong side. Can't you see that? He wants to take over the whole mountain. He wants to own every silver mine around our town."

"I signed on with Ralston," Morgan said standing. "A deal is a deal. Unless he crosses me, I'll have to stay with him. Thanks for the cinnamon roll. They're the best in town." Lee turned and walked away from the table and he was sure the pretty girl behind him was crying.

That afternoon Sam Plummer laid out the job.

"We move on the Desperation Mine at dusk. It's owned by a man named Gus Jacobs. One of the smallest mines. They only have about ten men working for them. But they have a good vein, so don't damage the place too much."

Lee sat back and listened. This was what he had been hired for, strong arming and shooting. He was good at it. It was also exactly what Colleen O'Reily said Ralston would try to do. He was beginning to get a bad taste in his mouth.

Yes, he'd killed men before and enjoyed doing it,

getting a thrill that he never could quite describe let alone understand. Usually those men had deserved to die. Often it was kill or be killed.

This looked a hell of a lot different. Big guy against a little guy.

"Morgan, your first job is to burn down the equipment shack. It's about fifty yards from the main shaft and the office building. They've got a steam lift works at the mine. That we don't want damaged."

All four of them would be in on it, as well as two more men with torches to do the burning.

Hardin snorted. "We just playing bonfire or do we do any shooting?"

"Depends," Plummer said. "We show them our hand, burn down the equipment barn and then palaver. They can walk out and live or stay there and fight and get burned out and half of them killed. We put on a good show up front, we can scare the hell out of them and not get our skins shot up."

"Hell, yes, if it works," Cassidy said. "I ain't one to pick a fight with a dozen rifles."

"We'll have our own rifles along," Sam said. "Any questions?"

There were none. Sam stood. "Come on down to the weapons room and we'll draw rifles, Remingtons, some Henry repeaters that you can shoot all fucking day before you reload."

Morgan picked up an Evans repeating rifle and a hundred of the .44 rim fire cartridges. The Evans had a tubular magazine one and a half inches in diameter extending from the butt plate to the receiver. It formed part of the butt framework and the small of the rifle stock.

In the magazine was a four fluted cylinder along which was coiled a spiral wire with pitch equal to the length of the cartridges held in the magazine flutes.

It had a screw feed principal and worked. The most important aspect was that the magazine could hold 34 of the .44 caliber rounds. This one could really be fired all day without a reload. The piece fired by a hammer under the breech, cocked by motion of the trigger guard between rounds.

The whole mechanism was delicate and complicated but treated right it could be a whirlwind of a weapon. The magazine on his was full.

Lee went with the other three men and two fire starters. They walked east and timed it just right, arriving at the small mine works just at dusk. The darkness would be the only cover they had. Here and there was a rock large enough for cover, but they were in the wrong spots.

"Burn down the equipment barn," Sam told Lee. He took one of the torch men with a gallon of kerosene and slipped around back of the shed with no one seeing them. The torch man doused the coal oil along the back side of the raw wood building. It had a lot of pine pitch in the wood and would burn like a bonfire.

They both lighted the ends of the kerosene soaked wood, made sure it had a good start, then faded back just as darkness closed in solidly.

The shouts of "Fire!" came quickly, but the three men who ran from the mine called out that it was too late. They had only a few buckets and no good water supply. They stood and watched it burning.

Plummer fired a rifle round over their heads.

"You men down there watching the fire. It's moving day. You have ten minutes to get every man out of your tunnel and out of the area. If you don't we're burning down everything above ground and starting fire to the tunnel mouth. You hear me?"

Two men turned and ran into the darkness away from the mine and toward town.

The third one rushed back into the office building.
Five minutes later nothing had happened except
the equipment shed was still roaring as fire ate
through the roof and sent the free shingles flying.

Plummer sent a rifle round crashing through the
window in the office. Six rifle rounds answered him.
He yelped and rolled quickly away from the spot.

"You bastards are asking for it!" he screamed.

"Morgan, get around back and lite fire to that
office building. Hardin, take the other torch and that
five gallon can of kerosene and pour it into the main
tunnel and fire it. We'll fry those bastards!"

Morgan motioned for the torch man and they
hurried off into the darkness. When they were out of
hearing of Plummer, Morgan touched the man's
shoulder.

"Wait a minute," he said. The torchman stopped.
Lee's Bisley slammed down across the man's temple
knocking him out. Morgan tied him with his own
boot laces, then hurried toward the mine entrance.

He spotted the torch man lighting the five gallon
can of fuel oil. He was outlined by the fire from the
shed. Quickly Lee pumped two rounds from the
Remington at the torchman, smashing his right leg
with a round and dumping him into the grass.

Hardin bellowed at Plummer that his man was hit.
Plummer yelled something Lee couldn't hear. The
coal oil was the key. He searched the area where he
had shot the torchman and in the background light
saw what he figured was the square can outlined by
the fire. He pulled down on the can and fired twice,
heard the bullet hit metal and puncture he hoped.

A string of profanity rumbled from where Hardin
had been and Lee saw him flash past the back light
as he ran up the hill toward Plummer's position.

He'd hit the coal oil.

Lee had rolled up hill after shooting at the coal oil

can. Now he surged another twenty feet and tried to figure out where Plummer and his two men were.

Lee knew what he had done. As soon as he slugged the torchman with him he had crossed a bridge that he could not venture back on. He was through with Ralston, and he had just picked up three fast guns as newly sworn enemies.

"Shit, in for an ounce . . ." Lee whispered. He sent four rounds slamming into the area where he figured Plummer and company could be, then rolled down hill to get away from his own revealing muzzle flashes.

Return fire came almost at once from three different spots. Smart, they had dispersed. There would be no way to find them in the darkness. But he could stand as an outside guard over the mine. He had heard sporadic fire from the office, but now no muzzle flashes that would indicate return fire by Plummer's crew.

Lee lay in the grass and dirt and rocks of the Nevada hillside and waited. A door squeaked below. A minute later, Lee could make out the movement of a man coming toward him and toward the mine tunnel.

The darkness was like a coal mine at midnight. Lee could barely see his hand three feet from his face. The Desperation Mine man slid by in the darkness six feet from Lee and didn't see him. A few moments later Lee saw his shadow slide into the tunnel entrance. There was no closure of any kind on the open tunnel. It stood over seven feet high and had tracks coming out of it for ore cars.

A small operation but evidently with a good potential. The lifting works sat to one side, a building that housed a steam rig to provide power to lift a cage up and down in the deep shaft.

Lee waited in the darkness. A sudden barrage of

firing came from up the hill. The Remingtons and Henrys. Lee fired a half dozen rounds from his Evans, then hugged the long gun and rolled away from his firing position.

There had been a dozen shots of return fire from the office as well. He had been surprised when six rounds blasted from the tunnel mouth. At least the miners were putting up a fight. Lee figured he had checkmated Plummer, at least for tonight. He didn't have the troops to storm the tunnel or the office building.

Without coal oil he would have a harder time burning down the office, and the mine would be tougher yet to set fire. Plummer would not risk his high priced men in a flat out assault. Chances were he was outgunned and knew it.

A half hour later, Lee heard movement across the way and figured Plummer and his team were retreating.

An hour later nothing had happened. Lee worked his way down to the office building and rapped gently on a window that hadn't been broken.

"Desperation Mine? A friend out here. Open up."

There was a long silence.

"What the hell you mean, a friend? You're trying to kill us!"

"You heard that first rifle over on this side before your man went to the tunnel. That was me. Who the hell you think kept this place from burning to the ground?"

Another silence. Whispering inside.

"Yeah? What's your name?"

"Names don't matter. You better put out a 24-hour guard around your place and keep it tight. Plummer and his friends have orders to burn you out. He'll be back, probably tonight."

"That figures."

"Put out some lanterns that'll burn all night. You got a night shift?"

"Hell no, this ain't the Silver Strike."

"Get some men back, get some shotguns, or you won't have a mine to defend by morning."

"I'm Gus Jacobs. I own this hole in the ground. I'm coming out. You gun me and you get four rounds of double-ought buck which should do damn bad things to your body."

"No gun play, Jacobs. We need to talk."

A door squeaked open down the front of the building and a shadow edged out. The man held a shotgun.

"You still there?"

"Yep."

"Say it was Plummer and his three guns?"

"True, but only two other guns now. I was the third. I just quit the team. How many men you have right now?"

"Damnit, just four."

"I make five. Set out ten or twelve lanterns, as many as you can scrape up, around your office, your lift works and the mine. Try to dig up some more men with guns. Could be a long night."

"You that guy, Lee Morgan, the gunsharp?"

"Yep."

"How I know you ain't setting us up for dead?"

"If that was true, you'd be dead already, Jacobs. There's one of Ralston's men up by the tunnel with one or two broken legs, and another man behind your office here tied hand and foot. Better do something with them first."

Two hours later the lanterns glowed brightly. The Desperation Mine had seven men stationed around the buildings in a circle twenty to thirty yards from the frame building. They had a perimeter defense. About two A.M. the kerosene ran out in one of the lanterns.

A man ran toward the lantern as it faded and a rifle shot slammed into the ground near him. He spun around and dove back into the darkness.

It was the only action by the attackers for the rest of the night. They figured there was a defense by then, and evidently held well back away from the defenders.

With daylight, Jacobs and Lee walked the site and found the brass from the rifle firing. They worked out a three man guard force for daylight hours, and five men at night.

"Figure I better put half my crew on guard duty or I won't have no god damned mine to dig in," Jacobs said. Lee was surprised at Jacobs' size when the sun came up. He was short and thick as an oak tree, with arms the size of many men's legs, and shoulders that would move a mountain all by themselves even if it was a bucket of ore at a time.

Jacobs took off a battered hat and stared at Lee. He scratched his beard and snorted.

"You say you was working for Col. Ralston, came with them last night to burn us out and switched sides. Christ, you ain't got a chance in hell of living out the day! All three of them gunsharps gonna be out hunting you down. You done cut your throat here last night, Morgan."

He held out his hand. "I got to thank you while I can do it when you're standing up."

"I've been hunted before, and by some men far better than this trio. I don't have any plans to run or to die."

"Good!" Jacobs said. "Colleen been talking about an association. Guess it's time. Long as you gonna be our security chief and head gunslinger."

"We'll see about that. Right now I could use some breakfast and then some shut eye."

"You can have breakfast down at my house. Missus will be more than glad to provide. Eggs, bacon, fried taters and lots of bread and jam and coffee sound interesting?"

It was. An hour later, Lee pushed back from the table, thanked the short, thin little woman who had cooked the food, and adjusted the Bisley on his hip. He hefted the Evans repeating rifle and marveled again at the 34 rounds that could be loaded in the magazine. At nine pounds it was about the weight of most rifles. He decided to keep it.

Lee held out his hand. "Thanks for the breakfast, they couldn't have done better in St. Louis's finest hotel. Keep on your guard."

Lee walked out the door and took a round-about way down the hill toward town. The Desperation was between the two large mines, and there was no cover whatsoever. He jogged aways, came behind an ore wagon working down the hill and slid in behind it to shield himself from the Silver Strike Mine.

He was halfway down Nevada Street when a buggy pulled sharply toward him and he had to jump out of the way to keep from being run down. For a moment his temper flared but when he looked in the rig he saw Colleen O'Reily motioning to him.

"Get in here before you get yourself shot down," she scolded. "I heard what you did for Gus Jacobs last night."

Lee stepped into the buggy but made no move to take the reins to the sleek black that pulled it. Colleen skillfully swung the rig around in the roadway and headed back up Nevada Street and toward the O'Reily Mine.

"How could you hear so quickly?" Lee asked watching the small woman who this morning would not lose the frown on her pretty face.

She glanced at him. "Jacobs sent a man over early to tell me. We keep up on the news. But you are a puzzle, Mr. Morgan. You start out a paid killer, ordered to burn out a small mine and slaughter everyone there if need be, but you change sides, shoot up the attacking force and fight them off the rest of the night. You are a complete puzzle."

"No puzzle at all, Colleen O'Reily. If you'd just smile once for me, I'd explain."

"That cheap?"

"Precisely."

She sighed, then looked at him and let a marvelous smile break out around her dark eyes and that pug nose and delicious rosy lips.

"Better, much better," Lee said. "Now, your reward. A fair fight I don't mind, a little bullying and pushing people around doesn't hurt one hell of a lot. But mass murder is where I draw the line. I had no intentions of letting those men die last night. If changing sides is what it took, that's what I did."

"Gus tells me he hired you as the new association's head security agent and gunslick. Is that true?"

"I did a job for him and he paid me."

"How much?"

"Best breakfast I've had since I left Idaho."

Colleen laughed. "You are not as tough as you make yourself out to be, Mister Gunslick Lee Morgan." She looked over at him as she pulled the rig into a stable in back of the house that stood near the O'Reily Mine.

A small stamp mill pounded away fifty yards from them.

"My offer still stands. We want you to be Security Chief for the Silverton Miners Protective Association. Right now we have two members, Gus and me. I hope to have seven more members by the end of the week. We'll pay you $75 a month for your services.''

Lee Morgan held out his hand. "Boss, it's a deal, considering my current unpopularity in some circles in this town.''

"Good, you'll stay here in my house. We can work together better that way.''

"Begging your pardon, Miss O'Reily, but I can't do that. I'm a target. Three gentlemen are going to be gunning for my hide 24 hours a day. I'd put you in danger that way. I'll put together a poke and get some supplies and camp out along the river. Could you get me a horse and saddle?''

She nodded. "Yes, that does seem the best way to handle it. Would you suggest I put up guards around my mine and headquarters?''

"Yes, Miss. Twenty-four hours a day. If you could see your way clear, wouldn't hurt any if you could lend four men to Gus for a spell. Shouldn't take too long. My three friends with the colonel are going to demand a showdown with me quickly. I'm sure they have some kind of takeover schedule for the smaller mines as well which the colonel will hold to.''

"So I better do my missionary work with the other mine owners. Good. I'll get started this morning. There'll be a saddled horse at the small hitching post at the rear of the house. You come in and my cook will fix you up with some camp food.''

She hesitated and he thought he saw the touch of a blush. "Mr. Morgan, it wouldn't hurt any for you to come around after dark for a good supper. We can make sure everything is going all right.''

"Yes, miss, whenever it's practical. I'd expect some of my days will be spent here, too.''

That's when he remembered his possibles were all in the room over on Mountain Street. Not a chance in hell of him getting them now. He'd need some clothes, shaving gear . . . later.

They had left the buggy and walked to the back door of the O'Reily house.

"Come in and I'll draw a map for you of the rest of the small mines and put down who owns them. My guess is that Ralston will try to squeeze out the small mines first. I'll go to the little outfits at once."

She drew a rough sketch and outlined the nine mines from the Diablo west of the Silver Strike, to the O'Reily and then the Winner Mine at the far east end of the vein. No silver had been found beyond the Winner shaft.

"That's the spread," Colleen said, looking up at him where he stared down at the paper over her shoulder. For a moment her face was only inches from his. She hesitated, saw the grin on his face and looked down again, then slid away from him.

"The mines are too far apart for one defensive circle," Lee said, his voice not quite normal after the surge of feeling when she had been so close to him. "Which means each mine owner is going to have to set up his own 24-hour defense. Three to four men during the day, and twice that many at night. Shotguns with double-ought, pistols, and rifles. Warn everyone that anybody who moves around a mine at night is liable to get blown full of holes."

"I agree. What's first?"

"First we set up your own defensive system. How many men do you employ?"

"About 150."

"Have your foreman find five who can use a rifle and get them topside for their new day time job. I'll want a tour of your place to figure out defensive positions."

They took the tour. The Nevada hills outside the timber zone are almost naked. A little grass, a few small sagebrush shrubs, and that's about it. Along the river there is a corridor of brush and a few cottonwood trees. But up on the slopes it's as barren as Great Aunt Matilda.

The slope of Desperation Mountain rose behind all of the mines. Here at the O'Reily, there was a bit of an indentation that really couldn't be called a gully.

An hour later, Lee had the men do the only thing practical: they dug three foot deep holes to sit in while on guard. Anything less and they would be sitting ducks for a rifle shot from cover.

When he had the men situated, it was past noon. They were to stay in their holes until relieved at dusk. It was a twelve hour assignment, but at least they didn't have to shovel silver ore.

He found the saddled roan at the back door that afternoon. The cook, a black man named Philip, had a flour sack of "traveling" food ready for him. He borrowed a box of .45 rounds for the Bisley and told Philip that he would get a small camp established and be back just after dark.

Philip grinned. He had taken an instant liking to the gunman, no matter what anyone said.

"Yes sir, Mr. Morgan. I'll tell Miss Colleen. She done went out to talk to the other mine owners about the association."

That was when Lee gave Philip a twenty dollar gold piece and asked him to buy some goods at the general store. Shaving gear, a small carpet bag, some work pants and work shirts and a few other essentials. The black man grinned, said he'd do it first thing, and waved as Lee rode away.

Lee silently wished Colleen luck with her talks with the other mine owners and turned south toward the East Walker River.

4

The East Walker River was good sized at Silverton, good sized that is for a mountain desert setting. It did spawn some thick brush along the near side and a few trees that birds must have seeded in years past.

On the horse, Lee had found a ground cloth and two thick blankets which he was sure that Colleen had arranged for. He rode a quarter-of-a-mile upstream, crossed over in knee deep water and found a spot he liked. It was against a modest bank, had thick willow brush and a few tall alders to one side and a heavy almost impassable upstream barrier of creosote brush. The cover was more than deep enough to hide him. He found a place to tie the horse, a young roan that was lively and ready for a long run.

"Not today, lady," he said, rubbing her ears. "Maybe soon. You'll be the first one I tell."

He laid out his ground cloth, scratched out a flat place and kicked free a spot for a fire, then brought rocks from the stream to put around it so it wouldn't get out of hand. He gathered dry, smokeless driftwood from the stream where high water had left a deposit of various sized dead sticks and twigs and a few good sized limbs. They made a stack for future use.

Then he hung his sack of grub from a limb of an alder so it was six-feet off the ground to outwit any prowling coyotes. He flushed out a Nevada creeper bird and then a flicker as he worked his way out of the brush on the roan.

He had a base camp. Now to do some scouting. He wondered what the enemy was doing, but had no chance to find out. On an impulse he rode back to the O'Reily house and found Philip there with his new carpet bag and clothes and other gear.

"Thanks, Philip. I didn't have much chance of doing any shopping. Now I have another problem. My black snake whip is still with my other gear over at Ralston's second house on Mountain Street. You have any idea how a smart man could get hold of it?"

Philip grinned. "Maybe a house burglary." His eyes rolled as he laughed. "Or maybe I know a man who works over there. Let me pay a friendly visit this afternoon and see what I can do."

Lee toured the guard posts on the O'Reily Mine, found them occupied and the men alert, but they had been looking into the O'Reily area. He convinced them the danger would come from the other direction, and soon he had them all facing outward.

He talked to the mine manager, Warren Quade. The man was tall, dressed in a black suit and vest and seemed straight out of a Boston men's store. He was stuffy and formal.

"Mr. Morgan, I can't really say that I'm happy

that Colleen hired you. Another fast gun in town can't help matters. But, since she did and you're here, I'll cooperate. First, I would guess that you'll need six men for night guards. We'll talk to the men as they come to work this evening at seven. Get volunteers and you can instruct them at that time."

"Fine, Quade. We have the men out there now with rifles and shotguns. Do you have enough equipment here to cover two more men?"

"I do."

Lee watched the man a moment and saw that he was uncomfortable, nervous, maybe a little frightened. Lee decided to twist the knife a little.

"Quade, you've made it clear you don't like me and don't want me around. Let me get one thing straight. Miss O'Reily is the boss here. I'll deal with her whenever possible. Also, you're the type of man I've never liked, nor trusted. So you deal straight with me and with Colleen—or you'll be answering to me."

"See here now!" Quade began. Then he glanced down at Lee's holstered weapon and he stopped. He turned and went back to his desk and became exceedingly busy with some papers.

That evening at seven, Lee walked into the O'Reily house's back door and asked Philip about supper.

"Be ready in five minutes, Mr. Morgan." He grinned, reached behind a partition and pulled out something and tossed it to Lee. He caught it: his black snake whip. It was exactly as he had left it, neatly coiled and fastened with the leather band and snap. It wasn't that he couldn't find a new one, but this one was broken in and he knew precisely the balance and reach and he could dot an "i" with it in a newspaper.

"Thanks, Philip, I owe you a favor."

The big black man grinned. "You also owe me a dollar. I had to pay my friend a dollar to steal the whip. We figure if'n he took the whole carpet bag, they miss it. But jus' the whip, they not know for days, maybe not at all. We a couple of smart ex-slaves."

"Sure are," Lee said, giving the man two dollars. "That other dollar is for wear and tear on your shoe leather."

Philip shook his head. "I can't take that, Mr. Morgan." He looked at the gunslick and saw the frown and the start of a counter protest. Philip shrugged. "Well, maybe just this one time, since you a friend and all. Right in this way to supper."

Lee found three men around the table with Colleen at the head of the spread.

"Mr. Morgan, let me introduce you to three of my top management men. We have a dinner meeting once a week to talk business. I hope you don't mind."

She introduced the three men. Two were in their twenties and one in his forties. Warren Quade was not one of them.

They had been talking when he came in and now returned to the business matter at hand.

"We should run that lateral another hundred feet," one eager young man said. "It's my belief that the vein will begin again down that way. It has all the right signs."

The food came in then, carried by Philip and a Chinese man, named Han, who Lee had seen in the kitchen. He was the handyman. It was served family style and there was plenty to eat: a vegetable and beef stew, as well as fried chicken, two more kinds of vegetables, and all the slabs of fresh bread and country butter that a dozen men could eat. A big metal pitcher with a top on it held almost a gallon of coffee.

They didn't talk business as they ate. It was a quick no-nonsense meal. When the three men were finished they discussed two other points about the mine, then thanked Colleen for the dinner and excused themselves.

When they left she looked up at Lee quickly. "Don't go, Mr. Morgan. We have some other business to discuss. I talked with three mine owners this afternoon. Two will join us, the third one laughed at me and said he'd take care of himself. The man was Dan Streib over on the Diablo west of the Silver Strike. Dan is quite sure he can defend his own place."

"Who were the other two?"

"Ivan Foley from the Mary Lou just off Mountain Street and Oliver Newton, our closest neighbor over west at the Deep Shaft Mine."

"So you've got four so far. That leaves four to contact."

"Yes. I think you should know that we're assessing ourselves twenty dollar a month for security."

"My pay check is secured. Did you ask the new mine owner members to set up security for tonight around their own operations?"

"Yes, both are ex-soldiers and said they knew what to do. I told them you'll stop by tomorrow to check out their places and make suggestions."

"Lanterns are always a good deterrent. Put half a dozen lit lanterns around buildings."

"Should we do it here?"

"Nope. The smaller ones, they'll be the first targets."

Colleen nodded and stood, walked in back of her chair and stopped and stared at him for a moment. He noticed now that she had on a dress, with fluted sleeves and showing a portion of her neck and upper chest. It was a dress up dress that clung to her small breasts and swept in at her waist.

"There's something else I want you to do," she said.

"Can't be done."

"You don't even know—"

"You want me to prove the Ralston gunhands murdered your father. Not a chance of doing that now. The score can be settled in other ways, however."

"No! I don't want any more killing. That makes me and you just as bad as Ralston and his killers."

"Not the same. If I settled the matter it would be in a fair pulldown, not a back shooting."

She closed her eyes for a moment, a stab of pain showing on her face. "I . . . I didn't mean to imply that there would be anything dishonorable . . . I . . . I . . . Is there anything else that I can do to find justice?"

"You said this county doesn't have much law. Isn't there a sheriff at the county seat?"

"For all the good it does. He lets Ralston *take care* of Silverton."

She came around the chair to where he sat. He was at eye level with the enticing swell of her breasts. He stood.

"Mr. Morgan . . . Lee, I know I'm asking too much, but I so desperately want to see those men who murdered my father punished!"

There was a mist of a tear. He brushed it away from her cheek.

"It will be taken care of before this is over. Trust me."

She watched him from cool black eyes, then took a deep breath and let it out slowly. At last she nodded.

He lifted her chin with his hand, bent and kissed

her lips gently. When he pulled away he saw her
eyes were closed. She opened them slowly.

"Don't do that," she said in a whisper. "I never let
my employees kiss me."

He could read nothing on her face so he bent and
kissed her again. This time her hands came up and
held his arms. He was the one who broke away.

"In this case it's all right. I won't tell anyone." He
grinned, then stepped back. "Time I was making an
inspection tour of the four mines we have in the
association."

"Uh huh."

Lee grinned. She still had a far away look in her
eyes. Slowly she came back to normal. "Yes, tour
them. So far nothing else has happened. Just forming
the association may be enough to slow down Ralston
and his dastardly plans."

"Let's hope so."

About midnight when Lee was talking to the
guards on the Mary Lou, they heard two rifle shots,
then a barrage of fifty or more shots from the
direction of the Diablo.

"I was afraid of something like this," Lee said. He
told the guards at the Mary Lou Mine to stay alert
and jogged across the side of Desperation Mountain,
over the road that led to the Silver Strike and
another three hundred yards west so he could see
the shadows of the Diablo Mine a hundred yards on
up the hill.

A fire broke out in one of the buildings but there
was no hue and cry to put it out. He worked closer
through the darkness and soon saw two shadows lift
from the ground in front of him and strike a match.
Somewhere near the Diablo mine tunnel he saw the
flare of one match, then another.

The men in front of Lee turned and trotted toward
the Silver Strike Mine buildings. He moved slowly

up the hill. The fire grew brighter as it leaped through the one story wood frame building that must have been the headquarters or office of the small mine.

Lee remembered his first visit to the mine only a few days ago riding with Sam Plummer. Dan Streib had made a strong stand, and given a warning, but now there was no sign of Streib, living or dead.

Lee saw two more men lift up from the ground and jog toward the Silver Strike Mine. A form ran through the fire light ahead and vanished into the darkness as the man headed east toward the large mine.

Morgan halted just outside the area lit by the fire. Now he could see two bodies in the dirt; one outside the burning building, another next to the mine tunnel. There was no chance that he could do the Diablo Mine owner any good now. If Plummer and his men had been here and left, the owner himself must be dead and his defenders scattered.

They had been too late for Streib, Lee felt sure. If he wasn't dead he wouldn't be able to operate his mine. It had been a money making dig, and was worth stealing. Ralston had raided it and tomorrow would probably have a bill of sale. The signature would be forged, but if Dan Streib was missing, who could prove the mark on the paper wasn't his?

Lee watched the Diablo until the fire went out. Then he moved closer, checking carefully as he went. He could smell only death. Two horses were down and dead. Besides the two bodies he had seen before he found two more near the mine tunnel. One corpse was sprawled over an ore car where the man had evidently hidden. Five men dead, probably more. One of them could be Streib himself.

A half hour later, Lee moved silently up behind a guard at the Desperation Mine and tapped him on the shoulder.

The miner turned guard screeched in surprise and whirled around, his rifle up. Lee caught the rifle and chuckled.

"Leastwise you've got the brains to be scared. If I was coming after you, you'd be dead by now. You can't stare in one direction all the time. Keep looking around, changing positions."

"Christ, but you scared six years off my life! You this Morgan guy we met before?"

"Yes. Better me than Sam Plummer. You heard the shooting tonight?"

"You bet!"

"My guess is that the colonel's men hit the Diablo Mine tonight. Somebody sure as hell did. At least five dead up there and the office burned into rubble. Keep alert and don't let that happen here. Being dead is no fun at all."

He talked to each man there, then went on to the Deep Shaft and talked to the guards. It was two hours until sunrise when he finally slid into his blankets in the willow brush along the river. He had left the horse a hundred yards farther along the stream.

He lay down, put one hand under his head on the blanket and went to sleep at once. If anything larger than a mouse moved within fifty yards of him, he would be awake at once with the Bisley in his right fist ready to do battle.

Early the next morning Colleen drove her buggy to the Diablo Mine. She had heard it had been attacked the previous night. An armed guard blocked her way into the trail that led the last twenty yards to the burned out mine office.

"Sorry, no one is allowed beyond this point," the guard said.

"I've come to see Mr. Streib. Is he about?"

"Wouldn't know, Miss."

"Who is in charge here?"

"Right now, I am, Miss."

"You work for Mr. Streib or Col. Ralston?"

"Col. Ralston, Miss. You have any questions, he's the man to talk to."

"How many men were killed here last night?"

"Wouldn't know, Miss. You'll have to—"

"I know, have to talk to Col. Ralston."

She touched the buggy whip and wished she were good enough with it to snatch the rifle from the man's hands, but she would only bungle the job. She stared hard at the guard, then turned the rig around and drove east and on up the hill to the Silver Strike Mine.

She left the rig in the yard and walked to the entrance of the office. Inside a foppish young man came toward her but the back door opened and Col. Ralston peered out through smoked glasses.

"Miss O'Reily. How good of you to pay a social call."

She stopped six-feet from him, the derringer weighing heavily in her reticule. For a moment she wanted to pull it and shoot the man dead. The surge of emotion passed and she frowned.

"I understand your gunsharps attacked the Diablo Mine last night, killed everyone in sight and burned it to the ground."

His face flamed for a moment and his eyes watered more than usual. His hand rose instinctively, then slowly descended.

"Miss O'Reily, I can see you're overwrought. Do you wish to sit down in my office?"

"No! I don't sit down with rattlesnakes. Did your men shoot up that mine last night or not? A simple yes or no will be enough."

"I'm under no obligation to answer such a ridiculous charge. If two more persons heard that remark I could bring slander charges against you."

"In what court, the Ralston Criminal Court of Ralston-Silverton? Don't be ridiculous, Corporal."

"That's Colonel, Miss O'Reily."

"Not to me it isn't. You even look like a Corporal. I'm warning you, Corporal, you try to burn me out, or kill my men, and the first person who dies will be you. Your three gunsharps, no matter how good, can't beat two-hundred rifles. Just remember that when you're planning your military campaign to wipe out every mine owner in Silverton, *Corporal!*"

Colleen spun around, marched to the door and slammed it as she went out. She climbed into her rig and turned the mare down the hill. The buggy had no brake and the single tree pushed against the mare's legs as she walked carefully downhill to Main Street.

Colleen had some shopping to do, looking for a new colored scarf to go with her brown dress. She wasn't sure why she suddenly had a need for a scarf to brighten up the dress, but she did. It certainly had no connection whatsoever with the fact that Lee Morgan probably would be having supper with her that evening.

She had just come out of the dress shop with her orange scarf and settled into her rig, when two mounted men rode toward her. She knew one was Sam Plummer and guessed the tall one was Bob Cassidy. They stopped thirty-feet away.

"Miss O'Reily," Plummer said. "Colonel Ralston sends his regards and requests that you drive up the hill to continue your talk with him. He had some suggestions you didn't give him time to make."

"No," she spat.

"Don't think you understand, Miss," Plummer

continued. "It ain't exactly a request."

She pulled the derringer from her reticule and fired at the men. She knew the range was too great and saw the round hit the dirt well in front of them.

"Now, no cause to do nothing like that," Cassidy said, moving forward on his mount.

Colleen swept a blanket back on the seat beside her, lifted a sawed off Greener. She aimed it over the men's heads and pulled the trigger. One or two of the big slugs thudded into the top of the Silverton Bank building in back of the men. Somebody yelled up the street and people began moving in her direction.

"That's double-ought buck, boys. You know what it can do a body at this range. I can put both of you on the ground with the second barrel full. You'll be bleeding from half a dozen holes. If you want it that way, you try to draw or you keep moving ahead. One of you sure as shooting is gonna be plumb dead. You buying in, boys?"

Plummer mumbled something and the pair pulled their horses' heads around and walked down the street, then kicked into a canter and soon vanished from sight.

Three men on the sidewalk gave a small cheer.

"Would you have gunned them?" one of the men called from the sidewalk.

She lowered the weapon, pushed out the used shell and put in a new one from a box on the seat. When she looked up at the man she nodded. "Absolutely. I'd just think of them as being rabbits, and pull down on them and fire. Any more questions?"

She grabbed the reins and drove the rig back down Main to Nevada Street and quickly up to her mine and house. The sawed off Greener lay across her lap as she drove.

When she stopped the mare, Colleen sat where

she was for a minute. She was not sure she could
walk to the house. She was still so keyed up and
angry that she wondered if her knees would hold
her up. At last she stepped to the ground, smiled
when her knees stayed in place and walked quickly
to the office.

The only lawyer in town was a man by the name
of Beauford Lawrence, a portly gentleman who had
learned how to live well on a minimum of work and
a maximum of money. He glanced up from his desk
as Lee Morgan stepped inside and locked the door
behind him.

The Bisley came into his hand at once and
Beauford stood and raised his hands.

"I don't keep any money here. I have maybe five
dollars in my pocket. Robbery is not a good idea.
You could get twenty years in the territorial
penitentiary that way."

"Shut up," Lee barked. "When I want legal advice
from you, I'll beat it out of your ears. Answer some
questions and stay alive, agreed?"

"Yes, indeed." He squinted at Lee. "Ain't you that
new gunman in town who quit employment with
the colonel?"

"Right, and you work for the colonel, so you are
not one of my favorite people. I'd guess that you
have the mining claim for the Diablo Mine.
Correct?"

"I really can't say, that's confidential . . ."

Lawrence didn't remember seeing the gunman
move, but when he looked down he saw the man
beside him and the big weapon's muzzle pushing
upward in the soft flesh under his chin. The muzzle
pushed higher and higher until Lawrence thought it
would tear through into his mouth.

"Again, the last time I ask before I pull the trigger.

You do have the mining claim papers for the Diablo Mine. Correct?"

"Yes."

"Show them to me."

Lee pulled down the weapon and pushed the muzzle into the oversize belly. "Get them now!"

Lawrence reached on his desk, flipped open a file and took out three sheets of papers fastened together and with official looking seals on the front page. On the back was a transfer of ownership section. It had been dated two days before, duly signed by two parties, one of whom was Dan Streib.

"How could the man sign the paper after he was dead?" Lee asked.

"He signed it two days ago, look at the date."

"Anyone can write in a date. Anyone can forge a name. Where is Mr. Streib now?"

"I believe he took the morning stage to Carson City."

"You believe wrong. The only two passengers this morning were women."

Lee tore the official claim papers for the Diablo in half. Lawrence gasped.

"That's a felony, sir, destroying mine ownership papers."

"Who's going to charge me?" Lee took out a packet of stinkers, tore off one, struck the match and lit the papers, letting them burn one-half page at a time and dropping the ashes on the wooden floor.

"I'd suggest you tell Col. Ralston only that the papers for the Diablo Mine are missing, that you are searching for them, and that he can't officially take over the property until you find them and get them forged."

"I could never do that. I don't lie well, and—"

"Better practice. As a lawyer, that's half your job. You tell Ralston what really happened here, and he'll have Sam Plummer use you for target practice.''

Beauford Lawrence rubbed his face with one hand and sat down in his chair. "You, sir, are probably truth-saying. But I hate to see the face of the man when I tell him. Best I got is that it was burned up in the fire they set. Yes, yes, that might do it.''

"In the meantime, I'd suggest that you advise the colonel to get his guards away from the Diablo. The Mine Owners Association will take it over until the rightful heir can be found.''

"Oh, Lordy, but the colonel is not going to like that.''

"Tough shit. He's got it coming. Stay right where you are and don't move for five minutes, or you'll get some lead through that new suit of yours.''

"Yes sir.''

Lee backed up to the door, unlocked it, opened it and slid outside. He walked down Main to the alley and ran down it to the first cross street, then toward the O'Reily mine.

The lawyer was a guess, but a logical one.

He walked along toward the O'Reily mine thinking. Hell, why not. Today was as good as any other day. He swung around and walked back to Main Street where he went into the Silverton Hotel and borrowed an ink pen and some paper and wrote a short note. He sealed it in an envelope, wrote Sam Plummer's name on the outside, and went back to the boardwalk. Lee found a boy to deliver the message for a nickel.

Now Lee walked faster back to the O'Reily house where he had left his horse and rode along the river east. That morning he had spotted a good sized white barked pine that had been lightning struck and splintered off fifty-feet in the air.

That was where he had invited Sam Plummer to

come for a showdown. There was open land for a mile around, so there was no spot for a sharpshooter to use for bushwhacking. He left no time either so there would be no chance for Plummer to set up a back shooting.

"Just you and me, Plummer. Let's get this over with and find out who really is the fastest. I know I am, and I'll prove it to you. Today at one o'clock."

That's when he remembered he didn't have his Waterbury. It was still at the jeweler's getting cleaned. Close enough. He had the Evans repeating rifle in case Plummer came with a rifle. His Bisley was clean, oiled and in top mechanicl condition.

As he rode the two miles to the big pine, he remembered an Indian saying: *Today is a good day to die!*

Lee never thought much about dying, except at times like these. Death came to every man, but the timing of it was what was important. Would this be the day he would be a hair slow, or his automatic eye-hand aim a bit off? Would Plummer work his magic just a fraction of a second quicker and straighter?

At last Lee shrugged and looked at the land around him. Not quite a mountain desert, but close. He could see wild iris, a few wild peach blossoms showed along the river. There was red Indian paintbrush and blue lupine and a tangle of wild roses with four simple petals.

Every man had to die.

He listened to the call of the mockingbird, saw a jay swoop down from a tree, then a flicker called lustily and a thrush swept by him surprised at his closeness.

It was a good day to be alive!

Lee let it go then, what would be, would be. He was enough of a fatalist to believe a man did everything he could, fought and clawed and battled with all his might, skill and brain power. But after all that, there was a time to let go and see what happened.

That was how he felt now, loose, ready, free, knowing he might never make the ride back to town.

Ready.

Yeah, he was ready.

It was nearly a half hour after he arrived at the base of the lone pine tree that he saw a rider coming toward him. He scanned the land behind the man and on each side for half-a-mile. There were no more trails of dust. Just one rider. There had been no time to set up a backshoot, no chance to do a bushwhack.

This time Plummer had to play it straight and honest. A year or more of taking the easy way out could wear away at a man's speed. It could take away that sharpness that rested in hundredths of a second. That would be a good thing to remind a man like Plummer about. Remind him and get him thinking about it, so he might not be paying enough attention to the matter at hand: living or dying.

Yeah, he would remind the gunsharp.

Lee Morgan sat down against the pine and closed his eyes. Might as well get in a little rest before the man arrived.

It was a great day, a wonderful day to stay alive!

5

Lee felt more than heard the gunman coming. He opened his eyes where he sat next to the tall single leafed pine. Man and rider were still 300 yards off. Lee stood, so the gunsharp could see him, then faded behind the pine's thick trunk in case Sam Plummer thought he could get frisky with a long gun.

"Get down and stretch out," Lee said when the rider came within earshot. "I hate to kill a man all tightened up after a couple of miles on a horse."

"Worry about yourself, drifter," Plummer said.

"Been thinking some on you, Plummer. Fact to face is that you ain't been too active lately in real gunfights. You had a pair of backshooters to do the tough work while you fronted and took the glory. Doubt if you ever fired a shot on some of those famous kills of yours."

"That got you scared, Morgan?"

"Not a whit. I can tell a rusty gunman when I see one. You're rusty, Plummer. Got red coat all over your gun hand, but you're too close to it to see the color.''

"You gonna jaw all day, or can we get on with it?''

Plummer eased down from his horse, getting off slowly on the right side so he wouldn't be shielded by the mount. The critter sidestepped nervously for a moment, then dropped her head where the reins ground tied her.

"You ready to die, Plummer?''

"Not a chance. I've seen you draw. This ain't no fancy beer bottle breaking.''

"Just for the record, was it you who back shot old man O'Reily a year ago, or was it Johnny Hardin?''

Plummer snorted. "What the hell you care? That's over and done. That girl ain't gonna hurt me none. But, case you want to know before you die, I was out front. My round hit him first before he cleared leather. Then the boys got excited and took some action from the rear.''

"Figures.''

The two men stood thirty feet apart, feet spread, hands hanging at their sides. Waiting.

"Anything else you want to confess before you eat dirt and die, Plummer?''

"Not a damn thing. Just a small bet. Bet you ain't even got your hands on that Colleen O'Reily's tits yet. Right?''

Lee felt a twinge of anger, but pushed it down. That was Plummer's try to rile him, so he wouldn't be ready.

Lee stared at the other gunman. There was no eye movement, no hands quivering, no advantage.

Always draw first in a face-down, Buckskin Frank Leslie had taught Lee. It gives you a split second advantage as the other man sees your move and starts his own. Sometimes it's enough to keep you alive.

Plummer knew the same fact.

Lee started his draw first, his right hand snaking up to the butt of the Bisley, lifting it backward and up just enough so the muzzle would clear leather. At the same time his thumb dragged back the big Bisley hammer so easy to find, cocking the weapon. Then the automatic lifting and aiming by the pointing method and eye-hand coordination that put him on target.

In these few hundredths of a second his trigger finger closed across the cold steel and squeezed the metal tang gently, continuously, so the movement wouldn't distort the aim.

Less than a second. He felt fast. Lee Morgan was not sure how fast but he heard his weapon go off a thin fraction of a second before he heard the second roar.

Through the haze of the black powder's bluish smoke from his gunbarrel, Lee could almost see the flight of the heavy .45 caliber slug as it spiraled on its way. The lead tore through the gambler's vest Plummer wore and bored into his flesh.

At the same instant, Lee felt a whisper as hot lead slammed through the air not an inch from his right side. Overaim, he thought in a millisecond. Then he saw Plummer slammed backward by the force of the big round.

Time seemed to freeze in hundredth parts of a second as the body eased backward. The gunman's left hand flew in the air. The .45 in Plummer's right hand came out of his fingers as his whole arm jolted outward in a try to save his balance.

The lead slug had broken through a rib, shattered the entire right side of his heart and dumped the corpse of another fast gun into the rocky dirt and tufts of grass on the high Nevada mountainside.

Lee stood there, welded in place, his weapon still

aimed at the spot where Plummer's heart had been.

He saw the gun fly from the dead hand. Knew the shot had been on target. Watched the body crumple in the dirt and never move again.

Now he knew. Lee Morgan was faster than Sam Plummer. At least this time he was faster. The only one that counted: the last time they faced each other. Slowly Lee let the heavy Bisley swing down to his side.

He carried the weapon low but ready as he walked slowly up to the remains of Sam Plummer.

"You lived like a bastard, Plummer. At least you died in a fair fight."

It was probably the only epitaph Sam Plummer would ever get.

A half hour later, Lee walked Plummer's horse into the end of Main Street and whacked it on the rump. Plummer was tied head down over his saddle. The horse walked down the street for a block, looked at the McGraw Livery but kept on walking toward its own barn up at the Silver Strike Mine.

At Nevada Street somebody ran out and grabbed the reins.

"Christ, it's Sam Plummer dead as a dormouse!" the man shouted.

Colleen rested an hour in her house after her confrontation with Ralston and the second one with his gunslingers, then she washed her face and combed her hair. She put on a bonnet and went to see Nance Kincaid at his mine south and east of her, the Last Chance.

It took her half an hour to talk him into joining the Miners Protective Association. He gave her a twenty dollar gold piece and had her sign a receipt for his first month's dues. He had heard about her run-in with the gunmen and congratulated her.

"Nance, we do what we have to do. *Corporal* Ralston is going to get more desperate the more we organize. Be sure to get out guards tonight around your claim."

She continued on to the Shovelful Mine to the northeast. It was a four man operation. The four men were partners and had no other workers. She talked to Page Ingram who was topside dumping out buckets of useless rock from their twenty-foot deep shaft.

"Heard about your group," Page said. "Like to join but we can't afford the twenty. Be glad to do anything else that might help."

"Keep a rifle within arm's reach whenever you can, Page. And start carrying a six-gun. Can't hurt."

They talked a bit more and then she walked back toward her own mine. It was somewhere after noon time. She heard men shouting in town but had no idea what it was about. As she came to the house she saw Morgan riding up. He looked a little grim.

He waited for her and held the door open. Inside the kitchen she seemed a little flustered. She wore the brown dress with the orange scarf and Lee grinned at her.

"Been out on the missionary circuit?"

She told him her halfway success.

"Better than nothing, we're making progress."

"What was all the shouting about down on Main Street?"

"Oh, seems they found a body."

"Where?"

"Tied head down over a saddle horse."

She pinched her face into a small frown. "Lee, do you know who it was and how the man happened to die?"

"Yep."

"Would you tell me, please."

He told her as they sat at the table and sipped at cups of hot coffee.

"There was nothing illegal. It was a fair shootout. He happened to lose. He also admitted that both Cassidy and Hardin were involved in your father's death."

"So why can't we file charges?" She closed her eyes and then slammed her palm against the table. "We have no confession now that Plummer's dead. And the other two won't admit a thing. Damn!"

"I'm afraid so. At least Ralston has one less gunman."

"And the other two will come after you as fast as they can."

"Maybe, but they'll be less enthusiastic now. They know I'll try to get a fair fight, and they don't like that."

She stood. "Lee, please be careful. I don't want anything to happen to you. Especially since I'm the one who got you involved."

He stood beside her. "Beautiful lady, I don't get involved with anything I don't want to."

She nodded. They stood close together.

"Lee, about before, when you . . . you kissed me. I shouldn't have let you do that."

"Didn't you like it? I sure did."

"Of course I liked it. That's not the point." She looked up at him.

Lee bent slighty and moved slowly toward her lips. She had time to pull away, but didn't. He claimed her soft lips and kissed her gently, then harder and felt her respond. Her arms came around him and he felt her press her body firmly against his. Her breasts seemed to throb through the clothing.

The kiss lasted a long time. She gave a little mewing sound when he leaned back, so he kissed her again. She pulled away and buried her face against his chest.

"Lee Morgan, you're impossible. I don't know what to do with you. You're not at all the kind of man I want to . . . to . . ."

"To get involved with?" he finished.

She looked up at him and nodded. He could feel the heat of her breasts through his shirt.

He kissed her ear and she wiggled. "Make you a deal, beautiful lady. I won't kiss you again, unless you want me to. Fair enough?"

He looked down at her and she smiled and nodded. Then he bent forward and pulled her tightly against his hard body and kissed her lips hard, demanding, his tongue brushing against her lips, but she didn't open them. This time he broke the kiss and stepped back from her.

She smiled at him, a warm, open, wonderful expression and she laughed softly. Her hand went out and touched his chest just to be touching him.

"Now I've got a whole new problem," she said watching him. "But it's a nice kind of . . . situation to think about. Oh, lordy! you do get me all flustered!"

"Good," Lee said. He kissed her cheek. "I better make a round of the member mines to talk up security before it gets dark. I'll be back in time for supper."

He left by the kitchen door and Colleen watched him go. She gently touched her lips with her fingers and smiled.

Outside, Morgan made sure that the Evans repeating rifle was in his saddleboot, checked his Bisley and reloaded the empty cylinder, then put a box of twenty rounds in his blue jeans pocket and stepped into the saddle.

He rode north past the Deep Shaft Mine and then north again passing a worked out or abandoned mine that was a falling down frame building, a tunnel entrance and piles of overburdened and worthless rock. There were a dozen or more empty

holes like this one in the area. He moved on toward
the Desperation Mine and angled down that way
hoping he wouldn't attract the attention of anyone
from the Silver Strike. He wasn't sure what kind of
security Ralston would have put on. He ran into a
guard at the Desperation Mine a hundred yards
uphill who was braced with a shotgun.

He identified himself and the guard put down the
weapon where he sat in a three-foot deep hole on a
wooden box. He saw the remains of a sack lunch. It
took him only a minute or two to make sure the man
was doing his job, then he rode on toward the
second perimeter man.

A rifle shot slammed into the thin air and Lee felt
the air part as a lead slug passed close to his head.

"Never try for a head shot, son," Buckskin Frank
Leslie had always told him when they were shooting
at game. The same thing applied when hunting men
and Frank hadn't needed to say it. The sound of the
shot came from the Silver Strike side, and Lee heard
the man he had just left return fire with a rifle.

Lee spun the mount around and rode northeast,
away from the Silver Strike. He looked back and
saw two mounted men riding hard from the Silver
Strike claim.

Ralston was striking back faster than he had
guessed. Cover? Where could he find some
protection? He saw a worked out mine and raced for
it, bending low over the mount's neck to make as
small a target as possible. He heard more rifle fire,
and felt a round nick his mount.

The guards at the Desperation Mine were firing
now, too, forcing the attackers to swing wide around
the Desperation land. He had no chance to get to one
of the guard holes. His only protection lay in the old
mine.

Another minute and he was there, jumping off the

mare and running for the mouth of the tunnel. The building here had fallen nearly flat and offered no cover. The mine tunnel had not been closed in any way. Equipment, even a broken pick and sledge lay to one side.

He stepped into the darkness of the tunnel and hefted the Evans rifle. If they came at the front of the tunnel, there was almost no protection. He'd have to work deeper into the mine. Quickly he checked for torches, found two unburned ones when he remembered where they usually were left.

Three rifle rounds slammed through the mouth of the old mine and drove Lee to the ground. These men knew what they were doing.

He was in the mine, but could see no targets. Slowly he worked toward the mouth again and saw one of the men. He was Bob Cassidy. The man lay behind an abandoned ore car, but one foot stuck out.

Lee lifted the Evans rifle and sighted in. He pulled down carefully and squeezed off the round. The aim was true and he heard the scream of pain, then a dozen pistol and rifle rounds hammered into the tunnel mouth as fast as the two men could lever their repeating rifles and pull pistol triggers.

Lee was forced back. Just before he moved he saw the sputtering sparks of a dynamite fuse and turned and ran into the darkness, grabbing the two torches as he sprinted into the gloom.

The dynamite explosion near the mouth of the tunnel multiplied its effect as the shock wave billowed through the narrow space. The force of the blast hit Lee in the back like the kick of an unshod mule and drove him to his knees. His ears rang. Dust and rocks sifted down from the unsupported dirt roof of the tunnel. A swirling cloud of dust followed the shock wave and for a moment he couldn't breathe.

Lee staggered to his feet and turned toward the dim light at the far end of the tube when he heard firing. Rifle bullets zinged and whanged through the cavern, ricochetting off rocks and the slender steel rails.

Over a dozen rounds blasted into the tunnel and Lee threw himself to the floor near the wall with his boots toward the firing.

When the booming sounds of the shooting stopped, it was unearthly quiet.

Lee heard someone laugh.

Some indistinct words filtered through to him. Then it was quiet again. How did they intend to keep him in here, stand guard all day?

Lee began moving cautiously back toward the entrance. The light grew stronger now and he saw a shape ahead of him still thirty or forty yards away. The figure bent over at the side of the tunnel, then stood.

The words came clearly now.

"It's lit, Cassidy, it's lit. Let's get the hell out of here!"

"Yeah, goodbye Lee Morgan!"

In the dim light he could see what they were talking about. The sputtering dynamite fuse sparkled brightly in the darkness.

Lee ran away from the bomb.

He charged down the blind tunnel another thirty yards before the explosion tore through the tube.

The first one had been a warmup for this blast. It knocked him flat on his face, and half the air in the tunnel seemed to be sucked out. His ears hurt so bad he screamed and then the dust and waves of rocks showered down from the ceiling.

He lay where he had fallen until the rocks and dirt stopped dropping on him.

Lee was in total blackness. He had held on to one

of the torches through his run. He felt around on the floor of the tunnel until he found the torch, a rough limb with one end that had been wrapped with gunny sacks and soaked with coal oil. It would burn for an hour and not burn up the sack, just the oil.

Lee sat in the tunnel floor and felt in his pocket for the stinker matches. He broke one off the stick and struck it, then lit the torch.

He soon found out that the tunnel was fairly intact. The fall from the ceiling had been minimal because the rock was hard and solid overhead.

He stood and began to explore with the torch. First he checked the entrance. There was a chance it hadn't been blocked by the bomb. He had little hope, but it was the first move. Fifty yards ahead he found only a large pile of rubble, rocks and dirt that extended to the roof of the tunnel. No way out there.

Now he retraced his steps, watching for drifts or laterals off the main tunnel. Quickly he found seven, all less than ten yards deep, all exploratory they looked like, in a search for a vein of silver or gold.

He found an abandoned pick and carried it with him.

For a moment he leaned against the cold rock wall. This mine was dry, no water on the floor, little seepage around the rocks on the ceiling or walls. One point in his favor.

What now?

Check out the rest of the tunnels. So far there had been no shafts that dropped down into the earth. They would do him no good anyway, unless they connected with more laterals. Another fifty yards into the mountain the tunnel turned as if it were going at right angles. Then it turned again. Now he found more activity.

An ore car that was loaded stood on the tracks as if waiting for a mule or men to pull it ouside. He found drifts every four or five yards and now and then a vaulted room where ore evidently had been mined and removed.

For a moment each drift looked the same. How could he be sure? He found some chalky stone on the floor and used it to mark on the drifts, the side tunnels, when he had examined them. He used arrows to show his direction of travel.

Again the tunnel turned and by now, Lee was not sure what direction it headed, deeper into Desperation Mountain with more hundreds of feet of rock over his head, or toward the down slope.

Now and again he found a shaft dropping straight down in the middle of the tunnel which had been widened to allow the tracks to pass by straight.

Twice he tried to check his watch, but the Waterbury was still at the jewelers. It had been after three when he went up to the Desperation Mine. By now it had to be at least five. It would be dark in another two hours. That made little difference to him.

He kept searching.

The torch began to sputter, then to burn the sacking.

Up the tunnel, he found a place where an ore car had damaged a square set that held up the rock ceiling. A piece of the 12 x 12 timber had splintered off.

Lee grabbed it to use as a torch when his branch had burned in half.

Most of an hour later, the last of the splintered wood had about burned up. Ahead he saw a larger room and he investigated it. Here he found three bunks, a table, two chairs, and what was left of some tinned food. He also kicked two rattlesnakes out of the tunnel and into a shaft. He had forgotten that snakes loved to winter over in caves, old mines, wherever they could get underground.

In the room he found more torches. Two of them had dried out, with the coal oil evaporated off them. In the corner he spotted a square five gallon can and sloshed it. Coal oil and half full!

He would have light.

Lee soaked one of the torches, and put it beside the first bunk. It had no mattress, just boards. He checked it carefully to be sure there were no snakes on it, or under the boards, then for just a moment he lay down on the rough boards.

He'd rest for five minutes, then move on.

When he woke up he didn't know where he was. The darkness was total.

Then he remembered. He lit the torch and wondered how long he had slept. When he touched the pine board that he had been using as a light, he found the charred end of it cold. Hours must have passed while he slept.

Again Lee moved along the tunnel, exploring, searching for he didn't know what.

A half hour later the tunnel began to narrow and the ceiling came down so he had to bend his head as he walked.

Ahead he saw another vaulted room where ore must have been taken out. Here he found some tin dishes and silverware, a small charcoal brazier, even a tin of something that bugs had eaten the label from.

For a moment something startled him.

What was it? There was no sound.

Then he felt it again.

Fresh air!

He could feel the fresh, warmer air on his face. That meant an opening. He moved one way, lost the air, moved the other and felt it stronger. At the end of the vaulted room the ceiling went higher. He looked closer and saw that the ceiling merged with a kind of natural chimney, a void in the rock formation that soared upward.

He held the torch near the walls of the room and saw where steps had been cut in the sides. A stairway?

Lee tried and found he could walk up the steps along the wall toward the smaller opening above. He broke the torch shaft in half so he could carry both it and the Evans rifle easier, then climbed up the wall steps. When he was ten feet upward, he saw the chimney plainly. Huge slabs of rock had fallen together leaving a crevice.

It looked as if the miners had found it at the top of the ore vault, and widened it as an air shaft.

Clean, warm air poured down on his face as he looked upward.

Climb! There might be room enough to work his way to the outside!

He used the torch as long as he could, then there was no way he could climb and hold both the rifle and the torch. He dropped the torch. Slowly his eyes grew used to the fainter light. With each upward thrust he found more light.

The steps were gone, but there were grooves and chips out of the rock slab that looked like they had been used for footholds.

He worked upward with them, then at last he could put his feet against one side of the shaft with his knees bent and press his back against the other side. Slowly he inched his way higher.

The shaft became smaller, but still with enough room to climb. Then it widened and that made it harder. The notches were there again, as if someone had planned the shaft as not only an air vent, but an emergency escape hatch as well.

He climbed. The light was stronger now. He couldn't see any sky, but he was sure it was up there. The vent was no longer formed due to the slabs of tumbled boulders. Now it twisted and turned as it moved upward appearing almost like a steep water course. One time it went almost level for ten-feet before angling sharply upward again.

He fell.

The shock of a rock handhold breaking lose made him slip and slide downward nearly ten-feet before he caught himself. The Evans rifle wedged between the sides of the shaft stopped his fall.

Gingerly he regained footholds and hand holds, but left the rifle in place. It had served him well. He could get another. The upward climb was gradual but easier now, the last fifty feet an easy 45-degree climb that resembled more than ever a dry stream bed.

At last he saw blue sky. It was daylight.

He edged up to the level at the surface and let only his head and eyes lift up to look out. Cassidy and Hardin might be watching for him. They might know of this air vent.

He saw only the back of the Desperation Mine. No one was in sight. Slowly he lifted out of the shaft and lay on the ground. He knew his clothes were dirt caked. Somewhere he had lost his hat without realizing it. His rifle was gone, but the Bisley was still in place.

He lay there for what seemed like an hour, gathering his strength, resting, watching the country. To the far left he saw a horse near a mine shack. He wondered if it were the one he had ridden. The sun was well up. He figured it was about ten in the morning. He had been in the mine all night.

He looked at the tumbled down mine shack and decided he had to go in that direction anyway. To the right he saw the Silver Strike works. No one would be watching this direction. Hardin would

report to Col. Ralston that the troublemaker was
sealed up and dead in the old mine.

Lee stood and walked along the side of Desperation Mountain, dropping down gradually until he
was on the level of the horse. At once he saw that it
was the place where he had entered the mine and
that this was his horse.

He mounted and rode up to the mine entrance.
Ten-feet inside he saw the pile of rubble and rock
and dirt where the tunnel had been blocked.

Cassidy and Hardin knew how to handle
dynamite, he was sure of that.

Lee turned and rode slowly ahead along the slopes
of Superstition Mountain and then down to the
O'Reily Mine and stable.

As he moved to the house, he knew what he had to
do. Both Hardin and Cassidy had to be dealt with.
The moment they knew he was alive, they would
come after him again. He could be of no value to
Colleen or the Association as long as he was hiding
to save his scalp.

Hardin would be next. First he wanted to clean
up, to have enough food to feed a team of mules, and
then a full night's sleep, preferably on a soft
mattress. It would not be dangerous for Colleen if he
stayed at her place tonight. Cassidy and Hardin
figured he was already dead.

When Colleen came in, he hadn't moved out of the
chair he had sagged into in the kitchen. Philip was
heating up bath water for him, and had brought him
two huge roast beef sandwiches and a pot of coffee.
He ate both the sandwiches and knew he could
down two more.

"What in the world happened to you, Lee
Morgan?" Colleen said from the living room
doorway. "Gracious, I thought I told you to be
careful."

He told her where he had been and she shuddered.

"I still don't like going down in the mine. I'm just not used to it. I send Warren down. If that had been me and I knew the only way out was blasted shut, I would have sat right down and died."

"Now you know what I have to do, don't you?" he asked.

"Cassidy and Hardin?"

"Exactly. My way. Now it's personal. I owe them, and I'm going to pay them off the only way they'll understand."

Colleen watched him a long moment, came into the room and touched his shoulder and a scrape on his forehead. The touching seemed important to her.

"Tomorrow," she said. "You can start doing that tomorrow. It's nearly noon already. You need to rest. Don't do anything about those men until tomorrow. I want to nurse you back to health."

Suddenly, he was too tired to argue. He nodded. "Anything you say, doctor. Anything you say."

6

Philip moved a portable copper bathtub into the room Morgan would use while at the O'Reily house, filled it with three buckets of hot water, and left a cold one nearby. He grinned, tossed Lee two big fluffy white towels and a bar of soap and left the room.

As Lee eased into the hot water, he decided there weren't more than one or two of his bones and joints that didn't ache from his difficult climb and then the battering fall in the mine. A good long soak would work that out, and after a fine night's sleep on a real honest to god mattress, he'd be ready to take apart Cassidy and Hardin tomorrow.

He leaned back in the tub, one of the long kind that you could almost stretch out in, but not quite. His legs extended up the gently slanted end of the device, but the water came up to his neck.

He soaked.

The warm water soothed his aches and pains.

Slowly he washed off his face and neck with a cloth and lots of soap, then he wet down his hair and washed off the dirt and sand he had picked up in the mine.

The effort tired his arms which had taken most of the wear and tear moving up that chimney. For a moment the hot water lulled him, dulling his senses, until he drifted into a delightful nap. The dream came quickly, someone massaging his tired neck muscles. It felt wonderful. Then he caught the scent of a violet perfume.

His eyes blinked open. The perfume smell was still there. So was the neck massage. Colleen.

"A little to the left," he said, sighing delightedly and without looking around.

She laughed, her voice sounding pleased, excited. "Is that better?" Her hands worked a new spot and he moaned in satisfaction. "You had a little nap. I didn't mean to sneak up on a naked man in his bath."

He caught her hands and gently tugged her around beside the tub. She knelt on the floor, and he smiled to see her bare to the waist. Her breasts were small, but sized with the rest of her tiny body. Her areolas were deep pink topped by dark red, extended nipples. He bent and kissed one breast and she purred like a contented tabby cat.

"I know I'm a brazen hussy to come to you this way. I guess as the boss of the mine, I've been used to taking the initiative, telling men what I want them to do. Now I'm not telling, I'm asking, begging, pleading."

He reached out and kissed her lips. They were soft, inviting and opened at once. After a moment she pulled away.

"Are we going to finish your bath first, or not? I'd much prefer to help you do the scrubbing."

He grabbed the cloth and began washing himself furiously. She picked up a second cloth and worked on his back. When he got up on his knees, Colleen smiled and took the soap from his hands. His erection was full grown.

"This part I'll wash myself," she said and did so with great care and tenderness.

"Easy!" he said sharply. "We don't want the cannon to fire before everything is ready."

She laughed and eased her washing.

A few minutes later he stepped from the tub and caught a towel she threw at him. As he dried, she slipped out of the skirt, three petticoats and tight, white drawers that extended from her waist halfway down each leg and were decorated with pretty pink bows made of narrow ribbon. Colleen unbuttoned the sides and sat on the bed as she wiggled out of the tight undergarment.

She stood, as naked as he was, not the least embarrassed. She held out a hand and he walked over to her, his excitement obvious.

He kissed her and they fell on the bed, she half on top of him. He kissed her breasts, teased them and licked her nipples until she yelped in delight. Then he nibbled on them until she fell hard on top of him, her hips pounding against his as she whimpered through a searing climax.

She pushed up from him, a sheen of moisture on her forehead and between her breasts. Her whole chest was flushed from the satisfaction and she slowly brought her breathing down to nearer normal.

"I've never been so fast that way ever before. You're terrific! Now it's your turn."

She laid down and pulled him over her, taking his erection in her hand and licking the purple head. Then bit by bit, she sucked him into her mouth and began moving back and forth. She pulled on his hips urging him to move in and out of her.

"You really want to do this?" he asked.

She nodded and settled into a rhythm. A good mouth job was seldom offered, and Lee threw himself into the delightful task with his wholehearted cooperation. Her hands found his scrotum and gently squeezed his balls as the pressure began to build deep in his loins.

Colleen made small little noises in her throat as she sensed his excitement growing. She squealed as the first load jetted into her throat, then she was busy as he ground gently again and again squeezing every drop of juice from his pulsating tool. She came away from him smiling, kissed his lips gently, then rolled him on his back.

"Rest," she said. "The afternoon is just beginning."

She slid off the bed and padded in barefeet to the door and opened it a crack, then full, and pulled inside a serving cart. On it were three kinds of fruit, two varieties of cheese, and two bottles of wine.

"I thought we might need some kind of nourishment for a long session. Philip fixed this for us, and will have supper delivered here as well."

She watched his surprise. "Don't worry, Philip is the absolutely most trustworthy person I know. I have no secrets from him. No, he isn't my lover, but a wonderful friend. Yes, I pay him too much, but he's free to move on anytime he wants to. He's been with us for almost four years now. Do you think I'm talking too much? I've heard that when I get sexy, and satisfied, and expectant, or just fucked and wanting that big prick of yours inside me the first time, or again, that I get to talking all crazy and strange and without stopping."

Lee took a ripe peach from the tray of snacks and

pushed it into her mouth shutting off the stream of
verbiage. He inspected the wine, opened a bottle of
white from California, and sampled it. He'd had
much worse. He poured two delicate stemware
goblets full and handed Colleen one.

"To a success, both in and out of bed," he said.

She giggled, touched his glass with hers and they
both drank.

Then she sobered. "Mr. Morgan," she said
formally. "I feel so at ease, so natural, as if this is
what you and I are supposed to be doing. I'm not a
woman who jumps in bed with every man I like. But
with you there was never a doubt. It was just a
matter of when. Does this make me promiscuous, a
really bad woman, a tart, even a slut?"

He put down his wine glass and pulled her bare
body to his, crushing her breasts to his chest and
then kissed her with all the passion he had ever felt.
When the long kiss ended he still held her and she
gloried in it.

"Miss O'Reily, you are every inch a lady. You are
regal and proud and yet can get just sexy as hell! You
are in command of a man's kind of business, yet delightful and inventive in a bedroom. You are
woman, you are lover, you are mine owner. You are
complete!"

She frowned.

"No," she said in a tiny voice. "I never wanted to
run the mine, it just became my responsibility when
daddy died. Mother had passed away years ago with
some nameless fever that the doctors couldn't even
figure out. All I really want is to get married and
have at least six children and love my husband and
let him support me for the rest of my natural life. Is
that too much to ask for?"

"Of course not. It's every mother's daughter's
dream. But you're so much more than that."

"No. I have no education. I've been lucky with the

mine because daddy had it so well in hand and so
many loyal employees. It should be called the Lucky
O'Reily #1." She took his hands and placed one on
each breast, then stared up at him with a winsome
smile.

"Mr. Lee Morgan, will you marry me?"

Lee kissed her on each cheek, then on the mouth
and both her eyes.

"Sweet Colleen. I'm a traveling man. I'm not the
kind any woman should marry. Maybe someday I'll
settle down again, somewhere. Maybe even raise
horses again. But right now I'm just a gun for hire, a
roving, rambling fiddlefoot. You don't really want to
marry me. It's just a woman's flight of fancy when
she's beautifully bare and her breasts are being
caressed and she wants something deep inside
her."

He took the wine glass from her hand, moved her
to the middle of the bed and spread her satiny legs,
then lifted her knees and knelt between them.

He spread himself over her, touching her body
with his lightly and kissed her lips, then her breasts.
His hand massaged her upper thighs, then worked
higher to the bushy covered triangle and gently
stroked across her moist, secret heartland.

Small yelps of delight drifted from her as she
arched her back and stretched her hands out
sideways. His fingers worked through the
moistness, found the tiny node and rubbed it back
and forth a dozen times. Quickly her breathing
surged, her hot breath came on his shoulder and
then she was rushing headlong into a grinding,
moaning series of spasms that shook her slender
body like a rag doll.

Four times the spasms jolted through her, each
time almost stopping, then his fingers on her clit
triggered a new round until she was exhausted and
panting from the spent energy.

She looked up at him, focusing for the first time in several minutes, and nodded.

"Wonderful, tender, husband-for-the-day Lee, please do it now. Put your big cock deep inside me right now!"

She lifted her legs more and Lee moved closer, then touched the soft wet spot and eased into her slot gently, letting the juices smooth his way inside her tight little tube yet without the hint of a burn.

Colleen's smile blossomed. "Oh, god, I can die now! That is so perfect, so wonderful. Wonderful! Oh, lord but that is the most awesome, thrilling . . ."

She stopped then, and her hips began to lift and thrust against him as he began the ages old game of man and woman. He had held back so long the second time that he thought he might be fast, but he wasn't. At last he lifted her ankles and put them over his shoulders and then plunged forward. After a dozen hard strokes that jolted her higher on the bed each time, he felt his own explosion coming, and roared with release as he climaxed and pinned her frame to the bed with each final thrust until he was done and spent and he fell on her, sinking them both into the mattress.

Her arms went around his shoulders.

"Darling Lee, you probably can't even talk right now, but I'm going to hold you inside me just forever and ever. I'll never let you go. I know, it's the sex talking, and tomorrow we'll both feel differently, but for today and tonight, I'm pretending that we're really married." She gave one last hump with her hips, then closed her eyes and drifted off into a joyous nap.

Two hours later when Lee heard a gentle knock, he got up and opened the door into the first floor hallway. He found another serving tray sitting on a stool. It was dinner, all hot and ready. He pulled it in and they ate with a raw hunger that amused them both.

After dinner they had more wine and cheese, then sat naked on the big bed and played poker. By eight o'clock, they had lost the cards in the blankets, crawled under the sheet and made love again.

It was sometime early in the morning when Lee woke up and realized that he was hard and that the small girl with the dark eyes was working at his crotch.

"One more time," was all she said, then she moved over on top of him and eased his lance into her willing scabbard and rode him like a bucking bronco in the breaking corral.

They got to sleep again just before dawn.

For breakfast, they dressed. Lee put on the new clothes that Philip had bought for him at the general store. Colleen slipped down to her room and when she appeared in the kitchen she was so radiant that anyone seeing her would know at once that she had been loved to complete satisfaction the night before.

Philip didn't seem to notice. He had flapjack batter ready and the skillet hot. When they came in he flipped the cakes and heaped bacon and sausage on their plates, along with coffee and homemade butter and lots of hot maple flavored syrup.

"Philip, you know I'm supposed to be dead," Lee said. "For a dead man, I've never had a better tasting breakfast."

"Thank you, Mr. Morgan. I appreciate." He rolled his eyes at Colleen who glanced up and saw him. "Some folks you just never know about."

She laughed with delight. "Philip, you know I think you're the best cook this side of the Mississippi. If I complimented you on every dish, every meal, first thing I know I'd have to start paying you. I like the slave idea better."

"Yessah, Missy Colleen," Philip said putting on a thick darkie accent. They all laughed.

After breakfast, Lee sat at the table with a stub of a pencil and a penny tablet working out a message. He did it in block letters as if he couldn't write the usual way. At last he had what he wanted and copied it once more, shortening it.

The message said:

"Mr. Hardin. Jist got to town, heard you here. I owed you twenty dollars on a bet in Dodge. I don't want trouble. Be glad to pay up. I'll be at Main Street a hundred yards out east of the livery at 9:30 this morning. I don't want no trouble." He signed it Amos.

Lee asked Philip for an envelope and put the note inside and sealed it. On the outside in the same block letters he printed the name, Johnny Hardin.

He took the note and the black snake whip outside and got his horse saddled. The whip went on the saddle where a cowboy usually carries a rope and looked natural enough coiled there.

Lee rode up Main Street toward the general store and found two boys about ten years old. He gave them each a nickel if they would deliver the letter to Johnny Hardin, into his hand personally.

"You might find him up at the house on Mountain Street, or on up at the Silver Strike Mine," Lee told them.

"I know where that is," one youth said. "My pa works up there all the time."

Lee went to the watchmaker and ransomed out his Waterbury. It had only needed cleaning. He paid the fifty cents charge and slipped the watch in his pocket. It was just after 8:30.

He rode out of town then, cantered out to the east past the McGraw Livery and looked over the country. The East Walker River came within fifty yards of the stable. He decided that was the best spot and rode into the willow brush there and tied up his horse. He adjusted his Bisley in its leather, and then unsnapped the black snake whip.

He swung the whip once, to check his arm, not his aim. His arm was only slightly stiff from where he had fallen on it yesterday. He found a tree he could lean against and watched through the screen of brushy cover to see who came out east on Main.

When he wrote the note he wasn't sure if Hardin would take the bait, but before he sent it by messenger, he decided Hardin would come. Twenty dollars was a month's pay for lots of men in Silverton. Then too, Hardin would wonder who it was who ran out on him owing him twenty dollars. His curiosity might be the biggest factor. He'd come, and alone. He wouldn't want to share the money, or the satisfaction, with Cassidy.

Twice Lee looked at his pocket watch. The first time it was 9:15, the second time 9:35. He watched the street and saw several men on horses, but none coming his way.

When Hardin came five minutes later it was from the north, down past McGraw's Livery and on foot. He ran from one bit of cover to the next, checking each way carefully. He slipped into the brush along the river about fifty yards east of where Lee stood and worked his way slowly back toward town.

Hardin was alone but well armed: he had two six-guns in twin holsters, and carried a sawed off, double barreled shotgun. The gunsharp was taking no chances.

Lee had hidden his horse in the brush fifty yards toward town, so the gunman would not run into her as he moved toward Lee. Now, Lee stood behind the thick alder waiting, the whip out and ready.

The brush could make it hard to use the whip, but

just in front of Lee there was a clear place to the
water line, a ten yard stretch where only grass grew.

Hardin did not crash brush, he moved like an
Indian, making no noise, stepping quietly through
the dry growth, the shotgun up and ready.

Lee chanced a quick look around the alder from
ground level. Hardin had just stepped into the
cleared area and now moved forward slowly, with
no cover.

He was only ten feet from the alder when Lee
stepped out, the black snake whip already in the air,
wrapping around the barrel of the scattergun and
Lee jerked it out of the gunman's hands. Before
Hardin could draw his six-gun he stared at the Bisley
already in Lee's left hand.

Hardin swore. "Knew the fuck it was you. But I
wouldn't tell Cassidy, wanted to bring your head in
a bucket to Ralston on my own."

The whip had dropped the long gun and cracked
again, jerking one six-gun from Hardin's right hand
leather.

"Toss away the other iron, easy with your left
hand," Lee ordered.

"If I don't, what you gonna do, shoot me?"

"Not right away. First I'll cut off your ears, then
slice off your nose . . ."

Hardin moved his left hand slowly, lifted out the
six-gun and tossed it into the brush.

"I don't enjoy being buried alive in some damn
mine," Lee barked.

"Didn't seem to hurt you much. How'd you get
out?"

"An air shaft, when I finally found it."

The whip sang out and tore a three-inch gash
down Hardin's right arm.

"You son-of-a-bitch!" Hardin screamed. "Wait
until I get my guns back!"

"Was blasting the tunnel closed your idea or Cassidy's?"

"Cassidy's mostly. Should have killed you."

"Damn near did. You've been busy in town, Hardin. I hear you back shot old man O'Reily when he was doing a shootout with Plummer."

"Yeah, so what? O'Reily was dead meat anyway."

"So are you, Hardin."

The whip cracked twice, the first time spun the gunsharp's hat off his head and the second one sliced his left ear off neatly without touching his head.

Hardin screamed in pain. "Bastard!"

He charged Lee. The whip sang out again, tripping Hardin, then a second time tearing through his pants and cutting a six-inch gash down his leg.

The gunman surged to his feet and tried to run away. Lee tore half the back out of his shirt, leaving a long red blood line, then tore flesh off his right shoulder. The third lash of the whip coiled around Hardin's left leg and dumped him into the grass.

When Hardin came to his knees to get back to his feet, Lee stood over him. He reversed his hold on the whip and swung the lead weighted handle down on Hardin's shoulder, smashing it, then swung it again from the side shattering the bones in his right wrist and hand.

Hardin bellowed in pain and tried to stand, but Lee wasn't through. Hot, angry blood pounded in his temples. He swung the whip handle again blasting into the gunslick's left hand, breaking the fingers and crushing the two dozen small bones in the back of his hand.

Lee delivered one more blow, a stinging, slanting jolt along the side of Hardin's head dumping him in the grass. Lee hit him once more with the deadly lead weighted handle, wanting to go on smashing the man's head until it was a bloody pulp.

This time he stopped. Even if Hardin could get himself patched back together, he would never be able to hold a six-gun again, not in either hand.

Lee stood over him a moment more, kicked his side gently and took a deep breath to slow his racing heart. The man had deserved to die. He was a killer, a bastard gun for hire who always took the wrong side. More important, he had tried to kill Lee Morgan and failed.

Hardin had deserved to die a dozen times for trying to bury Lee alive in that dark, ugly mine.

Enough.

Damn well enough for Hardin. Lee coiled the whip and carried it as he found the sawed off shotgun and then walked down to his waiting horse. He looped the black snake whip in place on his saddle and rode back to the O'Reily house. He'd get a note to the doctor. There must be one in town. He didn't want Hardin to die, he wanted him to live, unable even to cock a weapon, and to suffer every day for the rest of his life.

When he got to the O'Reily house, Colleen wasn't there. She came in shortly so angry it looked like she was breathing fire.

"We lost one more mine today," she shouted at him across the kitchen. "Upton Bryce sold out the Winner Mine to the Silver Strike. I saw him down at the bank. He said he got a good price and he couldn't afford the uncertainty of a long fight with Ralston. I told him we almost had it won. He and his family are moving to Carson City in two days."

Lee sipped the coffee Philip had fixed for him. He got up and poured Colleen a cup and she smiled briefly, thanking him and touching his hand so he knew she wasn't angry at him.

"I'm not unhappy with you, Lee. I'm furious at

Ralston. He thinks he can win with gunslicks and by buying out mines before they have a chance."

"That part, the purchase, we can't do anything about. Far as I know, it's still legal."

She took the coffee and then set it down and put her arms around him.

"Right now I need a hug. I know it's all legal to buy out a competitor, and that's what makes me so *damn mad!*"

Lee hugged her and felt her relax a minute.

"I know how I could really get you relaxed," Lee whispered in her ear.

She looked up, grinning at him, but shook her head. "This is one little problem I have to meet head on. I think I'll take a drive and talk to the mine owners we have now. I don't want to lose any. You come with me for moral support?"

"Would, but I have some shopping to do. Some clothes. Philip did fine, but I can't become a fashion plate with only two shirts, especially since I tore that one yesterday. You know these people, you'll do fine. I'd guess we have your favorite *Corporal* on the run. You know how much a full Colonel hates being called a Corporal, don't you?"

"Not really, I was trying anything that day." She spun around and the skirt slid upward showing an ankle. She grinned and headed back outside to her buggy. "You be home for supper, you hear?"

Lee said he'd make a point of it and headed downtown, the Bisley on his hip. One thing he had to buy was a new hat, a Stetson if he could find one in light tan with a band of blue diamonds around it.

Colonel Cleve Ralston marched up one side of his den and back the other. The two people who sat in chairs in the middle followed his movements with special interest. He waved his arms at them, and

shouted more than talked. They both had heard
everything he said as he went over it again and
again.

"Cassidy, how could you let Hardin be suckered
into a showdown that way with Morgan? What am I
paying you for anyway? First I have four men who
are supposed to be professional gunmen. Now I'm
down to one."

He marched again, lit a cigar and blew blue smoke
into the air. His eyes watered and he threw the
smoked glasses on his desk, then wiped at his
swollen eyes.

"Cassidy, I want Morgan gunned down today.
You get any help you want, and you do it anyway
you want to, but you put him dead and in the dirt
before sundown. You do that or you get on your
horse and ride because I don't want ever to see your
face again!"

"What if I can't find him, Colonel?" Cassidy tried.

"Then you're fired, through, finished. I'll tell
everyone that Morgan ran you out of town. Your
reputation will take a quick nose dive into the
muck!"

Cassidy stood.

"Sit down, Captain! I'm not through with you yet.
When I'm through, I'll dismiss you. Christ, no
discipline at all around here any more."

He saw Debbie Sue grinning at Cassidy's anger
and embarrassment at being scolded.

"Don't laugh, slut, or you'll be the next one I
throw out. Remember where I found you, parting
your thighs and humping your little cunt for a dollar
a throw!"

"Temper, temper, Cleve. Remember your fainting
spells. You should know by now that nothing you
can say touches me. You'll have to do better than
that."

He glared down at her where she sat, then slapped her face hard. Her head jolted to one side and she laughed at him, her eyes sparkling.

"Did that touch you, slut?"

Cassidy stood. He knew what was coming and didn't want to watch it as he had to once.

"Colonel, sir. Do you have any other instructions for me?" Cassidy asked sharply.

Col. Ralston turned to him as if surprised he were still there. "No! Damn your eyes, no! Just be sure that Morgan is dead before the sun sets, or die yourself. Get out! When you come back I want his head in a bucket!"

Cassidy left the room as quickly as he could. As he closed the door he saw Col. Ralston swing his hand at the woman who was smiling.

Debbie Sue took the blow on the side of the head, spilled off the chair and sprawled on the floor, the smile on her face more intense than before.

"Come on, *corporal,* you can hit me harder than that. I won't even try to play with you unless you can do much, much better. Are you slowing down? Is the rheumatiz getting at your bones? I remember when you were strong . . ."

He kicked her in the side and she gagged for a moment, then sat up. He tried to kick her again, but she caught his boot, twisted it, dumping him on the floor on his chest. She leaped on his back, slamming him against the carpet, then grabbed his arm and bent it behind him.

She pushed it upward until he shrilled in pain. Through the pain there was a weird smile on his face.

"Yes, yes, now you're getting the hang of it."

She let him go, stood and helped him to his feet. His fist hit her right breast and he scratched her face.

Debbie Sue cheered and laughed. "Now you're getting started, sweetheart. You can do it!"

Ralston wiped his eyes on his shirt sleeve then grabbed the woman's blouse and began tearing it off her body, slapping and punching her as she cheered him on.

7

Lee Morgan liked his new Stetson. It settled on his head at exactly the right angle, was the perfect size, and had a good feel to it. Something about a new hat always brightened his spirits. Now all he had to do was find Cassidy. The gunman had to be the next order of business, before Ralston. Without Cassidy, Ralston would have to rely on local gunhands who would not be the quality of a Bob Cassidy.

Lee started across Main Street. The broad expanse was either a mire of mud or a strip of two-inch dust. Now, due to a long sunny stretch, the street was in its dust stage. He walked around one of the numerous piles of horse droppings and as he did, he stepped into a pothole that steel rimmed wagon wheels had pounded out of the hard dirt.

At exactly the time his foot hit the hole and he stumbled forward, a rifle boomed from the alley ahead of him beside Ruth's Stitchery Store. The bullet came so close to his head he could hear it, and also hear the window shatter behind him in the Silverton Hardware Store.

The stumble turned into a diving roll as he hit the dirt on his right shoulder, rolled and came up to his knees. He had started to draw the Bisley as soon as he heard the roar of the rifle. He fired three times into the alley mouth toward the bushwhacker before he came to his knees, then twice more and saw the gunman running down the alley.

Lee jumped to his feet and raced after the man who now shot once behind him with the rifle, but the unaimed round went high. At the end of the alley the gunman had left his horse. He leaped on board and rode away to the left around the back of the jeweler's store.

Lee darted back to Main, called to a man who had seen the gunplay who was about to step into his saddle.

"Need your horse!" Lee shouted.

"Shore enough, grab her. Get the damn bushwhacker!"

Lee caught the horse, started it moving and vaulted on its back. He saw there was no rifle in the boot and kicked the animal into motion down the alley north. He rounded the jewelry store and saw the rider at a gallop passing the back of the General Store in the alley heading west.

Lee laid the ends of the reins against the horse's flanks as a whip and the little roan stretched out in a fast gallop. There was no chance the shooter could get away unless Lee's horse broke down. There was so little cover on the mountainside that he could see for three or four miles in every direction.

Only the brush and trees along the East Walker River provided a strip of green brush and willow and alder and a few white barked pine and some mountain hemlock.

As Lee rode, he took stock. He had only his Bisley, the twenty rounds in his belt and the five in the weapon. Twenty-five shots. He would conserve his rounds. No wild shooting. As he assessed the situation, two shots barked into the clear, thin air from ahead. They came from the bushwhacker's iron and neither slug made it the fifty yards back to Lee.

He set his mouth and continued riding hard. It had to be Cassidy. If the man had not let his pride get in the way and had used a shotgun with two barrels loaded with double-ought buck back in town instead of a one-slug rifle, his target would be down and probably dead by now. Thank god for the man's pride.

They rode for three miles, following the low land along the sides of the river. Once the rider ahead started to cross the stream, which was little more than knee deep, but he backed out and rode west again.

Slowly, Lee gained on the other man. Without warning the bushwhacker ahead came to a stop, lifted the rifle and fired. Lee heard the shot, jogged his mount to the left and flattened out behind the roan as much as possible. Two more shots sounded ahead and Lee felt one of the bullets hit his horse.

She went down with a scream of protest as Lee grabbed his Bisley and kicked free of the animal. The roan was as good as dead. She had shattered one leg and now screamed and kicked through her death throes.

He heard a laugh from ahead as the rifleman began riding toward Lee. The hunted had become the hunter once again.

Lee was thirty yards from the brush along the river. He ran for it, zig-zagging to disrupt any aim Cassidy would try. Two rifle slugs came close but both missed. Then he saw the rider stop for a better aim. Lee dove for the ground, did a shoulder roll and came up running again at an angle to his other line, then he turned and dove once more into the brush as three angry long gunshots sounded behind him.

Lee crawled through the light brush to a pine tree and stood behind it watching for Cassidy. He stayed well back out of hand gun range. He believed thirty yards was safe, but Lee had done a lot of damage with the heavy Bisley at that range. He moved slightly, working toward the front of the brush line for a better chance at a killing shot.

A horse made a big target. He had no worry at all about killing a horse. If it was him or a horse dying, there was no choice. He worked closer as the man he now identified clearly as the tall, slender Cassidy, rode back and forth watching the brush.

Lee decided he would get off five shots as quickly as possible, hoping one would find the mark, and then retreat to the cover of the pine.

He sighted in, gave the elevation he thought he'd need and fired three shots rapidly, saw none of them hit, lifted the muzzle a little more and fired twice more. The horse and rider both bellowed in pain and the animal spun around in a circle like a bucking bronco, pitching Cassidy off, then it screamed and galloped hard back toward town. There was no chance for Cassidy to catch the animal.

Lee reloaded his revolver with six bullets and watched the downed man. Somewhere he had lost the rifle. Lee couldn't let him look for it. He fired again, then ten seconds later again. It took one more shot that came close to the gunman before Cassidy lifted up and ran farther west where the brush line was closest.

Cat and mouse. Cowboys and Indians. Cattlemen and sheep men. It had come down to a stalking game through the lush growth of the East Walker River, and the prize was life. The man who lost the game died.

Sixteen rounds left.

A good gunman counts his shots, knows exactly how many rounds he has before he needs to reload. In a running fight Lee had always left one round in the chamber while he reloaded. Then if he were surprised he had one killing shot left.

Lee remained totally still, listening. Cassidy was crashing brush ahead going away. He was not the woodsman that Hardin had been. Lee moved ahead quickly by stepping out of the brush and running alongside it. He ran for thirty yards, then stopped and listened.

More brush crashing, still ahead but closer. He ran again and stopped. No sounds. Cassidy also was listening. A battle of nerves. Cassidy broke and ran fast. Lee slammed a shot into the brush where he heard the gunman.

Fifteen rounds.

The wasted round was worth it for its scare effect. Now Cassidy knew Lee was close and coming after him. The crashing continued as Lee followed along outside the brushy area. He could move much faster than Cassidy.

Then the brush thinned on this side of the stream. Only an occasional alder stood along the bank. Lee slid behind brush at the edge of the void and watched the trees.

He brought up the Bisley, aiming between the two alders which were large enough to cover Cassidy.

A figure ran from one tree toward the next.

Lee tracked him and fired. Cassidy yelped in pain, turned and searched for Lee as he ran but couldn't locate him. There had been time for only one round.

Lee wanted to run up on the bushwhacker and

empty his gun in him, but Cassidy was still armed and deadly. Position and cover, a man had to have both. Cassidy ran again but Lee wasn't ready. By the time he got his weapon up and fired, the round was low and caught Cassidy in one leg.

He dove into cover and screamed at Lee.

"Fucking bastard! Nobody is that good a shot. Lucky bastard! Just wait. I'll kill you yet."

The void without brush meant Lee had no cover or concealment to move ahead. He waited until Cassidy ran into heavier brush, then he surged across the open place to the concealment of the brush on the far side and listened again.

Nothing.

He waited. Cassidy could be hurt too bad to run any more. Lee knelt behind an alder for five minutes but there was no sound at all. Could Cassidy have stepped into the water and waded downstream silently? Possible.

Lee worked his way without a sound through the ten yard width of brush and trees to the water's edge. Ahead thirty yards he saw Cassidy working slowly downstream along the muddy shore. Lee fired a shot at him. Cassidy looked back, waved a fist and slid into the underbrush.

Twelve rounds left.

Lee reloaded as he ran back to the open country and then forty yards forward where he stopped and listened.

Once again, Cassidy worked through the brush along the stream.

Lee did what he had considered before. He ran fifty yards ahead in the open, then quietly worked his way into the brush, found protection and settled down to wait for Cassidy to come through the brush toward him and into his gun sights.

It took fifteen minutes for Cassidy to come up to

where Lee waited. Only he came up behind him and only an errant step on a dry branch gave him away and ruined his chance to backshoot Lee and kill him.

When the branch broke Lee dove to one side, spun around and fired four times at the spectre of the gunman who loomed out of the sun and brush. He fired wildly emptying his own revolver.

A moment later Cassidy's six-gun ran dry and the men stared at each other through the soft blue smoke haze. Then Lee dug rounds from his belt and Cassidy turned and ran to the east through the brush, floundering to get away as he pulled rounds from his belt loops to reload.

"Damn!" Lee growled as he let out a little of the pain. One of Cassidy's bullets had hit him in his left shoulder and he wasn't sure how bad it was. It was bleeding, but at least he could still move his arm.

He shoved more fresh round into his weapon.

He had eight rounds left, six in his Bisley, two in his belt loops. He had to nail Cassidy's hide to a tree before dark or the bushwhacker would get away. There was no chance he could trail the man in the dark. Why was he heading this way? Why didn't Cassidy go back to Ralston's mine for cover and support?

Lee returned to the method that had worked before. He gained the edge of the brush and ran forward, stopped and listened. Brush crashed for a minute or so, then stopped.

Ten minutes later there had been no movement. Lee knew he had to go find Cassidy now. He knew the man must have figured the same thing and would have a good position and his weapon ready with six rounds.

Lee moved cautiously the way he had learned from the Indians. Slowly, never putting weight on his foot until he was sure whatever was underneath would make no noise.

It took him ten minutes to edge through enough brush so he saw what he decided must be Cassidy's position. It was beside a two-foot thick giant alder, with a fallen log beside it. He could stand or sit and have good fields of fire.

Lee wished for a dynamite bomb he could toss over the log. No such luck. He had to work around behind the tree. That took him another eight or ten minutes. At last he could see one of Cassidy's boots extending from the cover of the log.

He moved closer, his Bisley up, his finger on the hair trigger.

The shot from behind surprised Lee.

Instantly his Bisley spun from his hand and he thought his trigger finger must be broken.

"Shit, I missed!" Cassidy roared behind and ten feet to the right. He pulled the trigger twice more but the hammer only clicked on fired rounds. Cassidy swore again, threw the empty weapon at Lee and charged into the brush.

Lee saw the bloody pants leg. The man was wounded. The weapon? Where was his Bisley? He found it nearby but the cylinder had been smashed to one side by the lucky shot. It would need a gunsmith to make it work again. Cassidy's weapon! There were still two rounds in his gunbelt.

He searched for the weapon for a minute, perhaps two, then realized it was lost in the brush and leaves and mulch. He had to follow Cassidy.

Now the cat and mouse game became more basic. It was mind and muscle against mind and muscle. After five minutes, Lee caught up with the tall man who brandished a knife keeping Lee back. Lee's shoulder began to throb. He could hardly lift his left arm now.

Cassidy limped along, fifty feet ahead, not bothering with the brush now, walking along beside the willow in the open.

Lee wished he had the hideout he often carried, a small derringer, scaled down into a .22 caliber size. It fit in the palm of his hand but at close range was deadly.

All he had was the knife in his boot. He'd save that for the first close up chance he had. The tall man moved slower now. The sun was an hour from setting. Two hours to dark. There would be a final confrontation before then. Lee would not let Cassidy get away in the dark. Even with one arm he would battle the gunman at close range with knives if it came to that.

The woods deepened ahead and Cassidy limped into them and out of sight. Lee hurried forward, rushed past a clump of willow and past an alder.

The thin man had the five pound rock lifted over his head and he crashed it down toward Lee from three feet away. The rock missed Lee's head, but slammed into his right thigh, driving him to the ground.

Cassidy had his knife out and was about to leap on Lee when Lee lifted his own knife, the sharp point glinting in the dappled sunshine.

"Be damned," Cassidy said, stepping back. "Didn't know you had a sticker."

He reached for another rock and Lee grabbed one off the ground and threw it at him, hitting his shoulder. Cassidy snorted and pulled back. "See you in hell, Morgan."

He limped away into the brush.

Lee felt his leg. He prayed that it wasn't broken. Gingerly he lifted up on his good foot, then gradually put his weight on the left leg. It hurt but only from the bruise. He could walk. He found a four foot long limb that was dead and strong to use as a cane.

Lee gritted his teeth and moved ahead. He would
not let Cassidy get away.

The two men moved downstream along the river
for an hour, never more than twenty yards apart,
sometimes closer, neither wanting to make the first
deadly confrontation without some kind of an
advantage. Cassidy had turned into a better woodsman than Lee first thought. Twice he had slipped
around Lee and worked a ways back west before
Lee caught him and they moved east again.

Now Lee came to a thicker section of woods and
he walked ahead cautiously. Cassidy had been
twenty yards ahead when he vanished. There were
more pines here as they dropped down from the
higher elevations. Lee walked slowly forward where
he had seen Cassidy go. A pine stood to the left and
brush and a dozen small alder to the right.

He stepped ahead beside the pine, then past it and
only then did he see the trap but it was too late to
avoid it completely. Years ago a pine had ripened
and toppled, broken and rotted and turned back into
humus on the woodsy floor. But a section of it had
balanced precariously against the larger pine and
one of its lower limbs.

Cassidy had seen it and climbed the pine six feet
off the ground. When Lee stepped into the right
spot, he had pushed the two foot thick pine log,
unbalancing it and sending it crashing down to the
trail and on top of Lee.

He was brushed back by the decaying log as it slid
down the tall pine, then rolled forward and pinned
both his legs under it.

If it had been green it would have crushed his legs
beyond repair, but it was twenty-years broken and
dead, and dry rot had robbed it of most of its weight.
Still Lee could not move his legs. He held only the
knife and his walking cane.

Somewhere to the right, Cassidy laughed.

"Well now, looks like our mighty gunslinger has been bested in his game of hide and seek. You're it, Morgan, and a slit throat is the prize. Welcome to hell, you'll be there in five minutes."

Lee tried to push the log off his legs, but it wouldn't budge. He had no leverage. He was pinned tightly. He grabbed the walking stick and looked at it, then he took his knife and began to sharpen the inch-thick end of the stick. It was hard and tough and difficult to cut. Slowly he made headway forming a point.

"Your idea to dynamite that cave entrance, Cassidy?"

"Yep. My idea. Should have killed you. How the hell did you get out, dig through all that rock and dirt?"

"Air shaft. Now all I have to do is kill you."

"No chance. I can stand back and stone you to death, or hit you with a club, or practice knife throwing on your back. Yeah, I could. But I specialize in slitting throats, Morgan. I promised myself if I didn't gun you down, I'd have the pleasure of watching your life flow out below that big talking mouth of yours, and laugh as you bled to death."

"For a no-talent gunman you've got a big mouth, Cassidy. It'll be an honor to kill you right here."

Cassidy laughed. "You and who else gonna do the job? You got a bad shot up arm, a bruised leg, both legs pinned under that log and that knife hand of yours will reach only so far. Course you could throw it and get lucky, but from what I hear you don't throw a blade none too good."

"Try me," Lee said. Anything to keep the man talking. He needed more time to make the point sharp and slender on the stick so he would have one chance.

"No use dragging this out, Morgan. I want to see

you die before it gets dark. Then I'll probably sleep over here before I walk back to town. Christ, we must have come out here seven, or eight miles. If I hadn't run out of rounds, I'd have nailed your ass two hours ago.''

"That word 'if' don't pay the taxes, Cassidy,'' Lee said.

Then the waiting was over. Cassidy came up in front of Lee and stared at him. The walking stick and its sharp point lay hidden by the two foot thick log.

"You ready to die, gunsharp?''

"This will be different for you, Cassidy. Heard you always back shoot men, that you never faced one down in all your misbegotten life.''

Cassidy laughed. "Can't get me upset now, you bastard. I got you by the balls and I'm cutting them off.''

Lee had the knife in his right hand. He saw Cassidy had a thick stick in his left. It was about a foot long. He would try to deflect Lee's knife with the stick and get in a killing slice with his own stabber.

From four feet away he lunged forward.

Lee dropped the knife, grabbed the walking stick spear with both hands and at the last moment lifted it.

Bob Cassidy's lunge continued. He saw the spear now, but was in mid air and couldn't stop. The point stabbed through the man's shirt, and into his chest. Cassidy's weight drove the lance back until it hit the dirt beside Lee, then the body came forward until the point of the spear broke out of Cassidy's back.

The inch-thick weapon penetrated Cassidy's left lung and tore out a section of his spinal column and he died instantly.

Lee rolled the corpse away from him. He was panting from the effort. For a moment he relaxed where he sat, then took a deep breath and tried to figure out how to get himself free.

The foot long stick Cassidy dropped lay near him and Lee picked it up. A lever!

He took the two inch thick stick and positioned it under the edge of the log and tried to pry upward with it. No luck. The lever was too short to give him any mechanical advantage. He looked at the sky which was beginning to darken.

Lee picked up his knife and idly stabbed it into the log. To his surprise the blade sank in three inches. The wood was pulpy. He twisted the knife and pushed downward and a six inch section of the log fell free.

He could carve out a tunnel for his legs and pull them out! Lee went to work in earnest and in fifteen minutes had one leg free and five minutes later had broken enough of the pulpy rotting wood away to pull his other leg out. He examined them closely. Neither seemed to be damaged seriously.

It took Lee five minutes to stand up and get walking. Both legs were bruised, both hurt. His arm still bled a little but he saw that the wound was not as serious as it could have been.

He put the blade back in his boot and began walking toward Silverton. With any luck he should be there in three hours.

It was after 8:30 that evening before Lee staggered up the steps to the front door of the O'Reily house below the mine and pushed open the door.

Colleen was there before the door closed. She rushed forward, caught his arm over her shoulder and helped him into the kitchen. She mumbled something as she sat him in a chair and stood back and looked at him. First she took off his shirt and checked the bullet wound in his upper arm.

"It went all the way through, good," she said half to herself.

Lee felt too tired to laugh, but he managed a short chuckle. "You haven't scolded me yet for not being careful."

"Won't," she said quickly. "Promised myself as I walked the floor here for three hours waiting for you to show up, that I wouldn't tear into you until I found out what happened." She reached in and kissed his nose. "So, gunfighter, tell me what in tarnation happened out there?"

She took out a pint bottle of rubbing alcohol.

He told her a condensed version of his bush-whacking and then remembered something else.

"I owe somebody for that little roan horse. Got to find out whose it was."

"We can do that tomorrow easy enough, now hold still." She sloshed the alcohol over the two bullet holes.

Morgan screeched like a stuck hog. "What the hell?"

Colleen grinned. "Price of being a gunsharp. It also helps a bullet wound to heal and kills the bugs that make things get infected. So don't complain. Now I clean out the hole a little and put on some healing ointment I have and bandage it up. Good as most doctors can do these days, leastwise out here in the wilds of Nevada."

"Maybe some of us would prefer a little infection."

"Too late now," She smiled. "At least this time you didn't lose your hat. It's a mess but it's still on your head."

Philip came in, took one look at Lee and began filling buckets of water to heat on the big kitchen wood range.

"You done it again," Philip said.

"This is the last time he does," Colleen said. "I'm gonna tie his boot laces together and then fasten him around the ear with a long string to my apron."

"Enough scolding. Where's my dinner?"

"First a bath, then if you're lucky maybe a sandwich and some coffee. How is that leg he hurt?"

"It is fine."

"Take off your pants so I can look at it," Colleen said grinning. He dropped his pants but the bruise wasn't showing yet and there was no blood.

He took his bath in the side of the kitchen while Philip hustled him up some dinner. As he soaked in the hot tub, Colleen brought him a water glass filled with half whiskey and half branch water.

"Figure you need a little pick up before dinner," she said.

Two hours later, he sat on the edge of the bed in his room as Colleen paced.

"So his gunmen are gone, what can we do now?"

"Now we work hard to keep the Association going, make it strong and honest. Get some kind of law and order in town that isn't run by Ralston. Gradually he'll see that he can't frighten the whole town and settle down."

"Not a chance," Colleen said. "I've looked into his eyes. He has to have it all or he won't even stay in the game. Winning is the only end game he knows."

She walked over and pulled down the bed covers.

"Inside, cowboy. Time for some recuperation. I'd love to snuggle in beside you for the night, but I'd forget myself and attack your body, so I better let you sleep alone."

"You have to learn to control your appetites."

She pushed his head down on the pillow and kissed his lips, then came away.

"I know I have to control myself, but I love eating you." Colleen grinned. "You have 24 hours to recuperate and then I won't be responsible for all sorts of sexy things I'm going to do to you."

"Fair warning," he said.

Then the hot bath and the good food and the second whiskey took their toll and his eyes drifted closed. Colleen reached down and kissed his lips gently, smiled and watched him sleeping for a moment, then slipped out and closed the door behind her.

For an hour she sat at the small desk in the parlor trying to work out a list of projects that needed to be done if Silverton was to become a normal, law abiding town again, where the miners could go about their business in peace. It started with either hiring a town marshall or getting a permanent group of Sheriff's Deputies stationed here to keep the peace. That was what she would work on first.

Tomorrow she would go see Sheriff's Deputy Kellen Gillette. He was the only Deputy Sheriff she had ever seen who wouldn't wear a gun. Said his job here was civil, deeds, wills, probate, bills of sale, and taxes. She would send a strong letter through him to the Sheriff at the county seat in Yerrington, thirty miles northwest. She wasn't even sure what the Lyon county Sheriff's name was now.

There had to be a way to save the town from Col. Ralston. The mines were important. She had a lot of hard working men who had been here for years. They deserved a fair wage, a peaceful town, and law and order.

Colleen was determined to get it all for them.

8

When Lee woke up the next morning he wished he
were dead. His arm ached like it was being burned
off in a campfire, his head pounded with a
monstrous headache, and he wasn't sure he could
move either leg.

It took him five minutes to get out of bed, and
another ten minutes to dress. After three attempts to
stand, he had to practice walking. Six turns around
the room and he thought he had it down. Moving his
left arm was another matter. It killed him to put on
his shirt and he couldn't button it. Trying to close up
his fly was impossible.

By the time he went to the front door, down the
steps and walked around the house six times, he was
almost mobile again. He managed to get his left hand
over far enough to button his fly but the shirt was
out of the question.

Inside the kitchen, Philip saw his problem and did
up the buttons.

"We best fix up that arm before breakfast," Philip said. He found a piece of muslin and fashioned it into a square, then a triangle and made a sling for the uncooperative and still burning left arm.

"Now, long as you can eat and drink with one hand, you'll get by today. Arm gonna feel better tomorrow. No fisticuffs today, Mr. Morgan."

"Lee, call me Lee. There never was a Mr. Morgan. There was a Mr. Leslie, but he was somehow never a mister either. Everyone called him Buckskin or Frank."

Lee saw the name meant nothing to Philip. He groaned as he sat down at the table, but the ham and eggs and hashbrowns followed by a bowl of oatmeal and raisins put him back in a good mood. The coffee was black and hot and not over boiled.

He asked about Colleen.

"She's been building up her nerve all morning. Said she was going to see that Sheriff Deputy and demand some law and order in this town."

Lee grinned. "Sure would like to be a mouse in her pocket and hear what she says."

Sheriff Elston Winner looked at Col. Ralston and shook his head. They both sat in the mine owner's fancy office at the mine and had just finished coffee laced with bourbon whiskey.

"Not a chance, Colonel. You showed me testimony of two witnesses who said they heard the two men in a confrontation on Main Street and a call out. Later one man turns up tied to his saddle head down and dead. No way in hell anybody could prove murder. Just can't do it."

"Sheriff, maybe I didn't make myself clear. I put a whole passel of votes in them boxes for you last election. This is the first time we met face to face, but I *delivered* this town and half the votes you got. I need a small favor. I *expect* that you will take care of it. I want Morgan arrested for murder, convicted and hanged."

Ralston took off the smoked glasses and polished them.

Sheriff Winner was surprised when he saw the man's eyes. They were watering and soft and weak-looking despite the man's six-foot three size. They spoiled the domineering effect of such a big man.

"Mr. Ralston, you ain't no fancy southern general now. You remember that. This is my county, elected fair and square, and I'll run it according to the laws of the state of Nevada no matter how much you threaten me. Is that clear?

"As far as your other man, Hardin, I'd rather give the gent who smashed up Hardin that way a medal. Hardin's been on more wanted posters than my dog's got fleas. Glad to see him out of the gunslick business."

Col. Ralston looked like he had been slapped in the face. "Aren't there some wanted posters on Lee Morgan? Arrest him and take him to Yerrington on suspicion. I just want him out of town."

"Don't remember no paper on a Lee Morgan. Don't arrest somebody less I got solid reasons. Did want to stop by and see you in answer to your letter. But not a thing the law of this county can do for you. You get me three witnesses who are reliable, and not saloon drunks, who can testify to back shooting or gunning down in cold blood, then I'll arrest this Morgan."

Col. Ralston put on the smoked glasses and stood near the half open curtains making the Sheriff squint to see him in the strong back lighting.

"Thank you, Sheriff Winner, for coming by. I'm sure you have a busy day here in Silverton."

It was a dismissal. The Sheriff rose and walked out

of the room without a goodbye. He had a definitely
bad impression of the mine owner, and at once
resolved not to do a thing about this Morgan—
unless it was to thank him for dispatching the
infamous Sam Plummer and breaking up another
wanted poster boy, Johnny Hardin.

Outside the mine, he joined his Deputy who'd
made the trip with him.

"Let's get down and see Deputy Gillette. He may
have some different kind of citizen complaints."

A half hour later, Sheriff Winner sat in another
mine owner's office. This one was drafty, there was
no window drapes, paneling or rugs on the floor. But
he felt a lot more comfortable.

"So, Miss O'Reily, our Deputy here, Gillette, tells
me you had a complaint this morning about law and
order. That's my job, would you give me the gist of
your needs?"

"Simply that, Sheriff Winner. We need either a
Town Marshall and about ten Deputies here, or we
need the county to send us a Sheriff's Captain and
ten Deputy Sheriffs to provide us with some real law
and order.

"Up to now the only imitation of law we've had
has been Col. Ralston's bully boy law. Your Deputy
here doesn't even own a gun."

Sheriff Winner nodded. He'd been worried about
Silverton for sometime now. He'd had citizen
reports. He peaked his fingers and firmed his jaw. "I
agree, we must have one of the two. Most towns this
size have City Police or a Town Marshal. That would
be best. You have a town council?"

"Not since Ralston's been here. He runs things."

"I strongly suggest that you elect a town council
and then appoint a marshal. That way you have local
control, speedy action."

He walked to the window and looked at the raw

pinewood built town. He shivered to think what a fire would do to the settlement. Wipe out ninety percent of the businesses built shoulder to shoulder out there.

"If you can't elect a council, or until you can do that, I'll send over a Lieutenant and five men. Part of his job will be to help you hold an election for your own Silverton town council."

Colleen was on her feet smiling. "Wonderful, Sheriff Winner. I'm so glad you came over here today. We now have a Mine Owners Association to fight Ralston, and we're getting some support from some of the larger merchants. We just might make it."

Sheriff Winner stood, knowing that he had cemented relations with a good contact. He'd write this pretty little Irish lass to head up his next election campaign in Silverton.

He shook her hand, carried his hat and stepped outside into the cool sunshine. Coming from Texas he'd known the burning hot sun, and frozen sun, but damn little cool sunshine.

The Sheriff and his Deputy served two warrants in a grand theft case, talked with the banker and three more merchants, then had dinner that noon at the Silverton Hotel and set out for Yerrington to the north slightly before one that afternoon. It was a thirty mile ride and if they pushed they could be home a little after dark.

They cantered out of town and had made good time for the first three miles northwest along the stage road that followed the East Walker River. The river made a mile long bend to the left but the trail forded the foot deep stream to save the two miles of distance.

Just as Sheriff Winner and his Deputy entered the water at the ford, hidden riflemen on both sides blasted a dozen shots at the lawmen. Both were blown out of the saddle. Not even saloon drunks and hangers-on could miss a man sized target at twenty yards.

The Deputy dropped into the water face down and didn't move. Sheriff Winner had been wounded in four places but not killed. He jerked out his revolver and got off three shots from where he sat bleeding into the East Walker River.

Three more rifle slugs blasted into his chest and one into his throat, dumping the Sheriff dead into the water.

The four gunmen came out of the brush and alders slowly, guns ready. Soon they relaxed.

A red bearded man with a black, low crowned hat, spat tobacco juice into the river.

"Yeah, that's done. Now we got to take care of the hard part. Drag them out over to this side."

As two of the men dug a hole in the soft soil along the side of the stream fifty yards down from the ford, the other two men pulled the bridles and saddles off the horses and slapped them on the hind quarters, sending them galloping up the trail north toward their home stable.

An hour later the four sweating men had the bodies and saddles and tack all buried deep alongside the stream. They covered the spot, then tramped down the ground and built a foot high mound before they dragged dead branches and leaves over the spot to make it look the same as the surrounding ground.

"Them two gents will never be found," one of the sweating men said. He handed the shovel to the red bearded man.

"Payday," the man said and held out his hand.

The man in charge reached in his pocket and pulled out a small leather bag and opened the draw strings. He took out double eagles, twenty-dollar gold pieces, and gave two to each of the three men.

"Now, the agreement was you'd keep on riding to Yerrington and then on to Carson City, right?"

The three agreed and went for their horses. The red bearded man watched them ride away, then turned and lifted into his saddle and rode back toward Silverton, the four double eagles still in the leather pouch deep in his pocket.

A mile outside of Silverton a rifle cracked and the red bearded man spun off his mount and flopped on the ground. Half of the back of his head had been blown away by a fifty caliber bullet from a Sharps 50-90. The weapon and the powerful round had been designed to bring down a buffalo at full stride.

A man sitting in the shadows with the big gun resting on a log smiled in satisfaction. There should be eighty dollars in the man's purse. Not bad pay for a few hour's work. Now all he had to do was report to the big man that the job was done.

As the rider came out of the brush with the big Sharps and rode on toward town, a thin young man astride a dun sat watching two hundred yards away. For the past three hours he had been witnessing men being murdered.

He had been coming toward Silverton when he heard the shots at the ford, and moved up close enough to see the final execution of the man in the stream.

Partly from fear he had remained hidden, then watched the careful burial of men and saddles. He saw the payoff, and followed the red beard back to his own execution.

Now a half hour later, he sat in the small office where Deputy Sheriff Gillette paced the floor. Colleen O'Reily had been in the office when the young man slipped inside and began telling his story.

The Deputy established quickly that the two men killed had been riding a roan and a sorrel, and gave exacting descriptions of the clothing they wore.

"The men were both lawmen, Lyon County Sheriff Winner and his Deputy," Gillette said with a groan of loss.

"Oh, lord," the thin young man said. "I was hoping the two were outlaws."

"Where did the last killer go when he came into town?" Deputy Gillette asked.

"Directly to the office of the big mine on the hill, the Silver Strike, it said over the door."

Colleen stormed out of the Sheriff's office. She had gone back there to find out the legal procedures for holding a local election, but found her new friend the Sheriff had been murdered. She also knew who had killed him.

She rode her buggy directly to Ralston's office building on the hill and stamped inside.

The pasty young man at the desk rose.

"Sit down and shut up!" she shouted at him. Colleen marched to Ralston's office door and unlatched it, then kicked it hard with her shoe slamming it open.

Col. Ralston looked up from a paper on his desk.

"Ah, the lovely Miss O'Reily."

"Shut up, you murderer! We have a witness. You won't get away with it this time. Those were two *lawmen* you had murdered. Then the leader of the four killers was blasted by a rifle as he came back to town. We know the whole thing.

"Just shooting my father wasn't enough. You had to want his mine and every one of the other mines on the hill. You're crazy, Cleve Ralston. *Corporal* Ralston, you aren't fit to run a shoe shine store, let alone a mine or to command men."

Colleen stood in front of him across the desk. She glared up at him. She was almost panting from her tirade. She pointed her finger at him.

"You are a dead man, Ralston! The law will settle your potatoes in a rush. I'm riding to Yerrington as soon as I can with a dozen bodyguards, so you better be ready for a fight. We're bringing the law down on you and we're going to hang you and the man who pulled the trigger.

"You're a dead man, *Corporal* Ralston!" She spun around and marched out the room, slammed the office door behind her and left the outside door open.

Col. Ralston watched her leave his office. He called sharply and two men came into the room.

"Follow her, grab her and take her out of town. There's a cabin south of the river somewhere. Use her all you want to, then kill her and bury her so deep nobody will ever find her body. Make sure she's dead before sunup tomorrow."

The two men hurried out the side door.

Ralston stood by the window watching her drive down the hill. Threaten him, would she! Try to bring the law down on him! Ralston trembled so badly that he couldn't walk. He leaned against the wall and closed his eyes.

He had not worked here for five years to see all of his efforts shot to pieces by one screaming little Irish *puta*! With a great deal of effort he caught hold of his nerves, calmed himself and walked back to his desk.

He would have to work out a quick legal way to take over the O'Reily Mine now that its owner was soon dead. He would talk with Beauford Lawrence. That asshole lawyer better have a good plan or there would be one less barrister in the county.

Three men on horseback followed Colleen as she left the Silver Strike Mine. They hung well back and the larger of the three, Willy, cautioned the men that there was no chance now to abduct the young woman without attracting a lot of attention.

"After it gets dark, lads. That's when we'll take the Irish lass and all three have our way with her, at least five times!"

The men grinned and split up, going by different routes, but shadowing the buggy as it bounced over the ruts in the dirt street and stopped at last at the back door of the O'Reily house below the mine.

Colleen flounced into the house. She was still so angry she could barely talk. The surge of screaming at Ralston had left her drained. He was so . . . so impossible! She would see him punished for what he did to her father, and to that nice Sheriff Winner! Ralston simply had to pay for his crimes.

Someone near the kitchen door chuckled. She looked up sharply.

"Lady, I've never seen you so ruffled. You came steaming in here like you were on a sulky race. Bet you didn't know that three men followed you."

"What? You're joking!"

"No, come look for yourself. I was at the front window when I saw you charging for home. I figured the devil himself was chasing you or at least a headless horseman . . ."

"Don't laugh at me. Show me the men."

At the front window he told her not to touch the curtain. He pointed out the first man who was off his horse now examining its rear hooves. He was fifty yards to the west of the house but in a position to see the front and rear entrances.

Another man sat in the grass on the far side of Nevada Street a hundred yards off, and a horse grazed nearby.

"Where's the third one?"

"Sitting in that buggy in front of the Johnson house. His horse is behind the buggy. They beat you down the hill and dropped off as you went past.''

"Why in the world . . .'' She stopped. "Oh, Lord, I've done it now. I was just on a friendly visit to *Corporal* Ralston. His men just killed the Lyon County Sheriff and a Deputy who had been in town this morning. A witness came into the Deputy's office while I was there finding out the election law. He saw the whole thing.

"I went flying up there and accused him of it and told him that I would see him dead, and scolded him something terrible. I guess I was shouting and screaming all the time. Those men must be from Ralston.''

"I don't think he likes you, Colleen.''

They walked back to the kitchen and she poured a cup of coffee.

"You're laughing at me again.''

"No, I'm proud of you. You just verbally spanked a man who has killed dozens of men only because they got in his way. Now for a person who he really dislikes—''

"Sheriff Winner said we should have a city government, and elect a town council and then hire a Town Marshal. I'm going to do just that. Then we'll keep Ralston in his place.''

"You'll need a strong man as Marshal. Chances are if Ralston is still around a Marshal wouldn't live long in this town.''

"Maybe by then we'll have Ralston in jail for murder.''

"Let's hope.''

Lee moved toward the window and a small groan of pain seeped from his tight lips. She looked up quickly.

"Goodness, I forgot to ask about my patient. How are you coming along? You don't look up to a hard fist fight.''

"I'm not. Just don't ask me to put my left hand over my head. Most anything else works after I get it started."

"Could you walk me up to the mine? I need to talk to Warren about some things."

He nodded, settled the Bisley in its place and reached for a rifle from the rack of four near the kitchen door. "I'll run the one watcher off. That's what they want us to do. We see him and get rid of him and then don't figure there are any more."

Out the back door, Lee lifted the rifle to his shoulder and strained to hold it with his left hand as he put a round within ten feet of the man to the east of the house.

"Get out of there, you're on O'Reily land!" Lee bellowed in his gruffest voice.

The man stood, shook his fist at Lee, then grabbed his horse and walked back down the hill.

Once Lee had Colleen safely inside the mill office, he checked the security positions, moved two of them and added a post for day and night so the O'Reily house was included inside the perimeter. That done he settled down in the house and began to lift his left arm, working it sideways, then up and down. He had to keep it from going stiff or it could be a long time before it came back to normal.

After ten minutes he relaxed and checked out the front windows. The other two men were still in position. As soon as it was dark, he'd surprise the men and send them on their way—or if they resisted, he'd kill them. It was time to get serious.

Every half hour that afternoon, Lee worked on his left arm. It was coming along. He could lift it straight in front of him now shoulder high without screaming.

Just after a big supper he worked his arm again, then slipped on a light jacket and loosened the Bisley.

"I'm going to make a round of the guard posts just to keep the men on their toes," Lee said.

Earlier he had made sure that Philip had a revolver and the sawed off double barreled shotgun that Lee had taken from Sam Plummer. Philip knew the danger that faced Colleen.

Lee started at the near side to talk to the guards. He had made the rounds before and they recognized his voice now as he talked his way around. At the far side below the mill he figured he'd take out the first of the Ralston men who watched the house.

It took him nearly an hour to make the rounds. When he came to the spot where the Ralston man had been, he was gone. Quickly he checked the buggy at the Johnson house. It was now empty, but there were droppings where the horse had stood behind it for some time.

A cold arrow stabbed up his spine. He forgot all about his tender legs as he broke into a sprint the fifty yards to the O'Reily house. He went past the guard with a shouted hello, then stopped suddenly. The guard lay in his dug hole at an odd angle.

Lee checked the man and found a knife wound in his back. He had been killed silently with a thrown blade.

Now Lee charged for the house, fearful of what he might find there, but already making guesses.

The front door was closest. He leaped up the steps and banged open the door. The lamps were burning as usual. The parlor was dark and empty, the dining room lighted but empty. He hesitated at the kitchen door then went in with a rush, the Bisley out, ready.

Philip lay crumpled on the floor by the range. A scarlet pool of blood below his throat which showed an ear to ear red slice.

Colleen wasn't in the house.

Quickly he took a lantern, made sure it was full of coal oil and hurried back to the dead guard. He used the light and circled the position three times, making each ring larger than the last. On the outside of the fourth circle he found the fresh hoof prints. Grass was still bending up from one of the horse shoe marks. Swinging the lantern slowly he found the other tracks. Three horses, one being ridden double from the indentations of the hooves in the soft ground.

He ran back to the mine stable, saddled his horse faster than he ever had done before and rode back to the start of the tracks. There was no way to predict the direction. He led the horse and swung the lantern as he walked watching the tracks. On the dirt street the three horses were easier to follow.

Night time bugs and small crawlers had already violated the impressions made by horse hooves during the day. The night time tracks were mostly clear of the small trails. The route led half way down Nevada Street, then slanted into the thin grass and headed east behind McGraw's Livery.

When the tracks hit the trail east along the river, Lee stepped into his saddle and galloped a quarter of a mile along the trail before he stopped and checked the dirt of the roadway for the three set of tracks. He found them at once and rushed on another half mile and lighted the roadway again.

The kidnapper's tracks were still there.

He rode for a mile this time, watching the land. There must be a house or cabin of some sort out here where they would keep her. What kind of ransom would Ralston expect? Or would he merely let the men have their pleasure with the woman before they killed her. More likely the latter.

He rode faster.

A quarter-of-a-mile ahead he saw a light blinking in the darkness. The blinking came as he rode past trees in front of the light coming from a window.

It was a cabin of sorts, half fallen in, but with what he guessed were two good rooms.

He left his horse a quarter-of-a-mile away and moved up softly, silently toward the cabin. They would have out no guard, expecting no company.

As he came toward the place he saw a shaft of light stab into the night from a door, then close and the shadow of a man walked a dozen feet away from the cabin and in the faint moonlight, Lee saw him stop and begin to urinate.

A dozen fast running steps later and Lee drove the broadblade dagger solidly into the man's left arm as Lee's good right arm circled his throat choking the breath out of him and stopping any sound coming from his throat.

There was a chance the man was a transient, innocent of any crime. A chance. Lee pulled the knife out of his arm, replaced the blade in his boot and dragged the man still in the choke hold back toward the window he had seen.

One look in the window was enough.

Colleen O'Reily hovered at the far side of the room, naked but with her chin up, her eyes darting fire.

"No!" he heard her yelp.

Lee tightened his grip on the shorter captive, lifted him upward as high as he could and then let him drop. At the last moment before the man's boots hit the dirt, Lee reversed the direction of his tough right arm and jerked upward with all his might.

The crack told Lee what he wanted to know. He had broken the kidnapper's neck. If he wasn't dead he would be within seconds. Lee pulled the knife from his boot and held it in his left hand as he drew the Bisley.

At the door he paused a moment, then kicked it inward and sprang in behind it.

A thin man with two days growth of beard and jagged black stumps for teeth stood in front of Colleen with his pants down. He turned, a revolver in his left hand.

Lee shot him through the forehead and spun to his left where he heard movement.

The man there looked up from a whiskey bottle. He saw Lee and threw the bottle at him, then scrambled across the floor toward a shotgun.

Lee shot him in the neck, then as he sprawled on the floor, Lee pumped another round into the man's heart and he lay still.

Before the sound of the last shot died, Colleen ran across the floor and threw herself into Lee's arms. He held her gently, kissed her head and patted her bare shoulder.

"It's over, sweet girl. The nightmare is over."

She sobbed against his chest, her small body heaving with the spasms of gasping breath and the washing away of the terror. Slowly her crying slowed and at last stopped. She leaned back a little and pulled his head down to kiss his lips.

"Darling Lee! I thought I'd never see you again! They said Ralston told them to kill me after . . . after they had used me all they wanted to. I . . . I think I nearly died just thinking about them."

Her face flamed with fear. "There were three of them!"

He patted her shoulder and kissed her cheek. "The third one won't hurt you any more." He held her tightly. "Maybe we should get your clothes."

"Yes, yes! I want to get away from here as quickly as I can."

Lee left the three bodies where they had fallen. Outside he stripped off two of the saddles and lifted Colleen onto the third horse. Saddles were easy to identify, horses much harder. He led the two horses

and watched the woman. Her skirt billowed delightfully around her thighs over the saddle.

"Don't worry about me," she said quickly. "I was
riding a horse in pants astride by the time I was
five."

An hour later they walked into the guard post east
of the house and Lee talked with the guard a
moment. He ran to the mine office and soon another
man left to replace the dead guard.

Inside the house he found Colleen kneeling beside
Philip, crying again. They were tears of anger, and
indignation, and fury, and telling an old and trusted
friend that he would be avenged. She looked up.

"They came in shortly after you left. They didn't
say a word. Philip lifted the shotgun and one man
threw a knife into Philip's chest. He fell and
dropped the shotgun and the other man cut his
throat. They made me watch.

"We went back the same way they came in . . .
and I saw they had killed the guard there . . ." She
shook her head.

"Is it worth it? All this killing. Dear Philip! He
would be alive if I hadn't screamed at Ralston this
afternoon. It isn't fair. He died for no reason. It was
nothing that he did."

Lee lifted her from the floor and held her. "I'm
sure Philip would say he died for an extremely good
reason—he was defending you with his life. I'm sure
he wouldn't have wanted it any other way." Lee led
her into the dining room and put her on the couch
and spread a crocheted afghan over her.

"You stay right here. I'll be back in a few minutes.
I'll take care of Philip."

Lee carried the gentle black man's body out of the
kitchen and up the hill to a small cemetery plot
where he had seen two crosses. He lay Philip on the
ground and covered him with a blanket. Then he

went back and scrubbed the blood off the wooden kitchen floor. Some of it would never come out.

He cleaned up and made a new pot of coffee, then took a hot cup in to Colleen. She was sleeping but awoke quickly.

"I want to bury him beside daddy. He had been with daddy for almost ten years. Philip had been a freed slave before Mr. Lincoln freed the rest of them. Yes, coffee, thank you."

She watched him. "Get a cup of coffee and just sit here with me for a while. I . . . I'm not ready to go to sleep by myself, not yet. Those three men . . . those damn savages!"

They sat and drank coffee and talked about nothing of importance. They touched and looked into each other's eyes. It was midnight before she asked him to come into her room. She undressed without embarrassment, put on a soft nightgown and asked him to sleep beside her that night.

He did. She cuddled up against him and cried herself to sleep. He put his arm around her but never had a thought of making love to her. It just never occurred to him.

9

Colleen put down her coffee cup and stood. "I tell you I feel perfectly fine. I'm still angry, and now is the time to get started doing what needs to be done."

"But after yesterday—" Lee began.

Her quick look stopped him. "I told you, I cried that out last night. They didn't hurt me, so they pulled my clothes off and grabbed me a little. I wasn't a blushing virgin, was I? Get your hat and look mean as you can and be my bodyguard."

Lee shrugged and led her out to the buggy. They drove down to the small Sheriff's station office across from the Archer Meat Market. Deputy Gillette was there.

"Miss O'Reily," he said with a broad smile. "I may be needing you as a witness when we go to trial on the death of Sheriff Winner. I sent a complete report to Captain Rawlings up at Yerrington. He's in command now. Also sent the witness so he can be on hand to get the legal wheels in motion."

"Thank you, Deputy. I'll cooperate any way I can. Today I want you to tell me the legalities of how we set up an election to pick a town council, so we can hire a Town Marshall. You were here when I talked to Sheriff Winner about it."

Morgan eased out of the office and leaned against the store's siding in the morning sun. It was warmer that way than walking. He checked the town. Things seemed to be moving along without pause, even though the three gunsharps were out of action, and Ralston had killed two lawmen.

Some town, somewhere, would continue after Lee Morgan got bushwhacked or gunned down by a faster hand.

Didn't look like Ralston would make another move for a while. He had some losses to absorb, some new men to line up to do his pistolero work.

As Lee thought it through, he knew there wasn't time enough left to get a town council elected and a Marshal brought in. Ralston could put a stop to that process any one of a number of ways. The man had to be dealt with in terms he understood—action and violence.

When Colleen came out of the office a half hour later, Lee knew exactly what had to be done. First he would try to convince her one more time.

She listened to him as they rode back to the mine. "Absolutely not! Mr. Morgan, I'm surprised at you. If we take up your gun against Ralston, then he drags us down to his moral level and we become as despicable and despotic as he is. There is a better way, the legal method. I'm getting the first step taken today. We'll form an election committee of potential voters here in town and get the business of organizing things started. In three months we can hold our first authorized election under the county laws."

"You realize what Ralston can do to this town in three months? He can burn out the other six mines including yours. He can frighten away everyone who wants to work for anyone but him. He can bring in a dozen fast guns and shoot down anyone who even looks crosseyed at him. He can hang each man on the election committee and stop your town before it gets started."

"He wouldn't dare! The new Sheriff would come in here with twenty Deputies and restore peace."

"That's a thin defense, a shaky, unsure and downright dangerous reason to be betting your life on, young lady."

At the house, a shotgun toting guard met them. Colleen bristled for a moment, looked at Lee and sighed. "I guess it's come to this. Leave him here."

"I have another armed man who will go with you from now on everywhere you go, even to the outhouse. We're not giving Ralston another chance."

"Yes, all right. I don't like it, but it won't last for long. Soon we'll have law and order in Silverton."

She went up to the mine office and the new bodyguard, a young man of about 25 who knew his guns, walked along beside her, watching everything in sight as they moved.

Lee settled down to look over the papers she had brought home. Setting up a new town wasn't that hard in Nevada. Getting it incorporated was the big step, but that could come later. He checked the printed regulations and realized that if they went about it correctly, the election committee could have an election called in three weeks, and vote a month after that.

Colleen could work on the committee, but being a woman she couldn't be an official member. Nor could she vote to form the town or for the town council members. If she lived in Wyoming she could vote. Women had owned the right to vote there since the area became a territory back in Sixty Eight.

The front guard came through the door and called to Lee.

"Some kid walking up the lane. You better come see what he wants, Mr. Morgan."

Lee went to the front door and down the steps. The boy was about twelve and marched along feeling important with a white envelope in his hand and a quarter in his pocket. With a quarter he could buy penny candy every day for a month. Almost. Not counting Sundays.

He came to Lee and looked up.

"Mr. . . . Mr. Morgan?"

"Right you are, son."

"I got this letter for you."

"Who gave it to you?"

"Dunno. Some big guy. Old. He came out of a saloon."

"What did he look like?"

"Dunno. Big, had a hat. No beard."

Lee took the envelope. "That big man gave you a dime to deliver this?"

"No sir, he sure didn't. Not a dime."

Lee found a dime in his pocket and flipped it in the air. The boy caught it, grinned and hurried back the way he came, only now he was skipping as he went down hill.

Back inside the house, Lee opened the sealed envelope and took out a piece of faintly lavender paper. A message was written in a tight, small hand. Precise. Neat.

"Mr. Morgan. I need to see you. I want you to help me get away from Cleve Ralston. The man is a beast and I can show you the bruises to prove it. I also want your hot body pressed tightly against mine!

"Come to the picnic spot just west of town on the Walker down there behind the Bottling Works. It's where the Baptists have their Sunday School picnics. I'll be there by one o'clock with a lunch basket. Please don't let me down. I need your help desperately." It was signed, Debbie Sue.

He had an hour. In the kitchen he saw that the handyman, Han, was the new cook. He was doing nicely. He said he had been a cook for a family in San Francisco for two years. He even knew enough English to communicate.

Lee warmed a cup of coffee with his hands and read the note again. When Colleen came from the mine, he showed the lavender paper to her.

"It's a trap. Ralston is using the girl to get you in the open so he can kill you. I won't let you go."

"Of course it's a trap. First he gets rid of me, then you, then Deputy Gillette and he'll have the town under his heel again. I'm going over there so he can't do that."

He laughed at her expression. "No, Colleen, I'm not walking down from the Bottling Works and making a perfect target of myself. When I go I'll know exactly the situation before I ever show myself. That area is near the river, so there must be a lot of cover along there. Right now I need to get moving. I always like to get to an execution early enough to get the second best view in the place."

"I don't . . ." She put her hand to her mouth and stopped. A tear misted her eye, then rolled down slowly over her soft cheek. "I'd just die if anything happened to you, Lee Morgan. You . . . you be just *damn* careful."

He kissed her cheek, made sure the Bisley was free and loose in his holster, then he walked out the front door and down the hill.

Lee went all the way down Nevada Street across

Main and to the end near the East Walker River.
Then he casually walked into the brush along the
river. He'd been in this same cover before and knew
how to use it. The bushwhackers would know, too,
and probably were already in place.

He moved along the inside of the brush, next to
the water line and worked west along the river as it
edged slightly farther away from Main Street.

When he could see the Bottling Works that formed
the west end of Main Street's businesses, he stopped
and listened. He worked silently through the brush
to the edge where the sparse grass and a few shrubs
grew in the natural little Nevada valley.

Nothing.

He watched for five more minutes. His Waterbury
told him it was twenty minutes until one. Debbie
Sue wasn't there yet, that was for sure. A movement
in the grass at the near side of a small bend in the
stream caught his eye.

He concentrated on the spot and soon saw the
grass move again.

One.

He judged the area and decided the man he had
spotted would be the one farthest this way. There
would not be another ambusher between him and
the man he saw.

Then he checked the other places around the
river's brushy bank but could not see enough of it.
He moved up silently toward the man he had
spotted. It took him nearly ten minutes to get into
the position he wanted.

As he settled in totally concealed and ten yards
behind the bushwhacker, he saw Debbie Sue get out
of her buggy at the back of the Bottling Works yard
and lift out a picnic basket. She looked into the
buggy and said something, then turned and walked
quickly toward the river.

As she picked out the exact place for the picnic, Lee moved forward toward the first victim. He guessed at least two, possibly three men would be there to gun him down. Ralston would not want to take any chances.

The mark moved again, coughed softly, then remained silent. Lee was now in willow and other brush, and moved slowly. He went past a fair sized alder and froze. The man ahead lifted up and stared through the brush toward the girl.

Lee could see the man plainly now. He seemed young, twenties, wore a brown hat and miner's clothes. The rifle he held was a Spencer seven shot repeater.

No chances at all.

Lee moved again. This time he had the broad-bladed dagger in his right hand, the Bisley in his left. Almost forgotten was the pain in his arm. Enough adrenalin now surged through his veins to overcome any weakness, any pain.

Lee did not have to plan what to do. In a battle or a shootout or a life and death fight, you have to know instinctively what action is needed. If a man has to stop and figure it out, he's dead before he strikes.

The miner/bushwhacker lay with the rifle poised beside him as he stared at the woman. The man's hand went to his crotch where he rubbed.

Lee surged forward, never exposing himself over the top of the two foot high grass and shrubs. He landed on the man's back, the Bisley coming down in his left hand across the back of the man's head.

His right hand whipped around the backshooter's throat and placed the blade against his flesh.

"Make a sound and you're dead!" Lee whispered to him. The slam on the head had stunned him, but as he came back to full realization he must have felt the knife.

"Nod your head yes or no. Understand?"
His head nodded.

"Did Col. Ralston send you to kill Lee Morgan?"
A nod.

"Are there three of you?"
A nod.

"Do you know if the girl is in on it?"
His head shook side to side in a 'no.'

"Point out the others. Where are they?"

A gurgling croak, the start of a yell spewed from the man's mouth.

Lee slashed down and across with the dagger, opening the jugular vein and carotid artery on the left side. The young man struggled for a moment, then relaxed. Thirty seconds later a long last gush of air came from his lungs, and Lee smelled the result of his bowels emptying.

Dead and gone. Another corpse. This one didn't bother him a whit. The bastard had been trying to kill him from ambush. Lowest kind of scum.

Lee took the rifle and moved six feet to a better observation spot and looked out. He was on a small sweeping bend of the little river that moved away to the left forming a gentle arc. Debbie Sue had spread a blanket and opened her picnic basket at the center of this arc and slightly outside of it. A perfect spot for crossfire from three rifles.

Now Lee concentrated on spotting the other two killers. He scanned the brush line again and again, but found no sign of the other two men.

A pair of crows sailed into the picture, dipped and swooped, then came to rest lighting in the top of a moderately sized alder on the far side of the small river bend. A moment later they lifted off squawking in anger at something below them.

Lee checked the ground cover there and at once saw a man moving. He was near the trunk of the tree but not using it as protection. Lee grinned, checked the Spencer to be sure one of the big .52 caliber rounds was in the firing chamber and sighted in on the man across from him.

Debbie Sue had been sitting on the blanket, but now stood and walked around it, waiting.

Lee checked his target again, and this time saw the glint of sunlight off a long gun's barrel. It was enough. It was a death warrant.

The Spencer lined up and Lee refined his sight, then squeezed the trigger gently. It fired. He rammed the operating lever down and up chambering a new round and found his target again. The man screamed and lifted up out of the weeds, his right arm hanging limply, already bathed red with blood.

Lee tracked his movement, centered the sights on his chest and fired again. The big round blew the bushwhacker back into the brush and out of sight.

Two down.

Lee watched the brush near the center of the arc of the river. Grass swayed. There was almost no wind in this spot. He watched, concentrating on the place the grass had been disturbed. The grass moved again farther into the brush.

Running for home.

Lee lifted the Spencer and fired the last five shots into the brush where he figured the third man had been retreating. He heard no cry of pain.

Lee looked at the girl who lay cringing on the blanket.

"Over here, Debbie Sue," he called.

She looked around.

"Here," he said again and she stood and walked toward the voice.

There was no one else in sight. A few rifle shots at the edge of Silverton usually didn't attract any attention. The woman came to the brush and stopped.

"This way," Lee said and she entered the willow and sagebrush growth until she was out of sight. Lee met her and watched her a moment. She shivered.

"You knew he was trying to kill me?"

"Yes, but he made me do it. I finally realized he must have told the men to kill both of us. I wanted to run, but I couldn't. I told you he beat me."

She opened her blouse and wore nothing under it, showing him her breasts. Both had ugly black and blue marks on the tender flesh. One of the large orbs was scratched.

"You know you can't go back to him."

"I know. Will you help me?"

He bent and kissed her breasts.

"Yes, of course. You can have me any way you want me. Then will you help me? I know he'll try to kill me. He's threatened me often enough. He's a crazy man."

They walked farther west until they were half a mile from the Bottling Works and found a soft grassy place screened with brush all the way around. Lee stopped and waited. She shrugged off her blouse letting her breasts swing free. Then she knelt in front of him and opened the buttons of his fly and reached inside.

"You're not even hard yet."

"I'm no fifteen year old boy. That's part of your responsibility."

She found his flaccid penis and pulled it out, massaged him, played with his balls, then licked the limp sword and sucked him into her mouth. Slowly he came alive and grew and came to full size.

She went on her hands and knees and lifted her skirt around her waist, pushing her bare buttocks at him.

"The top hole," she said, "the tight one."

She had left his member slippery with her saliva, now used more of her own spit to coat the pucker of her brown anus. He knelt behind her and edged forward.

"Oh Christ!" she bellowed as he penetrated the first tightness, then she moaned and fell with her head and shoulders on the grass as he inched in more and more.

"Wonderful, don't stop!" she shouted. He saw tears in her eyes and wondered if the bruises on her breasts were what she had wanted as well.

Then he didn't care. She had invited him in. He pressed forward into her bowel, came out and stroked again. He felt like a sixteen year old with the little neighbor girl behind the barn and both of them having their first fuck. She cooed and sang and pumped back at him now on every stroke and then thundered into a climax of her own which only increased Lee's excitement. He tried to hold back, to rest, but knew it was too late.

Again and again and again he slammed into the cushions of her buttocks as he sprayed his seed deep into her barren tube. She knew when he was through and collapsed into the green of the grass and urged him to stay in place and on top of her. He did. His hands crept around and found her big breasts which he caught and held.

A few minutes later she turned her head so she could see the side of his face. "Do you think he told them to kill me too?" she asked softly.

"You can bet on it. The Colonel does things up neatly. You're a loose end. You know too much of what he's done here in Silverton."

She was quiet for a moment. "Did you kill all three of them?"

"Two, I think one got away. He was smart enough

to run as soon as he heard me shoot."

"How did you know it was a trap?"

"That's not the way you would set up a love-making. Not in the middle of the day in a public place. And damn well not for a picnic. That's not what you like to eat."

She laughed. "You know I was . . . I am, a whore."

"Every woman's a whore in a way. Women marry for security. They give out sex for security. How is that different than two dollars a pop upstairs?"

"My kind of a man! I think I better get up."

Lee rolled away, and she went into the brush a dozen feet. When she came back, Lee was ready to travel.

"Where to?" she asked slipping on her blouse and buttoning it to the top.

"Ralston will know it if you stay at a hotel. You better come up to the O'Reily house."

"That girl won't like it."

"She's smarter than that."

"You fuck her?"

Lee watched Debbie Sue for a minute. Then nodded. "But don't mention it. It was honest, loving."

"Okay, but she'll know about us. She'll sense that you just balled me. Women can tell."

"Like I say, the girl has a good head on her shoulders. We won't worry about her. Our big problem is to get you on the morning stage headed for Carson City without Ralston knowing it."

"I don't have any money."

"You need any?"

Debbie Sue grinned. "Fuck no. I can earn my way. But it might be a little obvious if I fuck the driver right there on the driver's outside seat before we leave."

"Obvious, but I could sell some tickets."

She stuck her tongue out at him and they walked east along the far side of the river past the little town, then crossed the shallow water and went up the hill on the other side of the McGraw Livery. They climbed up the virgin slope of Desperation Mountain toward the O'Reily mine and house.

Lee opened the back door for her after waving at the shotgun guard. Colleen met them in the kitchen. She looked at the disheveled, buxom redhead, put on a polite smile and held out her hand.

"I don't think we've met. I'm Colleen O'Reily. You must be Debbie Sue. Welcome to my house. I'd guess Cleve Ralston wouldn't exactly put out the welcome mat for you at his house now." She shook the hand Debbie Sue held out.

"Pleased to meet you, Miss O'Reily. Lee said it would be all right if I came here."

"He's right . . . as usual." She turned and hugged Lee and kissed his lips lightly. "Now, as for you—well at least you didn't get shot again. I'm glad. What's the plan?"

"Debbie needs some traveling clothes, a bag of possibles and a ticket to Carson City. From there on she says she can manage quite nicely on her own."

Colleen nodded. She knew the moment she saw the big breasted, red-headed woman that Lee had just made love to her. Knew it and figured that was all right because he was still alive and the girl would be gone soon. Now she nodded as she looked frankly at the other woman.

"A carpet bag we can find, and some of the necessities. I'm afraid my clothes just wouldn't . . . I mean, I'm just not that big, anywhere!"

They all laughed.

"I do have a traveling cape that would work. It's always been too big for me, and a bonnet." She grinned. "Yes, and I have some things we can alter.

I'm a good hand with needle and thread."

"Enough of this girl talk," Lee said gruffly. "What about some food around here? We didn't have time to eat the picnic lunch Debbie Sue brought."

Colleen punched him in the shoulder. "We saved you some. My new cook is named Han, and he has some fried potatoes and onions with some red peppers mixed in along with some warmed up roast beef, gravy and fresh peas just in on a freight wagon."

As they ate, Colleen told Lee about her progress on the election committee.

"So far I have four men on the committeee. All we need are eight. Then we are going to get at least half a dozen men to run for the town council. If we do the vote to have a non-corporate town, we can elect town officials at the same time, if the town vote passes. That saves us another two weeks."

They talked votes and council and who to get for the Town Marshal for the rest of the afternoon and evening. Lee made his run around the Mine Association member guard posts, and found everything quiet. Nothing had been heard from the Silver Strike. Lee didn't expect any retaliation from them until the next day, when Lee planned on making a courtesy call on the ex-Southern general himself.

When he came back to the O'Reily house and checked the security, all was well. He went inside and found Colleen sitting with a cup of coffee in front of the living room fireplace. The fire was burning brightly. He hadn't seen a fire there before.

"Thinking?" he asked as he sat on the floor beside her chair.

"Uh huh. Debbie Sue went to bed. She was exhausted. I'm trying to figure out some way to lasso you and tie you to a chair and keep you here."

"Come up with any good ideas?"

"Not as good as Debbie Sue did when I brought up the idea."

"She said what?"

Colleen turned and grinned at him. It was her little girl, I'm gonna talk naughty grin. "She said I should fuck your brains out every night until you gave up and stayed."

Lee chuckled. "Worth a try."

"You're probably too tired out after your romp in the grass."

"Who told you that?"

"The grass stains on your pants legs helped. You didn't even take your pants off. Besides, I could just feel it, the way she looked at you. Woman stuff."

"Happens."

"We just going to sit here talking dirty all night or are you going to come to bed?"

"About time somebody asked me nicely."

"Nobody will even shoot at you if you come quietly."

"Good."

Colleen grinned. "First time, I don't even want you to take your pants off, just open your fly."

He did.

The stage was due out of the Wells Fargo office that morning at ten. A half hour before departure time, Lee bought a one way inside ticket to Carson City and had a long talk with the driver. The man who controlled the six horses, took Lee's five dollar gold piece and nodded.

Later that morning, Lee drove a closed black buggy out a half mile west of town and waited. The stage pulled up even with the buggy and then began to slow. A quarter-of-a-mile farther along it stopped and Lee pulled up beside it.

He handed Debbie Sue into the coach, told her

goodbye and closed the door. The stage raced away
from the spot and Lee watched it go, then turned his
buggy and drove back through Main and up to the
O'Reily Mine.

The house was busy. Six buggies sat in the front
yard and two in the rear. He went in the kitchen
door after waving at the shotgun guard out front.

Voices came from the parlor. Han waved at him
and hurried into the parlor with a large pot of coffee.

Lee edged up to the parlor and looked in. Nine
men sat around the room, all but one puffing on
cigars. Colleen stood in front of them and seemed to
be in charge.

"Then it's agreed, gentlemen, all of you have
voted to turn Silverton into a legal town in the
county, though unincorporated. I'd appreciate a
show of hands."

Nine hands went up.

"The next order of business is to elect, appoint or
suggest a chairman of the committee. I'd like to
nominate our Silverton banker, J. Ambrose
Buleton."

"I second," a voice said.

"Think we should close nominations," another
man said.

Everyone laughed.

"All in favor of closing nominations for chairman
of the Silverton Town Committee, say aye."

A chorus of aye's came.

"All opposed, same sign."

There was only silence.

"Done!" Colleen said with a small note of pride.
"I'd like to turn this gavel over to the new chairman
of our town committee, Mr. J. Ambrose Buleton."

Everyone cheered as Buleton took the gavel. He
was a slender man, with an open, hard working
face, an up by the bootstraps kind of guy.

"We can do it," he said softly. "Four mine owners and five merchants. All we have to do is get a copy of Yerrington's town charter and adapt it, have our election and get to work. I suggest we start right now. Who can go to Yerrington tomorrow to bring back a copy of that charter?"

Lee moved away from the door and went to his room. He'd have a nap, at least until Colleen came in all excited to tell him about what a good start they had made on the *town* of Silverton. He agreed. It was a first good step. But one large problem still remained.

That problem was his job. Tomorrow.

10

Lee Morgan woke up slowly, delightfully. Someone was kissing him. He kept his eyes closed, then grabbed the small woman as she lay on top of him.

"Gotcha!" he said.

Her eyes were wide, her pretty face smiling. "Yes, I know, but the question is, do I have you? Did I do what Debbie Sue said I should when I came in last night? Did I really fuck your brains out?"

"Yes, you did."

"And what am I going to do this morning?"

"Fuck my brains out?"

"Yes! And I won't let you get your pants on until you promise to stay in town and make an honest woman out of me and maybe at the same time be our Town Marshal."

"Let's try the first part first," he said.

"Can I be hopeful?"

"There's always hope."

She pushed up and dropped a breast into his

mouth and started telling him exactly what she was going to do for him and to his body to keep him in town.

It was almost an hour later before they went to the kitchen for breakfast. Han had everything ready, hash browns, eggs, coffee, flapjacks, and a plate full of crisp bacon and the never empty coffee pot.

"Damn sight better than trail food," Lee said taking his third helping of everything.

"This is all part of the exciting job offer you'll be getting later on," Colleen said.

"Board and room . . . and everything?"

She grinned. "Yes, everything. Salary, too. But the committee hasn't figured that out yet. I'm hoping that the 'everything' will help convince you."

"Best offer I've ever had, a real attractive package of employee benefits." He finished and pushed back from the table. "But I have one small item to take care of before I can even consider such an offer."

"What item?" she asked, her face showing worry.

"Not to be concerned. When I come back we'll talk some more about the package."

He bent and kissed her lips gently, then settled the Stetson on his head at precisely the right position and checked the Bisley.

"I'll be back," he said and went out the kitchen door.

He walked. It was a good morning for some brisk exercise. It got his system functioning, his mind alert. He'd need both in top form. A rim of clouds clung to the far mountains. There was a new, stronger nip of cold in the air this morning. Fall was coming. The high Sierra Nevada was no comfortable kind of place to winter over.

First the business at hand, then the decision. After all, a Town Marshal was little more than a gun for hire job. Wyatt Earp had done it, so had half the big name gunslingers of the past ten years. It was a possibility. Those damn side benefits were outstanding. But then he'd be a lawman—again. He wasn't sure he wanted the responsibility. He'd have to report to the town council. *Answer to them.* Lee shuddered and walked across the side of Desperation Mountain past the Deep Shaft and Mary Lou mines, straight for the Silver Strike.

He had figured there would be no guards out, and they wouldn't know who to stop anyway. He was right.

Five minutes later he turned the knob on the office door at the Silver Strike and stepped inside.

The pasty faced young man looked up from his books and stood, his face curious.

"Aren't you . . ."

"Ralston here?" Lee asked in his deadly flat voice. It was a tone that demanded an immediate answer.

"Yes sir."

"Good, sit down and shut up."

The sallow faced man dropped into his chair.

Lee loosened the Bisley in its leather home and strode toward Ralston's office door. He turned the knob and thrust the panel open hard. It swung in and banged against the wall.

Ralston sat at his big desk patting his eyes with a soft linen handkerchief. He dropped it, looked up and squinted for a moment, then stood slowly.

"Yes, Morgan, I more or less figured that you would come. So you beat all three of my gunsharps. I didn't think you were that good. Want to work for me now?"

"Ralston, shut up. You have two choices, you can get on the afternoon stage and run for your life, or you can sell out your holdings here at a fair price and move on quietly to another town and take out your misplaced and wrathful anger on the poor souls there."

Ralston slipped on his smoked glasses. "That's really not much of a choice, is it, Morgan? You do have a flair for the dramatic, even if you are a hard man to get rid of."

"Ralston, you're through in this town. Law and order is coming, not Ralston law, real law. You can't fight everyone in town. Offer to sell out to the Silverton Miners Protective Association. Your best move."

"Don't be stupid, Morgan. I have a man covering you right now through the left door with a shotgun. I lift my right hand over my head and you're a dead man."

"Good try, but it's a bluff. Anyway, look at the door. You're in the direct line of fire. I saw that when I came into the room. You've killed your last man in Silverton. With me it's personal. Your latest try to gun me down was pathetic. Your gunmen are not even good beginners. You must be scraping the bottom of the barrel around here."

"Morgan, we can strike a bargain. I'll pay you five hundred a month to work for me. That's six thousand dollars a year. That's more cash money than you've ever seen. It's twenty times as much as a miner in my tunnels makes!"

"What would my first assignment be, to gun down all of the men on the election committee?"

"What committee?"

"You're slipping, Corporal. But then any man who has to beat up a woman to get her is well over the hill. You're dead, you just haven't fallen over yet. You better sell out before you drop over dead there at your desk."

Ralston seemed to fade before Lee's eyes. Gone was his bravado, his anger, his fury. He reached one hand toward his eyes, then took off his smoked glasses.

"May . . . may I get a handkerchief to tend to my

eyes?''

Lee nodded.

Ralston moved his right hand slowly, opened a top drawer on his desk. When his hand came out it was quickly and it held a derringer. Lee's Bisley blasted a shot so fast, Ralston didn't have time to get his finger on the trigger. The .45 round slammed through Ralston's right wrist, spewing blood over his desk and jolting the deadly little pistol out of his hand.

Ralston screamed at Lee, then turned and ran out the back door of his office. Lee didn't shoot again. Where could the man run? Lee moved to the door, saw it opened to a hallway that led to the back of the building.

Ralston was just rushing out the door. Lee followed him. At the doorway he could see Ralston heading across the slope of the mountain looking back. He stopped a man and took a six-gun from him, then ran on toward what looked like a mine tunnel.

Lee rushed after him now, not wanting to lose him in the mine itself. Ralston looked behind at the advancing Morgan, and pulled open a wooden door and stepped into the mine tunnel.

When Lee got there he saw that the tunnel was abandoned. There had been no activity here for perhaps years. The wooden door had not been locked. Lee pushed it with his foot and jumped to one side. As the door swung open, a shot blasted from inside and the lead whistled through the void where the door had been.

Lee fired one shot into the tunnel, then ran through the opening and stepped to one side out of the light and crouched.

He was totally blind for a few moments. There was only the light coming in the open door. The

weak eyed Ralston must be totally blind. Lee
waited. He heard movement deeper into the tunnel.

As his eyes adapted, Lee checked the front of the
tunnel. He found what he wanted. In most mines
they keep torches in the front for emergency use. He
found three here, and all had been recently soaked
with coal oil. He took one, lit it with a stinker match
from his packet and held it well away from him.

Almost at once a shot boomed from the tunnel
ahead. The closed space made the shot sound twenty
times as loud, and the concussion brought dust and a
few small rocks down from the tunnel ceiling.

"Might as well come out, Ralston, you've got no
place to run. You don't know the tunnels. You'll get
lost in there within half an hour."

Lee had ducked low at the far side of the tunnel
when he shouted the words. Another shot slammed
through the tunnel quickly but missed. When the
sound faded out, Lee could hear swearing and
footsteps that grew fainter ahead.

He took the torch and moved down the narrow
tracks in the center of the tube. It was eight feet high
at this point, and he walked quickly.

The tunnel was a damp one, with drips hitting his
face and shoulders now and then. Lee held the torch
low by the tracks and he found footprints in the inch
deep dust on the floor. The tunnel had not been used
in a long time. He followed the footprints.

Twice they took turns into short drifts that had
been exploratory or had held ore that had been
worked out. There was little shoring of the ceiling,
and here and there a rock fall had piled dirt and
rocks three feet high in the tunnel. Lee worked over
them, found the footprints on the other side and
continued.

A shot suddenly ripped through the eerie silence
of the tunnel, and came close to Lee who had not

expected it. He dropped the torch and jumped away from it as dirt and rocks fell from the roof of the tunnel.

Another shot jolted through the cave, this one hit the torch and kicked it two feet to the rear. More rocks fell.

As the second shot came from ahead, Lee saw the muzzle blast and returned fire with two rounds of his own at the target. As the sound of the three shots slowly faded, he heard a bellow of pain ahead.

"Bastard! You'll be courtmartialed for that! Nobody shoots at his Commanding Officer. Sergeant, arrest that man!"

Gradually the sound of the rambling words faded, and Lee knew the man had moved deeper into the tunnel. Fifty feet ahead, Lee came to a shaft dug straight down in the side of the tunnel. It was deep. He dropped a rock in and it took several seconds before it hit bottom with a splash.

Rotted protective timbers around the shaft fell away as Lee pushed one. He checked the ground beyond the shaft and found Ralston's footprints. He must have stumbled by and missed the shaft by blind luck.

Lee saw something moving ahead. It slithered away from the light and then coiled. A rattlesnake. Lee passed it and continued forward. Ralston had fired five times. He might have one shot left. He had not taken the man's gunbelt or he would have 16 to 20 more rounds in the loops.

The roof of the tunnel dropped gradually, until Lee had to bend over to walk. Another fifty yards and the top of the tunnel was so low that the narrow ore car rail tracks stopped and Lee bent in half as he moved.

Ralston's tracks continued.

Fifty feet ahead the tunnel roof raised again, and a

side tunnel slanted off at right angles. The new one had tracks as well. Lee studied the footprints. They went down the new tracks for aways, then wandered and at last came back and continued forward.

Lee's torch was burning brightly. It should last for two hours. The footprints turned into a drift, and Lee followed them although he could see another set of prints coming out of the drift. At the back a large room opened where ore had been taken out.

In the dust he saw where Ralston had fallen. He crawled on his hands and knees for a while, then stood and walked out of the drift to the main tunnel and moved forward.

Ahead he heard a man crying.

Lee moved quicker now, hoping the trail was about ended. But he found no one. The footprints continued.

After what Lee figured was about fifty yards of careful walking ahead, he heard a scream. He ran forward, the torch out in front. The tunnel was eight feet high again, and here and there he saw signs that it had been used.

The scream he heard continued, then turned into a wail and a high keening that he had heard only once before when an old Indian woman lay dying.

The footprints continued ahead straight down the middle of the tunnel to a barrier around something. As he came up on it he saw it was another shaft sunk straight down in the middle of the tunnel. The rail tracks swung around it and continued. He could see where a barrier on this side had been broken and half of it carried away.

The wailing and screaming and sobbing came from the shaft. Lee edged up to it and peered over the edge. The torch light showed that the shaft had only been started. It was not more than ten feet deep, but the sides smooth and vertical.

The light shown to the bottom when he held the torch low and for a moment he wasn't sure what he saw.

Ralston lay on the bottom, sprawled over a mass of something. But it seemed to be moving. Then he saw the motion as the triangular head of a rattlesnake struck at Ralston's hand, hit it and pulled back.

Looking closer, Lee realized that the whole bottom of the pit was one rolling, squirming mass of a ball of rattlesnakes, coiled together for warmth.

Lee shivered watching them. Something slithered across his foot and he kicked at it, sending another rattler over the edge into the pit.

He watched Ralston. The man flailed at the snakes with his hands, used the revolver and kept pulling the trigger without firing any shots. Then he slashed at the striking snakes with the metal weapon.

His keening continued, a high, desperate, life-ending wail that chilled Lee to his bones. Now two of the rattlers struck Ralston's arm and hung there not able to release.

Masses of snakes began squirming and moving, not used to the sudden foreign thing that fell on them, and half blinded by the bright light.

One snake struck Ralston's cheek, and the Colonel bellowed out a scream of stark, unbelievable terror. Another sunk its fangs into Ralston's nose. Ralston's eyes cleared for a moment to see the deadly reptile, then his eyes rolled up and his arms fell to his sides on the snakes.

The keening stopped.

Cleve Ralston, late a General in the service of the Confederate States of America, had died of shock before the venom in his bloodstream could kill him.

Lee stared at the tableau for a moment, kicked at another snake coming across his foot and walked back the way he had come, following the footprints in the dust so he wouldn't lose his way.

When he came out of the tunnel, the sun hurt his eyes. He leaned against the closed door and waited for his eyes to adjust again. Then he put out the lighted torch he still held and walked back to the Silver Strike mine office.

The pasty faced young man rose when Lee came in the door. He looked as if he was ready to run.

"Do you have a mine superintendent here?" Lee asked softly.

The youth nodded.

"Go get him, at once!" Lee's tone carried a sharpness to it that sent the man rushing away.

Ten minutes later, the youth and an older man with a limp and one mangled hand returned. The elder man held out his good left hand.

"Charley Jones. I run this mine, the Colonel only owns it."

Lee liked the no-nonsense working man. He gripped the hand and motioned to the Colonel's office. Inside they both stood.

"Mr. Jones, your employer is dead. He ran into an abandoned tunnel after trying to shoot me. I chased him. He had no light and fell into a shaft where he was met by about a thousand rattlesnakes. It was too late by the time I found him."

"God! What a way to die!"

"That's true. But perhaps that made up in some small way for the terrible way he lived."

"Amen to that. I worked for the man, but I didn't agree with the way he ran the hole, or how he treated his people."

"That can change now. You're in charge until you can find any relatives or heirs he might have. Know of any?"

"He had a sister in Atlanta. I should be able to get

ahold of her.

"Damn, so the old bastard is dead. The workers will be notified at the end of the shift. Going to be a lot of cheering about this."

"Wouldn't argue with that."

The two men looked at each other, both liking what they saw. Lee broke the silence. "The Silver Strike seems to be in good hands. Oh, I'd suggest you join the Silverton Miners Protective Association, so everybody can take down their guards and get back to digging out silver."

"That I'll do. Is it that nice Miss O'Reily who runs it?"

"Yes. And there's an election committee formed to organize a town here and set up a Town Marshal. That will mean some real law and order for a change."

"Glory be! All of this at once may be more than Silverton can stand."

"I think it'll work out just fine. Oh, one thing. If the Colonel had any more gunsharps on his payroll, send them back to the tunnel face or move them down the trail. This town doesn't need their kind any more."

Charley grinned and looked at Lee.

"Including you, Mr. Morgan? I know about your Pa, met him once. I hear you're almost as fast as he was."

Lee laughed. "Almost is the key word there." He started for the door. "I better get back and see what else I have to do before I get all choked up here."

Both men laughed, and went into the main office. Lee left Charley to tell the clerk about his new boss and went out the door and headed back to the O'Reily Mine.

About four o'clock that afternoon, Lee talked with

the Election Committee and Colleen. While she wasn't an official member of the committee she was listed as "clerk," and kept minutes and had an unofficial vote and could speak her mind.

She had just recommended that when they get their town organized that they hire a Town Marshal and pay him a hundred dollars a month to maintain law and order. She strongly suggested that they ask Lee Morgan if he would take the job. They had asked him and he stood to reply.

"Gentlemen, I thank you for your offer. That's a handsome salary that most any lawman in the state would jump at. But I'm not the man for the job. It will give folks here and around the state the wrong idea about Silverton.

"Gunslinger, yes. I know what people call me. You don't need a fast gun in this town. You need a good, honest lawman who will keep a firm grip on the rowdies, urge out of town those who won't obey the laws, and generally take care of the law abiding citizens who want to live here and raise their families.

"I've done a little law work in other states and territories. I wasn't at all happy doing it. That's definitely not the way I want to spend the rest of my life, or even the next year or two.

"I'm a fiddlefoot, I like to keep moving. Although there are a lot of good reasons I could stay here, including all sorts of benefits. It just isn't right for me. Thank you."

He sat down and the men looked at each other. A tear rolled down Colleen's face.

Gus Jacobs from the Desperation Mine got the floor.

"Mr. Morgan, I for one, and I'm sure the other miners and store owners in town, appreciate what you have done for us. When you rode in, this town was getting ready to fly apart. Ralston would have taken over by force, and everyone figured it was coming.

"Now we've got a real chance at making something of our town, and working out our claims for whatever they are worth. I want to go on record as making a motion that the election committee vote one Lee Morgan, a profound debt of gratitude for his services to this community just before it became a real town."

There was a second and unanimous agreement.

Lee thanked them, winked at Colleen and left the meeting which was being held in the Silverton Bank.

Outside the sun was getting low. He stretched in the warming rays and then found a chair in the sun and leaned it up on the back two legs and rested against the wall of the Silverton Hardware Store.

The sun was warm, the work done, now all he had to do was figure out what he was going to do next.

Before he worked it out, the meeting was over in the bank and Colleen came out and tipped down his chair. He recovered just before he sprawled on the boardwalk.

"That, young lady, means you get a spanking," he said softly.

"That was one of the things I was hoping you would do to me," she said with a wicked little smile. She handed him an envelope. He looked inside and saw U.S. banknotes.

"What's this?"

She linked her arm in his and they began walking toward her house.

"That is your hundred dollars payment from the Mine Protective Association, and another payment of a month's wages from the Election Committee for services rendered."

"Oh."

They walked along aways and Lee touched his hat rim as two women went by.

"They probably think I'm a fallen woman, what with two men living in my house and all. But what do they know. Now, don't tell me you won't take the money. You earned it, more than earned it. Half the mine owners owe their lives and their claims to what you did these past few days."

Lee was deeply touched by what had just happened. It had been a long time since strangers had treated him like an honest, normal human being. It felt damn good!

For just a moment he considered staying in Silverton, taking the law job and hanging on to it for as long as he could stand it. But just as quickly he stomped down the idea. He'd hate it, and the people would soon dislike him and then ask for him to be kicked out, and that would not be good.

This way he could leave town with a good reputation behind him.

That left one small problem, the feisty, sexy little wench who now held his arm so tightly as they walked up the steps into her house.

"Hey, rich lady, you haven't said much just now about wanting me to stay. Any new ideas?"

"Yes, into my room."

Inside she giggled like a school girl as she put her arms around his neck and kissed him deliciously.

"My idea right now is to fuck your brains out again. And then again, and to wear you right down to a nub. That way no other woman will have you, and you'll have to stay here in Silverton with me."

Lee laughed. "Hell it's worth a try."

They tried that afternoon.

After supper, they tried again.

They had midnight sandwiches and coffee and

tried again until nearly morning when Lee at last fell asleep in her arms.

"I won," Colleen said, but she knew it was only their little 'who will go to sleep first' battle, and not the whole war.

In the morning he was gone when she woke up and she sat up in the bed with a small scream. He wouldn't ride away without saying one final goodbye, would he?

Her answer came through the door before she could get out of bed.

"Young lady, since you won the bet last night, here is breakfast in bed. No, no, you won fair and square. Now enjoy. You eat your breakfast, while I nibble on your ears and your bouncing, perky breasts and maybe, if you get damn lucky, even lower down."

"You are crazy, but I like you. We have to go on a horseback ride and have a long talk. Besides, I want to get you all sexy in the grass along the river."

"Sweet Colleen, it won't change my mind. Like I told the men yesterday, I'm a fiddlefoot. I'm a gun for hire. I can't stand the lawman way of life. Hell, I'm even on a wanted poster or two. How would it look if some bounty hunter came riding into Silverton, arrested the Town Marshal and hauled me back to Idaho or California or somewhere?"

"It would make a nice item in the newspaper." She made a face at him. "Oh, late yesterday we hit a new vein in the mine. It's the one we lost a year ago. It's still on our claim, it's turning back into our land, and it's twice as good as anything we've hit so far. You stay here, I could make you a rich husband."

He kissed her around a piece of bacon she nibbled on and shook his head.

"Look, I know I can't explain it to you. Hell, I've never been able to explain it to myself. Sleeping in a

nice warm, soft bed all the time makes me jumpy.
Just being nice to people all the time can get me so
nervous and angry sometimes that I don't know
what I'm going to do.

"You know in the past I haven't always been on
the right side of the law. It's hard when somebody
wants to hire your gun and he turns out to be not the
greatest citizen the town has ever seen. Like Ralston.

"Hell, I try. Right now I still want to get back to
my Spade Bit ranch someday. Maybe raise horses
again, who knows? First, I better check in at Denver
and see if a contact I have there has had any mail
waiting for me. Could be a job. Somebody out there
somewhere must need a gun for hire."

"Oh, damn!" Colleen said. Then she kissed him.

CALIFORNIA CROSSFIRE
BUCKSKIN

Special acknowledgement to Madelyn Tabler and Mae Miner without whose help this book would never have been written.

1

Screams ripped the summer air and drowned
out even the sound of the big Concord team's
two dozen hooves hitting the packed dirt of the
street. The screams reverberated over the
stage's wheels, grinding to a stop.

Lee Morgan stepped from the coach and lifted
his gear down from overhead, a tattered carpet
bag and his black snake whip.

A man's voice commanded, "Come 'ere, bitch!
You ain't goin' nowhere."

Another scream split the air.

What the hell's going on in this place?
Morgan wondered.

He had no chance to glance around the dusty
little town of Lost Canyon before he heard the
woman cry out again.

She screamed over and over, long frightened
wails, then screeched in desperation. "Help!
Someone help me." Another scream, then, "Let
me go! Won't anybody help me?"

Morgan spun toward the sound and saw the
slender creature in the grasp of a great hulk of a
man. Stringy dark hair hung long and lank from
under his dirty hat. His arms bulged like hams
out of his rolled-up sleeves. His massive hands
held the woman by her upper arms and shook
her.

5

Morgan couldn't hear at that distance what the man said to her. It was hard to figure what he was trying to make her do, or perhaps tell her, there in the center of town.

Not many people were around, but the place was by no means deserted while this scene played out. A woman in a bonnet carrying a basket on her arm turned to look. Some men lounged against the front wall of the hardware store. No one moved to help the woman. Morgan wondered where the sheriff was. No one lifted a hand.

The woman was young, beautiful, Morgan could see from where he stood. Her auburn hair was pulled together into a cluster of ringlets at the nape of her neck. Wisps of curls escaped around her face. She wore a long blue print dress with lace at the sleeves and hem. It was tucked in at her tiny waist.

Morgan dropped his gear at the edge of the boardwalk and uncoiled the black snake whip, his right hand behind him. The tied-down Bisley Colts on his hips would be of no use to him right now; he couldn't take a chance on hitting the woman struggling in the brute's grasp.

Trailing the black snake whip, he took a step or two in the direction of the big man and his captive.

When the woman stopped screaming long enough to take a breath, Morgan called out, "That your husband, Missus?"

"No!" She sounded a cry of revulsion at such a thought. "No. No!"

Morgan took a couple more steps toward the two and warned, in a deadly level voice, "Let the lady go, Mister. Now!"

The victim's dark eyes were wide with terror

and pleading as she turned her face toward Morgan. His heartbeat accelerated just looking at her. It would sure as hell take a whole posse of men, even bigger than that one, to keep Morgan from helping this enchanting female.

"Mind your own fuckin' business." The man released one hand from the terror stricken woman and threatened to draw. "Ease off, stranger, and stay alive."

Morgan heard squeals of fright from some other women, apparently seeing the threat of gunplay as they boarded the stage behind him.

He took one more step toward the man whose hand darted for leather and drew a forty-four out of its holster.

With an arcing movement of his right arm, back and up, which bystanders might have been led to believe was raising in an attitude of surrender, Morgan brought the black snake whip into action.

He heard the stage start off. He heard the crack of the black snake, and the report as the other man's forty-four discharged.

"Ahhhh!" It was like a cheer from several people on the boardwalk lining the street.

By the time the weapon fired, it was pointing toward the ground with the whip tearing a bloody trail across the back of his gun hand. The gun dropped to the street. He howled with pain, let go of the woman, and grabbed his injured hand.

With a flick of his wrist, Morgan recoiled the whip. "Now what the hell were you saying, tough guy?"

"I'll get you, you son of a bitch." The man's face contorted in fury. "You haven't heard the last of Brant Corson."

Morgan went closer. "That may be, but this lady better have heard the last of you."

Brant Corson started for the gun lying in the dirt. Morgan moved into his path and bumped the larger man with his shoulder. Corson swung a left. Morgan ducked, nudging the forty-four aside with the toe of his boot, and in turning gave Corson a left jab which bloodied his nose.

The big man snorted like a maddened bull and rushed at Morgan with both fists clasped and raised to hammer him into the ground. Morgan side-stepped, but not quite far enough. He took a glancing blow to his left shoulder.

In too close to use the black snake, Morgan dropped it and pounded his right fist into his enemy's mid-section. Corson grunted but his knuckles clipped Morgan below the eye. Morgan could feel the warm fluid start down his face and knew his adversary had drawn blood.

Regaining his balance in time, Morgan came back with a left uppercut to the giant's jutting jaw.

It stopped Corson long enough so that Morgan could kick the man's forty-four farther into the street.

Corson got his breath and came at Morgan again. The great bulk of the gargantuan figure could have crushed anyone he landed on, but Morgan, tall, lean and agile, was too fast for the heavier man. As Corson lunged, Morgan feinted and slid to one side, leaving only a booted foot in the man's way to trip him. Corson sprawled heavily in the dust cursing loudly.

Glancing around, Morgan found that the woman had completely disappeared. A pang of disappointment flicked through him. He wanted to see her, to know who she was, to make sure she was all right. He wanted to touch her, to know she was real. But she was gone, fleeing from the man she feared.

Since the lady was no longer in danger, Morgan swung around and retrieved his Stetson which had fallen to the ground. He slapped it against his leg to clear off the dust. Picking up his whip, he recoiled it, then gathered his carpetbag from where he'd dropped it and headed up the boardwalk toward a sign that said: Doubloon Saloon. Morgan glanced back once to make sure Corson, retrieving his firearm, was heading the other way.

Been in town about ten minutes and already made an enemy, Morgan thought.

He would not have been in this town at all, if he hadn't owed Hank Broom a big one. He had known Hank for years and they met now and again. Hank had a hair-trigger temper, which had given the two of them trouble more than once.

But Hank had also saved Lee Morgan's life, and it only took one of those to make Morgan obligated. So he was here in answer to his old friend's telegram. Besides, the way the wire read, it might be worth something, and if it turned out that way, he could use the money.

He took another look up and down the broad dusty street along which stood a couple of other saloons, a general store—General Emporium, the sign read—a hotel, and far down the other side a livery stable. He would check out the rest of the place when he found out why he was here.

He pushed through the swinging doors and walked into the Doubloon Saloon.

Morgan stood for a moment adjusting his
eyes to the dimmer interior, then checked out
the saloon's other customers. Not many were
there in mid-afternoon on a weekday; a couple
of men leaning on the bar about three-quarters
of the way down, and three others arguing at a
table at the far end of the room.

Hank Broom, the man Morgan had come to
meet, stood talking to the rotund barkeep at the
near end. Broom looked up as Morgan came in.
" 'Bout time," he said.

Broom was half a head shorter than Morgan.
His weatherbeaten face, below a bush of salt
and pepper hair, wore a frown.

Morgan put down his gear and stuck out a
hand. "Good to see you, Hank. What's it all
about?"

"Draw him a beer," Hank told the barman. To
Morgan he said in a lowered voice, "You didn't
come here to rescue damsels in distress,
Morgan. You were supposed to keep low."

"Hells bells, Broom, keep low? This town's so
small people'd notice an extra flea on the local
dog."

"Yeah, well . . . try not to put on any more
theatrics."

The barman slid the beer across to Morgan
and went on down the bar to wait on his other
customers.

Broom and Morgan took their mugs over to
one of the tables. Morgan dragged his gear
along and dropped it on the floor beside his
chair. The lead weighted grip on the two-foot
long handle of the black snake hit the floor with
a loud clunk. Morgan stuck out his foot and
drew it in closer to him. The whip had saved his
neck more than once both by lash and by using

the handle as a cosh.

When the two men were settled at their table and had taken a couple of swallows of their beer, Morgan asked, "Now what's the big hush-hush proposition that got me to Lost Canyon?"

"We won't discuss it here," Broom told him. "Soon's we wet our whistle, we'll go down to the hotel and get you into a room. Then we can talk."

"Fine," Morgan said. "I hope it's worthwhile. I made the trip all the way from Denver to this place on California border. Lost Canyon, never even heard of the place. What there is of it."

Broom said. "It's okay in the summer. Don't want to stay around when winter comes, myself. I know this town from way back. In spring that dusty street out there is a river of mud from snow melting down from the mountains. Pretty hot in summer, but this is better than later, when you're either ass deep in the snow or can't get a grip on the ground for the ice."

"Never cared a hell of a lot for snow and ice, myself," Morgan agreed. "We gonna finish our business before summer is over? Only one person I might be interested in around here."

Broom snorted. "Never mind the women. But some interesting people go through here. And some of 'em never leave."

"Don't know as I want to be one of those, if you mean what it sounds like."

They finished their beer. Broom waved to the barman. "We'll be in again, Moe."

Morgan picked up his gear again and they strode down the street. A faint breeze rustled the big trees behind the buildings on the opposite side of the street. A boy and a dog tore past them and the boy suddenly came to a stop. He turned and stared at Morgan, his gaze transferring from Lee's face to his black snake whip. The youngster looked as if he wanted to say something, but changed his mind and ran on.

They reached the hotel, a recently painted white two-story building, which had a long veranda running the length of the front. The men went up the steps and across the porch making loud hollow sounds with their boots.

Hank Broom introduced Morgan to Jeb Rowe, and Morgan signed the register and paid for a room.

"I'm the owner along with my wife, Essie, here," the hotel man said, turning the book around to see Morgan's name.

"How long will you be with us?" the owner's wife inquired.

"Can't be sure, ma'am," Morgan told her and picked up his gear.

"Same thing your friend here said, a few days ago." She smiled. "If your room isn't all right, just tell us."

"Oughta be all right," he said. "Lucky number. Twenty-one. What are chances of gettin' a bath in this town?"

Essie nodded. "Just give us a little warning and we'll have Nelly fill the tub at the end of the hall on your floor. Twenty-five cents extra and the towel and soap are furnished."

"Thank you, ma'am. Hour or so from now'd do fine." He glanced at Broom to verify his time schedule. The shorter man shrugged.

Broom and Morgan went up the wide staircase to the second floor. "Where you located?" Morgan asked.

"Downstairs. Room six," Broom told him. As they stepped into Morgan's room and shut the door, he added. "Now we can have a talk. You ever hear of Hex Downs?"

"Downs? Don't think I ever knew anybody by that name personal, but seems to me I might've heard it sometime or other."

Broom glanced around the room. "You got the best room. Look at the size of it, and this one even has a fireplace."

"Well, since I don't plan to stay and wait for winter, I guess it don't matter if it has a fireplace or not." He took off his tan low-crowned hat, dusted the black band with the red diamonds against his forearm, and laid it on the bed. Then he methodically put his change of clothes into a bureau drawer, laid a couple of brushes on the dresser top, and washed his face in the basin with water from a large crockery pitcher.

"Hex was a train robber," Hank Broom said. "He was the one, in fact, who took care of stashing the loot. There were just two of them. One got shot dead during the robbery, and Downs took off to hide what part of the gold he managed to keep a hold on."

"Gold?" Morgan repeated.

"That's right. He likely got away with at least four ten-pound bars, a couple of 'em in each saddlebag."

Morgan whistled. "Just one of those would damn near pay a ranch hand's wages for ten years. Where is this fortune in gold bars?"

"The last place Downs was seen was here in Lost Canyon. In fact, he died in a gunfight right out there where you were putting on your little show earlier today."

"You think you know where the gold is stashed. And you think we're going to find it."

"Have an idea how to find out where it could be," Broom said. "Want your gun help."

Morgan went over to the lace-covered window and brushed the curtain aside. The Sierra Nevadas rose majestically in the far distance. The lower slopes, covered with Ponderosa pines, glinted green in the late afternoon sun.

He gazed down at the street where he had scuffled with Brant Corson. He rubbed his left shoulder. He could still feel where the massive fists had hammered him. If the blow had landed on his head, as intended, it could have broken his neck.

He could almost see the woman with her auburn hair, curly wisps blowing around her face. He tried to imagine how her face would look in serenity, or in passion, instead of terror. He could visualize her long blue print dress swirling around her ankles when Corson let her go to draw his forty-four.

Morgan could feel a hunger in his lower belly and between his thighs. He wished he could see that auburn haired woman coming up the street looking for him. But she was not out there. Maybe he would be able to find her before he was finished in Lost Canyon.

"So that's it," Broom said.

"Huh? Oh, sorry," Morgan mumbled.

"Thinking about that woman again?"

"What do we do to get this gold?"

Broom sighed. "Damn, I should have known better than to ask *you* to come to a town where there'd be any type of female. I should have told you to meet me at some large boulder out there at the bottom of the foothills."

"All right, tell me. I'm listening. What's the story?" Morgan let the curtain swing back over the window. He sat on the edge of the bed and faced Broom who had begun to pace the room. "Shoot."

"There's somebody else in town looking for the same gold we're after. That's one reason I wanted you along, in case there's trouble." He stopped pacing and sat in a chair beside the bed.

Broom took out his fixings and rolled a cigarette. When he had it lighted, he went on. "Hex Downs visited an old man who lives in a beat-up shack about eight or ten miles out of town. First thing tomorrow morning, we get a couple of horses. There's a livery right down the street. We go to see this old gent and find out what he knows."

"What are we going to do with this gold when we get it?" Morgan wanted to know. "Who did it belong to before Downs and his outfit came by it?"

"The U.S. Government. There's a reward . . . if we decide to tell 'em we've found it."

Morgan thought about that for a while. This would have suited his daddy to a tee, he thought. Sometimes his natural father, William Buckskin Leslie, fought on the side of the law and sometimes otherwise, but he always fought well and he usually fought fair. As long as he got his pay, he enjoyed it.

Frank Leslie's reputation was well known throughout the west. His fame fanned out from an Idaho ranch he'd finally settled down on about a half day's ride out of Boise. That was before he and Harve Logan had managed to kill each other with one simultaneous shot apiece.

Yes, Frank Leslie would have liked hunting for stashed gold. He'd have said something like, *Probably hell of a lot easier than panning for it.*

"Probably a hell of a lot easier than panning for it," Morgan said aloud. "You think this old gent we're going to see will be able to tell us something? If he knows, why doesn't he get it himself?"

"Can't say," Broom told him. "Maybe we'll find out in the morning. You gonna get something to eat before you turn in?"

"Soon's I find that bathtub," Morgan agreed.

He found the dressing room at the end of the hall. A buxom young woman, who told him her name was Nelly, poured two pails of steaming water into a tub in the middle of the room. A chair and two pegs on the wall served to hold the bather's clothes.

Morgan put his clean shirt and a change of socks and summer underpants over the back of the chair, hung his gun belt on it, and moved it closer to the bathtub. Then he sat down to take off his boots.

Nelly came in with another pail of hot water and a pail of cold water, and poured both into the tub. "That ought to be about right, Mr. Morgan. Usually is."

Morgan took off his shirt. "You plan to stay and scrub my back for me, Nelly?"

"That doesn't come with the price of the bath, Mr. Morgan." Nelly's cheeks were already rosy and when she blushed they got redder. But her eyes sparkled above her flirty smile as she left the room and shut the door behind her.

When he was clean and dressed, Morgan met Broom for their evening meal. The only cafe in town was apparently the best. Most of the tables were filled and only a few places were open at the counter. They took a couple of those and Broom recommended the stew. It was served with great chunks of hot sour dough bread and coffee.

"Coffee is great," Morgan told the counter maid.

"Have our own well. Deepest well in town and the best water in the west."

Later, after he and Hank Broom had finished eating and had ogled the counter maid some more, they stopped at one of the three saloons to toss down a brandy to cap off the day. They both managed to stay out of the brawls that broke out and back at the hotel, Lee Morgan made his way back to room twenty-one.

He brushed his low-crowned Stetson and laid it on the bureau, took off his gun belt and hung it on the straight chair within easy reach.

He was just about ready to strip down and get into bed when he heard a soft tapping at the door. "Yeah?" He drew the bolt and opened the door.

Before him stood the auburn haired woman.

This time she wore a soft gray dress, the bodice of it laced up and cupping her small breasts so that enticing white mounds showed above it. In her hand she carried a small carved leather grip, a one-of-a-kind satchel that had the look of something valuable. The bag was about a foot-long and eight-inches wide with two buckled straps around it.

Her dark eyes gazed up at Lee Morgan and she smiled tentatively. "May I come in?"

Morgan stepped back. He could scarcely trust himself to speak. She was even lovelier than he had thought.

"Yes," he finally managed. "That is, uh, certainly. Come in."

She brought an intoxicating scent in with her. Morgan closed the door and shoved the bolt quietly into place.

2

She moved like a cloud. Stepping into the room past him, she looked around her. "They seem to keep a nice hotel. It's a pleasant room."

Morgan nodded. He seldom encountered a woman, a lady, his mind amended, who left him feeling so like a schoolboy in short pants, so tongue-tied.

"I wanted to thank you in person," she said, turning to face him.

"You're welcome." He sounded like a school boy, to himself at any rate.

"You risked your life," she went on. "That man is a bully and a cold blooded killer."

"That's about the way I had him pegged," Morgan agreed. He didn't know whether to ask her to sit down or not. He liked the way she looked just standing there.

"I located you through Essie Rowe, down-stairs." Her smile made the sunset seem insignificant. "I have found that Essie has a habit of knowing most everything. She saw the whole thing, the way you rescued me and all."

The gray dress she wore was soft, velvety, with a fitted top laced at the waist with silver cord. When she took a deep breath, the shape of her breasts rose. Morgan quickly stopped staring at the lovely petal soft glow of her bosom and looked instead at her dark eyes with their long curving lashes.

"Essie says your name is Morgan."

"Lee Morgan, at your service, madam." Saying his name began to make him feel more like himself. "And yours?"

"Celia Fair."

"Your name suits you." He hadn't meant to say it aloud. How fair she was, with her pale clear skin and auburn hair.

"*Miss* Celia Fair," she said.

Morgan was glad to hear that. He had not been above helping himself to some other man's woman in times past, always providing the woman was willing. But this one! He was somehow glad to hear it was Miss.

"But thanking you isn't all I came here for." Her eyes shot arrows into Morgan's heart and other vital places. "I came to ask another favor."

"Ask, by all means. Do you want to sit?" He removed his gunbelt from the chair and hung it on the bedpost.

"No. Thank you." Celia Fair shook her auburn curls. "I wanted to ask you to keep this for me." She held out the leather bag.

Morgan noticed again the carving in the leather, hand-tooling that could only have been done with loving care by an expert. "Did someone you know do that leather work?" he asked.

"My brother. A long time ago." There was a tone to the answer that said 'don't ask anything more about it.' She went on to explain the favor. "It would be only for a few days. If you could hold onto the bag, keep it safe for me, until the next stage comes through."

He accepted the bag. It was heavy. He thought he should not have left her standing there holding such a heavy burden.

"The next stage? You're not going away?"

She smiled up at him, warming him all over. "Not right now."

Morgan set the bag on the chair. "I'll find a safe place for it. It must be important to you."

"It is." She did not tell him what it contained.

He glanced around the room thinking where it might be best concealed, while he was out gold hunting with Broom. He would keep it safe for Celia Fair. He walked to the fireplace wall and started checking bricks. Around the corner beneath the mantel, he found a slightly loose one.

After working at it for a few moments with a knife he took from his right boot, he removed the brick and the one below it. There was a hollow space behind them. He took out four more bricks to make enough room for the bag to slip in. The bag fit as if the space was made for it. He pushed it back hard, and replaced the bricks so they looked as if they had not been moved.

Celia Fair stood close by watching every move. Morgan swept up the mortar dust he had dislodged and pinching bits of it up between his fingers, spit on it and then worked it around the brick.

He returned to the fireplace and picked up the hearth rug. He drew it across the spot on the floor until all trace of the dust was hidden away under the rug.

"Aren't you clever!" Celia exclaimed. She stepped to the corner of the fireplace and looked at the place where Morgan had replaced the brick. She dusted a tiny spot with her finger. "If no one actually put hands on it, they would never know."

His job done, Lee returned his attention to Celia.

She stood there before him, looking up at him, charging the room with her beauty and her scent. They stood close together, only inches separating them.

She raised her hand and touched his cheek. "You were hurt in the fight."

"Not much. Just a scratch." The cheek was warmer where her fingers made contact. He could imagine the split skin healing at her touch.

They gazed into each other's eyes. He took one of her hands in both of his. "You are lovely. I feel as if I had known you always."

Her answer surprised him, thrilled him. "I have known you always, too." She hesitated only a moment, then said, "And I want you, Lee Morgan."

He took her face in both his hands and kissed her ever so gently. She responded and the kiss became demanding. His arms encircled her and hers reached up to him.

In moments his lips went from her lips to her eyelids, to her ear lobes, to her slim elegant neck. Her breath came more quickly, she arched her body to his, and he kissed the mounts of the white breasts above her velvet bodice.

She drew away from him and he experienced a momentary panic, thinking she was going to leave. Instead she led him to the bed, pushed him gently into a sitting position and knelt before him.

"You saved me from that beast, the least I can do is make you more comfortable." She reached behind the heel of one of his boots and using her other hand on top of his foot, pulled the boots off, first one then the other. She peeled off his socks.

Thank God for the bath and the clean clothes, Lee thought.

When she had freed his feet, she stroked them with her dainty hands, sending lightning bolts clear up to his throat.

In a moment, she rose, sat beside him and took off her own black shoes. Reaching underneath her skirt, she unfastened things and slipped off one silk stocking. She must be a city lady. He wondered how long she had been in this town and how she got mixed up with Brant Corson. But she was here now.

Celia removed the other silk stocking and dropped it on the floor beside the first.

Morgan's heart pounded so loud he thought she would hear.

In a moment she stood again and faced him. He regained his feet and again put his lips down to hers. Her arms went up around his neck and their kiss clung from sweet, through insistent, to passionate. Again he tasted her ear lobes and kissed his way down her neck and found the crevice between her breasts. Her scent was light yet overpowering.

Finding the ends of the silver lacing, Lee pulled and loosened the velvet bodice that kept him from those tempting globes. As the nipples came into his view, they sprang to attention, the tips hardening before his lips reached them.

Celia's fingers combed through the hair at the back of his head, and drew him closer, then traced around his ears down his neck to unbutton his shirt. He let go of her long enough to snatch his shirt off and in moments they both were naked and again reaching out, each pulling the other close.

Morgan held the whole silkiness of her against himself, feeling every smooth soft inch of her on his body, once again kissing her lips. He felt the rapid beat of her heart against his chest, the rise of her breasts with their hard nipples. He kissed them again and tasted them with his tongue and lips, making gentle sucking motions.

He ran his hands over her smooth back, past her slim waist, and over the slight flare of her hips, feeling her shudder with pleasure at his touch.

Grasping her firm round buttocks, he pulled her tightly against him as he felt the rising pressure in his groin. He kissed his way down to her navel and circled it with his tongue, feeling goose bumps rise on her legs as he bent and let his hands traverse the rest of the way clear to her ankles.

He rose again and sought her lips. Celia's hands felt both soothing and exciting as they traced his contours, down his back—slowly, teasingly, caressingly—then circling his buttocks and up his sides and to his chest. His nipples contracted at her touch, as hers had to his.

Lee went down to one knee on the carpet and when his kisses reached the red-gold furry mound hiding the love place he sought, Celia's legs trembled. In a moment he stood and in the same motion lifted her in his arms and deposited her on the bed. He took a moment to gaze at the loveliness of the feast before him. Her eyes sparkled with eagerness.

He began at her breasts again and his kissing, gentle biting, and sucking made her squirm with pleasure and raise her lower body to invite him. His own organ urged him too, but he took his time.

Making his way again to the love nest, he parted its outer lips and let his tongue make dartings and sippings, over and over again. She was becoming damp with readiness, but he had flavors to taste before the main course.

He licked and tickled and sipped until she thrust herself harder into his face. He leaned in to her and thrust his tongue as far inside her as it would go, savoring the essence of her.

She yearned for more, for the real thing, and her fingers found his jewels and gently touched and fondled, then encircled his rod and coaxed it into even more hardness and length, until he understood her desire was as great as his own.

He was going to give her what she wanted, push it into her, because he was becoming eager too. But as he straightened above her, she deftly turned her body head to foot, so that while he could continue his tasting, she put her lips to his groin, kissing all around the base of his organ, fondling his balls with one hand, stroking and kissing up and down the length of his turgid penis with her tongue and lips.

Her tongue drew a path up the back of his rod, the most sensitive side. When she reached the tip, the end of her tongue circled it. Her touch was light at first, then became more firm and urgent.

Again Lee sent his tongue into her love hole. She shuddered and momentarily seemed to forget what she was about. She moaned as her opening made an involuntary grab at his tongue. Then she put her mouth over the end of him and nibbled with her lips, like a mare taking a sugar cube from a man's hand. The exquisite torment of holding back was almost too much for Lee, but before he could make a move, she twisted around again.

She pushed gently so that he lay on his back. She mounted him, holding his organ in her delicate hand as she lowered herself onto it, sighing with pleasure as she sat all the way down on him.

Then she rode.

She rode him like a delighted child galloping across a pasture. He put his hands up to clasp her bouncing breasts. He pressed his buttocks upward until her knees no longer touched the bed as she rode. She balanced herself with her hands on his chest and clamped her knees to his sides.

Her tempo fit his and he urged her to continue with his hands at her buttocks.

She romped merrily, smiling, throwing her head back and giving little laughs and joyful cries.

Then suddenly the world exploded in ecstasy. His whole being seemed to burst out into her. He thought he would never finish before he died of the exquisite release. Celia cried out with joy.

They pushed together hard, desperate to hold the moment, until finally she collapsed forward onto him. He put his arms around her to hold her close on top of him feeling a glorious pulsing, hearts pounding, and the sighing breaths of fulfillment.

After a while, they rolled over, nestled their bodies close together and sighed audibly again. They kissed softly and fell asleep.

When Morgan came awake in the morning, light pushed through the lace curtains showing through his eyelids into his soul. When had he slept so? Deep delicious rest.

He stretched, remembered, and reached out feeling for her across the bed.

Celia Fair was gone.

He lay there for a long moment wishing and wondering. But he knew women were like that. Here one moment in all their glory, and then gone. He had thought from time to time of settling down. Once in a while a woman came along that made settling down seem desirable. Celia Fair could have turned out to be one of those.

Morgan shook himself out of his reverie. The fair Celia was not here now. He had other things to do.

Morgan had to meet Broom to go out and see what the old man could tell them about the gold. He dressed, strapped on and tied down his Bisley Colts, and left the hotel.

The sun oozed over the eastern horizon making a long shadow of Lee Morgan's tall frame as he covered the fifty yards of the dusty main street of Lost Canyon. He mounted the three steps to the sand-whipped front door of the General Emporium.

Denims, stacked on a log table, filled one corner of the store, and sheepskin jackets for sale hung on nails pounded into the wall. Dried beans in an open sack leaned against the tin covered counter where an aproned clerk weighed sugar on a scoop scale.

Morgan needed a rifle. He ran his fingers along the barrel of a .52 caliber Spencer, checked the sighting twice and nodded. He laid three tubes of ammunition beside it and paid. A pretty girl entered the store. Morgan smiled and tipped his tan Stetson.

Morgan picked up his purchases and was ready to leave as Hank Broom stepped briskly into the Emporium. "Thought I'd find you here."

For most of his forty years, Broom had lived by his gun, and sent a few men, good and bad to their maker. He was still quick as a fox. Sometimes too quick for his own good, Morgan thought.

The two stopped at the cafe for coffee, eggs, steak and hash browns. They said little as they ate, intent only on getting set for their morning errand. As they got up from the table, Morgan slipped a couple lumps of sugar into his pocket.

"I've got it," Broom said and paid for the meal.

It was Broom's show, so Morgan didn't argue.

Outside, an eddy of dust swirled and Broom pulled his hat forward to shield his face. They turned toward the livery. "There's a fair looking bay for sale, stabled beside my mount, a gelding. Young, strong, don't know the price. Stable hand says a fellow sold it for a stake in a poker game. He lost."

"I'll take a look."

The gelding suited Morgan. He added a saddle and dickered the stable owner down to a suitable price. After paying the man, Morgan saddled his new horse and looped his black snake whip over the saddle horn, then stepped to the horse's head. He stroked the bay's muzzle. "We'll get along fine. Won't we, fella?" The horse poked his nose forward. Morgan reached into his pocket and brought out the sugar cubes. The bay accepted one, then the other. Morgan patted the horse's neck and mounted up.

He and Broom headed out of town.

"This old timer you think might know something about where the gold is hidden, he got a name?"

"Ole, but everybody calls him Gramps. For some reason, Hex Downs, the one who hid the gold bars, got friendly with Gramps. I was in town the day Hex arrived. Close mouthed. Wouldn't even give his name at first, then finally said he was Hex Downs."

Broom paused to motion a slight change in direction. "I had just come in from Sacramento. The papers up there were full of the train robbery. No names were mentioned, just that one got away. The story said which way they thought he headed." Broom grinned. "Not many newspapers come to Lost Canyon. Don't suppose most of the people can read anyhow."

Morgan gazed ahead at the cool green trees on the side of the mountain a few miles ahead. "How did you find the cabin?"

"Followed Downs up there. After Hex died in the gunfight, I went up and talked to the old fellow. He's smart and wary of strangers. I doubt anybody puts much over on him. He's a good man, and fair. I didn't get it out of him, but I think Downs told him where he hid the gold."

Broom took a long drink of water from his canteen and offered it to Morgan. The morning had begun to heat up.

An hour later the trail led the two men into the trees. Live oak leaves rustled in the breeze and covered much of the ground. Suddenly the trail all but disappeared. Now it skirted the oak, then turned north back into the high desert.

When they reached the pines, only hoof tracks showed them the way. "Gramps have horses?" Morgan asked.

Broom squinted at the tracks. "The Indians do a little hunting up here, jackrabbits that wander up from the desert, now and then wild turkey. The old Chief is peacable enough, tolerates the white man. But he's got a son who hates us. Wants the Washos to be fighting warriors, as they have in the past."

This was new country to Morgan, and he listened for foreign sounds. Nothing stirred that he could detect.

They were most of a mile into the timber when an arrow skimmed Broom's shoulder and lodged in a Ponderosa Pine. Birds flew up in a flurry of movement. Both men hit the ground at the same time.

Quiet. Deep dead quiet.

"Damn," Morgan muttered. "You can't hear them and you can't see them."

Crouched low, they led their horses into the trees and took shelter behind two downed trees. Both leveled their rifles in the direction the arrow had come from and waited.

Morgan knew they were being surrounded. He could feel it by the cold chill that crossed his neck. He rolled toward Broom. "See anything?"

Broom pointed first in one direction, then in another. "Could be half a dozen of them, probably after our guns and horses."

"Washos?"

Broom nodded.

A dry leaf crunched. Morgan fired. Two arrows skimmed the top of the log where Morgan crouched. He went lower just in time.

"Cover me." Morgan plunged into a stand of pine a few yards away skidding on his stomach the last few feet. Two more arrows twanged into the ground where he'd first hit the dirt.

He crouched, eyes boring through the trees. A gust of wind rippled through, making false sounds. He held his fire. He could hear Broom's rifle shots zinging over his head.

A horse whinnied. Morgan turned. Broom's .45 pistol exploded. An Indian yelled, then dropped a few feet from the horses. Three arrows returned fire. One pinned Broom's shirt sleeve to one of the downed logs. His shirt ripped when he jerked loose. Blood showed on his shirt; he was hit.

Morgan made a slow careful circle attempting to get behind the Indians. There had to be at least three left. How many more? Thick brush blocked his view. Slowly he got to his feet behind a tall pine.

He scanned the thick stand of trees. He listened for some telltale sound. The bastards could be anywhere, and Broom couldn't make a dash for the protection of the thicker stand of trees without cover.

Morgan backed stealthily toward another tree. He sensed a presence. He whipped his Bisley from his holster and turned just as a brown arm reached for his neck. He could smell the Indian's sweat. A knife, aimed at his chest, glistened in a shaft of sunlight.

Morgan fired. The Indian dropped without a sound, a hole where his nose had been. The knife slipped from his fingers. Morgan kicked it away.

Morgan picked up his hat and set it back on his head. For the next half hour he crept through the trees. Because of the arrows shot at Broom, there had to be at least two more. He thought about returning to where Broom still lay between the two downed trees, but until he got those last two bastards they couldn't go on to the cabin anyhow.

A bird sound close by warned him, because it wasn't a bird call, it was a signal. Morgan pushed his rear into some thick brush and backed in until he was out of sight, but he wasn't fast enough. An Indian, his face contorted with rage, plunged at him with a war ax raised to strike. Morgan lifted his Bisley and fired. The Indian stopped mid-plunge, a bullet between his eyes. He dropped to the ground.

Morgan let the air swish out of his lungs. Damn, he hated fighting Indians. They were sneaky and so silent.

He glanced toward Broom's spot between the downed trees. He was gone. How in hell had he gotten out of the tight spot he was in? A shot from a forty-five sounded, then another. Morgan waited.

In a moment, Broom emerged from the trees; the spot of blood on his torn shirt sleeve had not widened. He hoisted his rifle over his shoulder and called out to Morgan. "Must be slippin'. I didn't get him. But he was moving out fast. I think that's the last of them."

The two men made their way back to the horses.

"The Washos want guns, and now and then they get a few." Broom shoved his rifle into the saddle boot. "But they didn't get ours."

Morgan motioned toward a rise. "We better make sure that last one was headed for home. I don't want any arrows in my back."

Broom agreed.

For several minutes the two men, astride their mounts, watched the valley below. A galloping horse, carrying one Indian, with three riderless horses tethered behind, grew rapidly smaller going away along the lower trail.

Morgan and Broom headed back to their path to the cabin.

"How's that arm?"

Broom reined in and waited for Lee. "Just a nick, I'll clean it up when we get to the cabin. I got a glimpse of that Indian that got away. I think it was the old Chief's son."

"Did he see you?"

Broom nodded. "And if he's anything like I've heard, he'll be after me. I'd better keep my rear covered."

"Don't you usually?"

The trail widened and Broom and Morgan rode side by side.

"Tell me something about this Hex Downs," Morgan said. "I gather he was a good shot, but he went down in a shootout?"

"He was shot in the back. Nobody, including the sheriff seemed to figure out who or why."

"Why did he come to Lost Canyon in the first place, and what made him stay?"

"He was here only a month or so." Broom frowned thoughtfully. "I didn't get well acquainted with the man. Don't think anybody did really. But I watched him. I would say he came to Lost Canyon by accident. The train was robbed this side of Sacramento. His partner

was killed in the robbery and Downs ran."
Broom shrugged. "It's only a guess, but I think
he figured there were a lot of lawmen in
Sacramento, and he'd be safer to go east."

"There's nothing east of Lost Canyon but
desert."

"That's right. Once he hit this settlement, he
didn't dare head on down into the desert alone
in the middle of summer. It not only skirts the
Washo Indian camp, but he couldn't carry
enough water to get him through. Not with
forty pounds of gold in his saddle bags."

"Did he make friends with anybody in town?"

"No. He sat around in the bar with Corson,
the fellow you horsewhipped." Broom grinned.
"I think Corson was trying to get close to him.
But I don't think they were friends, least not
friendly enough so Downs would tell Corson
where the gold was hidden. Once he met
Gramps in town, Hex spent a lot of time up
here."

Morgan could understand why. The altitude
and the pine trees changed the summer heat of
Lost Canyon, which was a couple of thousand
feet lower elevation, to a cooler mountain
temperature. He glanced at the wide flat valley
below. Heat rose in waves from some areas far
beyond them and to the east.

They stopped to rest the horses from the
steep climb of the last few miles.

"This Hex Downs could have been anybody,"
Morgan said. "Maybe he was passing through
and liked the town. Decided to stay."

"You know me better than that. I don't chase
wild hares." Broom frowned at Morgan. "Hex
Downs was the man with the gold, all right.

Now all we need is to find out what he did with it."

They resumed their ride and an hour passed before the cabin came into sight. It was a one room hutch, maybe twelve-by-fifteen feet, neatly built of logs. A lean-to held fire wood, and a tethered mule brayed as they approached.

The cabin door stood open.

Morgan didn't like the wary feeling that assailed him. From habit his right hand slid to his tied down Bisley Colts. Fresh hoof prints from shod horses stood out in the dirt to the left of the door.

Broom dismounted, rifle in hand. So Broom felt it, too.

Silently they approached the open door, one on each side. Broom stepped boldly forward. Morgan held up a hand, then shook his head. Broom stopped. They both listened for any telltale sound that could designate danger inside.

Silence.

Could the old man have heard the shots earlier from this distance and expected trouble? From what Broom had told him about Gramps, Morgan didn't think he was the kind of man to shoot before he knew who he was shooting at.

"Gramps?" Broom called out.

No answer.

Broom lowered his rifle. "He's not even here. Probably down at the spring."

They edged their way into the cabin, Morgan still held his Bisley Colts ready to use.

"Damn!" Broom exploded. "Look at this mess."

They stood inside for a long moment to

accustom their eyes to the gloom. Chairs were overturned, boxes dumped on the floor, and the plank table lay on its side.

On the bunk in the far corner of the room lay Gramps. Blood covered one side of his face. His eyes stared at them in death.

Morgan felt for a pulse even though he knew the old timer was dead. The body was still warm. Morgan closed the man's eyes.

"Looks like you weren't the only one, Hank, who figured Gramps knew where the gold was hidden."

3

Lee Morgan set a log chair on its feet and straddled it, leaning his forearms on the back. He ran a finger along the smoothly crafted chair back, feeling the workmanship. "Whatever Gramp's killer was looking for, he didn't find it."

"That figures. They probably killed the old man tryin' to make him talk, then tore the place up looking for the gold or something that would lead them to it." Broom picked up four books that had been dumped to the floor and set them back on the shelf. "It's obvious the old fellow could read, maybe he could write too and wrote something down about the gold."

"I think he was too smart for that." Morgan's gaze took in the empty shelves and the spattered floor. Sticky preserves ran together with tomatoes and cut green beans. "Every jar has been broken and searched and every box has been dumped." He indicated the pile of clothes with turned out pockets. "They even went through his clothes. No, I'd guess they found nothing. But that doesn't mean we can't find something that might tell us who did the killing. At least we know one thing for sure."

"What's that?"

"Somebody else knows that Hex Downs brought gold bars to Lost Canyon."

"When we find out who killed Gramps, we'll know."

Lee gently spread a blanket over the old man's body. "Wonder who the old fellow was protecting by keeping silent. Downs is dead, and somehow I can't believe the old gent wanted the gold for himself, or he'd have already had it and gone off to spend it."

"Gold is a mighty powerful magnet." Broom began a close search of the far side of the cabin. He added to his philosophy on gold, "Some people, even honest folks, can't resist the pull."

Morgan gave a muffled chuckle. "Even honest folks like you and me."

Morgan combed the side of the room where Gramps lay dead on his bunk. It was beginning to look like their prime lead would get them nowhere. He ran his fingers along all edges of the bunk, hoping for a secret compartment, or a niche, anything the killers had missed.

Morgan's fingers stopped. "Broom, I may have found something." Down on one knee, he examined a scrap of leather wedged between the two birch logs that formed one side of the bunk.

Broom leaned down to look, his salt and pepper hair fell across his forehead. "Could be." He lessened the tension of the logs and Morgan pulled the piece of buckskin free. They examined the three inch strip, about a quarter of an inch wide, turned it over.

Morgan ran it between his fingers. "Feel this, it's soft, too soft for home tanning, I'd say. I've got an old buckskin jacket back in Idaho."

Broom nodded in agreement. "Didn't see any

clothes here with that sort of trim." He paused a moment, then said. "Well, hell, guess we'd better get the sheriff notified, so we can bury the old fellow."

Morgan slipped the scrap of leather into his pocket, dusted off his Stetson, from habit, and set it firmly on his head. "Coming?" He opened the cabin door and took one step. A volley of gunfire pushed him back fast. "Damn! Now somebody else wants us dead."

Morgan's Bisley Colts jumped into his hand and he returned four shots into a clump of trees a hundred feet away. He glanced at Broom sighting his rifle through the small window. "Think it's the Indian back with reinforcements?"

"If they had revolvers they would have used them the first time." He pointed toward a neat circle of shots, head high, that the gunman had made in the cabin door. "That's good shooting for close to a hundred feet. That was no Indian."

"I'm going out the back window and try to get behind them. We haven't got enough ammunition to last an hour in here. Keep 'em occupied." Morgan dumped the spent shells from the Bisley Colts, loaded in six new rounds and dropped a handful of shells into a pocket. He picked up his black snake whip and disappeared over the sill of the back window.

Morgan heard Broom's two well-placed rifle shots plow into the clump of trees. A dozen, maybe more, shots answered, hitting the cabin above and below Broom's window. Then more shots from the trees, even when Broom didn't shoot back.

Morgan circled behind the clump of trees,

giving it a wide berth. Inch by silent inch he crept toward the sound of the gunfire. He could smell the gunpowder, even taste it on his tongue. Whoever was doing the shooting, meant business.

He crept closer. He'd have to take them one at a time.

Behind an enormous rock, a battered brown felt hat bobbed first one way and then the other, avoiding splinters from the rocks that Broom targeted with his rifle.

Morgan listened for firing from some other location. There was none. For one gunny, he sure raised a ruckus.

Morgan crept closer behind the pistol-packing assailant. He wasn't in the habit of shooting men in the back, not even killers.

Morgan raised the black snake whip. He wanted this one alive. If he knew anything about the gold, Morgan planned to squeeze it out of him.

The tip of the black snake circled the gun, whipping it to the ground. Without missing a beat, the man spun around, his other gun firing at where Morgan's head would have been had he not dropped to the ground and rolled.

Morgan came up squeezing the trigger of his Bisley. The other man's gun clicked, clicked again. Empty. He could not fire again without reloading.

A breeze lifted the other man's hat. It floated to the ground. He shook aside a shock of sun-bleached hair.

Morgan's trigger finger froze. "My God, you're nothing but a damn kid."

"I'm not a kid. I'm eighteen, and I'll get you if I have to . . . to . . . ."

Morgan came closer. The kid didn't back away. He had guts all right. The kid had guts. His Bisley Colts still aimed at the kid's chest, he took the useless pistol from the boy's hand and tossed it into the brush. The gun on the ground, he kicked it out of reach. "You'll get me if you have to what?" Morgan snapped.

The boy stood straight and tall. He wore bib overalls over a blue-gray cotton shirt. Morgan would bet a night's stake in a poker game the kid had never even shaved.

The boy's eyes blazed with fury. "If I have to hang for it. Gramps was my friend. You killed him."

"Or you did."

"Me! Gramps was all I had in this rotten world. He raised me up from a little kid. Taught me everything I know."

"Sit down," Morgan ordered, and pointed to a patch of grass in the shade. Warily the boy sat down, not taking his eyes from Morgan for a second. Morgan dropped down beside him. "You got a name?"

"Jason. Jason Isley."

"Jason," Morgan said. "I didn't beat your Gramps to death, and neither did Hank Broom, my partner. How did you know he was dead? He was still warm when we got here."

"I found him." Jason's eyes clouded with grief. "I heard somebody coming, and I jumped through the back window and ran. I thought it was the killers coming back."

"Didn't you see anybody going down the mountain? You must have seen something. Whoever did this had to go down." Morgan looked beyond the cabin. Only a small rocky rise showed the top of the mountain. "There's no place to go up to. Broom says it's a sheer drop on the other side."

"There's a trail that goes all the way down to the high desert, but it's hard to find. Somebody would have to know his way around."

"And who might that be?"

Jason frowned impatiently. "How would I know? I never use it."

"Seems to me you don't know much of anything except how to shoot a gun at anybody you see."

"I heard you and your friend coming."

"What about the Indian fight. You hear that?"

Jason nodded. "I saw Burning Arrow scoot for camp with three horses behind him. Did he leave any dead Indians behind?"

"Three."

"That's right. There could be trouble. But I suppose as long as his son didn't get hurt, the old chief won't start anything. He's old and he wants peace with the whites. It's Burning Arrow and a bunch of young braves who think the tribe should still be warriors."

"So Broom told me."

Jason glanced at Morgan. "Gramps and the old chief are . . . were, friends."

Morgan got to his feet and motioned to the cabin with his head. "Come on, we'll tell Broom who you are, then you go down and get the sheriff. Broom's been around here longer than I have, and he says to be on the safe side, we can't bury your Gramps until the sheriff checks it out."

"I heard Sheriff Taylor telling somebody that you're a dangerous gunny and that you and Broom used to be partners holding up banks.

Did the ranchers outside of town hire you?"

"Hank Broom and I were never partners in any such thing, just friends from a long time ago. Why would the ranchers hire me. Have they got rustler trouble?"

Jason seemed relieved. "I should have known the sheriff wasn't telling the truth, he lies to everybody."

"Even to the ranchers?"

"He doesn't even try to catch the rustlers."

Morgan let Jason get his pistols out of the brush. "Can't let 'em lie out here and rust." Then they headed for the cabin.

Morgan pushed open the cabin door. Broom sat across the room, his rifle leveled. He let it fall to his knee. "Hello, Isley. Where are the others, dead?"

Morgan grinned. "Wasn't anybody else. This one-man army did all the shooting."

"Waste of ammunition," Broom said. "What did you plan to do when you ran out?"

"I separated you two, didn't I? Made one of you go out the window. Once I got you, I planned to go after the other one."

Broom shook his head. "You'd need eyes at the back of your head to watch both of us."

"Okay, cut the lesson in strategy," Morgan growled. "Jason, who knew Hex Downs spent a lot of time up here, besides you?"

"I don't live up here now. I live in a room behind the cafe downtown, I work there. I never saw Downs here. But Gramps said Hex came up now and then."

"This is a long hot ride from town. Did he tell you why Hex came up here?"

Jason glanced warily from Broom to Morgan. "Does there have to be a reason?" He slapped

his worn felt hat on his head and loaded his
pistols. "I'll get the sheriff. I'd like to bury
Gramps before nightfall."

"Take my horse," Morgan said.

"No. Mine's over behind the rocks."

Jason walked a good piece into the timber
before he permitted a quiet tear to slide down
his cheek. Gramps was dead. It was like he'd
lost a mother and father at the same time. He
walked faster hoping the awful ache would go
away.

In the distance, Jason's horse, Felipe,
whinnied. He was up wind from the horse and
Jason wondered absently how the animal could
know he was coming.

With no sense of caution, Jason called out.
"I'm coming, Felipe, keep your shirt on."

Jason rounded the boulder that shielded the
horse from view. All thoughts of Gramps
vanished. The smell of danger permeated the
air. He dropped to the ground a half second
before a rifle shot cracked against the rock
behind him.

Jason had flipped a rein around a flat ground
rock to keep Felipe out of sight after he had
discovered Gramps' body.

It was a good place to hide a horse. Two
thirty-foot boulders formed a wide V. At the
narrow part, they almost came together, leaving
a six foot deep hiding place. When he was a kid
he used to hide from Gramps when it was time
to do his reading and numbers.

Now Jason crawled along the sandy ground,
using his horse as a shield. The rifle shot had
come from a stand of trees fifty yards away. A
bullet skidded across the ground. Felipe
whinnied and pulled back as far as the

anchored rein would permit.

Jason reached for the flat rock. Another shot skipped across the hard dirt landing useless against the rocky wall.

He had to get Felipe loose so he could get away. Gramps had given him Felipe on his birthday the year he was twelve. He couldn't bear to lose Felipe now.

Crawling forward, Jason jerked the rein loose, then plunged for the small hiding place and protection. The horse raced for freedom. He would go home to the stable in Lost Canyon, or maybe just back to the cabin.

A barrage of gunfire erupted from the trees. Jason unloaded both his pistols at the clump of greenery, then backed into the narrow rock opening to reload. Morgan had called him a one-man army. Jason hoped the man with the rifle would think he had more than one man to shoot down.

He backed deeper into the narrow space. The gunman took advantage of the seconds Jason was silent. Three rifle shots in quick succession hit the inner edge of his hiding place.

Jason stepped back. All hell broke loose. Bullets flew in every direction ricocheting from one side of his hiding place to the other. Jason dived out the other side to keep from getting killed.

When the barrage of stray bullets finally stopped, Jason aimed both guns at the trees. He squinted into the noonday sun.

For just a second a face emerged from the trees. Corson. Why was Corson trying to kill him? Jason didn't fire.

He heard horses coming then. They came from the direction of the cabin. Probably

Morgan and Broom. They had likely heard the shooting.

Movement in the trees brought Jason's attention back to Corson, then an ominous quiet. Had Corson heard the approach of horses, too? Cautiously Jason moved from his hiding place. No firing came from the trees.

He stepped onto the trail. Morgan and Broom reined in their mounts, settling them down from the sudden stop. Morgan looked down at Jason and shook his head. "Can't you get even a mile on your way without getting shot at? Did you get him?"

"No." Jason spat indignantly. "But if you hadn't come pounding down the trail, I would have. It was Brant Corson. He ran. I saw him."

"Horse came up to the cabin with no rider. We didn't figure you preferred to walk to town." Morgan's forehead wrinkled thoughtfully. "So Corson tried to kill you. He also tried to do something to Celia Fair. Looks as though he's the man we have to get. He must know about the gold. When he couldn't get information from the old timer back there, no doubt he intends to get rid of anybody else who knows."

Broom nodded. "Corson. Turd. He'd kill his own mother for a double eagle. Wonder who he's working with, or if he's goin' it alone."

"Do you think he killed Gramps?" Jason asked.

"When we got to the cabin," Broom answered, "there were footprints in the dirt, looked like two horses."

Morgan dismounted and handed Jason the reins. "Take my horse back up to get yours. Be careful, Corson could be waiting for you to start down the hill. He's out to get you, and he might not be the only one. Don't trust anybody in town, and I mean nobody until we get this sorted out. Now go get the sheriff and stick close to him all the way back up here. At least with him you should be safe."

Back at the cabin, Morgan motioned to Broom to sit on the step. For several minutes the two of them sat quietly soaking up the beauty of the trees, the cool shade, and the cloudless sky where it showed through. Broom rolled a cigarette and lit it, making sure his match was out instead of just throwing it in the brush. It had been a dry year so far. A few feet away, Broom's horse stood beside Morgan's, munching the crisp green grass.

"The old fellow owned what must be the only decent patch of green in the area," Morgan said. "Must be twenty degrees cooler up here than it is down in the middle of that burning town." He turned abruptly. "Do you think the gold is up here? We'd better keep looking before Jason gets back with the sheriff."

Broom stood up. "No, I don't think it's here, but if we get off our butts and really look, we may find another lead. When I telegraphed you to come, Gramps was the only lead I had. That and some talk around town."

Morgan grinned and got to his feet. "I didn't exactly plan on fighting Indians or getting into a race with half a town to locate a few gold bars."

"Nothing comes easy, Morgan, you should know that by now." Broom winked. "Not even that Celia Fair. You seem to be having a hell of a time keeping up with her."

For the next several hours, they searched for some clue that would lead them to the gold. Outside, Broom dug at the base of every tree

with fresh dirt marks around it. When nothing
led anywhere they began all over again in the
one-room cabin.

"Books," Morgan said. "The old fellow
seemed to set a lot of store by books." One at a
time he leafed through them. Through Dickens,
and a History of Sweden. Ole Olmanson was
written in the fly leaf of some of the books.
Must have been the old man's whole name. A
Swede. There was a worn Bible, with names and
dates written. All the dates were too old to
mean anything.

A beginning reader. Morgan smiled. He'd
learned some from the same reader when he went
to school.

Next he picked up a threadbare dictionary. He
fanned the pages. A thin oilskin folder dropped
to the floor. He opened it and found a leaf of
yellowed papers. "Hey, Broom, look at this."
Morgan read aloud. "Being of sound mind I
bequeath all my earthly possessions to Jason
Isley." There was more legal jargon, describing
the cabin and the land surrounding it and any
and all livestock. "It's witnessed by Jeb and
Essie Rowe. They're the ones who own the
hotel?"

"That's them." Broom reread the paper. "It's
even been made up by a legal man. He's dead
now. Used to be a judge."

"At least the kid will have something besides
washing dishes and the like in the cafe."
Morgan looked out the door. "Here he comes
now with the sheriff. Should we give the will to
the sheriff so he can finish making it legal?"

"No!" Broom exploded. "Give it to Jason,
later. Let him decide who he wants to show it to.
Probably should take it up to Sacramento and

have it recorded right and proper. That way nobody's gonna cheat him out of it."

Morgan quickly folded the papers back into the oilskin and shoved it into his back pocket.

It was nearly four o'clock by Morgan's pocket Waterbury, when Jason and the sheriff reined in their horses and came inside the cabin.

The sheriff jerked back the blanket that covered the old man, then dropped it back into place. "That's him. Beaten to death, huh?" The sheriff dropped his ample body into the one easy chair in the room and pushed his expensive gray Stetson to the back of his head. A shock of black hair fell across his brow making his oily face appear swarthy. "Anybody see who did it?"

Jason looked away. "He was dead when I found him, Sheriff."

"I can see that." He shot an accusing glance at Morgan. "You're a professional gunny. Did you try to beat information out of the old codger?"

Morgan didn't bother to answer, but Broom did. "Morgan is a friend of mine, and he did not beat Gramps to death. We found him together, and he was dead."

"Good thing you got Broom here to vouch for you, Morgan, though he ain't much better. Otherwise, I'd lock you up in a minute. Strangers, that's what causes trouble around Lost Canyon. Strangers poking their noses into things that are none of their business."

He got up and walked to the door. "Go ahead and plant him."

Jason jumped to his feet. "Aren't you going to try to find out who killed Gramps? You haven't even looked around the cabin, for footprints or something."

"All in good time, boy. I figure it must have been a stranger coming through who counted on the old man having a few double eagles tucked away. Probably never see him again, unless he comes back."

"Brant Corson isn't a stranger in town, but he was out back shooting at young Isley," Morgan said. "Just after noon time, before the kid left for town to get you."

"You're just trying to get Corson into trouble because you had a run-in with him," the sheriff said.

Neither Broom nor Jason Isley argued with him.

The sheriff pointed a threatening forefinger at Morgan. "You, Morgan, I want out of town. We don't want the likes of you shooting up our town and riling up the Indians. You better not be here tomorrow."

When the sheriff had gone, Broom and Morgan helped dig the grave. They wrapped Ole Olmanson in a blanket and lowered him into the earth.

They stood for a moment before shoveling the dirt back over him, Jason a little apart from the other two.

Morgan mumbled to Broom in a low voice. "Suppose we should say something?"

"I guess so. You want to?"

"You. You're the preacher's son."

Broom accordingly bowed his head and asked the Lord's blessing on the old man's soul. He used his name, Ole Olmanson, and then said, "Known and liked by all as Gramps. Amen."

Jason said, "Thank you."

They took up their shovels and filled in the

grave, smoothing it up around the sides. Then Morgan and Broom returned the tools to the shed, leaving Jason alone.

4

Jason Isley felt empty. He stood alone under the trees beside the mound of newly turned earth. All the rest of the world was out there and he was here, alone.

The brief informal ceremony was over, the poor old man's body was in the ground. It had been kind of Lee Morgan, he thought, to suggest that they should say a few words for the old man. Jason guessed he wouldn't have thought of it himself. Or perhaps he would have when it was too late.

Gramps had been the only person Jason could remember who had seemed like family. Other boys had a mother and a father, sometimes brothers and sisters. But Jason had only Gramps.

The man, who Jason was later told had been his father, had never made a home for his wife and child. He rode away one day when Jason had not yet reached the age of two, and was later hanged as a cattle thief. As Jason reached the age of reason, he learned about his father. Since that time he grew up wanting nothing to do with law-breakers of any kind.

Old Gramps had been able to see the good in most anyone, but Jason saw right and wrong.

He barely remembered his mother. He had a picture of her tucked in with his meager belongings. She had been a pretty lady. Maybe not a very good lady, but a pretty lady. She had died giving birth to another baby, who also had a hit and run father, just as Jason did. But that baby died with their mother.

Jason was about four years old when she died, and Gramps had taken him in. He could not remember any home but here in the cabin with Gramps.

Gramps taught Jason to ride before he was big enough to get on the horse alone. He had taught him other things, too. He read to Jason from books and magazines and newspapers that came from big cities back east.

When Jason was about six, Gramps had given him a horse, and had insisted that Jason ride the horse to the one-room school house on the edge of town where there was sometimes a schoolmarm or a school master. When there was no teacher and no school, or when the winter snows were too deep to get through, Gramps taught him.

Once Jason asked Gramps where he got his learning and Gramps just said, "Here and there. But that was a long time ago."

Jason was one of the few in town who had graduated the eighth grade and had taken all the tests. Gramps said that learning was an important thing.

When Jason turned sixteen, he had moved out of the cabin and got himself a proper job at the cafe in town so he could earn his own way. He came to see Gramps often and sometimes brought him supplies from town. If he had been living here still, maybe this wouldn't have happened. Maybe Gramps would still be alive. Or maybe they would both be dead.

Surely Jason would have been able to do something to prevent whoever it was from killing the poor old man.

After a little while, as the breeze pushed at the thatch of sun-bleached hair falling over his forehead, Jason took a deep breath and turned away from the grave. He walked a little way toward the cabin and then stooped to pick up a small round stone about the size of a silver dollar. He held it and looked at it, then found another and another.

He gathered a handful of the worn pellets, rounded by weather and boots tramping the path. Smoothing them in his hand one by one, he thought, Gramps had always appreciated things like this, smooth stones, weathered wood, the way a hawk soared across the sky from one great tree to a rock on the side of the mountain.

Jason returned to the mound and placed the stones in a circle at the head of the grave in front of the wooden cross that Hank Broom had set into the dirt.

"Jason." He heard Lee Morgan's voice call.

Without answering, Jason made his way back to the cabin.

"We were picking up some of this stuff before," Morgan told him. "You'll be interested in this paper here. Seems to be the old man's will."

"Gramps left a will?" Jason looked at the paper. The document was typewritten on a legal looking form. It had Gramps' signature: Ole Olmanson, and some other signers had put their names to it, one of them with curliques at the ends of the letters.

"And there's some other stuff here that tells the lawyer's name who drew up the will." Morgan handed the rest of the papers over. "Broom says he was a judge, but he's dead now. You probably should go to Sacramento and get it registered, or something. You ever been to Sacramento?"

"No. I've never been to a big city. Always thought I'd like to some day." Jason sighed. "I don't have money enough to go there. But I could write a letter to the circuit judge. He'd be able to tell me what to do." Jason's mind raced with what he had just read. He owned land. Gramps had left him the land, the cabin, even old Rocky, the mule, because it said, *any and all livestock.*

"I wonder when he did this?"

"It's dated, isn't it?" Hank wanted to know.

"Oh, yes. That was a long time ago." Jason had trouble taking it all in. "Did Gramps think he was going to die way back when I was a little kid?"

"Guess he just wanted to be prepared, in case." Morgan patted Jason's shoulder. "Guess he really thought a lot of you, kid."

Jason folded the papers and put them back into the oilskin in which Morgan had found them. "I wonder why they didn't take these. Whoever killed him, I mean. The land's worth something. Couldn't they have had it instead of me?"

Hank Broom snorted. "Wasn't what they were after. They wanted information. Don't guess they got it, or they wouldn't have tore the place apart like it was."

"Probably didn't look through the books."

Morgan added. "Or even if they saw them, they'd likely think the boy here knew about the papers and the lawyer."

Broom agreed. Then he told Morgan they had best get back into town. "You comin' along, kid?"

"No," Jason told them. "I'll feed the mule and decide what to do next. I'll be on in soon. Got to go to work early in the morning."

Morgan put out his hand. "Good meeting you, Jason Isley. Sorry about your Gramps."

The younger man shook hands. He liked Morgan. "Thanks. Sure had you pegged wrong when I saw you ride up. You've been a help. Gramps probably woulda liked you, too."

"Sure you don't want to ride on into town with us?" Morgan asked. "Besides the trouble we had with those renegade Indians, whoever killed the old man might be looking for you."

Jason had avoided telling Morgan and Broom anything he knew about the gold, which was practically nothing. He knew that's what they were looking for too, but they weren't going to kill for it. "I can't tell them anything," he said. "Gramps probably knew. But he never told me."

"They don't know that," Broom said.

More thinking aloud, than actually telling, Jason said, "Gramps could have told Miss Celia."

"Celia?" Morgan asked.

"Well, he knew her. He talked to her, I guess about her brother."

"What brother?" Morgan pressed for more information. "You mean Celia Fair?"

"I guess that's her name. I don't know anything about it." Jason felt he had already said too much. "What are you guys going to do with that gold if you find it? It was stolen, wasn't it? Whose is it supposed to be?"

"Maybe we'll get a reward," Broom said smoothly.

Jason didn't believe him. He was sure that Broom and Morgan would never do something like kill a defenseless old man, but he didn't think they would turn in the gold if they found it. "You guys go ahead," he told them. "I'll see you in town. I'll be okay. Don't worry about me."

Finally Broom went down to the spring, filled the canteen and watered the horses. Then the two men set out on the return trip to town. They kept a sharp lookout but saw no one else anywhere along the trail on the uneventful ride back.

"Think the kid knows more than he's telling?" Broom asked once on the way.

Morgan shook his head. "No. But somebody else could have the idea that he does. Maybe we can track down those somebodies before they do any more damage. Might start with Brant Corson."

They rode out of the timber and down to the high desert feeling the afternoon heat start their sweat glands pouring before they reached the valley town of Lost Canyon.

They made the usual necessary arrangements and stabled their horses at the livery. Broom asked the stableman whether any other mounts kept there belonged to men recently arrived in town. The man didn't have a lot to say, so they learned nothing.

"The sheriff already asked you about that?" Morgan wanted to know.

"Sheriff and me don't talk much."

Morgan gave it up and followed Broom outside.

As they stood by the door deciding what they wanted to do next, the young boy and his dog that they had seen the day before, came around the side of the building. This time the boy didn't just look as if he wanted to say something.

Staring at Morgan, he said, "Hey, Mister. You're the guy what whupped old Brant Corson, ain't you?"

Morgan shrugged. "You might say so."

"Wished I could do that." His gaze slid to the black snake whip Morgan carried with him when he left the horse and saddle.

Broom laughed. "Maybe you could teach the kid something, Lee."

Morgan shook his head. "Doubt I'll be around long enough to give out any lessons."

The boy's wideeyed admiration shifted again to Morgan's face. "Bet you could even whup Sheriff Tyler."

"Would you like that?" Broom asked him.

The stableman appeared in the doorway. "Willy, you shut your mouth."

Willy tucked his head. "Aw, Pa." The boy and his dog shot around the side of the livery stable out of sight.

Morgan and Broom walked over to the hotel.

"Don't seem to be a lot of people in love with the sheriff in this town," Broom said.

"Probably a lot of people in this town have good sense. Sheriff Tyler seems like real shit. You known him long?"

"Wasn't sheriff last time I was in town. Never met him before."

They went on into the hotel.

"Gotta figure out what's next, I guess," Broom said and followed Morgan up to his room.

Opening the door, Morgan stopped dead. "What the hell!"

The room had been ransacked. Whoever did it had not taken care to cover his actions. The bureau drawers had been flung onto the floor, along with Morgan's few clean clothes. The bed had been turned up, the mattress dragged to the floor, blankets yanked every which way. His carpetbag lay on top of the pile of bedclothes.

It was the same sort of mess they had encountered at the old man's cabin. Except that Morgan didn't have as much stuff in his hotel room, so whoever had done it didn't find as much to toss around.

"They must have been mighty disappointed that you were traveling so light," Broom said, shoving his hat back and scratching his head. "What'd they think you had? You didn't rob a train on the way out, did you?"

"Nope."

There was only one thing that Morgan could figure would have caused this. He had rescued Celia Fair, and Celia had come to him to leave something that she obviously treasured.

Broom was no dummy. He apparently had some thoughts about the matter too. "Something to do with that woman and that guy Corson, right? Why would he do this sort of thing, just to get even?"

Morgan didn't answer.

"You don't even know her, do you?"

"Don't have any idea where she is," Morgan said.

"I didn't ask if you know where she is. I asked if you know her."

"Depends on what you mean by know her," Morgan said.

"You hound, you've got yourself involved already."

"Don't worry, we'll find the fuckin' gold," Morgan growled. "But gold or no gold, I'm going to find the son-of-a-bitch who wrinkled my clothes."

"Good," Broom said. "Let's go get something to eat. Maybe we'll think of something else."

"Go ahead. I'll join you in a minute. Just want to check through my stuff and sling the mattress back onto the bed. I'll be right along."

When he was alone in the room, Morgan bolted the door, then checked the fireplace to make sure the intruder had not discovered his hiding place. The bricks appeared undisturbed, looked natural, but Morgan brought the crockery wash basin from the stand on the other side of the room and held it beneath the brick to catch the crumbling mortar. He removed one brick and was relieved to find the leather bag still intact.

Carefully replacing the brick, he again moistened the dusty mortar and tucked it realistically into the cracks.

He stood there wondering where Celia Fair was. He thought about the night before. God, it made him hot just thinking about her. Her silky smooth body and her delicate talented hands. He licked his lips, but tasted only salt and dust.

He wondered how he could get in touch with her. Someone must know. The trouble was, he couldn't take a chance on asking the wrong person.

Dusting out the basin, he poured water in it from the pitcher and washed his face and hands. Then he dried off, went out into the hall, and locked his door.

At the desk downstairs he dropped off the useless skeleton key at the desk. Anybody could get into the room, if you weren't there to slide the bolt on the inside.

Nelly was behind the counter. "Everything all right, Mr. Morgan?"

"Not exactly, Nelly. You see anybody go into my room today while I was gone?"

"No, sir." She looked alarmed. "Has someone been in your room?"

"You might say that. Tore the place all up."

"Oh, dear. It was all right when I made up your bed at ten o'clock, Mr. Morgan." Nelly wrung her hands, her excited voice raised with anxiety. "I'm the only one that was in there. But I didn't muss anything up."

"I know you didn't. But if you get time, you can make up the bed again. I tossed the mattress back on the bed, but the blankets could use help."

"The mattress was off the bed? Wait, I'd better tell Mr. Rowe."

Jeb and Essie Rowe had already come out of an office somewhere behind Nelly. "What's all the fuss about, Nelly?" Essie wanted to know.

"Morgan?" Jeb said.

"Someone got into Mr. Morgan's things, in his room," Nelly said. "I made up his bed this morning. Honest. I didn't move anything. It wasn't a mess then."

Jeb and Essie insisted upon going up with Morgan to see the problem.

"I already put away the bureau drawers and such," Morgan said. "Don't know what they wanted, but someone tore into everything. Not that I have much with me."

"Did they steal something?" Jeb inquired.

"No. I didn't find anything missing. Don't think we need to call in the law or blab it around," Morgan told them. "I wouldn't have mentioned it to Nelly, but I hoped maybe she'd tidy up the bed. I'm not much for bed making."

"Of course, she'll make it right up," Essie said, starting to do the job herself.

Morgan thought they both seemed relieved that he had not wanted to notify the sheriff. He wanted nothing more to do with the damn sheriff. He got the feeling that the Rowes felt the same way.

He thanked them for their help in the matter and went on over to the cafe to meet Hank Broom.

Over their early supper they spoke quietly about the events of the day, glancing around occasionally to make sure no one was near enough to take in their conversation. They reached no conclusions, except that they wanted to find out more about Brant Corson and what he was up to.

They made the rounds of the three saloons to see if Corson was around, but they didn't see him. Morgan got propositions from three different voluptuous bar girls, joked with them, smiled a lot, and rejected all three. He had never felt the need to pay for giving women joy and satisfaction. Better they should pay him. Broom, however, left Morgan to finish his last brandy alone, disappearing with a highly rouged night creature on his arm.

Morgan thought he saw someone watching him from the end of the alley as he made his way back to his hotel. He slowed down to see if they might want to follow along, but they didn't take the bait. He decided he had taken something personally that had nothing to do with him. Probably whoever it was had been watching everyone that went by. There didn't seem to be much else to do in the town except drinking and doxies.

5

After taking his clothes off and cleaning up, Morgan lay on the bed thinking about the things that had taken place. It had been a long day. The Indians, the old timer dead and buried, and Jason Isley. Morgan wondered how much more young Jason knew about the gold than he let on.

But soon Morgan relaxed and began to doze off. In and out of a sort of half sleep, he dreamed about Celia Fair.

He roused suddenly and sat up trying to figure out what had wakened him. It came again. A gentle tapping that made his heart race. Could it be?

He pulled on his pants, buttoning them part way up. Then he stopped short, and before going to the door, took his Bisley Colt out of the holster hanging on the bedpost.

Standing close to the edge of the door, not directly in front of it, he asked, "Yeah? Who is it?"

The tapping came again and a whispered answer. "Celia."

He drew the bolt and opened the door. There she was. He could scarcely believe she had actually reappeared.

This time she wore an ankle-length dark gray

traveling suit that had a white blouse with a bow at the neck. The jacket of the suit fit her perfectly, made with long lapels and two buttons at the pinched in waist. She carried a plush gray carpet satchel with large yellow roses and green leaves patterned on the sides. From one wrist hung a moleskin bag of the sort women sometimes carried their knitting in. On her head she wore a bonnet that matched her suit.

This time Lee Morgan didn't have to be asked if she could come in. He drew her into the room immediately, took the carpetbag and set it aside, and returned the Bisley to its holster on the bedpost.

"I was thinking about you!" Lee said, taking hold of her hand.

"Is that why you are practically undressed?" Her laughtered tinkled out at him, making him laugh too.

"But you," he held her at arm's length and looked her over, "you're dressed for travel."

"I'm leaving in the morning. I had to stop and pick up my bag that I left with you."

Morgan shook his head. A troubled frown crossed his brow. "You're leaving?"

"Not until morning, Lee." Celia touched his face with her hand. "I also had to stop because I wanted to be with you."

He put his arms around her and held her close to him. Breathing a sigh of relief he told her, "I want you to be with me. And I want to be with you."

She drew away momentarily. "You kept my leather case safe?"

"Of course."

He strode over to the fireplace, shoved the

hearth rug into the right spot to catch the crumbled mortar and once again removed the bricks. He carefully took out the leather bag and dusted it off with a used towel. "There you are. Good as new. And every bit as heavy as it was when you brought it in here."

She took the bag and set it with her other things. "Thank you, Lee. I was sure you would know how to keep it safe for me."

"We picked the right hiding place," Lee told her. "When I got in from some errands yesterday, someone had torn the room apart searching for something."

"For my bag?" Concern clouded Celia's face.

"I don't know what they were looking for." He smiled at her, walked over to the door and made sure the bolt was securely in place. "But they didn't get it. Aren't you going to look in it to make sure it's all right?" He wanted to know what she was carrying.

She picked up the bag again, undid the buckles and opened it. "There they are. It's my jewelry. Heirlooms handed down through my family." She took out a necklace and held it up. It glittered in the lamp light.

Morgan got a quick look over her shoulder before she returned the necklace and closed the bag. Could be a fortune in gems in that bag. She refastened the buckles.

"I brought them with me, because I thought I might have to sell them to help my brother."

"But you didn't have to?" Lee asked her.

"When I got here he was already dead."

"Oh. I'm sorry."

"It's over. I hadn't seen him in a long time." She sighed. "We weren't close. There is nothing I can do about it now."

Celia took off her bonnet and placed it carefully on top of the bags on the floor. She unbuttoned her jacket and hung it on the chair, then sat down and took off her shoes.

She smiled up at Morgan who stood watching her. Her movements, so full of grace, and so sensuous, fascinated and roused him.

As before, she sneaked up under her skirts and slowly, as if teasing him, peeled off the expensive looking stockings, first one and then the other.

"Where are you going on the morning coach?" Morgan asked.

"Salt Lake City. Then on the train. Chicago. Boston." She untied the white bow of her blouse and unbuttoned the buttons, slowly, tantalizingly.

"Why must you go?"

"I have to take care of my father's business." She drew her arms out of the sleeves and dropped the blouse on the chair. "But that's not until tomorrow. Let's not think of those things now."

Morgan stepped closer. He didn't want to think of those things now. In a moment he was helping her out of the rest of her clothes. He shed his pants and finally they embraced. "You feel even better than last night."

"So do you," she murmured.

They kissed, a long tender kiss full of promises. Then Celia's lips found the indentation at the front of his neck, between the ends of his collarbone. Her kiss was feather light and thrilled him. He never knew that spot on him was so responsive.

He bent to kiss her again, but she said. "Come lie down."

They went to the bed, and she told him to lie on his stomach.

"What for?" I can't hold you if I'm lying on my stomach.

"I'll show you," she promised.

He lay down on his stomach as she took a tiny bottle of oil from her moleskin bag and brought it to the bed with her. "Relax," she said. She got on the bed beside him and knelt sitting back on her heels. She leaned over and kissed the middle of his back, sending a shiver up his spine.

In a moment she began to massage his legs with the oil. It felt good. She went from his legs to his back, smoothing the oil with firm strokes from his buttocks to his shoulders, then lighter strokes back down again, her fingers scampering and tickling on the way.

His muscles relaxed, except for one on which he was lying. That organ grew longer and harder.

He felt relaxed and euphoric, yet excited. "Your hands are stronger than they look," he said. "Where did you learn to do that?"

"From my Swedish nanny," she said. "She taught me many things. Do you like it? Your skin is parched from the dry air, and thirsty. It drinks up the oil."

"My skin isn't the only thing that's thirsty. I'm thirsting for you."

After massaging on up to include his shoulders and the back of his neck, she said, "If you're still awake, you may turn over now."

He turned over and she laughed delightedly. "There's something sticking up, here!"

She put aside the little bottle of oil and walked her fingers up his legs, past his excited organ, and all the way up his chest, where she tweeked his nipples.

Lee grabbed her and rolled over with her, pinning her down and kissing her passionately. She returned the kiss making little humming sounds to show her pleasure. She squirmed against him, exciting him even more.

"Put your hands on me," she whispered. "I love to feel your hands on me."

He knew how good her hands felt to him, so he obeyed. While he kissed and suckled her breasts, his hands traversed her smooth skin over her sides, her belly, her thighs. Then he paused. His hand lay there, just touching, making her wait.

Her body made an urging move, tensing, beseeching.

Lee's fingers moved to find the exciting erectile point at the upper tip of her inner labia. He put his thumb on the love button and slowly put a finger into the hole. Adding another finger, he moved first the fingers and then the thumb, and she raised her body trying to take the fingers in farther. The fingers slipped easily, wet with her juices.

Celia stretched a hand trying to reach his groin, but Lee was in the way. He teased. He moved the fingers again, and then the thumb.

"Oh." Her audible sigh. "Oh, please. Please."

He couldn't disappoint a lady, so he raised himself above her, she opened her legs wide, and he thrust his organ into the warm moist place he had prepared for it. She accepted him and moved with passion wanting it deeper and deeper. It seemed to grow even larger after it was inside.

She raised her legs and circled his body,

clutching him tightly as they thrust together, their rhythms sending them to a higher and higher pitch of excitement.

"Now," she cried. "Now. Oh, now."

The release came intensely, lasted forever, and they both moaned in ecstasy, clinging to one another, as her love hole contracted over and over, squeezing his member, making additional thrills chase one after the other up through his body.

When they finally relaxed she stroked his hair and his face and murmured, "You are wonderful, Lee Morgan."

They slept, and when morning came to Morgan, it woke him angry. He found she had gone. She had dressed, picked up her things and gone, while he went on sleeping.

"Damn, woman!" he exclaimed aloud. "How could you go without saying goodbye?" He had wanted to talk her out of it.

Morgan got up, did the morning things, and got dressed. He looked out the window at the street below and saw nothing worth seeing. A couple of riders went by, heading east. Morgan didn't recognize them as anyone he had seen before. A horse was tied at the rail across the street in front of the cafe. There was no stage. He didn't know when it was scheduled to go through Lost Canyon, or if it had gone. He went downstairs.

The night man was still at the desk. He snored loudly. Morgan couldn't think why the Rowes paid him to sit there with his feet up and sleep.

Turning from the desk and going down the hall, he pounded on the door of room six. "Go away." Hank's baritone sounded hoarse this morning.

Morgan went away. He went to the cafe across the street.

There was only one other customer who sat at the counter silently shoveling his eggs into his mouth.

Morgan decided on a table, and the waitress came to him.

When he had ordered breakfast, he asked the sleepy-eyed girl, "What time's the stage today?"

"East or west?" she wanted to know. "This is the day we have two."

"Oh, damn, wouldn't you know." Then he remembered. Celia had said Salt Lake City, Chicago, Boston. "East."

"That one's gone. We got our supplies off it at the crack of dawn. Only a couple people out there." She stood with one hand on the back of the chair opposite Morgan, leaning, ready to stop and chat a while. "Guess there were two or three people already on it, coming through. Didn't stop long enough for them to come over and eat though."

"Who got on from here?" Morgan wanted to know.

"There was an old man, looked like he was going to go back home to die, he was so old. Folks do that, you know. They come out here and they want to go back where they started from, when they get old."

Morgan nodded. "Makes sense."

"I wouldn't want to go back. I grew up here." She poked at her hair, a preening gesture. "I'm going to go clear to the Pacific Ocean one day."

"Who else got on from here?"

"There was a lady, city clothes, so pretty. She stood there talking to a big guy. I don't think he wanted her to go."

"A big guy?" Morgan asked. "Corson? Long hair?"

She nodded. "Ugly."

"Did he hurt her?"

"No, they were just talking. Like I said, I didn't hear anything, but it looked like he wanted her to stay. I know he didn't get on the stage. But she did."

But she did, Morgan thought.

Before Morgan had finished his breakfast, Hank Broom came in and joined him. "You bang on my door earlier? Did you find out something?"

"Sorry," Morgan said.

He had found out nothing. Celia had told him what was in the leather bag. He had loved, and slept, and learned nothing more.

"You look worse than I feel, Morgan," Broom growled. "What the hell's crawled up you?"

"She's gone."

"Damn." Broom exploded. "Just when I was gonna tell you I thought she might be of some use to us. The Isley kid said something about her knowing the old timer. I thought you'd find out something about that."

"I didn't. I let her get away. She came out here to help her brother, but she said he was dead when she got here."

"You think she might have known this Hex Downs character?"

"I don't know."

All Morgan knew was that he hated the idea of Celia having gotten on the stage and leaving town. He hated the idea of Corson talking to her. But at least the son-of-a-bitch hadn't gone with her.

Suddenly another thought hit him. Broom

was right, Jason Isley had said Celia knew the
old man. "My God, you don't think that was her
brother? Jason said Hex Downs went to see the
old man, and Celia went to see the old man. But
she isn't married and her name isn't Downs."

"People can change their names," Broom
said. "Downs might not have been his right
name. Wish you'd have asked her that."

"So do I," Morgan said, feeling even worse.
"Could that have been what Corson wanted
with her? To get her to tell what she knew about
Hex Downs?"

Celia Fair would have given almost anything
to have stayed. Lee Morgan was the first man
she had ever met that she could have remained
with forever. But she had to go back. Her
father's business came first. He had become old
and feeble and, he had signed everything over to
her.

"I've educated you like a man," he told her.
"I've taught you everything about the business.
Now I'd better sign it over, before I get so I can't
sign at all."

So Celia Fair was president and chairman of
the board of Fair Lumber and Ores. Her brother
Hex would have been, but he had gone astray
years ago. Their father had written him off as
the black sheep of the family. "You were always
the smart one, anyhow, my darling Celia," her
father said.

The big Concord stagecoach raced along over
the trail east not making a lot of noise. But like
Celia, everyone inside seemed to be deep in
thought, not wanting to hold conversation with
strangers.

It had been that way coming out, too, but

after many miles, they would loosen up and exchange life stories, destinations, show pictures of children and grandchildren. There were two other women and a man who had been on the stage when it arrived in Lost Canyon. An old man, now apparently sleeping through the bumps and jounces, got on when Celia did.

She had been afraid that Corson wasn't going to let her get on, that he would shake her and drag her away as he had the first time, the day that Lee Morgan had rescued her. At least something wonderful had come out of that frightful experience.

Where would she ever come upon another man so sensitive to a woman's wants and needs? A little shiver went through her just thinking about it. Where would a woman ever find a man who had any idea that a woman could enjoy it, too? A man who would not be shocked to find a decent woman, not a bar girl or a whore, who knew her way around a bed? Lee Morgan, she thought, I hope we meet again.

Suddenly gunfire sounded. The coach swerved and picked up speed, swaying crazily from side to side. The passengers clung to whatever hand-holds they could find. Fear filled the inside of the stage like a fog.

Several more shots were fired, galloping horses' hoofbeats sounded alongside them. Men shouted. The people inside the stage clung to their seats, bouncing as the stage went off the beaten trail.

There were more shots. Then the Concord slowed and stopped.

A man's voice shouted, "Don't do nothing foolish, up there."

A second man added, "Just sit tight and

nobody'll get hurt."

A man with a kerchief tied around his face, so he wouldn't be recognized, stuck his head inside and ordered, "Everybody out."

One of the women began to weep, whimpering, "Oh, no. Oh, no," over and over.

The passengers stepped down one by one. Some of them held their hands up. Someone murmured a prayer. "Hail Mary, Mother of God. . . ."

The old man who boarded in Lost Canyon squeaked, "Don't shoot me, I'm goin' home."

"Nobody's gonna shoot ya, old man," one of the bandits said. He stepped toward them and took Celia by the wrist. "This is what we're after, right here. Where's your bag, lady?"

Celia tried to pull away, then not wanting to get someone shot, pointed to the top of the stage. "The one with the roses. You can have it."

The driver threw it down. "Can't help you, lady. We got orders not to get ourselves killed."

"Smart." The bandit holding onto Celia's wrist picked up the bag.

His partner, holding a rifle, rasped, "Why can't we get a little bonus here?" He poked at one woman's purse. "Pick up a little extra cash, some trinkets."

"Shut up, Axel. We'll take only what was ordered." He waved the passengers back into the stage. "You can go now."

As soon as the others were inside, the driver whipped up the horses and tore away leaving only a cloud of dust and Celia in the hands of the two gunmen.

"What do you want of me?" she asked, trying to control her voice.

The man with the vise grip on her wrist said,

"Just followin' orders." He put his pistol in its holster.

The other rammed his rifle into the holder at the side of his saddle and mounted up. "Want the little lady to ride with me?"

"Get back down here and tie up her hands, stupid."

"I'm not going to run away from you on foot in the desert without any water," Celia said in a reasonable tone, sounding much more calm than she really was. "Where are we going?"

"Shut up," her captor said.

The one called Axel dismounted again and said, "How's she gonna hang on with her hands tied up?"

His partner relented. "Okay, just put her on behind me."

The other man got on his horse and Axel cupped his hands for Celia to put her foot in. "Come on. Unless you want me to grab you and hoist you on."

She complied. There was nothing else to do. In a moment she was on the horse with her skirts hoisted clear above her knees and one of her stockings ruined in the process. She wondered whether she would live to see another pair, or anything else.

Axel gave an appreciative leer at her shapely leg, fastened her carpetbag to his saddle horn, and mounted up. They started back in the direction from which she had come on the stage.

They rode in silence for a long time. The sun beat down on Celia's head, the bonnet helped shade her face, but it made her feel hotter than if the breeze created by trotting along had been allowed to blow through her hair. Perspiration ran between her breasts. The rough ride and sitting in the awkward position behind her captor, having to hang on to him around his waist, made her legs and back ache. She was so uncomfortable she could scarcely feel the fear she knew was inside her. There was no one to save her this time.

Had that loathesome Corson spoken so quietly to her earlier just to point her out to these men, and then sent them to take her? What was going to happen to her?

At least they didn't have the right bag. Her leather case had her name and address on it. The stage company would hold it for her. Her jewels and Hex's note would go on to Salt Lake City to wait for her. If she lived to claim them.

When Celia thought she could no longer bear it, they reached a ranch. The men approached an outbuilding and dismounted. As her captor lifted her down, she practically fell into his hands.

"Better get this little lady a drink of water."

"Me too," the other one said and set off toward a windmill some distance away.

Celia sat on an old bench beside the shack and removed her bonnet. In a few minutes Axel returned with a tin cup of water. He spilled it on her skirt while handing it to her. She didn't care. She felt completely hopeless by this time, but the water revived her. She said, "Thank you," automatically, then wondered why.

They took her inside the shack and pointed to an open steamer trunk. Her heart beat madly. What were they going to do with her? Bury her alive! She would die.

"Get in and lie down," barked the one who always took charge.

She stood still shaking her head. Celia was not a woman who cried easily, nor was she easily frightened. But tears welled into her eyes and terror gripped her insides. She started to scream, but the man's dirty hand stopped her. "Nobody around to hear you, anyhow."

"Hey." He took hold of her arm. "It won't be for long. Nothing's gonna happen to you. We don't want anybody to see you come back to town. If you're going to raise cain, we can always dope you up. Or hit you over the head."

There was an old quilt on the bottom of the trunk. The man urged her forward with a grip on both her arms.

She made a slight move to fight back, but he lifted her easily into the trunk and pushed her so that she lay down on her side, curled up. "I won't be able to breathe."

"You'll be able to breathe, but it'll go hard on you if you make a lot of noise before we get there."

He closed the cover and she heard the hasp click down and something push through to secure it. She realized she was holding her breath. She started to breathe again with a sob.

They picked up the trunk and moved it, setting it on something, possibly a wagon, which then began to move. It was a sore and bumpy ride. It went on and on forever. It hurt her shoulder and her hip. Her head drummed with pain. The trunk was getting stuffy. She was going to die after all. She started to call out. She made only a small noise, but she kicked with her heel at the back of the trunk.

The wagon stopped. The lid opened. She started to sit up and tell them she couldn't breathe. Suddenly a rag was clamped over her face. She tried to fight it off.

Chloroform was the last word she thought of.

She woke dizzy, nauseated and tied to a chair. There was a gag in her mouth so she couldn't speak.

She tried to take slower breaths so she wouldn't be sick with the horrid rag bound into her mouth. She stared around trying to see where she was. The lace curtained windows across the room showed the dimming light of late evening.

Lace curtains? The hotel! The same hotel where Lee Morgan had a room? It must be. She was in the hotel in Lost Canyon.

She must try to get her senses clear, so she could think. She must find a way to bring help.

Someone put a key in the lock and opened the door. It was the bossy kidnaper. "Axel's bringing you something to eat. Then there's someone who'll want to talk to you."

Celia suddenly realized, with a shock of fear, that these men had pulled the bandanas down from their faces as soon as the stage had left her with them in the desert. They had not cared from then on that she could see their faces. She didn't know who they were, but she could see them. They would kill her at the end of whatever they were after, so she wouldn't recognize them later. She was going to die.

"We're gonna take this out of your mouth. If you scream, I'll fix you so you'll really have something to scream about. You got that?"

Celia nodded.

He took the gag out of her mouth. He untied her hands. Axel came with soup and bread and coffee. "I didn't spill much," he said.

She took a sip of the coffee, at least getting

the rag taste out of her mouth. She thought she would be sick, but somehow managed not to be. "Why am I here?"

"Somebody wants to see you."

"Could I wash my face?" Her hands shook so she had trouble holding the coffee cup. She set it down. She couldn't think well enough to know what to do. If they untied her feet from the chair legs, would she be able to find a way to get away? Or would they put her back to sleep?

6

The sleepy-eyed waitress came to take Broom's order for breakfast, but she directed her smile at Morgan. "Can I get you anything more, Mr. Morgan?"

"Maybe more coffee."

"Yes. Yes, right away. Sorry, I should have refilled your cup sooner." The flustered waitress hurried away for the pot.

"You never fail to charm them all, Morgan." Broom directed a sly look at his friend. "Especially Celia Fair?"

"I didn't charm Celia enough. She left."

"Think she could be Down's sister? If she is, there's a good chance she knows something."

"And she's taking what she knows back to Boston."

"Maybe she doesn't care about the gold or maybe. . . ." Broom frowned. "Maybe she didn't know why her brother needed help, if he was her brother."

The waitress flirted openly with Morgan when she refilled his cup. Then, as if it were an afterthought, poured more coffee into Broom's half full cup.

"Thanks for the great service, Florrie," Broom said. "Now I'll have to put more sugar in." He laughed. "And I won't know how much, you've got me all mixed up."

The burly man over at the counter finished his breakfast and paid. She thanked him profusely for the generous tip. "Just want to be friendly, little lady," he said and eyed the young girl from her slim waist to her neck.

Morgan watched, amused. She was a friendly kid, probably not yet seventeen. Her eyes reflected a kind of loneliness not unfamiliar to him.

Morgan's glance roamed around the restaurant. The six other tables, covered with worn oil cloth, were empty except that each held a can of condensed milk, punctured with two holes, and shakers of pepper and salt. No one sat at the counter now.

Florrie leaned against the jam of the door leading to the kitchen, where now and then a dish clattered as if it were being stacked with others to dry.

Morgan sipped at his coffee waiting for Broom to finish eating. Not much of a breakfast crowd. He dragged out his Waterbury. Nearly nine o'clock. Probably most had come and gone.

Through the glass in the door, he saw Corson approach. Automatically he felt for his Bisley Colts, then relaxed. He noticed Broom did the same. Morgan chided himself. They were both getting jumpy. That was a fast way to get yourself killed. Corson had as much right to come into the cafe as anyone else.

Corson came into the restaurant and slowly, it seemed to Morgan, closed the door behind himself. Damn, he was an ox of a man, and the anger that screwed up his ugly face was not reassuring.

Corson came straight toward their table. Like cracking a whip, he snaked his forty-five from its holster and pointed it at Morgan. Lee heard Florrie start to cry out, the end of her cry muffled, as if she had put her hand over her mouth as she retreated to the kitchen.

Corson leveled his gun at Morgan's head. "Celia said she left her bag with a friend. She didn't have a lot of friends. Ole is dead, that leaves you. I want it."

Morgan's mind whirled. Had Celia told Corson that when she left this morning? What if Corson was her brother? No, she'd said her brother was dead. If she told him she'd left the bag, why hadn't he come on to Morgan sooner, like in his room right after the stage left? There, he wouldn't have had an audience. "Is that why you tore up my room yesterday?"

"I didn't tear up your damn room. That bag is your death warrant unless you turn it over."

Corson had the drop on them. Morgan tried to look nonchalant, but he sure didn't feel that way. "I don't have any bag. She probably took it with her when she left on the morning coach."

He saw Corson's finger tighten on the trigger. "Now, you son-of-a-bitch," he barked, "I want that bag!"

Lee felt Broom tense beside him, felt the miniscule movement of his hand toward his gun. Broom was fast, but didn't he realize he couldn't outdraw a man with a forty-five already in his hand?

Corson must have seen Broom's movement. He aimed the gun at Broom's head. "Try it and I'll splash your brains all over the floor."

Broom tried it. Two simultaneous shots exploded. Morgan dropped to the floor and whipped out his Bisley. Corson had been right about Broom. The forty-five had blown a hole in Broom's brow and splattered the back of his head all over the floor behind him.

Morgan raised his Bisley Colts to gun the killer down.

He squinted at Corson in disbelief. Corson, shocked surprise on his face, clutched at a neat round hole in his chest, just over his heart, and slowly sank to the floor.

Broom's hand still gripped his pistol, only halfway out of the holster.

Morgan rolled, landed crouched, but on his feet. "Who the hell. . . ?"

The only other person in sight stood at the kitchen door, a weapon still in his hand. "Jason!" Lee bellowed. "Put that damned thing away."

"He was going to kill you," Jason babbled. "He wanted to kill both of you."

Outside people yelled. "Shooting. There's a shooting in the cafe."

Morgan sprinted toward Jason. The door to the cafe opened slowly, as if the person on the other side didn't want to be a victim too. Morgan grabbed Jasons gun and tossed it underhand. It thudded almost noiselessly into the kitchen garbage bucket. "Keep your mouth shut," he ordered.

Jason backed away, apparently still in awe of what he had done.

Morgan went back to the table, bent over and jerked Broom's gun from its holster and let it drop on the floor. He and Broom went back a long way. Later, there would be time for remembering. Right now he had to convince the sheriff of a downright lie.

Corson groaned.

He wasn't quite dead, but he soon would be. Morgan stooped down beside him. "Where's the gold, Corson. It won't do you any good now."

"Doctor," Corson rasped. Blood trickled from the corner of his mouth.

"You're dying, Corson, you know you are. Maybe your partners arranged it, whoever sent you in after me. Tell me where it is, and I'll see that the greedy bastards don't get it."

Apparently Brant Corson realized it was over. "Don't know." His next words were almost inaudible, but Morgan leaned close and caught them. "Celia knows," he said. Then his eyes rolled up, and Corson was staring blankly at the ceiling of the cafe.

Sheriff Bert Tyler, brandishing a bulky revolver, pushed the spectators aside and plunged into the cafe. "What's going on in here?" he demanded.

Morgan holstered his gun. "Guess they were enemies from way back," he said calmly.

The sheriff looked at Broom without flinching, then down at Corson. "He never was very smart," he said.

By then a dozen townspeople crowded into the cafe. At the kitchen door, Florrie, the waitress, her eyes round with shock, stood beside Jason. Morgan caught Jason's eye and gave him a silent warning to keep out of it.

The sheriff holstered his gun. "Any witnesses?"

"Just me, I guess," Morgan said. "You know Broom was fast. Corson should have watched him closer. I thought Corson had him beat."

The sheriff pointed a finger at Morgan. "You seem to be right in the middle of every killing

lately. I told you to get out of town. If I see you
again, I'll run you out." He paused. "Or maybe
I'll run you in. You got no proof you didn't do it,
if you're the only witness."

"My gun hasn't been fired." He held it out in
the palm of his hand.

The sheriff felt of the barrel, shrugged and
turned to a couple of the townspeople who still
stared at the dead bodies on the floor. "You
two," he said, indicating two rough-looking men
nearby. "Get these bodies out of here and over
to the undertaker." Then he turned and left.

When he was out of sight, Jason rushed over
to Morgan. "I . . . I never did that before," he
stammered. "I never killed. . . ."

Morgan shushed him, then looked down at
Broom. "Old Hank should have known better
than try to draw when Corson had the drop on
us."

"He was trying to save your life."

"I know. He's done it before."

Morgan pushed Jason back into the kitchen.
"Get your gun, you may need it. Where did you
learn to shoot like that?"

Jason dug his gun out of the trash can and
wiped it off before holstering it. "Gramps
taught me. He believed everybody should know
how to shoot straight. Do you think Corson
intended to kill you?"

"He looked like it."

"I think he was really after Broom," Jason
said. "Anybody who knew Broom knew he
could be reckless if he was provoked and there
was bad blood between those two. I think
Corson wanted to kill Broom ever since he got
to town."

"Or without Broom to back me up, maybe

Corson figured I'd get out of town."

"Think the sheriff meant what he said?"

"Guess I'll stay away from my room at the hotel for a little while, just in case the sheriff or anybody else gets any ideas. You got a room here in town I can use while I get my thoughts straightened out?"

"Sure. I've got the back room here at the cafe, come on." Jason led Lee to a storeroom behind the kitchen. One small window let in a little sunlight, showing a neatly made cot and boxes stacked to make shelves for his clothes. "It's not much, but I get it as part of my pay for working in the kitchen."

Morgan sat down on the edge of the cot. The blanket was clean, and he noticed the floor had been swept. Gramps had taught Jason more than how to shoot a gun and read a book.

With Broom and Celia gone, Morgan thought, he had no friends in Lost Canyon. He'd have to watch his back every minute. Maybe he should move on. But he could sure use that gold if he could find it, and he still hadn't found the son-of-a-bitch who ransacked his room.

Jason sat on the one chair in the room, which looked like a spare from the restaurant. Morgan noticed him squeezing his hands nervously. He couldn't leave the kid alone. If the sheriff got hold of him, he'd break and admit to the shooting, sure as hell, wrought up as he was.

Florrie burst through the door. "Corson's brother Joe, and three of his ranch hands just rode in to town. They're at the undertaker's place."

Jason jumped to his feet and shoved a worn felt hat on his head. "I'll face them. I'll tell big Joe how it was."

"And you'll get shot down." Morgan gripped Florrie's shoulders. "We're leaving by the back door. Corson's brother will be over here. Stick to the story that Corson and Broom shot each other, if anybody asks. Can you do that? If you don't, it's all up for Jason."

Florrie's gaze flew to Jason. Morgan wasn't surprised at the warmth it displayed. "I can do it." She pushed Jason and Morgan toward the back door. "Stay behind the buildings to the livery and nobody will see you."

Jason hesitated. The front door of the cafe burst open, and Florrie ran to serve them. "Where's the tall guy who saw the shooting? The bastard who said Broom shot my brother. He's a damn liar! He's the one Brant was after."

Morgan shoved Jason out the back door. "Come on," he growled. "There are times when honesty is not the best policy."

Once outside, Jason's hesitation vanished. "They think you did it." He lowered his head to stay out of sight through the back window of the saloon, and ran ahead of Morgan to the end of the row of buildings and across the street. They found cover again behind the buildings on that side until they got to the stables.

"Let them think it."

Inside the stable, Willie, the ten year old with the dog smiled broadly when Jason and Morgan came in. "You gonna teach me how to use the whip today?"

"Not today. We've got to leave as fast as we can." Morgan stooped down and talked earnestly to the boy. "If anyone asks you if you've seen us, will you tell them we haven't been here?"

The boy nodded solemnly. "I won't tell." Then

he scurried around helping them saddle up. "I promise I won't tell, no matter what, and Pa's not here. I'm in charge."

Jason patted the boy's dog before he and Morgan cautiously led their horses out the rear door.

"We can't go up to the cabin, not with close to four miles of open ground to cover before we get to the timber." Morgan pointed. "How about those trees? What's beyond them?"

"The quarry. There's caves up there."

Without further comment, Morgan spurred his horse into a gallop and in minutes they were within cover of the live oaks. Then he let Jason lead the way.

They followed rusty iron tracks, obviously put in to cart rock down to the town, for close to half a mile through the trees, then they stopped on the rim of the quarry. Endless piles of broken rock littered both sides of the stretch of tramway. At the end of the tracks three holes, that appeared to be caves, offered them cover.

Morgan reached for his canteen and shook it. "The kid must have filled them. Is he a good friend of yours?"

"There's not much to do evenings after the cafe closes. We play cards some. And we went rabbit hunting together a couple of times."

They headed for the far cave. The horses' hooves raised an acrid dust. Morgan could smell it and taste it on his lips. "How long since you've been up here?"

"Been a while. I used to come and watch them blast rock from the side of the hill. The town built a new jail with the rocks, but the mortar didn't hold and two men escaped. That about ended the rock business."

Jason led the way to the mouth of the cave, dismounted and led his horse inside. Morgan followed. "This is the deepest one," Jason said. "It will keep the horses out of sight."

Inside, Morgan stared uneasily at the rock walls and ceiling. Several long cracks suggested danger of a cave-in, especially if they were disturbed by gunfire. And Morgan had no doubt that Corson's brother and his three ranch hands would come looking for them. They hadn't covered their trail.

At least Jason and Morgan had time on their side. It would take a while for Joe Corson to figure out where they had gone.

They sat down on the floor of the cave, far enough in to be out of sight, but still able to see any approaching riders.

Jason fiddled nervously with his gun, making sure it was fully loaded, checking it again. "I never killed a man before. I feel creepy all over. Does it ever go away?"

Morgan leaned back against the wall of the cave and perched his tan Stetson on his knee. "Sometimes it never goes away, especially if you feel you made a mistake."

"Did I make a mistake when I shot Corson? He would have killed you, too. I'm sorry about Broom. He was your friend from a long time ago, wasn't he?"

"He saved my life once." Morgan smiled remembering. "I hung around his place for a spell after that. But yes, that was a very long time ago."

Morgan sighed and was quiet for a while. Then he began again. "He got a gang together and they held up stage coaches and robbed a bank or two. That's when he wouldn't see me any more. Told me to be on my way. I might have joined his gang, but he wouldn't let me, said I was too young. Said I was too soft for killing."

"Are you?" Jason asked.

"Not when it's necessary."

Morgan dragged out his Waterbury and checked the time. Nearly two o'clock. It was cool in the cave, so he couldn't tell it was mid-afternoon. He didn't want to talk any more about Hank Broom, it made his gut hurt. Soft? Broom's big heart, standing up for a friend again, did him in.

Suddenly Morgan stiffened, every sense on alert. "Horses," he whispered. "Do you think Willie talked?"

"Not unless his pa beat him half to death."

"Is his pa a friend of Sheriff Tyler?"

"No, he hates him, but he's scared of him, and he hasn't got the guts to stand up to him."

Felipe, Jason's horse whinnied. Jason jumped to his feet and clapped his hand on the horse's muzzle. "Quiet, boy," he soothed. Felipe quieted down.

The sound of hoofbeats came closer. Morgan took the Spencer rifle out of his saddle boot. Guns cocked, Morgan and Jason took places just inside the mouth of the cave.

The riders, Joe Corson and three of his ranch hands, stopped at the rim of the quarry. Their horses pawed the sand, eager to advance. The men talked, but there was no way Morgan or Jason could hear what they said from at least a hundred yards away.

The riders separated, two taking one side of the quarry, the other two advancing along the rock wall of the other side. Once again, Morgan glanced at the long cracks in the rocks inside their cave.

Jason noticed. "We could get buried alive, couldn't we?"

Morgan nodded. "I suppose. Don't fire unless you have to."

"Maybe they won't know we're here."

"They know. All they need to do is look at the fresh prints in the sand. But they obviously don't know which cave we're in."

"This is the only one big enough to hide the horses."

"We're not sure they know that." Morgan didn't want the boy to panic. He was in a bad enough state over his first kill. "We'll just be quiet."

They watched two men dismount and creep to the edge of the far cave. Gunfire exploded. They were testing.

Lee and Jason remained quiet.

The two men on the opposite side of the quarry galloped along the rock face toward their friends. Morgan and Jason edged back out of sight as they passed within ten feet of them. The four men disappeared into the other cave.

Jason moved back into place to see better. "Wonder what they're doing in there." he said softly. "Maybe they're looking for the gold."

"Was Brant Corson that close to his brother?"

"Joe's a ranch owner. Brant worked for him sometimes, but mostly Brant hung around town, around Sheriff Tyler's office."

"Brant knew about the gold, so the sheriff probably does, too. If the others who know have figured out that you know, you better watch yourself."

Two of the men emerged from the far cave, then the other two followed. They walked, kind of bunched together, toward the mouth of the second cave.

"They're getting too close," Morgan whispered. "Aim carefully, so we don't get too much return fire. Don't shoot to kill, unless you have to. Get them in the leg or thigh or the hand, just enough to send them running."

Morgan raised his Spencer rifle. Jason took careful aim with a hand gun. "Now," Morgan ordered. A volley of shots exploded, as fast as the two could fire.

None of the men had time to draw, they were busy hopping around, holding a shot-up foot off the ground, or cursing and grabbing a shoulder. Only Joe Corson, who brought up the rear, appeared not to be hit.

The three injured men dropped to the ground, all trying to hold their injuries and draw their guns at the same time. These were ranch hands, not expert gunnies. For several seconds, Joe Corson crouched behind them. When he realized his men could not protect him, he attempted to make the long dash for the cave they had just left.

Morgan placed two rifle shots against the rocks in front of Joe. He skidded to a stop. He looked around frantically for cover. There was none. He grabbed his horse, mounted and leaned in over it. The horse moved fast. Lee held his fire. From that distance and a fast moving target, he would probably injure only the horse. He didn't want to do that.

When the three ranch hands saw Joe heading out, they scrambled for their horses as best they could, holstered their weapons and rode away.

Jason leaned against the wall of the cave and let his breath out in a long sigh of relief. "Think they'll be back?"

"No. I don't think Joe Corson is anxious to get himself killed even to avenge his brother. He moved pretty fast out of here." Morgan glanced at the sun. Mid afternoon. "I think we better get out of here too, before somebody decides to tear up my room again."

"Your room? When?"

"Before we got back from Gramp's cabin."

"What did they take?"

"They didn't find what they were looking for."

Jason frowned. "Could it have been the same person who killed Gramps? They tore up his cabin looking for something, you know."

"It all boils down to one thing," Morgan said. "The gold. A lot of people in this town seem to know about it, including you. If we're going to catch whoever killed Gramps, you have to tell me everything you know about the gold."

They were through the trees and the town of Lost Canyon lay ahead, before Jason finally spoke. "I don't know how your friend, Broom, found out about it, but Gramps told me some gold had been stolen off a train near Sacramento. He read it in the newspaper. He gets them . . . I mean, *got* them late, after his friend in town has read 'em. Gramps said he figured Hex Downs was the robber that got away."

"But he didn't turn him in to the sheriff. I thought Gramps was a law abiding citizen."

"Nobody trusts Sheriff Tyler, especially not the ranchers. They've been trying to get him to leave, but he won't go. And nobody wants to go up against his fast gun, or his cronies." Jason shrugged. "So I guess he'll just stay until he decides to leave."

"That's it? That's all you know?"

Jason was silent. Morgan had the feeling that although Jason liked him, he had not yet decided whether to trust him.

"Well, the sheriff wants to see me out of town." As they rode into the main street, Morgan headed for the livery stable. "I have to go see the undertaker. It's over at the furniture store isn't it?"

Jason nodded. Then as they dismounted, he stood close to Morgan and said. "I think Gramps knew things he didn't tell me. He thought it could be dangerous for me."

It could be dangerous for anybody who knew too much. Suddenly, Morgan was glad that Celia Fair had gotten out of town.

7

Morgan found the undertaker at the funeral parlor connected to the furniture store. Called Goodrun, he was a long lean old fellow in a black suit who spoke in a monotone. Morgan talked with Goodrun about the proper arrangements for his friend's burial.

"Hank Broom's been in town before for different spells. He's acquainted, that is, *was* acquainted with more people here than I am," Morgan said. "Suppose some of them might want to know."

"They'll know," the old undertaker said.

Morgan returned to the cafe.

Jason had been watching for his return and came out of the kitchen to meet him. "You aren't leavin' town, are you? On account of Hank Broom gettin' killed and Corson's brother coming after us?"

"Hadn't planned to just yet," Morgan growled, and in an even lower voice, he drawled, "For one thing, that Sheriff Tyler is too eager to have me go. Outside of him and the Corson gang, the rest of the townspeople I've met so far don't seem to find me objectionable. Believe I'll hang around awhile and figure out why the sheriff feels the way he does."

Jason drew himself up as tall as possible and grinned broadly. "I was hopin' you'd say that!"

"Yeah?"

"I want to help you find the you-know-what." Jason glanced around to see who was close enough to hear.

"Well, I suppose that would be all right. If you think I need help."

"The way things around here been going, you'll need somebody protectin' your butt, Jason declared. "Or at least someone who knows the territory."

"You have a point there. When do you get through working today?" Morgan wanted to know.

"I'm all caught up for now. I might have to come back." They sat at one of the tables in the almost empty restaurant. The young waitress, Florrie, brought them steaming cups of coffee and smiled sweetly at Jason.

When she had left them alone, Morgan asked, "What do you know about it anyhow, Jason?"

"You mean the gold? Nothing."

"Not just the gold, but all the people that might have had something to do with it. Might have had their hands on it or wanted to get their hands on it." Morgan pushed his hat to the back of his head. "Hex Downs came to see your Gramps. Celia Fair went to see your Gramps. What did they have to do with each other?"

"Hex was dead by the time his sister got here."

"His sister." Morgan nodded thoughtfully. "I wondered about that. She said something about coming to help her brother and that he was dead by the time she got out here. She just failed to say who her brother was." He gazed out the window for a long moment.

People who went by outside slowed to stare in, as if the news of the shooting had made its way around town.

Finally Morgan continued speculating. "It's possible that Hex Downs told the old man something and the old man in turn told Celia."

"I don't know," Jason insisted. "Gramps never said."

"No, but Corson obviously thought she knew something about it, because that was the last thing the bastard said. With his dying breath."

"It must be true, if he said it when he was dying," Jason said earnestly. "They always tell the truth then."

"I suppose." Morgan stood up. "When can we go back out to your cabin? We've got to see if there's something hidden out there."

Morgan paid for the breakfasts he and Broom had eaten before the shooting.

"I knew you wouldn't forget," the waitress told him. "I'm sorry about your friend. But I can't say the same about the other one."

"Right."

"Minute I saw him come in, before I even knew he had his gun in his hand, I went right out to the kitchen and told Jason."

Morgan nodded.

" 'There's gonna be trouble,' I told him."

"Appreciate that, Florrie," Morgan said. "Maybe you saved my life, who knows. You and Jason, here. If he hadn't got Corson, I might have been next."

"And I appreciate you not saying anything different to the sheriff, too," Jason put in.

"With Sheriff Tyler, it's just as well to let him think what he thinks," Florrie said scornfully.

"He's never been known to be right, yet, has he?"

Jason gave Florrie a shy grin and followed Morgan out of the cafe. They stood in the sun in front of the building for a moment. "Think we could ride out there some time today? Your Gramps could have had the gold stashed away for Hex Downs all along. Only nobody has looked in the right place yet."

"I've been thinking about that, Mr. Morgan."

"Drop the mister, kid."

"All right, uh, Lee. Anyhow, what I thought was that Gramps didn't have the gold. But he might have known where it was. He could have left some kind of a clue. He was a clever old guy." Jason smiled remembering. "We used to play games. He'd make up games for learning stuff, like 'rithmetic games and spelling games. And if I couldn't get the answers right off, he'd give me clues to help me figure things out."

"Sounds like a possibility all right. When can we go back out there?" Morgan clapped the boy on the shoulder. "I don't want to go prowling around *your* place all by myself."

"I'll get the time off. I haven't taken any time for a while. When you want to go?"

"I'll go over to the hotel, get my gear and meet you at the livery stable, if you're sure you can fix it up to get off work."

As they stood there, two riders left town at a canter heading northwest.

"You know those two?" Morgan wanted to know.

Jason shook his head. "Could be some more of Corson's brother's ranch hands. The Corson ranch is closest one to town. But it's east of town, opposite of what they were heading. No, I don't know who they are."

"Didn't look like any of that lot that were after us," Morgan commented. "Besides, those sorry s.o.b.s need time to heal up."

They parted and Morgan went over to the hotel. As he started for his room, Essie Rowe called to him from behind the reception desk. "See you for a minute, Mr. Morgan?"

"Sure." He went over to the desk and took off his Stetson. "What can I do for you, Mrs. Rowe?"

"I heard about Hank Broom."

Morgan nodded. "He owing some on his room when he died?" Morgan reached into his pocket. He probably had barely enough left to pay his own way.

"No, no! It isn't that," Essie said. "Goodness, no. We wouldn't think of. . . ."

"With the number of people passin' away around here lately, you could go broke not thinking of that," he told her.

Although there was no one else in the hotel lobby, Essie lowered her voice. "He left something for you."

"He did?"

"When he first checked in, he left this package." From under the counter, she drew a thin packet wrapped in butcher paper and tied with a string. "He said if anything happened to him, we were to give it to you. So I wrote your name on it and here it is."

Morgan took the package. It had his name on the outside, in Essie Rowe's neat penmanship. "Thank you."

"He must have been real sure of your coming, because it was before you even got here. We hadn't even met you. He told us your name and said you'd be here, and if anything ever happened to him, you were to have it."

"Yes, ma'am. Will you be needing any help with getting his things out of his room?"

"No. He had a steamer trunk and it's addressed to his papa, the Reverend Mr. Broom in I-ow-ay. So we'll send it on the Wells Fargo, whenever they come through. Probably Tuesday week."

Morgan nodded and picked up his hat from the counter.

"Don't usually have people to bring trunks with them," Essie chatted on. "But another man came in with one just yesterday. Had a friend helpin' him lug it in. Looked to be heavy."

"Maybe he brought his books along. Books are heavy," Morgan said. "I knew a professor fellow once, lugged his books wherever he went."

"He didn't look like any professor." Essie shook her head. "But I'm glad this one had help with his. Don't want Jeb's back going bad on him again."

Morgan nodded, put on his hat and went upstairs to his room.

After bolting the door, he sat down on the edge of the bed and untied the string, laid back the butcher paper, and found bank notes. Hank had left him a wad of money.

There was a message on lined paper in Hank's labored scrawl. *This is so's you won't of come for nuthin in case somethin hapens to me.*

Hank was not big on spelling. But he had certainly called it right. Something had happened to him.

If you go ahead for the gold, watch out for a guy named Corson.

Corson was dead, Morgan thought. But then Hank had written the note before that. He had written the note before he even knew that Corson would be the first man Morgan would tangle with when he came into the damn town.

Folding the bank notes along with Hank's message, he shoved them deep into a side pants pocket. There was enough there to keep him going for a while, and maybe even to take care of a decent burial for Broom. Now, Morgan thought, if he and Jason could just get close to that damned gold!

Morgan picked up his black snake whip and his rifle and headed for the livery stable. The sun was high in the sky and there wasn't a cloud anywhere.

Jason was already there, horse saddled, waiting for him. "Don't have to go in again until late tomorrow. I brought along some grub." He patted a saddlebag.

"Good. Let's go." Morgan got the bay gelding ready and mounted up.

Riding up to the cabin, Morgan kept a sharp look out. He didn't relish the thought of another run-in of the type he'd had making the trip with Hank Broom. It didn't take them as long to get there, since they had no Indian fights or other trouble along the way. But as they neared the property, they found fresh hoof prints on the trail.

"Has there been more traffic along here than I remembered?" Morgan asked. "Or am I skittery?"

"Somebody's up there right now," Jason said. "I can tell by the way Felipe acts."

"You've had that horse a long time, I'll bet," Morgan guessed. "When you have a horse a long time, he'll talk to you. So I'd believe the horse."

They slowed and peered through the trees. Although they saw no one, Jason dismounted. "Let's go round back."

Morgan agreed and they led their horses for a way, then looped their reins around a couple of low limbs, continuing without the mounts. Morgan took his rifle with him. Jason had one of his revolvers in hand.

They crept quietly through the trees being careful not to make unnecessary noise in the underbrush. About a hundred yards out in the timber, as they came even with the back corner of the building, they could see the shed and the area at the rear of the cabin.

Behind the cabin were two men. They appeared to be the two that Morgan had seen riding out earlier. One of them was about to climb in through the rear window.

"Hold it, right there," Jason shouted.

He was premature with his demand. They were still a little too far away. However, the startled man fell back out of the window. The other one ran for his horse.

Jason fired, although he was out of range. The man on the ground scrambled away crabwise, trying to regain his feet. Morgan took aim with the rifle. He got off one shot when he realized that Jason was running toward the cabin.

"Get down, you fool," Morgan yelled and took another shot at the man who had dropped to the ground still scrambling.

The intruder finally made it to his feet and as he started to run, he turned and fired once before he got to his horse. His shot was short and went wide as well.

Morgan saw red spurt from the man's

shoulder. I may have winged him, he thought.

Jason ran for the cabin, firing and yelling. But the two men had already reached their horses and made good their escape around the corner of the building and out of sight down the trail on the other side.

Morgan strolled on up to the back door of the cabin looking disgusted.

"Oh, well," Jason said, kicking at the dirt with the toe of his boot. "I've shot enough guys for today anyhow."

Morgan relented and grinned at him. "I like a man that can laugh at himself when he makes a bone-head play like that."

"I guess I should have been closer," Jason admitted sheepishly.

"At least we came on them before they got in. So they didn't get anything."

"Probably took them a long time to find their way," Jason said. "I'm glad it did."

They went back to where they had tied their horses and brought them around behind the shed where there was a water barrel and fresh grazing.

Jason said nothing the whole time. Morgan could see his mind was busy with memories of Gramps and their years together, so he let the silence be.

When they'd taken the saddles off and put their gear inside the lean-to, they went into the cabin. Everything was as they had left it the day before.

It was almost nightfall by the time they had gone through everything in the cabin again, searched the shed, and come up empty.

"I can't understand it," Jason said finally. "I thought sure there would be some kind of sign, some clue."

"How did your Gramps usually make these clues when he was teaching you stuff?"

"Oh, he'd draw a picture, something like that." Jason's face took on a faraway look again. "Sometimes in summer, like it was today, we'd be out under the trees with a breeze ruffling the book pages and the papers."

"You studied in the summer?"

"Sure. Gramps said it was always good to be ahead when the next schoolmarm showed up. And he never let me give up." He shrugged, as if trying to relate to Morgan instead of Gramps. Finally he straightened. "Well, we don't have to give up either. Let's have something to eat and stay here tonight."

"Sure. We can go out and see that the horses have a good place for the night. And maybe we can have a look around on the outside, before it gets too dark."

They went out and while Jason took care of the horses and the mule, Morgan walked all the way around the cabin, admiring the way it was built. There were marks that showed where the logs had been checked to set together. Nicks and scratches and chisel gouges that had lasted through the years. Then he found something that had nothing to do with the way the logs went together and although it was not that fresh, neither had it weathered for years.

He studied it for a moment, then called Jason over. "What's this supposed to be?"

Jason frowned and ran his fingers over the carving in the wood. "I never saw that before. Done with a knife. Like you'd carve your initials in a tree."

"Looks recent. But not today or yesterday."

"Done since I lived here."

"What is it supposed to be? Can you tell?"

"It's like an Indian picture. It could be a hill. No, a rainbow. With an arrow at one end," Jason said.

"And a tepee," Morgan finished for him.

"At the end of a rainbow, there's supposed to be a pot of gold." Jason jumped up and down. "It's the clue. I bet Gramps put it there after Hex Downs was killed. Wish he'd a told me."

"From here, the arrow's pointing to the northwest. Is it supposed to be aiming at the tepee?"

"Maybe toward the Indian camp," Jason said.

"Those Indians Broom and I had a run-in with?" Morgan thought they would not have a hell of a lot of luck if they decided the gold was in one of those tepees.

"Gramps was friendly with the Chief. Gramps always got along fine with the Indians. Especially with Chief Greatfoot."

Jason pulled out provisions he had brought along from the cafe, and they went back into the cabin. The boy made a small fire in the old stove and put on a pot of water for coffee. They lit the kerosene lantern, ate cheese and bread and meat, and drank coffee.

"How the hell we going to find out?" Morgan wanted to know.

"There's one Indian from the tribe who works in Lost Canyon. He's read the law. He even makes speeches sometimes. And he's been clear to Washington to see the president. Maybe we can get him to take us to the chief."

"I sure want to talk to that chief," Morgan said. "Can you see this guy when we get back to town in the morning?"

"First thing," Jason promised. "If he's not

gone on some business out of town. He's gettin'
to be a real big shot, even if he is an Indian.
Name's Grey Stoneagle."

Jason got them some blankets and they
bedded down on the floor. Although they didn't
speak of it, neither of them seemed to want to
sleep on the bed where they had found old
Gramps.

Morgan put his black snake whip and his
gunbelt with the Bisley Colts, along with the
rifle, by his side and lay down. He thought
about the gold for a little while, wondering
about the Indian chief and what good it would
do to see him.

In a little while he began to think about Celia
Fair and wishing she hadn't gone off on the
stage to Salt Lake City, to take the train to
Chicago and Boston. He was feeling horny again
already, and she had been so good.

So beautiful and so good. She'd learned it all
from her Swedish nanny? He didn't like to think
of her wasting it on some other man that she
might meet in Chicago. Or Boston. God, what
ailed him, anyhow. Lee Morgan didn't go
mooning around after some woman he'd had.

She was gone. She'd had her fling and left to
take care of her father's business. He would
probably never see her again, so he had better
forget her and get on with his life and his search
for the gold.

8

Morgan and Jason woke late and had coffee and biscuits, then saddled up for the ride back to town. Before they went, they found some paper and a stub of a pencil with which Morgan made a sketch of the carving he had found on the log at the back corner of the cabin. He studied it for some time after he had drawn it on the paper. He compared it to the symbols carved in the log and decided it was near enough. Then he folded it and put it in the pocket with Hank's money and note.

Why would anyone want to hide gold in a tepee? Would Hex or Gramps, either one, have trusted the old Indian chief that much? After all, the Indians could have used the gold. They might not have had as much know-how about where to have it melted down and put in more exchangeable sizes, the way Hex Downs would have, but Morgan couldn't imagine either himself or Broom trusting an Indian like that—not even a Chief.

Maybe it was just the secret that lay with the chief? Or another clue? They would have to find a way to meet with him to discover whether he had any such information.

While Morgan was making the drawing,

Jason took a broom and whisked at the dirt by
the back door, across the trail as it led up to the
front door, and anywhere else he thought
hoofprints would show up, if someone came to
the cabin before he did the next time.

"Good work," Morgan said. "You're a smart
kid, Jason."

"Sometimes I have an idea or two," Jason
said. "Sure can't figure out why Gramps would
leave what we're looking for with the old chief.
'Specially with his son being such an enemy of
the whites and next in line to run the tribe. The
old chief could die off. . . ." He let that thought
fade, apparently thinking again of the fact that
his Gramps was gone.

It was afternoon when they finally got back to
Lost Canyon. Morgan said, "You're going to get
together with this dude Indian that lives in
town, huh?"

"I'll find him. I told you, his name is Grey
Stoneagle. He lives over the barber shop, I
think. I'm sure he used to. Anyhow, the barber
will know."

"If you find him soon enough, maybe he'll be
able to take us to see the chief by tomorrow.
What do you think?"

Jason nodded. "I'll try. Then I'll go to work,
so I can get off again tomorrow to go."

"Good. You sure this town Indian gets along
okay with the rest of them? That chief's son
might recognize me from before."

"He won't do anything about it if we're
escorted in," Jason said. "He does things his
father doesn't approve of when he's away from
the camp. But I don't think he'd defy him, if
Grey Stoneagle gets the chief's permission
first."

Morgan put his horse in the livery, took his black snake and started out the door.

Sheriff Tyler came stomping down the street and stopped when he saw Morgan. "You still here?"

"Gotta wait around till I get Hank Broom properly put under the ground, Sheriff." Morgan narrowed his eyes at the sheriff, daring him to try to drive him out of town in the face of his obvious concern for a dead friend's burial.

"Likely get that taken care of today, won't you? Awful warm this week. Wouldn't want to wait too long." The sheriff's lip curled into a sneer and he moved on.

The stableman's son, Willie, and his dog, stood at the corner of the building watching. The livery owner remained inside, but Morgan knew he had been within hearing range.

Morgan waited until the lawman was well past, then turned to the boy. "You know an Indian fellow, name of Stoneagle, that keeps a place here in town, Willie?"

"I might," the boy said, eyeing Morgan cagily.

"Just wondered where a person might get in touch with him."

The boy said nothing.

Morgan took a coin from his pocket and flipped it in the air, catching it and flipping it again.

The boy got to his feet. "I see him sometimes."

"Well, I'd like to see him, myself."

Morgan flipped the coin again, this time toward Willie who caught it and smiled broadly. "I'll probably see him."

As Morgan turned to leave, the boy called after him, "Had my druthers, I'd like to learn about that whip of yourn, Mr. Morgan."

"We'll see."

Morgan went down the street to the hotel. He stopped and asked at the desk whether Nelly was filling the tub that afternoon.

"She could do that," Jeb said. "Right away."

"Thanks. I'll get ready."

Morgan noticed a woman sitting in one of the lobby chairs. She wore a dark red dress with long sleeves and buttoned high at the neck. Her hair had been swooped up and pinned high on her head and with the afternoon sun coming in side windows of the lobby it made her look as if she wore a halo. She had sharp features, but was not unattractive. Maybe about Morgan's age, she sat quite still, holding onto her reticule and gazing toward the door. Morgan wondered if she were waiting for someone.

She didn't appear to notice him. Usually a woman would at least look at him, so he could nod or tip his Stetson. He went on up the stairs to his room.

Nelly brought water to the bathtub again. Morgan asked her who the woman sitting in the lobby was.

"Said something about Brant Corson," Nelly said. "But her name's not Corson."

"What is her name?"

"Rebecca Petersen," Nelly told him. "Think you know her from somewhere?"

"No, I don't think so. Yet—"

Morgan took off his shirt and winked at the blushing Nelly who picked up her pails and prepared to leave the room.

"Wait just a minute," Morgan said. After he had arranged for Nelly to get a bit of laundry taken care of for him, he gave her enough to pay for that and a small tip.

"Thank you, Mr. Morgan. I'll see these get done up right away."

She left, and Morgan bathed and dressed. Then he went back downstairs.

The woman still sat in the same position assuming the same attitude.

Morgan went up to her. "Excuse me, Madam. Do you know what time it is?"

She started, then glanced up at him. He eyes were bright blue. She looked younger than he had thought at first. Now that the sun was no longer shining in on it, her hair proved to be pale blonde and still looked like a halo, piled high on her head as it was.

"Oh . . . I . . . Maybe." She fingered a watch hanging on a gold chain around her neck. She stared at it, as if surprised to find it there.

"I think it's supper time," Morgan said. "Are you planning to eat your evening meal with someone?"

She shook her head mournfully. "Not any more."

Morgan sat in the chair next to her. "What do you mean?"

"He's dead."

"Oh. That's too bad."

Rebecca Petersen looked at Morgan, as if seeing him for the first time. "Well, maybe it's too bad. He was too bad, too. Did you know him?"

"Who?" Morgan asked.

She was really quite pretty. If, as Nelly had suggested, she had someting to do with Brant Corson, she had something in common with Morgan. They both were left with someone to forget on this pleasant summer evening, just dipping into night.

"Brant Corson," she said. "Did you know him?" she asked again.

"Only by sight," Morgan told her. "I heard he. . . ."

"He was shot." She was quiet for a moment, then added as an afterthought, "Probably with good reason."

She sighed a deep shaky sigh that sounded as if it came clear from her pointy-toed buttoned shoes. The sigh apparently opened the way for more words. "I came over from Reno. I thought Brant had struck it rich out here. He was going to. Instead, I come and find out he's stone dead. I should have come earlier. Damn Bert Tyler!"

Morgan was sure he wanted to hear more about that last remark. "Come across the street and have some dinner with me," he suggested. "We've both been left on our own in a strange town."

"You're alone, too?"

"My friend left town," Morgan said. He stood and put out a hand to help Rebecca Petersen to her feet.

Rebecca accepted. The top of her head came about to Morgan's nose. Just a nice fit. She was thin of waist and hip, but had an ample bosom, outstanding, in fact.

They went over to the cafe and found a table in the back corner. Morgan held Rebecca's chair, then sat where he could watch everyone who came or went. It hadn't done much good to be able to see Brant Corson when he came in the day before. But he liked to be able to see anyhow.

"Little wine to start out with?" Morgan asked. "Or a beer?"

When the woman had tasted a glass of wine, she seemed to relax a little. "I'm going to head for San Francisco when the next stage comes that's going that way."

"You have kin in San Francisco?"

"My daddy lives there. He was right. I never should have left home in the first place."

"So this Corson who was shot yesterday was your—" He let the sentence dangle.

Rebecca picked it up and finished it. "Man. He was my.man. We were together in Reno and did right well, till he got this big idea about coming over here."

"What did you do there?"

"I danced. They had a fancy saloon there with dancing shows. Brant was good at cards and other things."

They were quiet for a stretch during which Florrie came over with the food they had ordered.

"Hope everything is all right," Florrie said, setting down Morgan's plate.

"Everything will be fine," he said. "You always work from morning to night?"

"Pretty much," Florrie didn't sound as if she minded.

"Florrie, this is Rebecca, visiting town from Reno."

The two women acknowledged the introduction.

Morgan asked Florrie, "Jason working this evening?"

"Yes, but he has tomorrow off. Said you might want to know."

"Good."

Florrie left them and Morgan turned his attention to Rebecca Petersen. "How's it going?"

"Fine. I'm feeling better, thanks to you, Mr. Morgan."

"Call me Lee, please."

"All right. If you'll call me. . . ." She hesitated, as if remembering what Corson called her.

"I'll call you Rebecca, if that's all right."

"That's my name. I really don't like nick-names, do you, Lee?"

"Luckily I haven't had to deal with any," he said.

"Corson called me Rebby and I didn't like that," she admitted. "I guess I shouldn't cry about him being gone, or carry on too much. There were a lot of things about Brant Corson I didn't like. But I think Bert Tyler was to blame for all Brant's troubles."

"The sheriff?" Morgan asked, trying to sound surprised.

"We knew him in Reno," Rebecca said. "He wasn't any sheriff then."

When they had finished eating, Morgan asked what she would like to do. "I suppose we could sample some of the great night life in this teeming metropolis of Lost Canyon."

They laughed together. She had a nice laugh, throaty and enduring.

"You're fun . . . Lee." She hesitated before saying his name.

"I like talking to you, too. Maybe we could go somewhere quiet. Find us a bottle and have a little nightcap," Morgan suggested.

Rebecca sat up straighter, raised her eyebrows and appeared to have a brilliant idea. "I have what they call over in Reno, 'an excellent bottle.' It's in my room at the hotel." After hesitating a moment she added, with a smile, "It's brandy. I stole it in Reno before I came here."

Morgan laughed with her again. "That's the best kind." He liked her down-to-earth manner, now that she had relaxed enough to let it out.

He paid the bill, said good night to Florrie, and offered Rebecca his arm as they left the cafe.

They went into the hotel and both picked up their keys at the desk. There was no sense in scandalizing the Rowes by advertising that they were both going to one room.

Rebecca had room twenty-nine down the hall from his, right next door to where he bathed. Actually it was right next door to where everybody on the second floor bathed, the ones who did.

They went in and left the door open while Morgan lighted her kerosene lamp for her. Then Rebecca closed the door and slid the bolt into place. She dug the bottle out of her bureau drawer and to Morgan's surprise brought out two small brandy snifters as well.

Her blue eyes twinkled and she nodded. "Yes. I stole those, too. Thought I was going to do some celebrating."

Morgan opened the bottle for her and poured. "We will do some celebrating. We'll celebrate our new friendship."

She sat on the edge of the bed and Morgan sat beside her.

He ran the brandy glass back and forth under his nose. "Smells darn good to me. Here's to friendship."

She touched her glass to his and sipped. "Ooo. That's warming, isn't it?"

"Smooth," Morgan said, drawling the word

out.

The silence grew for a minute or two and Rebecca took a couple more sips of her brandy, as if trying to relax again. "I guess I'm sort of nervous."

"That's because the friendship we're drinking to is so young," Morgan told her. "Incidentally, how young are you?"

"Didn't your mama ever teach you not to ask a lady's age?" she asked. But she began to smile again.

"I wouldn't want to try to give you a kiss, if it would get me into too much trouble," Morgan kidded, grinning back at her.

"You're kinda good looking," Rebecca said, scanning his features. "I had a friend in Reno who used to say she was old enough to know better."

"But too young to resist?" Morgan shot back.

"I'm nineteen. But I'll be twenty in a day or so."

"Then I guess I'll kiss you before you get too old," he said. He reached across her and set his glass down on the bedside table, took her glass out of her hand and set it beside his.

Her blue eyes gazed into his and a slight smile rested on her lips. He kissed her. A gentle testing kiss. A kiss that a young lady in a strange town wouldn't be able to resist.

She didn't resist.

He kissed her again, still tenderly, but more enduring. She slid her arms around his neck.

He embraced her holding her close and feeling the firm full breasts against his chest. He wanted to feel them next to his bare skin. But he had no idea how much experience she had had. He had no desire to frighten her.

On the other hand, she had said Corson was her *man*. Morgan moved a hand up and down her back, slowly. She responded by pressing her body closer to his and making her lips softer under his kiss.

Lee moved his lips from hers to her neck, just below her ear. Her high-necked dress didn't permit much maneuvering there, so he unbuttoned her top button. In moments they were both rapidly shedding clothing and almost instantly found themselves back on the bed naked.

He reached into her hair to pluck out a pin. She helped him, and the blonde silk cascaded down around her shoulders and back. "It's beautiful," he said.

She smiled and they embraced. He lay her back against the pillows and kissed her. Then he drew away and looked at her.

Her breasts were magnificent. He liked women with small firm breasts too, but this was a treasure trove. He fondled them, nursed them and caressed them. He couldn't leave them alone.

He straddled her and lay his rapidly growing rod between her breasts and squeezed them together against it.

Rebecca did nothing to prevent him. Her blue eyes gazed at him in wonder and the slight vaguely interested smile still played on her lips. He couldn't tell whether she was becoming aroused or not.

He swung his leg back over her and slid down beside her, giving her another kiss on the lips and then running his tongue between her breasts and on down her middle. She giggled.

Teasing her nipples with kisses and nibbles

while sliding his hand down across her flat belly to the furry mound below it, Lee felt the buds on her breasts harden and heard her murmur, "Mmmm."

He moved his main focus of attention to the slit in the furriness and agitated her love button with his fingers. His lips refused to leave the fantastic breasts. But she now became more obviously excited. The more he played, the more her body responded.

She finally put her hand out and touched his leg, then cautiously ran the hand up to find his throbbing organ. She clasped it in her hand and seemed to urge it toward her.

"Roll over," he said.

Lee told hold of her waist and helped her turn over, boosting her buttocks, so that she rested on her knees and elbows, showing her rosebud ass.

He got behind her on his knees and felt for her now moist and swollen hole. He gently slid his rod into the eager cunt, closed the space between them, and leaned over her so his arms went around her and fondled her breasts while he worked in and out of her, doggie style.

Before he got too far to control it, he wanted her ready too, so he moved one hand down the front of her and diddled her most excitable spot some more, while pumping in and out.

She emitted little cries of pleasure and lifted her rump to meet his pushes. Their efforts were at first slow and teasing and then became urgent, strong, and faster until Lee could hold back no longer. As he released his hot juices into her, she called out, "Oh, yes."

Presently they rolled over onto one side. Still

engaged, Lee held her closely in his arms. Cupped like spoons, they lay breathing deep satisfied breaths.

The lamp wick flickered. They paid no attention, letting it die out on its own. Before they fell asleep, Lee heard her sigh and murmur, "I never had it that good."

Sometime during the night, Lee felt Rebecca's silken hair fall across his chest as she turned and snuggled close to him. He put his hand on her breast and felt the nipple harden in his fingers.

His groin awoke and in a moment his rod was hard and ready again. They rejoined, in the dark. This time, he pulled her on top of him, afraid that he might crush her if he mounted her straight away.

He grasped her firm buttocks and rocked her as she leaned forward so that her two great globes touched his face. He took first one then the other by its tip sucking until finally he forgot them in the rush of another release.

Rebecca rested on top of him, her breasts pressing on his chest, her fine hair falling across his arm, her heart beating hard, and her breath again coming in gasps, as was his own.

"Oh, you!" she said. And again they slept.

In the morning, the sun was already beating in through the lace curtains when they woke. Lee opened his eyes to see Rebecca leaning on one elbow looking down at him. Her eyes were just as blue in the daylight as they had been at night. Her long pale hair hung to the side, over the arm she rested on.

"Aren't you a pretty sight to wake up to," Morgan said.

"We could stay right here all day," Rebecca said, then bit her lip, as if she thought she had spoken out of turn.

"That would be almost perfect, except for one or two things," Lee told her. "I have to go and meet someone. And I have to bury a friend today."

Rebecca gasped. "Oh, that's right. I did mine yesterday. Only I don't think his brother wanted me there."

Lee leaned over and kissed the girl, then got out of bed and started putting on his pants. "So what are you going to do?"

"I don't know. I guess I'll have to go and ask Bert Tyler."

Morgan made no comment on Sheriff Bert Tyler. She had known him in Reno, and possibly thought the sheriff would give her some of Corson's things.

"Well, I have to see about my friend that died the same day. His name was Hank Broom." He pulled on his shirt and tucked it in.

"Did your friend get shot too?"

Morgan just nodded. No use telling her that her erstwhile man shot his friend.

"I'll see you later," Morgan said. He smiled down at her. "I liked it too." Maybe it had been simpler, after all, when females ran off in the early hours before you woke, and you didn't have to think what to say or how to get away without making them feel rejected.

He glanced out the door to see who was about, not wanting to compromise the lady. Finding the hall empty he headed for his own room.

He had been inside only a minute or two, when there was a tap on the door. He hoped it wasn't going to be Rebecca getting clingy.

It was a tall Indian dressed in a dark well-cut business suit. His blue-black hair was cut to a modest length, with the back slightly longer than the sides. He removed a well-blocked gray felt hat and asked in cultivated tones, "Mr. Morgan?"

"Yes."

"I'm Grey Stoneagle. Young Willie said you were looking for me."

"Come in." Morgan stood back so Grey Stoneagle could accept the invitation. "Have you seen Jason Isley?"

"Yes. Last night. He told me what you want. But I wished to speak to you, before we go."

Morgan indicated the chair, but Stoneagle shook his head. "I'll be only a minute." He looked Morgan straight in the eyes. "We will go to my old chief in peace."

"Of course." Morgan had never known an Indian who spoke such perfect English, who had manners better than the last U.S. Senator he had known. Then he decided he had better level with this man who was about to help him and Jason with their mission. "We go in peace, but there may be one problem."

Stoneagle stood hat in hand waiting, attention.

"A few days ago, a small group of Washos set on a friend and me as we were on the trail up to Ole Olmanson's cabin. There was an exchange of gun fire."

"I know about it," Stoneagle said. "I have made arrangements. It will be all right. Chief Greatfoot will see you. We will go when you are through with your ceremony. We will meet at the stables." He didn't offer to shake hands, just nodded and left, putting his hat on as he went out into the hall.

Morgan watched Grey Stoneagle until he disappeared down the stairway. He moved like a panther. A panther in a business suit. Silent and smooth. And he knew everything that was going on. He would see Morgan after the ceremony.

Just before noon, the old cemetery, behind the church and partly enclosed in a forged iron fence, accepted the remains of Hank Broom.

A modest gathering of certain townsfolk heard the Reverend intone something about ashes and dust.

Jeb and Essie Rowe were there, having apparently left Nelly to hold the fort back at the hotel.

The barber had closed his shop for an hour and stood by, having done the same the day before for Brant Corson, according to Jason. Morgan couldn't imagine why the barber had attended the earlier service as Corson never looked as if he'd had his hair cut or washed in his entire lifetime. Perhaps going to funerals was a tradition with him.

A couple of highly rouged ladies from Hank's favorite saloon wept prettily into their hankies.

Jason stood next to Morgan and held Florrie's hand. Florrie had brought a little clutch of hand-picked flowers, as had Essie Rowe.

A group of kind and thoughtful people.

The sheriff stood on the periphery of the small assembly and watched. He left without comment as the first spadeful of dirt was returned to the six-foot hole. Morgan wondered if Tyler assumed he would now leave town.

If so, he assumed wrong.

9

Back from the cemetery, Morgan tried to put Broom's death behind him. There was work to be done, work that Hank had started and Morgan intended to finish.

Lee headed for the livery to meet Jason and Stoneagle. The Indian was an enigma, probably the product of some Indian agent who, as an example, sent him off to school to be educated. An example of what? And whose side would Stoneagle take in a fight?

He had promised to lead them to Chief Greatfoot. Jason and Lee would be two white men threading through hostile Indian territory, with only Stoneagle's word that the chief would talk to them in peace. By nightfall they could be two bloody scalps hanging in Greatfoot's camp.

Across the street in the sheriff's office, Morgan glimpsed Rebecca Petersen. He wished he were closer so he could overhear the conversation between Rebecca and Sheriff Tyler. Her gloved hands moved in animated gestures. Did the gestures designate anger or was she simply explaining something to Tyler? Perhaps she wanted to claim Corson's belongings. Maybe she was trying to find out

whether her man had struck it rich before he
died.

At the livery, Morgan's horse whinnied in
recognition when he spoke. Lee patted the
horse's shoulder, then ran his hand gently
across the animal's soft muzzle. The horse
nuzzled Morgan's fingers. "Now what do you
want? You've been fed. I know Willie fed you
this morning."

Morgan dug into the pocket of his denims and
brought out a lump of sugar he'd taken from the
cafe at breakfast. "This what you're after?" He
held the sugar in his palm and the horse
accepted it.

Morgan lifted his saddle from the rack and
secured it on the back of his mount, checked the
cinch a' second time, took the rifle out of the
boot and made sure it was loaded. Then he
turned to look for Jason and Stoneagle.

The Indian stood silently against the wall. Did
Morgan detect a ghost of a smile on Stoneagle's
face? Or perhaps it was a sneer. "Jason will be
here in a moment," the Indian said. "He is
escorting Florrie back to the cafe."

The Indian had changed from his business
suit to denims and a brown linen shirt, but he
still wore the straight brimmed black hat. Lee
noticed that boots, much the same as his own,
covered his feet. His gun belt held a Colt forty-
five.

Stoneagle disappeared for a moment at the
far end of the stable. He returned leading a
giant black stallion, complete with saddle and a
rifle in the boot. This Indian was either rich or
smart. It would take a year's pay to buy a
stallion like his, or the cunning of a fox to
capture him on the range and break him. Lee

had a feeling Stoneagle was smart.

Morgan leaned against the side of the stable. Why did he have misgivings about the Indian? If Jason trusted him, he would have to. There was no other means of getting through the Indian territory to Chief Greatfoot.

In minutes Jason arrived, his eyes bright and a little smug. Florrie must have permitted a kiss when he left her. "Hi, Grey," he greeted the Indian. "Everything all set?"

Stoneagle smiled at Jason. "We are ready to go. The messenger came before daylight. The chief will sit with you and Mr. Morgan."

The three riders headed northwest, in the same general direction as Gramps' cabin.

The sheriff now sat in a chair outside his office fanning himself with a white cardboard, probably a 'wanted' poster. Morgan felt the sheriff's eyes on his back and wondered if he would signal one of his boys to follow them. Rebecca was nowhere in sight. Whatever she had to say to the sheriff evidently was finished.

Out on the trail, Stoneagle led the way. Jason and Morgan rode side by side. "How long have you and Stoneagle known each other?" Morgan asked.

"Ever since I came to live with Gramps. He spent a lot of time at Gramps' place. I think he was kind of an outcast in the tribe."

"You trust him? I mean he won't lead us into an ambush, will he?"

"I'd trust him with my life." The indignation in Jason's voice surprised Morgan.

"You *are* trusting him with your life." He wanted to know more about Stoneagle. "Why was he an outcast?"

"I think his father was the son of a chief from

another band of Indians, who married a woman
from Greatfoot's tribe. Stoneagle can't be a
chief, but Greatfoot's son, Burning Arrow, has
always been afraid he might try to take his
place. Burning Arrow is always stirring up
trouble with the whites. Thinks he's a warrior."

"It must have been Burning Arrow and his
friends who attacked me and Broom the day we
found your Gramps."

"He and his bunch of renegade warriors have
killed a lot of white people. Some in the town,
but mostly they attack wagon trains and supply
trains. He hates whites. He kills everybody on
the trains."

"Why don't they go after them? Send the
army after them?"

Jason grinned. "Wait until you see the
entrance to the camp, then you'll know why.
Nobody can find it."

The summer sun beat down on Morgan's
shoulders. They should have left earlier. The
sandy trail they followed was clear of growth,
but low desert bushes dotted the ground on
either side. Up ahead the cool green of the
mountains beckoned, but Stoneagle led them
around the base of the mountain.

About two hours into the desert, Stoneagle
stopped and dismounted at what appeared to be
a tiny oasis. "We must rest the horses. Soon we
will climb a steep trail up there." He pointed to
a ridge of mountains in the distance. "I am
sorry there is no water here at this time of year,
but there will be plenty of water at the high
spring."

Jason and Morgan got off their horses and sat
cross-legged in the shade. Morgan's gaze
scanned the countryside for landmarks in case

he needed to come here without a guide. He noted a camelback rock on the crest of a hill.

Stoneagle smiled. "Finding Chief Greatfoot's camp would not be a problem for you, but you would never gain entrance without a guide, one already expected by the chief."

"Well guarded?"

"Even without the guards, you would not get in."

Morgan didn't pursue the subject. He had heard about Indian camps with entrances that were impossible to find. About beautiful fertile valleys surrounded by tall mountains loaded with game, deer and wild turkeys for food.

A few miles later, the upward climb began. With no trail visible, Stoneagle led the way. No wonder the white man often got ambushed. He always went the same way and wore a trail. Evidently Greatfoot's tribe never took the same path twice.

Up and up they climbed. Stoneagle led them back and forth like a million hairpins hooked together. Morgan and Jason dismounted and led their horses. Only a trained mountain horse could scale these rocks with a rider, without danger of falling. Stoneagle's stallion had no trouble.

At the spring, they stopped to water the horses and to eat the lunch Florrie had packed. Cheese and biscuits and strips of beef. The Indian appeared to savor their food. He had truly become a white man in everything but the color of his skin.

"Stoneagle, I assume you will interpret for us?"

"If needed. The chief speaks English. If he knows where the gold is hidden he will tell you.

It is of no value to him."

Morgan didn't mask his surprise. "So you know about the gold, too?"

"I would not have brought you here without knowing why you wanted to come." Stoneagle got to his feet. "We must go. The entrance to the camp is near by."

The Indian didn't mount his stallion, but led it along behind him. They must have gone a hundred yards, when suddenly out of nowhere, they were completely surrounded by Indian braves. One addressed Stoneagle angrily. "So the white Indian who is a coward has brought white murderers to our camp. I order you to take them away."

No one had to tell Morgan this young brave was Burning Arrow, the son of the chief. He'd seldom seen such hate on a man's face.

"You do not order me, Burning Arrow, I have a message of safe passage from the chief, your father, for these two men."

A half dozen braves stood their ground. Morgan's gaze scanned the long rock formation in front of them. They might be going in, but where?

Stoneagle advanced along the rock face. "Stay close behind me."

Burning Arrow jumped into Stoneagle's path. He raised his war ax. "One more step and I will kill you."

Morgan wondered at the force of the anger on the young Indian's face. No emotion at all showed on Stoneagle's. With a swift movement he reached forward and wrested the war ax from Burning Arrow. "You will step back and permit us to enter."

"I will kill you," Burning Arrow rasped

between clenched teeth, but he moved away and the three of them went on.

For several more yards, Morgan and Jason followed Stoneagle along the rocky wall. Suddenly the Indian disappeared. The two men stood alone. Jason scowled, ran his hand along the wall.

A bush moved and Stoneagle reappeared, his eyes dancing with amusement. "Thought you two were following me."

"We were, but—" Jason began. Then he grinned at his own stupidity. Jason and Morgan stepped around the bush and following Stoneagle, threaded their way back and forth through a maze of rock corridors.

When they passed the last rock into the trees, the fresh aroma of pine filled the air. They led their horses fifty yards or so down the tree covered hillside and stopped. Below, a long green valley stretched for maybe five miles. In the middle of the valley, at least fifty neat tepees formed a colorful circle.

Morgan whistled under his breath. Green mountains completely surrounded the Indian camp, giving adequate water to the lush grazing land.

Morgan heard a rustle behind him in the trees. His hand automatically reached for his Bisley. Had Burning Arrow and his braves come in and planned to trap them inside?"

"Put your gun away," Stoneagle said. "You have been granted safe passage. No one will attack you inside the camp. Not even Burning Arrow."

Morgan could almost taste the hostility of Burning Arrow as he and his men trailed behind them to the brightly decorated tepee at the center of the camp.

In front of the tepee, the chief, a grizzled man, near the age of Gramps, sat cross-legged on a buffalo robe. "Son of my gray-haired blood brother, please sit."

Jason sat down.

The chief indicated Morgan. "Is this your friend who wishes to speak?"

"This is my friend, Lee Morgan," Jason said.

Morgan and Stoneagle were invited to sit, and did.

"Jason's Gramps knew about some stolen gold bars. The man who stole them is dead. We want to find the bars. Did Gramps give them to you, or tell you where they were hidden?"

"We want to return them to their rightful owner, Chief Greatfoot," Jason said.

Morgan was having second thoughts about Jason. Did he really plan to return the gold to the railroad for the reward, or was he using a ploy to get the information? No, Morgan was sure Jason meant to return the gold.

The old chief sat thoughtfully for several minutes. "My blood brother spoke of the gold that his friend had brought to the village, but he did not give it to me. He told me he would tell his friend to hide it in a safe place."

"Did he say where he planned to tell his friend to hide it? Give you a message that might indicate the hiding place?"

"No. My blood brother would not endanger my people by giving me such a message."

Morgan sensed Burning Arrow's presence behind him, but tried to ignore the uneasiness it caused. He got to his feet. "I thank you for letting me speak, and for granting me safe passage into your camp. We must not keep you longer."

The old Indian nodded, but said nothing. Morgan and Jason, following Stoneagle's example, mounted their horses and headed for the exit from the camp.

When they were some distance away, Jason leaned toward Lee. "Did you believe him?"

"Yes. I think he's a truthful man. He could buy guns with the gold. Why did Stoneagle say it was of no use to him?"

Stoneagle rode up beside them. "The chief does not want guns, but Burning Arrow does. If he could find the gold, he would buy guns. The chief is old and losing his power. If Burning Arrow takes over the tribe, or even a part of it, you may be sure that many white men will die."

Morgan glanced around for the young would-be chief. He was nowhere in sight. Uneasily, Lee followed Stoneagle and Jason through the labyrinth of rocks out of the camp. He didn't trust Burning Arrow, or his young braves, especially in this timbered area where their horses would be accustomed to navigating the steep terrain.

"Let's get out of these trees," Morgan said. But he was too late. An arrow found its mark. Stoneagle slumped forward on his stallion, an arrow protruding from his shoulder. An Indian had shot Stoneagle in the back.

The stallion kept going, carrying Stoneagle down the mountain. In one quick fluid motion, Morgan and Jason abandoned their mounts and scrambled behind rocks. Their horses followed the stallion.

Jason glanced at Morgan beside him. "Good,

you got your rifle."

"Watch your back," Morgan warned.

Jason watched. Suddenly his Colt forty-five barked and a young brave toppled from an over-hanging precipice, falling face down practically at their feet. Blood spurted from his neck, blood and flesh had been spread across his shoulders, and the blood pulsed down his bare, coppery back.

"How many more?" Morgan whispered.

"Don't know."

"Over there." Morgan aimed his rifle. The shot missed. Two arrows glanced off the rock, inches from Morgan's head. "There's at least two more." He sensed the braves creeping closer. He couldn't see them or hear them, but he knew they were closing in.

He nudged Jason and pointed to where a leaf moved, but only one. Their vulnerable position made them an easy target if the Indians got behind them, but nothing nearby offered anything better. Morgan watched the leaves in that spot for several seconds.

One moved again. He fired, once, twice.

No arrow returned his fire. The branch the leaves hung on moved, swayed, and bent nearly to the ground. An Indian brave pitched forward. He lay motionless on the ground, his back blown open by Morgan's shot.

"You got him." Jason got halfway to his feet.

Morgan jerked him back to the ground. An arrow whizzed by where Jason had been. "There's at least one more."

Jason appeared shaken. "Let's get out of here."

"How? Burning Arrow is still out there. If we

make a run for it, he'll get one of us for sure. Just wait, he'll make his move."

They waited. Ten minutes passed, then twenty. Morgan's nerves threatened to explode. He could see that Jason's were no better. An old Indian trick. Wait. Wait until the opponent could no longer stand the strain and left his cover. Well, Lee and Jason wouldn't bite.

They stayed put behind their rocks, not moving, not talking, just watching in every direction. Finally Morgan edged a few feet to the left, motioned Jason to do likewise.

A sudden movement, not ten yards away, jarred their nerves. Jason raised his Colt. Morgan shook his head. "Decoy." He had fought hostile Indians more than once, and throwing an object, a rock or a limb, to get an enemy's attention, was an old trick. It gave the Indian a chance to reposition.

Several more minutes passed. An arrow from behind missed Morgan's head by inches and glanced off the rock.

Morgan spun around, fired several rounds into the trees. A noisy thrashing in the brush answered, then hooves pounded the ground. Morgan rose slowly from his crouched position and peered over the rocks. A horse, carrying a rider with blood trailing a thin line down the back of his bare arm, galloped toward the Indian camp.

"You got Burning Arrow," Jason said. "He wears that headband with the colors of the chief."

He's barely wounded. See how well he sits his horse?"

Jason holstered his gun. "Well, at least he's

going home. Think there are any others?"

Near the edge of the timber line, they could see three riderless horses drinking at the spring. Both men broke into a run, jumping from rock to rock and over tree roots that threatened to throw them headlong down the mountain.

Stoneagle lay beside the spring breathing raggedly. "Arrow. Bleeding," he gasped.

An arrow protruded from deep in his shoulder. Morgan stripped part of the Indian's shirt away. "Can't take it out, you'll bleed to death." He broke off a stick half an inch in diameter, and placed it between Stoneagle's teeth. "Bite down hard, I've got to break off the arrow's shaft."

Drops of perspiration wet Morgan's brow as he positioned the sturdy arrow between his closed fists. He gathered his strength, then in one quick motion bent the shaft. It snapped. He wadded up the torn shirt and wrapped the wound and the broken end of the arrow, then tied it in place. "You've got to travel now to get to the doctor."

Stoneagle nodded. Jason and Morgan lifted him onto his horse. Morgan took the reins and mounted the stallion, sitting behind Stoneagle. "We've got to move fast," he said to Jason. "Tie my horse behind yours and let's go."

The eight or ten miles ahead, under the desert sun, didn't look promising for Stoneagle. He'd lost a lot of blood, and the jarring ride could cause him to lose more.

For the first hour they moved along at a good gait. By grasping Stoneagle around the middle, Morgan could hold him in a somewhat upright position, but twice he accidentally bumped the broken shaft of the arrow, and the Indian had gasped in pain.

They stopped to rest the horses. Although the stallion was a mighty horse, carrying two riders in the afternoon sun could throw him lame. He thought of walking and leading the stallion, but Stoneagle could not sit his horse alone.

The next few miles of the trip became more difficult. Stoneagle could no longer raise his head to drink from the canteen. Morgan wet a piece of his shirt tail and laid it across the back of the Indian's neck. At intervals, he soaked it from the canteen.

They could see the shadows of Lost Canyon in the distance when Stoneagle, now unconscious, slumped forward against the neck of his horse. Morgan could no longer hold him in even a semi-sitting position. By now blood soaked the compress and the back of what was left of the Indian's shirt. Soon he could die.

They still had a couple of miles to go when Morgan signaled to Jason. "Ride on ahead and make sure the doc is ready for us."

"I'll find him and tell him you're coming in," Jason promised, and galloped into town.

Morgan poured the last of the water over Stoneagle's head. "We're almost home," he said.

Stoneagle moved slightly but didn't answer. At least he was still alive.

Morgan urged the stallion to go faster. All of Morgan's mistrust of the Indian had disappeared. He wanted Stoneagle to live.

When they came into town, Jason ran to meet them. He took the reins and led the horse to the steps leading to the doctor's house where he had his office. A couple of bystanders helped

Morgan and Jason carry Stoneagle up the steps.

The doctor took over and Morgan waited. If he'd had any sense he would have left the way Jason did, and had Florrie make him something to eat, but he waited until Doc removed the arrow and announced that Stoneagle would live. "Barring infection," he said. "Now Indians are shooting Indians, and in the back yet!" Doc shook his head in disbelief." He decided to keep Stoneagle there. "My wife and daughter will help tend him."

Stoneagle had regained consciousness. He signaled Morgan to his bedside. Pain etched his face, but he spoke clearly. "Do you know if Burning Arrow was killed?"

"I winged him, but he rode off after his braves were dead."

"Be careful, my friend," Stoneagle warned. "Unless the old chief can control them, this could bring many braves from the tribe down on the town."

10

Satisfied that Grey Stoneagle's condition had been attended to the best of the doctor's ability, that he would have someone on hand to care for him, and that there was nothing more he could do, Morgan left.

Jason had already hurried off to his room behind the cafe to get ready to go to work.

Morgan saw to stabling his horse and Stoneagle's and with his trusty black snake whip in hand walked back to the hotel. He picked up his key from Essie Rowe behind the desk and went on up to his room.

Throwing the bolt, he tossed his hat and his whip on the bed. This area was getting downright tiresome with that damn Indian brave coming down on him every time he turned around. And when Burning Arrow wasn't attacking him, it was someone else.

If it weren't for the gold, Morgan thought, he would leave right now. Maybe the gold wasn't worth it anyhow. Maybe he'd best just cut his losses, pack up, and take off. Say to hell with it.

He stomped over to the wash basin, poured in some water from the pitcher and washed his face. He felt agitated and restless.

As he finished toweling his face and head, he

noticed a small scrap of paper lying in the middle of the floor. He hung the towel on the peg and ran a comb through his hair, then picked up the slightly crumpled paper.

Straightening it out, he swore as he saw the hastily scrawled message: *Help me Celia*

Celia! His heart raced. She needed help. But where?

My God! What could this mean? Was Celia still in Lost Canyon? In trouble? Corson was dead. Who could be threatening her now? The men who worked with Corson to find the gold? The men who had killed old Gramps? The men who had chased him and Jason to the caves?

Morgan clapped his Stetson onto his head. He was ready to rush out the door. He'd go to that damn Corson Ranch and see just what the hell was going on. The last man to give Celia trouble had been Brant Corson. Now who else could it be but his brother? He'd go out there and show those bastards. He would kill every one of them if he had to.

He had his hand on the door knob, when he realized that he was about to go off half-cocked. He had always derided Hank Broom for doing that very thing. Jumping in before he was ready. He had to stop and think about this. How had the message reached him? Where had it come from? He went back and sat heavily on the bed and stared at the paper in his hand. Someone put it there. So someone must know.

Why would a call for help come like this? If she were still here in Lost Canyon, why didn't she come to him herself? Unless she couldn't. Somebody had her. But where?

Finally he got up and went down to the lobby. "Mrs. Rowe, I have a problem. Do you know who left this message for me?"

Essie Rowe looked startled. "What? Message? No I don't think we have any messages for you." Obviously flustered, she turned to search the boxes behind the counter. "No messages, Mr. Morgan."

"No, you misunderstood. I already have the message. I wondered how it got in my room." Morgan could swear the woman was trembling. He wondered briefly what was the matter with her.

Nelly came into the lobby from the hall leading to the rooms on the ground floor. "Room six is ready for occupancy now, Essie."

Room six had been Hank Broom's room.

"Oh, I'm sorry," Nelly said, apparently realizing for the first time that Morgan stood there.

"Nelly, will you take over the desk, please. Jeb wants me." With a murmured 'excuse me' Essie Rowe rushed out of the area.

"Have you been helped, Mr. Morgan?"

He frowned after Essie Rowe. "Wonder what's the matter with her?"

Nelly shook her head and shrugged. "Seems all right to me. Just been pretty busy lately."

He laid his key on the desk. "Nelly, did you see someone shoving a piece of paper under my door while I was away?"

"No. I haven't seen anyone near your door." She looked worried. "Did someone tear up your room again?"

"No. Nothing like that. Someone must have put a message under my door."

She told him she didn't know who it could have been.

Morgan headed for the cafe. This thing had

him rattled. He knew he wasn't thinking straight, maybe young Jason could come up with an idea. He strode on through to the kitchen without acknowledging Florrie's greeting.

When he heard what had happened and saw the piece of paper, Jason shook his head. "I thought she'd gone east."

"I thought so too, but why would a message like this be shoved under my door at the hotel? Who would know something about it?"

"Whoever put it there," Jason said. "The folks at the hotel don't know?"

"If somebody over there knows, they haven't said so."

Florrie came into the kitchen. "What's the matter?"

Morgan showed her the paper, too. He would show everyone in town, if necessary.

"Maybe the old woman where Miss Celia lived would know something," Florrie suggested, after thinking for a minute. "Mrs. Smith would be sure to know if Miss Celia is still in town."

"Where? What woman?"

"Mrs. Smith's Ladies Residence," Florrie told him. "Go one street back." She pointed. "Off Main Street. It's the big grayish house with the gingerbread."

"Gingerbread?"

"You know, the fancy scrolls and stuff. Decorations. Has a round room that looks like a tower, except it isn't up high."

Jason said, "Turn to your left at the barber shop and go up the path, it's practically the first house you see. The biggest."

Morgan hadn't done any exploring in the rest

of the town. He had scarcely found time to notice anything but the hotel, livery stable, cafe, and of course the trails out of town to the cabin, the rock quarry, and the Washos' camp. He followed Jason's instructions and found the Victorian house surrounded by big old trees and an expanse of lawn. There were wicker chairs on the veranda.

A small tidy plaque beside the door was engraved, MRS. SMITH'S LADIES RESIDENCE. He twisted the bell handle and heard it sound a metalic clatter on the other side.

A tiny gray-haired lady answered the door. She looked him up and down and inquired in a quavery voice, "Yes, sir? Are you selling something? Or did you come to call on one of my young ladies?"

Morgan removed his hat. "Name's Lee Morgan, ma'am. I wanted to ask about one of your roomers. A Miss Celia Fair."

"I don't call them roomers. They're guests."

"Yes, ma'am. Guests."

"But Miss Fair hasn't been here since, I believe, Tuesday."

Of course it was Tuesday, Morgan thought. She left here Tuesday and stayed all night with him before she got on the stage Wednesday morning.

"She has gone back home in the east. You're too late." The elderly woman looked him up and down again. "Shame, too."

Had he been less concerned, he would have smiled at the implied compliment. "She hasn't been back?"

"You don't get home and back that fast, young man. She's likely got about to Salt Lake

City by now."

Morgan held out the scrap of paper. "I found this piece of paper shoved under my door today."

"Oh, my." Mrs. Smith clutched a fragile almost transparent hand to her heart. "Oh, dear. I do hope it doesn't really mean it."

"I'm trying to find out anything I can about it." Morgan took back the paper and put it in his pocket.

"I think you should call on the sheriff," Mrs. Smith offered.

"I'd even do that if I thought it would help," Morgan muttered, replacing his Stetson and turning to go.

Would he do that? Yes, by God, he would. If that no-good lazy bastard could ever be forced to do his duty, this had to be the time.

In spite of a morbid feeling in the pit of his stomach and doubts of many kinds assailing his brain, Morgan went to the sheriff's office.

"What the hell are you hanging around for now?" Tyler wanted to know. He sat tipped back in his chair with his feet on his desk. The place smelled of cigar smoke.

"Not for any love of the place," Morgan growled. "But something has come up." He took the folded note out of his pocket and showed it. "I need to know what you think of this?"

"Thought you already helped the lady. First thing you did when you got to town, wasn't it?" The sheriff didn't change his position. He tossed the note down on the desk. "It's likely been blowing around the streets since before she left. Somebody probably picked it up long after its need was met."

"Seems to me it could be something else,"
Morgan said. "Maybe she didn't go on that
stagecoach after all."

"Well, now, I would have heard about it, if
there'd have been any trouble, like the last time
she started to leave." He made an offensive
sound halfway between a snort and a laugh.
"Corson was the one who was preventin' her.
He's dead."

Morgan couldn't trust himself to speak. He
snatched up the paper and left the office.

"You better be leavin' too, Morgan," Bert
Tyler barked after him. "I've warned you
before."

Morgan stopped at the livery stable. "Willie
around?"

Willie's pa shrugged. "Out back, I guess.
What you want with him?"

"Just wanted to ask him something." The
thought crossed Morgan's mind that the stables
smelled a lot better than the sheriff's office.

"Ask him what?"

"He does errands or carries messages for
people sometimes, doesn't he?"

The stable man shrugged. "Now and again.
You got a message you want carried?"

"Just wanted to ask him something," Morgan
repeated and made his way around the corner
of the building.

When he found Willie he found out nothing,
except that Willie still wanted to learn to handle
a black snake whip, and that was not news.
"Good luck," Willie said.

Discouraged and frustrated, Morgan headed
back to the cafe. He went in and sat at the
counter.

"Coffee, Mr. Morgan?" Florrie asked.

"I don't know."

"You haven't found out anything?" She set a cup of coffee in front of him. "You better have something to eat. You haven't been in here for a good meal all day. Taking your business elsewhere?"

"No. Haven't felt like eating." Morgan's gut feeling told him that the sheriff was all wrong. This note had been written recently and sent specifically to him. It meant that Celia Fair needed help. He had to find out how he could help her.

"I bet you could think better if you just had a nice plate of stew," Florrie insisted. "And I'll tell Jason you're here."

Celia heard them coming back. They kept her tied up most all of the time now. She never should have tried to get out the window. Now she would never have another chance. They tied and gagged her every time they left the room. And sometimes they were gone for so long she could hardly stand it.

She kept trying to keep her hopes up, that her message had reached Lee Morgan. But she hadn't been able to put enough in the note. He wouldn't even know where she was, if he got it. She didn't even know where she was. She was sure it was the hotel, but she didn't know which room. No one ever came to clean up. She wondered if the hotel people were in on this too. No. Not Essie Rowe. She was such a nice person. But didn't the hotel owners wonder what was going on in here?

The last time the men came back, they brought bread and cheese and cold coffee. The one called Axel had his arm in a sling. Celia wondered what had happened to him, but when she asked, the bossy one told her to shut her mouth.

This time, the two of them came in and after his usual warning about what would happen to her if she made a sound, the bossy one took the gag out of her mouth. But to her surprise he didn't start asking her things about her brother this time, and he didn't rant about her having stuck him with the wrong bag when she got off the stage. Instead, he tied the handkerchief around her eyes. What didn't they want her to see?

"Someone's here to talk to you," he said gruffly. "And if you know what's good for you, you'll tell him what he wants to know. He's a lot tougher than old Axel and me."

She heard the door open and close again. She assumed someone else must have come in, someone that she was not supposed to see. Did that mean she would know him, if she saw him?

"Well, now, Miss Highfalutin' Fair," a new voice snarled. "I want you to tell me what you did with the leather bag that Brant Corson wanted from you."

She said nothing. She didn't even realize for a moment that he was waiting for her to speak, she had been listening to his voice so closely. She had heard that voice before, but she couldn't place it.

He kicked at her foot, and said, "Bitch. Answer." It hurt her ankle where it was tied to the chair. She cried out. "Ow! What do you want from me?"

"Just told you. Want to know where that bag is. What was in it? It was the gold wasn't it?"

"What gold? There's no gold in it. Just some

jewelry that belongs to my family."

Why were they treating her like this? They
could have the jewelry, if they wanted it. If only
they would let her go. But she knew that wasn't
what they wanted.

They must want the note that Hex had written
her and left with the old man up the trail on the
side of the mountain. The note didn't mean anything to her, but it probably would to them. It
must have something to do with this gold they
were ranting about.

"Now we know that's not what was in the
bag." His threatening voice grated on her ears.
"It's going to go hard on you, if you don't tell me
where it is."

"It's probably in Salt Lake City by now, or
maybe on it's way to Boston." There, let them
know where it was. What were they going to do
with the information? If they found the bag,
would they let her go or kill her? How long
would it take someone to get clear to Salt Lake
City to try to get the bag? Would she have to be
tied up all that time, before they decided to kill
her?

The men withdrew to the other side of the
room. She could hear them mumbling.

Celia decided it was time to do something.
How could she hurt more than she already did?
She screamed.

One of the men stormed back across the room
at her and clouted her a blow across the face so
hard that it tipped the chair over. Now she hurt
worse. She thought the arm she landed on,
between the chair and the floor, must be
broken. And her head had hit the floor. The pain
was excruciating. She began to sob. She
couldn't help it. Now she was in worse shape

than before. Nobody had heard the scream
apparently. Nobody came pounding on the
door.

The handkerchief had slipped from her eyes,
but she couldn't see anything. Her back was to
the men.

She heard the third man's voice say, "Stupid
ass. Now look what you've done. I'm getting out
of here." The door opened and closed.

What would they do with her now? She
couldn't even think about it. The pain was so
great it crowded everything out of her mind.
The pain was making her mind go blank. Maybe
she would die of it.

After eating his stew, with Florrie urging hot
bread with butter melting on it and a cup of
coffee as well, Morgan returned to the hotel. He
saw Sheriff Tyler on the way. The man
obviously was too angry to speak to anyone,
even to tell them to leave town.

Morgan sat down in the lobby of the hotel.
What would he try next that would butt up to a
dead end? Nobody could, or would, tell him
anything. Should he go out to the Corson ranch
and ask them? If they shot him on sight, it
wouldn't help Celia would it? And he still
wouldn't know. He'd be dead.

He glanced up at the desk and saw that Essie
Rowe was back in her place. He thought about
how she had run off so fast when he tried to ask
her about the message. Why had she been so
frightened? Did it have something to do with
what he had asked her?

He stood and as he took his first step toward
her, she retreated and disappeared again into
the back room. He rang the bell on the desk.

In a moment, Jeb came out from the office in the back. "Yes, sir, Mr. Morgan?"

"Oh, never mind, I'll just pick up my key," Morgan said.

"Is there anything wrong?" Jeb wanted to know. "Had any more trouble with people invading your room?"

Morgan thought about that question for a moment and suddenly realized that someone must have been inside his room, otherwise how did that little piece of paper get to the middle of the floor.

Why hadn't he thought of that before? When you shove a letter under the door of a room, it goes only under the door, until you can't push the last edge of it any further.

"Mr. Morgan? You all right?"

"Not quite, Mr. Rowe." Morgan spoke slowly. "Can we have a word in your office?"

Just then Jason Isley came into the hotel lobby.

Morgan motioned for him to come with them as Rowe led the way to the back.

When they entered the office, Essie quickly got up to go back out to the desk. "I'll just take care of things," she began.

"I'd like to speak to you, too, Mrs. Rowe," Morgan said.

Essie looked positively terrified. "But there's no one on the desk."

"They can ring the bell," Morgan suggested.

"Essie, what's wrong?" her husband wanted to know.

She sat back down without saying anything, twisting the handkerchief she held in her hands.

Morgan got out the piece of paper once again. "I found this in my room." He handed it to Jeb

Rowe. "I believe your wife may be able to tell us how it came to be there."

Rowe studied the paper, frowning. "Essie?"

"Anyone could have put it under your door," Essie said, swallowing hard.

"If someone had put it under the door, I wouldn't have found it in the middle of the room."

"It could have blown to the middle of the room, when you opened the door." The woman was grasping at straws, trying to save herself from what? Who did she think was going to hurt her? Who had given her the note to put in there? The note was from Celia, and Celia certainly wouldn't scare anyone.

"Essie, what do you know about this?" her husband asked.

"What are you afraid of?" Morgan added. "Just tell me where you got the paper in the first place. Celia is in trouble, and I want to know how to help her." Damn the woman. She knew! She was the first person in the whole town that showed the slightest sign that she knew something.

Essie began to weep. "It was in their towels. I didn't know what to do with it. I didn't know what it might mean."

Jason who had been standing quietly just inside the closed door the whole time, finally spoke. "You probably did the right thing with it."

"Whose towels? Where did you get it? Where is she?" Morgan stood, almost shouting.

Jeb Rowe made a move toward him. "There's no call to get riled up. If someone is threatening my wife, I want to know why."

Morgan sat back down, trying to contain his

impatience and his fury. If he didn't find out in time to help Celia, he would strangle both of them.

"The people in that room don't ever want anyone to go in there to clean or anything." Essie's words came haltingly at first. "They made that clear. The man with the trunk. And they just throw the towels in a heap out in the hall when they want clean ones and we put a new pile by the door. Sometimes they take food in and set the tray outside the door when they're through."

"What door?"

"The towels were out there last night and when I took them to be laundered, that's when the piece of paper fell out."

On their feet, Morgan and Jason both spoke at once. "Which room?"

"Number eleven."

Jeb Rowe followed the other two men down the hall. "Now let's go at this thing right," he urged.

"You got a key?" Morgan demanded. "Or do we crash through it?"

"Wait a minute." Rowe stood close to the door and listened. "Sounds like somebody cryin' in there." He knocked.

A man's voice growled, "Who is it?"

"It's your hotel owner," Rowe said. "Got your fresh towels here."

"We already got fresh towels," the voice said. "We're okay."

Jeb put the skeleton key in the lock and turned it. The bolt was thrown, however, so the door wouldn't open. Morgan, with his Bisley Colts in his hand, ran at the door and crashed through. The other men followed close behind him.

Essie Rowe screamed from a little way down the hall. Shots rang out. Morgan saw the woman tied to the chair and lying on her side on the floor. He knew who it was. He shot the nearest man point blank. Blood gushed from the front of his throat, and the man went down before he could finish drawing his weapon. He would never draw another weapon, or another breath.

Morgan pulled a table over onto its side and ducked behind it as the other man fired several shots. Jason Isley fell to the floor.

"Drop that piece or you're a dead man," Morgan advised, leveling over the edge of the upset table at the man's head.

Apparently seeing his friend lying dead on the floor and having no available cover himself convinced Axel that he should end the battle there. "Shit." He threw the forty-five out into the middle of the room. "I've got shot up enough already for these stupid bastards." He raised his one good arm into the air.

Jeb Rowe picked up the gun from the floor and held it on the surrendering man.

Morgan went to the woman on the floor. It was Celia. He said nothing, just drew his knife from his right boot and cut her bonds. Then he turned her carefully, relieving her of the chair.

"Oh, Lee, you found me."

That was all she could say. The pain obviously caused her to faint. She looked like a wilted flower whose fragrance had faded to almost nothing.

Morgan picked her up and lay her gently on the bed. Celia came to and cried out as he felt the injured arm to see if it was broken. Then more tears came.

"You'll be all right," Morgan said soothingly. "You're safe now."

Essie Rowe, who had come running up to the door, cried, "Jeb, are you hurt?"

"Jason," Morgan asked, finally. "You hit bad?"

Jason slowly got to his feet. "Naw. It's just a scratch." His face was the color of the white lace curtains.

"I'll hold this fellow, Mr. Rowe," Morgan said. "Can you get the doc? He was in his office this afternoon."

"Think he had to go out of town. But the barber is pretty good. I'll get him."

The barber came with his first aid kit and checked Celia carefully. "Don't think the arm's broken, but it is bruised real bad. And you've got a nasty bump on the head. Might get a cloth wrung with cold water, Miss Essie."

Essie, having made sure her husband was unhurt, hurried to get spring water and a cloth.

When Jason's scratch, which included a sizeable chunk taken out of his denims and his thigh, had been treated with carbolic and bandaged, the barber pronounced them damn lucky.

Morgan sat on the edge of the bed beside Celia holding her hand.

Axel finally spoke up, pointing to his partner. "What you going to do with him?"

"You sit right there and shut up," Morgan told him. "Or I'll do the same to you as I've already done to him."

Sheriff Tyler, apparently alerted by someone hearing the shots, appeared in the doorway.

"Morgan, I ought to shoot you on sight. You're sittin' here with another dead man on the floor."

"No!" Celia cried. Morgan felt her tense and recognized terror in her voice.

"He's not going to shoot anybody," Morgan told her.

Jeb Rowe said, "This man here and the one on the floor are kidnappers, Sheriff. Held this young woman against her will, right here in my hotel."

"Why didn't you complain earlier?"

"Because I didn't know it. They toted her in here in that trunk over there, unbeknownst to us."

"How can you be sure?" The sheriff gave one of his snorts. "Maybe she was just paying these men a visit."

Celia started to protest. Morgan fumed but held his temper and soothed Celia.

"When you get up and around, Miss, you come down and make your complaint. I'll be in my office until time for the Friday night dance."

Morgan noticed that the sheriff was dressed up, wearing a string tie, a clean shirt and pants, newly polished boots and a snappy looking buckskin jacket.

Morgan fingered the thin strip of leather in his pocket and tried to see whether the sheriff was missing a strand of fringe. He wasn't close enough to tell, but it wouldn't have surprised Morgan to find out that Bert Tyler had been present when an old man was beaten to death in his cabin.

When Tyler had taken Axel away with him and promised to notify the undertaker, Celia clutched at Morgan's arm. "It was him. That was his voice! I'm not going to his office for anything."

"His voice?" Lee wanted to know.

"He was in with them. He was here when they blindfolded me. I was sure I'd heard the voice before."

"Stands to reason," Morgan said.

When she felt steadier, Celia cried, "I've got to get cleaned up. I can't stand it any longer."

Morgan carried her and her carpetbag up the stairs to the dressing room where Nelly filled the tub and offered to play lady's maid.

Before he set her down, Celia gave him a faint smile and a glint of the familiar twinkle momentarily came to her eyes. She whispered into his ear, "If I weren't so beaten up, I'd invite you in."

"I'll be right outside the door. You let Nelly help you this time."

He had no intention of leaving Celia Fair alone for a minute until he knew everything there was to know.

When she had finished her bath, she came out dressed in a long blue nightgown of the finest flannel. Her auburn hair was still damp. It hung around her shoulders and tight little curls framed her face.

He insisted Celia be put to bed in his room. "I'm going to guard her until we can get some outside help. The sheriff is not to be trusted."

Essie had a tray brought, and Celia managed to eat a little while Morgan wolfed down his share. Now that she was safe, his appetite had returned.

When they were alone, Morgan finally asked, "What did they want?"

"The leather bag."

"We have to get the whole story, Celia. These people aren't going to give up just because a couple of them are dead."

"I don't even know the whole story," Celia said. "I told you about coming here to help my brother. Now it sounds as if there was some gold involved." She lay back against the pillows and sighed. "From what has been said, I believe that my brother, Hex, stole the gold."

"That seems about right," Morgan said. "How come your brother's name was Downs?"

"He changed his name when he left home. Father wanted him to take over the family business." Celia looked as if she were going to cry again. "If Father had just let Hex be himself, just stay home and write his poetry, everything would have been all right. But Father didn't think that was manly."

"More manly to rob stages, I guess," Morgan said.

"So he went away and changed his name and got himself killed."

"What about the old man up the mountain? Gramps."

"I got a message and went to see him. He gave me a note from Hex." Celia stopped and wiped her eyes. "I don't even know what it means."

Morgan could almost feel the weight of the gold in his hands. He wiped one of his palms against his pant leg. "What did the note say?"

"It was like his poetry. It said:

Open so to see,
the book lies on the table.
Underneath them all
is the treasure of my fable.

Celia went to sleep in his arms. Morgan held her and thought of the things she had told him. An open book and a table? Underneath a book and a table? There hadn't been any books or tables in old Gramps' clue. There hadn't been any books or tables in Chief Greatfoot's tepee. Morgan couldn't make it add up.

He dozed and dreamed of books and tables. He dreamed of the books at Gramps' cabin and the hand hewn table. He dreamed of his father's library table at Spade Bit back in Idaho where the deed to the ranch was kept in the table drawer.

But in each place, in his dreams, on every table, every book he opened revealed only pictures of men with long stringy hair coming out of tepees and drawing down on him faster than he could reach for his Bisley Colts.

He woke with a start, wondering where he was and why his arm was asleep. The moon shone through the lace curtained windows lighting the room so that he could see Celia's face. He carefully withdrew his arm from underneath her. She stirred but didn't waken.

He still couldn't make any sense of the four-line poem Hex Downs had left his sister. She must have remembered it right. She even wrote it down so he could see how it had looked. It looked like a poem and it rhymed. But that was all he could say for it. What could it have to do with a rainbow and a tepee?

In the morning, when Morgan was up and dressed, he waited for Celia to waken. He wondered if she would still be here or where she would be when she got well enough to want to play again. He switched that train of thought off immediately. She had been through a lot, so he refused to entertain such heat-producing ideas. He had rescued her and made himself responsible for her welfare.

All he wanted to do right now was find the gold. Then whoever else was after it would no longer have any reason to bother Celia. And Morgan, himself, could get the hell out of this crap-filled town.

11

Celia winced slightly as she stretched, then noticed Morgan. "What are you looking so angry about this morning? And you're already up and dressed. Where are you going?"

"Nowhere without you. I'm not leaving you alone."

"I want to go."

"Go where?"

"Anywhere! Out of doors. I want to go outside."

She swung her legs carefully off the edge of the bed and sat up. "The whole time I was held captive, I had this horrible feeling that I'd never see the sky again. I guess I still have it." She nodded eagerly, as if having decided for sure. "I want to go outside."

"I'll take you out, if you're up to it," Morgan assured her. "We'll go to the cafe and have breakfast." He grinned down at her. "But I don't think you can go in your nightgown."

Celia put on the blue print dress that she had worn the first time Morgan had seen her struggling in the clutches of Brant Corson. She managed her clothing, but Morgan helped her with her dainty boots. When she had arranged her auburn hair in its usual becoming style, she

took a deep breath, stood somewhat unsteadily
at first, and then pronounced herself ready to
go.

They made it to the cafe, and Jason limped
out of the kitchen to say hello to Morgan and
congratulate Celia on her recovery.

"I told him he didn't have to work today,"
Florrie said. "But he insists he's all right."

After a leisurely breakfast, Celia still wanted
to walk some more. So they left the cafe and
started up the main street. Morgan enjoyed
Celia walking beside him along the plank
sidewalk of Lost Canyon. His boots made deep
clunking sounds and her dainty ones tap-tapped
along beside him.

He vowed again that he wouldn't let her out
of his sight until he had dealt with the man who
had been responsible for her kidnapping. Even
though he was fairly certain now who had
ordered her brought back in a trunk, without
proof he'd be a fool to openly accuse the fastest
gun in town.

Celia had been quiet, apparently thinking,
too. "If Hex had told me he needed my help to
dispose of stolen gold, I wouldn't have come to
help him," she declared.

"I'm glad you did," Morgan told her. "I'm
sorry about all the trouble you've gone through,
of course." In a moment he added, "There's a
reward for anyone who finds the gold, you
know. The federal government offers it."

As they strolled along up the main street,
Morgan saw Sheriff Tyler coming in the
opposite direction. He was walking and talking
with Rebecca Petersen. So, Morgan thought,
she was still here.

The sheriff stopped in front of them to say

that he was glad to see Miss Fair up and around. "Now you can come to the office with me, and we'll fill out that report before the circuit judge comes in. He should be here in a couple of days."

Celia ignored the sheriff and put out her hand to the woman beside him. "I don't believe we've met, I'm Celia Fair."

Rebecca gave her name, glanced briefly at Morgan, and then said, "Excuse me. I'm going into the church to light a candle."

The church was a few steps back in the direction from which she and the sheriff had come. Morgan had never really noticed the church before, but then he wasn't much of a churchgoer. Churches had more to do with mothers, he'd always thought, than with men.

Celia clung tightly to his hand. "Is that lady upset about something?" she asked.

Morgan's pride told him that Rebecca had looked just a bit jealous. But he wasn't going to tell Celia that.

Before either of them could say more, a man riding fast tore up the street. Stopping just past them, he dashed into the church. Immediately the church bells began to ring.

"What the hell's that for?" Morgan wanted to know, looking up at the steeple. "It's only Saturday."

"Indian attack!" the sheriff shouted and took off at a run in the direction of his office.

A shopkeeper and two customers ran into the street. The nearest saloon emptied.

"Indians! Indians!"

Suddenly there was a sound like thunder a long way off. Hoof beats.

"My God, they're right. Those damned

Washos again!"

Morgan practically dragged Celia to the church. He hustled her up the steps and inside. "Get in here. And stay put until I come back for you."

"Stay with me."

He kissed her quickly. "I'll be back."

More men came out of buildings, loading rifles as they ran and taking cover.

The hoof beats came closer and Morgan could hear the Indians' war cries. He ducked behind the corner of the church as a band of Indians made their first pass. Flaming arrows streaked through the air. The church was made of stone, it would probably not be in danger. The Indians swung left and he could hear them turn down the alley.

A hundred yards away and across the street, the livery stable roof suddenly glowed with flame. Willie, followed by his barking dog, led two horses through the side doors. He slapped their rears and dashed back into the burning barn. In seconds he emerged with two more. One of them was Morgan's bay gelding.

Morgan dashed across the street and made for the barn. Willie turned to go back into the building now engulfed in flames. Morgan threw him aside. He struggled to get back on his feet. "There's one more."

"I'll get him."

In seconds, Morgan returned leading a stallion. Stoneagle's black stallion. With a smack on his flank, he ran off down the field toward the other horses. From the tack room, they managed to save a few saddles.

"Anybody in there? Your pa?" Morgan asked Willie.

Willie shook his head. "Nobody. Pa's down at the Dubloon."

The Indians came down the street again making another pass. Morgan ducked behind a buckboard and dragged Willie with him. Men, rifles blazing, ducked for cover behind wagons or back into doorways.

Burning arrows flew overhead. One embedded itself in the roof of the General Emporium, smoldered for seconds, then the roof burst into flames. These braves sure knew how to make a mess.

An arrow went through a window at the hotel down the street and set curtains afire.

Three more Indians, apparently just arrived, galloped their Pintos across the clearing and into the Main Street, shooting with rifles at anything that moved. With his Bisley Colts Morgan dropped one that got close enough with a bullet into the neck. The Indian screamed, fell from his horse, and a fountain of blood gushed from his jugular.

The others kept coming. Rifle fire exploded from doorways and windows of burning buildings. Indians fell. Some tried to crawl to cover. Few made it.

"They've got guns, Willie. Stay down," Morgan warned. He marveled at the kid's guts.

"Those fire arrows are doing worse than the guns," Willie said. "They're wrecking the town."

Morgan scanned the perimeter of the buildings for some sign of Burning Arrow. He had to be the one behind the attack. But how many braves had joined him? Not the whole tribe, but they moved so fast, it was hard to tell how many there were.

He glanced across the street toward the church. No smoke appeared near the stone structure. So far, Celia was safe.

A brave rounded a corner. Morgan picked him off. His bow, already drawn, skittered an arrow across the dust.

Down at the center of town, about in front of the sheriff's office, a gun battle erupted. Rifles and hand guns blazed from windows. Return fire splintered a door.

Morgan traced the source of the outside shots. Two Indians appeared on the roof of the feed and lumber building pouring lead into the sheriff's office. Morgan's Bisley Colts wouldn't carry that far. But someone's rifle did. One Indian threw up his arms, and he and his rifle toppled from the roof, making a dull permanent thud heard the length of the street as he hit the ground. He didn't move again.

Smoke filled Morgan's eyes. The burning dry wood and hay in the building behind him nearly choked him. He lifted off his Stetson and ducked his head into the nearby watering trough. An arrow missed him by inches.

Morgan wanted to move but scanning the street for the next nearest cover, he found none. Burning buildings needed help, but they could do nothing about that until they got rid of the damned Indians.

Just then Morgan spotted Burning Arrow riding fast. The brave aimed the rifle just as Sheriff Bert Tyler appeared around the side of his office. As Morgan watched fascinated, from his spot behind the big watering trough, wondering which of his enemies would win this match, they both fired. Burning Arrow appeared to dive from his horse. He landed in the dust of the street and his mount thundered on without him.

As suddenly as it had begun, the attack ended. With their leader dead, the braves who were still alive fled. The street became quiet. Nobody moved for two or three long, still minutes.

Willie started to stand up, but Morgan grabbed him and pulled him down again. "May not be over."

The acrid smell of gun fire lay silently on the still air. Smoke billowed straight up, masking the sun, covering the town with an eerie gray pall. In the distance, receding horses' hooves pounded out of town. The attack was over.

Finally the populace came alive. Fire brigades formed. Water was brought to the fires any way they could bring it.

Morgan strode toward the spot where he had seen Burning Arrow fall. As he approached, he saw Tyler go out to Burning Arrow and give the carcass a vicious kick. Morgan heard the sheriff say, "Smart ass, knew too much anyhow."

Morgan pretended not to hear. He glanced around at the bodies, some red skinned, some white.

He joined a bucket brigade putting out the roof fire at the Emporium. It hadn't as good a start as some, so they were able to put it out before damage moved far into the store itself.

The stable and its supply of feed inside were lost, but the horses were safe, thanks to Willie's quick thinking in the beginning. Women, working from inside, had saved the hotel.

When the townsfolk seemed to have things under control again, Morgan hurried back to the church and Celia.

After the cacaphony of the battle, the church

presented extreme quiet. His eyes adjusted to the dimmer interior. Although there was smokey sun shining through the handcrafted, stained glass windows, it took getting used to.

He saw Celia sitting in a pew with her head bowed. As he went into the row, she looked up and smiled. "Oh, I'm so glad you're all right. Is it over? What happened?"

"It's over. We've tangled with Burning Arrow before, but he won't lead braves out to kill white men again."

"Did you shoot him?"

"The sheriff shot him."

They sat in silence for a little while. Morgan thought about the church. It had offered haven for Celia when the attack came. This was a place of sanctuary, topped by the tower with bells that not only called people to worship, but also warned of attack.

"Tower," Morgan said aloud. "Steeple. Spire. It could have been a steeple instead of a tepee."

"What?" Celia obviously couldn't make out what he was talking about.

"The old man, Gramps, left a clue. Jason and I thought the clue meant a tepee. He searched his pockets and found the paper on which he had made the drawing and showed it to her.

"What is it?" Celia frowned at the pencil marks. "I'm sorry, I didn't mean your drawing wasn't . . . nice," she finished lamely.

Morgan laughed at her trying to save his feelings. "It's a crude picture of the clue the old man carved into a log on his cabin. We thought it was a rainbow with an arrow pointing to a tepee."

She nodded. "It's sort of like that."

"But it could be a steeple, the spire of a

church, instead of a tepee."

Celia shrugged. "What is it going to mean, when you decide which it is?"

Morgan grinned at her, glanced around to see whether anyone else was near and smoothing the paper on his knee, said, "If the old man meant it to be a steeple, it could mean that the gold is somewhere in the church, instead of in an Indian tepee."

"Oh, the gold again." Celia sighed.

"If I can find the gold, the others who want it will give up trying to get information from you, information that you obviously don't have."

They sat for another quiet period, gazing around them. As he sat there in the stillness, his mind could see again the poem Hex had written, as Celia had copied it for him.

> Open so to see
> the book lies on the table
> Underneath them all
> is the treasure of my fable.

Suddenly Morgan jumped to his feet. "My God, it's right in our laps!"

He pulled Celia by the arm and headed for the front of the church.

On the altar table lay a large open Bible.

They went up the two steps to the altar and Morgan stared down at the Bible. Now here was a book from which came no gunslinging Corsons. Here was an open book on a table.

He took hold of the edges of the table to move it. It seemed to be fastened down. He squatted, examining the base of the table. It was like a cupboard with a small door.

He turned the small wooden hook and opened

the little door. Inside were two shelves, empty except for offering baskets. What made the table so heavy?

Celia stood by watching. Morgan glanced up at her, thinking about the way she had watched him in his hotel room when he was hiding her leather case which had contained the note about the book on the table. He was sure he had found that table. But how could he get under it?

Morgan felt around the bottom shelf inside and found two crudely formed, but clever, sliding catches. He pushed each of them back, then stood and easily lifted the table. He moved it to one side.

He knelt again and examined the floor.

"Ha!" He took his knife out of his boot and carefully sticking the point between two boards, raised one of them easily. He removed another board and reached into the space between the floor and the foundation rock. In a moment his hand touched metal. His heart thumped faster. He knew what it had to be.

He felt the size and shape of the cool metal he had encountered. He grasped it and withdrew a ten-pound gold bar.

Before he could reach in and bring out another, a thunderous voice froze them where they were.

"Knew damn well some son-of-a-bitch would lead me to it if I waited around this hellhole long enough." Sheriff Bert Tyler stood in the center aisle with a forty-four trained on Morgan. "Just go ahead and lift the other ones out of there. How many are there? Four?"

Keeping his eyes riveted on Tyler, Morgan reached slowly into the hole and removed another bar and, with great deliberation, set it on the floor. Then he carefully brought up a third. His mind raced trying to get an idea of how to get out of this with his life, if not the gold.

He pulled out the fourth bar and set it beside the others. "All yours, Sheriff, we were about to come and call you. You'll want to get in touch with the Federal Government."

"Sure, Morgan." The sheriff took a couple of steps closer. "I'll want to get in touch with the fuckin' undertaker, is who I'll want to get in touch with. Better draw out your old Colts there, so it will look as if I shot you in the process of robbing the church."

Morgan wondered whether there was a way he could draw and shoot without getting either Celia or himself shot up too badly. "Well, if that's the plan, Sheriff, this young lady had better get down out of the line of fire."

"Don't think that's necessary, you're both off to the happy hunting grounds along with that stupid brave I just took care of outside. Now take out your weapon, carefully. You can lay it down on the floor, there. So's it'll look like that's where it fell."

Morgan put his hand on the top of the Bisley. He knew he couldn't draw. He didn't know how long he could stall this lunatic in front of him before it would be over.

Suddenly another voice rang out in the house of worship. "No, Bert Tyler, that's not the plan after all."

The sheriff whirled to look at Rebecca Petersen who stood between rows of the back pews holding a large bore pistol in both hands. It was pointed at the sheriff.

Morgan drew and fired. At the same instant,

Rebecca discharged her oversized weapon. The kick of the heavy piece set her backward hard onto the seat.

Blood ran from the sheriff's head completely obscuring his features. Torrents of blood spurted from his chest as if pumped directly out by his heart. The sheriff's gun arm swung down, and he collapsed by degrees. It seemed as if all motion was suspended on a string of beaded movements. The sheriff's knees buckled, his head sagged, his rump reached the floor first, then his back and shoulders and head.

"You got my man killed," Rebecca said. "You're not going to get his gold." She spoke more softly now. "I'm claiming a share of that gold, folks." She sat there and reloaded the old pisto! and slid it back into her reticule.

Celia Fair had not screamed, nor had she fainted. She stared first at Rebecca, watching until the gun was safely tucked away. Then she turned her attention to the downed sheriff. After another moment, she looked at Morgan and smiled, as if something nice had just happened.

People began to come into the church, "What were the shots?" "Who shot the sheriff?"

"Lots of folks told him he should resign." It was the liveryman's voice, Willie's father.

Jason limped up the side aisle and came to Morgan's side. "You all right?" He looked at the sheriff, then stared down at the bars by Morgan's feet. "You found it!" He waited a long moment then asked, "Now what?"

Rebecca Petersen picked her way carefully through the group of people beginning to clog the center aisle. Some of them had probably come to give thanks for their survival after the Indian raid. Others wanted to know what the gun play in the church was all about.

"He was a bad man," Rebecca announced, standing in the pulpit as if ready to give a sermon.

Everyone stopped moving and talking. Every eye turned toward Rebecca.

Rebecca pointed down at the sheriff. "This man was going to kill two people, to keep them from giving that gold . . ." Again she pointed. ". . . to the Federal Government of this country. He planned to tell the people of this town that he had caught them robbing your church. A criminal hid the gold in there and now it has been found. The reward will be divided among those who found it." She moved away from the pulpit and stood beside Jason and the other two on the raised platform.

Morgan finally answered Jason Isley's question. "Now what? I'll tell you what." Picking up the gold bars, he handed Jason one. "Comes out just right. One for you. One for Celia. One for Rebecca. And one for me."

The undertaker came and had his men carry Sheriff Bert Tyler's remains away. No one seemed distressed about that.

The minister of the church was heard to remark that he had never drawn such a crowd on his best Sunday.

One man kept saying that he thought Lee Morgan would be a good sheriff.

Morgan stepped down and tapped him on the shoulder. "There's your man, if you want an honest, hard-working, land-owner for sheriff of Lost Canyon." He pointed to Jason Isley.

Celia told Jason they would telegraph her

U.S. senator and tell him the gold had been found.

Morgan dropped a light kiss on Celia's cheek. "Tell him *part* of the gold has been found." He took a last look at her and strode out of the church.

Her gold bar wrapped in a kerchief, Rebecca Peterson hurried after Morgan.

When Rebecca knocked on his door, Morgan was just ready to leave. By her costume, he would have taken her for a young boy, except for her awesome bosom.

"Did I hear you mutter something about San Diego?" she asked him.

Morgan nodded. "With a horse, and a canteen, you can make it. I plan to send young Willie a black snake whip from down there. I also understand you can get rid of most anything of value in San Diego."